The Wives of Bath

WENDY HOLDEN

headline

First published in 2005
by HEADLINE BOOK PUBLISHING

First published in paperback in 2005
by HEADLINE BOOK PUBLISHING

1

ISBN 0 7553 0068 8 (A format)
ISBN 0 7553 2629 6 (B format)

Typeset in Garamond by Avon DataSet Ltd,
Bidford-on-Avon, Warwickshire

Printed and bound in Great Britain by
Clays Ltd, St Ives plc

Headline's policy is to use papers that are natural, renewable and
recyclable products and made from wood grown in sustainable
forests. The logging and manufacturing processes are expected to
conform to the environmental regulations of the country of origin.

HEADLINE BOOK PUBLISHING
A division of Hodder Headline
338 Euston Road
London NW1 3BH

www.headline.co.uk
www.hodderheadline.com

For Isabella

Chapter 1

Hugo peeled his face from the white-coated chest of an exceptionally pretty woman. His rush through the hospital was such that he had failed to consider that the corner he was heading for might have someone coming round it.

'Sorry,' he grinned at her, thinking that, actually, he wasn't sorry at all. It wasn't every evening he got to bury his nose in something as luscious as . . . he squinted at her badge . . . Dr M. Watson, Consultant Paediatrician.

'Don't worry,' the doctor replied slightly frostily.

'You're not really called Dr Watson, are you?' Hugo looked her up and down flirtatiously, taking in the glossy black hair and large dark eyes. Confidently he waited for his own handsome face and commanding height to have their usual effect on a woman. To his surprise, he waited in vain.

'Are you looking for somewhere in particular?' The doctor's manner was polite but no-nonsense.

'I'm here for a class.' Hugo maintained his expectant smile. She'd crack eventually. They always did. 'An antenatal class.'

Dr Watson did not crack, however. But she did give him directions. After several more twists through the grey lino maze, Hugo finally found the door he was in search of.

He knocked and opened it to find Amanda sitting tense and annoyed amid a horseshoe of people. Next to her was an empty orange plastic chair.

'Sorry I'm late,' Hugo muttered.

In front of the horseshoe stood a thin-faced woman with wire-framed glasses and a bright, toothy smile. There was, Hugo thought, something over-eager, manic even, about the way her eyes shone through her lenses.

'Goot evening,' she said. 'My name is Lotti. Yes, you are late, but bedder late than never, as you say in this country, I think?'

Dutch, Hugo guessed, as, bracelets rattling on her out-stretched arms, the woman came towards him. He found himself bustled to a table and asked his name, which was then written on a badge and stuck to his lapel. Thus labelled, Hugo was free to stumble to the seat beside his wife.

He looked swiftly about him. The sight of so many pregnant women made him nervous. Their stomachs looked strained beyond endurance, about to burst any second. He imagined a huge cannon bang: a twenty-one-tum salute.

Lotti beamed round at the horseshoe. 'It's goot to see you all here tonight. You know, I hope you find these classes useful, not just for information about baby and birthing, but also to make frens? You know, couples who meet at these classes sometimes stay frens for years.'

Hugo stared fixedly at the floor. Nothing made his toes curl like forced social interaction. Like that bit in church when you had to offer each other a sign of peace.

'Now,' Lotti instructed, lenses glinting, 'I'd like everyone to stand up one by one and introduce yourselfs to the class. Please!' She gestured at the person nearest, who rose to her feet.

'Mel' – according to her name badge – was short and pugnacious-looking, with cropped grey hair. Hugo's glance flicked over her to rest approvingly on the woman she was next to: a very pretty, very pregnant redhead, with creamy skin, faraway eyes and an air of dreamy gentleness. She looked vulnerable, he thought, trying to catch her eye and wink at her. This must be why her mother was with her.

Mel gestured to the redhead. 'This is Saskia. My partner.' Hugo stopped winking at the redhead and gave her a look of comic reproach.

'That's great, Mel,' Lotti beamed. 'And can you tell the class what you do?'

'Saskia's a Home Office pathologist. I'm an organic gardener.'

'Baby's sure going to be lucky with the vegetables, ha ha. Nothing out of the jars in your house, ha ha.'

'No,' said Mel shortly, and sat down.

Next it was Amanda's turn. She bounced up, despite her bump, a dazzling, red-lipsticked grin stretched rigidly across her face. 'My name is Amanda Fine,' she breathily declared.

'Although it is more likely you'll have heard of me in my professional capacity. As Amanda Hardwick.' She paused expectantly.

'Are you that woman off *The Bill*?' a thickset man next to Saskia eventually hazarded. Amanda tightened her lips. 'I'm *quite* a well-known journalist,' she declared, as Hugo felt his fists tighten and his toes ball up with embarrassment. '*Very* well known in the States. But I don't suppose,' she added, looking round disparagingly, 'that anyone here ever gets *Style* magazine.'

'I do, sometimes,' offered a woman with heavy make-up, shiny skin, a large nose and wild brown hair. Her name badge read 'Laura'. 'You mean the one that comes with the *Sunday Times*?'

'No,' Amanda said freezingly. 'I do *not* mean that one. I mean the extremely prestigious and influential American one of the same name.'

Hugo was surprised she had brought up the magazine. Earlier that year – and in rather mysterious circumstances – Amanda had resigned from *Style*. On principle, she had told him. A disagreement with the legal department or something, he recalled. He hadn't realised until then that she had any principles. Her complete lack of scruples had been one of her attractions, initially.

Lotti's voice broke into his thoughts. 'Well, it's all very interesting anyway, Amanda. Thank you.'

Amanda sat down and gave Hugo a bad-tempered nudge. She was, he saw, staring at his lapel. Dismayed, he now saw that, positioned at a drunken angle on his suit, the crumpled white name badge read 'Yogi'. Lotti had obviously misheard 'Hugo'. But you probably didn't get many Hugos in Holland.

'Yogi!' Lotti trilled, inadvertently rubbing it in. 'Your turn now, please.'

Crossly, Hugo got to his feet. He had assumed that the covert glances from the rest of the class, particularly from the women, had been impressed and possibly flirtatious. The realisation he was the object of amusement was both unusual and unpleasant. 'Erm, well,' he began uncomfortably. 'The first thing I should say is that this badge isn't strictly accurate. My name's not Yogi.'

'Shpeak up, Yogi!' urged Lotti from the front. 'We can't hear you!'

'My name's not Yogi,' Hugo bleated. 'It's Hugo – Hugo Fine.' Bloody hell. Why hadn't he just stayed in the pub? Amanda had rung his mobile even as he raised the pint glass to his lips, demanding to know why he wasn't in the antenatal class.

'I understand you've recently moved from London, Yogi,' Lotti steamrollered on. 'Would you like to tell us why?'

Good question, Hugo thought. The same one he asked himself most mornings. He suppressed a sigh. 'Oh, you know. All the usual reasons. Better quality of life and all that.'

'And so much better for children,' Amanda energetically interrupted from beside him. 'Family life in the country, we thought. Real life. Quality time.'

There was a murmur of agreement from the others at this.

5

'Dandling angelic infants in the dappled sunlight under the apple blossom, that sort of thing.' Amanda flashed her red grimace again.

The murmur stuttered slightly. There were glances of surprise.

'So we're both thrilled to be here,' Amanda finished, in the manner of a visiting Royal. '*Aren't* we, darling?'

Hugo flinched at her violent nudge and nodded faintly.

In point of fact, and as Amanda well knew, he was not at all thrilled to be here. He had resisted fiercely her idea of moving out of London and into the countryside. An urbanite to the core, he had a terror of the deep middle of nowhere with its black nights and awful stillness. But Amanda, once pregnant, had insisted her city days were over.

The compromise was Bath. As well as halfway house between big city and rolling ruraldom, it had the additional benefit of being somewhere Hugo had actually heard of. It also had good London train links, not that he used them. He had imagined commuting to his old job as an estate agent in Islington. But his wife, it turned out, had decided his city days were over as well.

As a result he was now the wage slave of one Neil Dustard, boss of a small Bath property firm. He had seemed reasonable enough at first; the only agent Hugo had applied to that had taken him out to the pub to discuss prospects. At the time this had seemed evidence of the sort of laid-back friendliness that corresponded to brilliance in business.

What it turned out to be was evidence of the alcoholism

already hinted at by Neil's red face. As a result of which his character was as unstable as his company, which Hugo soon discovered to be as mired in lack of ideas as it was in lack of ambition. And he was mired there too, now. Bugger Amanda, for making him move here. And bugger himself, for letting her. He tuned back into the discussion.

'Of course,' Amanda was saying to the class, 'obviously Bath *is* a bit backward compared to London. But it's really not bad at all to look at – quite pretty in fact – and so *cheap*! We've got a *huge* family house here for the price of our flat. But then, it *was* in Notting Hill . . .'

The rest of the class was staring stonily at Amanda. Hugo clenched his toes again. Why did she have to say these things?

The flat had not been in W11, for a start. W10-and-a-half at the most. Not-quiting Hill, as he had thought of it.

Nor were Bath house prices cheap. Cheaper, yes, but hardly bargain basement. Some basements, in fact, were pretty expensive. Hugo, thanks to his job, knew this before they even moved there. But it had taken time for Amanda, with stormy reluctance, to accept that the five-storey Royal Crescent mansion she had imagined owning was way beyond their means. The house within them, Number Four Fitzherbert Place, was a distinct cut below and one she had initially refused to countenance. This had suited Hugo, who had no wish to live there either. Then suddenly Amanda, apparently accepting their financial limitations, had become full of enthusiasm for the fact Number Four was Georgian and 'bursting with original features', according to the estate agent's details.

Something, possibly original, Hugo thought, had certainly burst through the staircase wall and left a large damp stain. Other period features included a grimy fanlight, tall, difficult-to-clean windows and high, cracked ceilings. Basically, it was a battered, three-floored terrace on the side of a hill on the edge of the city. Basically, it was a mess.

'But it says here that it's got "huge potential for refurbishment".' Amanda stabbed the estate agent's details with a manicured forefinger.

'That's estate agent speak for "complete bombsite".' But Hugo knew he argued in vain. When, eventually, inevitably, Amanda prevailed and Number Four was theirs, he was left with the uncomfortable feeling of being the biter bit.

Just as, uncomfortably, he was recalling all this, there was a commotion at the class door and a man came in. Lotti trained her glasses on him. 'Hi. Welcome. Come in. You're a bit late, but never mind.' She bustled over to do the business with the name badges.

'We had to wait for a bus,' the man said defensively.

The newcomer was, Hugo realised, extravagantly handsome. From the Cherokee cheekbones to the dark hair curling carelessly round the base of the muscular neck, his were the type of film-hero good looks that aroused resentment in the most relaxed of men. And Hugo, standing up amid sniggering strangers, sporting a silly name badge, was feeling far from laid back at the moment.

'A *bus*?' echoed Amanda disdainfully.

The long-haired man looked at her. 'We don't do cars,' he said witheringly. 'We believe they're damaging to the planet.'

Lotti glanced delightedly up from her sheet of stickers. 'Hey, me too. I don't do cars either. I bicycle everywhere.' She brandished her marker at the bus fan. 'What's your name?'

'Jake. My wife, Alice, is here too, but she's in the loo throwing up at the moment.' He grinned at the women. 'Guess you know how it is, girls.'

Hugo's stomach tensed in dislike. The women, however, looked charmed. There was a sympathetic murmur from all except Amanda, who looked disgusted. She did not, Hugo knew, appreciate being reminded of pregnancy's less glamorous aspects.

Jake was now looking at Hugo. Or, more precisely, his name badge. There was a mocking gleam in his eye. 'Yogi, huh? As in Bear or Maharishi Mahesh?'

'Neither,' Hugo replied icily, suddenly loathing him. 'My name is actually Hugo. I'm not sure Lotti heard properly.'

Lotti was now fixing Jake's badge on his broad chest. Her manner was half investiture, half flirtation and entirely distracted.

'Do go on, Yogi,' she gasped, flushed. 'You were saying what is it you do.'

Hugo shifted to his other foot. 'I'm an estate agent.'

Was that a snort coming from Jake's direction? He looked challengingly at the new arrival. But Jake avoided his gaze, sneering instead at Hugo's pinstriped suit.

'Thank you, Yogi. You can sit down now.' Lotti's glasses flashed speculatively around before being drawn magnetically back to Jake. 'Jake,' she fluttered. 'Why don't you tell us a little about yourself?'

Jake, who had sat down, rose slowly up again. There was a stirring among the women as he unfolded himself to his full height which, Hugo had to admit, was impressive. He noted with irritation how confidently Jake stood in his battered lumberjack shirt and scruffy jeans. Handsome head tilted slightly back, he seemed at ease to an almost aggressive extent, rolling gently but constantly from one foot to the other.

'OK, well I'd just like to say,' Jake looked round with an intense, deep-set gaze, 'that I, for one, am not here just for decoration. I think we fathers should take an active part in everything to do with the birth. I mean, we're mothers too, in a way, and I personally don't have a problem with feeling that.'

Ecstasy lit Lotti's face. 'That's right, Jake,' she gasped, eyes brimming behind her glasses. 'If only more men felt like you.'

Nauseous, Hugo thought, was the only way to describe how he personally felt. Sliding a glance round the room, he divined similar sentiments in the other men present. Their expressions ranged from miserable to murderous.

The women, however, were sighing with admiration. And none more so than Lotti. 'Tell us what you do, Jake,' she invited.

'I run a magazine.'

'But that's marvellous!' Lotti threw out an excited arm in

Amanda's direction. 'Amanda here was just telling us about the magazine she works on.'

Jake looked Amanda doubtfully up and down. 'Can't imagine it's the same sort of thing. Yours is all celebrities, sex and make-up, right?'

'Sounds great,' interrupted Laura.

Amanda favoured her with a tight smile. 'It's a glossy, if that's what you mean,' she told Jake. 'Is yours a glossy?'

He shook his lustrous locks. 'Not likely. It's printed on eco-sustainable paper. It's a recycling magazine.'

'A cycling magazine!' exclaimed Lotti in delight.

'RE-cycling,' Jake's perfectly level brows drew together in irritation. 'It's called *Get Trashed!*. Available from health-food shops, Soil Association-approved organic greengrocers and by subscription from me.' He looked around challengingly.

'Recycling!' Lotti clasped her hands together. 'A very important subject. Isn't it, everyone?'

Heads nodded, Hugo's included. For what it was worth, he had religiously washed out his bottles and cans and posted them through the appropriate holes in the recycling container near the Not-quiting Hill flat. Amanda had been less diligent in this respect, although once, after a particularly lavish party, she had written to the council suggesting they provide containers with holes for magnums. So far as he knew, she had not received a reply.

'Our latest issue,' Jake informed the class, 'shows you how to build a house made entirely of reusable waste.'

Hugo snorted and tried to turn it into a cough. He was

rewarded with a bright smile from Lotti. 'You know, Yogi, maybe you ought to get together with Jake. You're an eshtate agent, right?'

'A house made of reusable waste?' Hugo mused as politely as he could manage. 'I'm not sure Dunn and Dustard have handled anything like that before.'

'And I don't think they're likely to,' Jake returned smartly. 'Unless you accept your commission in LETs, that is.'

'In what?' Hugo asked, his polite tones now strained.

'Local Exchange Tokens,' Jake growled impatiently. 'Another of *Get Trashed!*'s interests is phasing out conventional payment methods in favour of trading skills. Or benefits in kind.'

'I'd have to get back to you on that.' Hugo imagined Neil Dustard contemplating such a proposal. He felt the start of another snigger and tried to turn it into a sneeze.

Next to introduce himself was stocky Jim, who had imagined Amanda to be in *The Bill*. He was a carpenter originally from St Helens.

'How marvellous,' gushed Amanda. 'Is that in the Caribbean?'

Jim looked at her in amazement. 'Merseyside.'

Then it was Laura's turn. Hugo looked at her with interest. Besides thick make-up, she had a wide gap between her front teeth, giving her smile a bawdy appearance. She was wearing a lot of hot pink. Hugo wondered where her other half was.

'He's, er, too busy to come,' Laura admitted when Lotti brightly asked the same question.

'No father of a baby should be too busy to come,' Jake opined loudly. 'It's his duty.'

'Fergus works in advertising in London,' Laura snapped back. Jake rolled his deep-set eyes in disgust.

The door opened and a blonde woman came in. The room rippled with interest as it realised that this, presumably, was Jake's wife. Who had presumably been in the loo all this time.

She was, Hugo instantly decided, rather less glamorous than her partner. She was thin, despite being pregnant, and lanky. Cleanliness seemed her most distinguishing feature. She looked almost carbolically well scrubbed in maternity jeans and a white T-shirt, her long, calm face completely devoid of make-up. She looked, Hugo thought, extremely earnest.

Yet however unexciting it seemed to him, the woman's appearance had clearly had an electric effect on someone else in the room. Amanda, beside him, was breathing short and fast. 'It *can't* be,' he heard her groan to herself.

'My wife, Alice,' Jake was announcing. 'Feeling better?' he asked her solicitously.

Alice was not listening. She was staring at Amanda, in what could only be described as horror.

Lotti had picked up none of the drama. 'Tell us about yourself,' she beamed toothily at Alice. 'Are you working at the moment?'

Hugo heard Amanda hold her breath. He sensed that she was very interested in Alice's answer. Frankly, now he was interested himself.

'N-no,' Alice stuttered. Then, recovering, she added in a clear, soft voice. 'But until recently I was in the legal department of a New York magazine company.'

Hugo's head exploded with the pealing of loud bells. So that was the connection. *Style* magazine. Was this mousy woman, then, involved in Amanda's mysterious resignation? With her scrubbed face and mild air, she hardly looked the type to take on his formidable wife.

Lotti was looking expectantly round the class. 'OK. Right. Now we all know each other, let's get down to business. Does everyone here know what a uterus looks like?'

Chapter 2

Standing at the bus stop after the class, Alice and Jake watched Amanda and Hugo's gleaming four-wheel drive sweep by. Behind the tinted panes, the white blur of Amanda's face stared contemptuously out.

'That woman,' Jake remarked, 'seems to hate your guts, for some reason.'

'I think she does,' Alice admitted, hoping he would not probe further. She felt queasy again and another bus journey was not going to improve matters. She had imagined herself dreaming, or rather, in a nightmare, when she entered the antenatal class to find her old enemy there. It hardly seemed possible Amanda Hardwick was having a baby in exactly the same place and at the exact same time.

'So what happened?' Jake probed as the bus, with its customary obduracy, failed to materialise.

Alice groaned. 'She was the one involved in that libel case.

15

The one I packed the job at Intercorp in over.'

In the orange sulphur lamplight, Jake's eyes widened. '*That* was *her*?'

Alice nodded. 'But in a funny way,' she said consideringly, 'she did me a favour.' She squeezed Jake's hand. 'I would never have met you if it hadn't been for Amanda Hardwick. If she'd been just one tiny bit less horrible, I'd probably have stayed in New York.'

As they stood waiting, Jake holding her close, Alice's thoughts drifted back to the fateful fortnight when her life was changed for ever. It had all started when Sherry, her assistant, had knocked at her office door.

Sherry was pregnant. She was stroking her bump and smiling dreamily through the glass. Alice beckoned her in.

'What's up?'

Sherry wafted in, bulge first, panting, both hands pressed into her back. Never had Alice known anyone make quite such a song and dance about having a baby. Sherry, who was tiny and slender apart from her bump, not only wore the latest and tightest maternity clothes, but had persuaded an Intercorp magazine fashion department to get the image from her latest scan made into a special-edition designer handbag. She also took off at least one afternoon a week to attend what sounded to Alice like a series of increasingly cranky birth preparation classes.

'Brant wants a word,' Sherry smiled toothily.

'Oh. Right.' Brant was head of the Intercorp legal team and her boss. Alice rose from her desk.

Sherry paused. 'And I'd like one too, if that's OK.'

'Sure. Fire away.'

'Is it OK if I take the afternoon off to go to my breastfeeding support class?'

Alice hesitated. 'But you know I've got that conference call with Europe this afternoon. It's important you're here to make sure all the international dial-ins work.'

Sherry's pixie face fell.

Alice raised her palms in a reasoning gesture. 'I'm sorry, Sherry. Can't you get support about breastfeeding at any other time? I mean, I realise it's terribly important and all that . . .'

'Oh, the support's not for me,' Sherry said. 'It's a therapy session for my partner to help him cope with the psychosexual implications of my breasts' new role as nurturers rather than erotic focal points.'

'Can't he go on his own?'

Sherry sighed martyrishly. 'Oh, it doesn't matter. I just thought you might, y'know, understand, that's all.'

'Understand what?' Alice asked patiently.

'Well, that these issues are, like, psychologically so important? You know, to spiritually prepare yourself? But I guess,' Sherry looked pityingly at Alice, 'that if you're not pregnant, or not a mother, you just wouldn't understand.'

'I guess not,' Alice said, trying not to be hurt or offended. None the less, she was irritated. Pregnant women could be so bloody *patronising*. Along with everyone else, they assumed her childless state to be her choice.

17

If only, Alice thought, it was that simple. Yes, she was thirty-six, unmarried and child-free. But that didn't make her a baby-hating careerist. Alice had, in fact, always imagined that, at some stage, she would be a mother. She had certainly imagined being one by her current stage. But it hadn't happened. Among the cards destiny had dealt her, the marriage–baby one just hadn't turned up.

There had been flings, some of them heady; affairs, some of them passionate. The odd serious relationship, even. But nothing serious enough to add up to the sort of stable, committed, loving partnership that made babies a possibility rather than a pipe dream.

What she did have, on the other hand, was a high-powered career, a mortgageless, minimalist apartment enviably located on Central Park, and as many pairs of shoes as a woman could want. Should she wish, she could fly to the Maldives or Paris at the drop of a first-class ticket. Although in point of fact she rarely wished to. Nor did she particularly care about shoes.

So while other women her age brought up families, Alice had simply carried on working. She was now wealthy, successful and enviably free from commitment or responsibility. And while she was vaguely aware this wasn't everything in life, it was certainly something.

Sherry grumped out of Alice's office and Alice got up to go to Brant's.

It was obvious from her boss's face that there was trouble. His expression, habitually anxious, looked even more so than usual.

He regarded Alice gravely through thick horn-rimmed spectacles. 'Amanda Hardwick,' he intoned dolorously.

'Oh. Shit.'

'You could put it that way. But I'm hoping you can sort it out.'

'No time,' Alice said quickly. 'I'm up to my eyes in that recipe case.'

Brant looked blank.

'You remember,' Alice prompted. 'That cake where readers were told to put in fifty cups of whisky instead of five. There are a lot of angry people out there. And a lot with very bad hangovers. I've been working late nights to sort it all out.'

This was no exaggeration, as the shadows beneath her eyes attested. But late nights were nothing new at the Intercorp Magazine Company and the glint in Brant's glasses was steely. 'Someone else can take that over. Amanda Hardwick's English, and handling English is your speciality.'

'Thanks a bunch,' Alice muttered. New York, as Brant well knew, was full of English people, many of whom he dealt with every day of his life. It was just an excuse to give her the short straw. And as straws went, Amanda Hardwick was about the shortest.

Amanda was Intercorp's most celebrated or notorious journalist, depending on which way you looked at it. She wrote mostly for the flagship publication *Style*. Despite being based in London, where she was rumoured to have a husband, she seemed to be a constant presence in New York. Her fame, so far as Alice could see, sprang from her extreme nastiness to any celebrity foolish enough to agree to one of her interviews. The fact that so many did represented, Alice supposed, the triumph of hope over experience. Either that or the terminal stupidity of the famous.

Unfortunately for Intercorp's legal department, Janice Kittenburgen, *Style*'s editor, was impervious to suggestions that Amanda was a liability. Janice, who came from Maryland but had an ego the size of Texas, resented the smallest interference in the sacred editorial process. Her view, as much as she could view anything through the vast black sunglasses she affected indoors, was that the more legally complicated a piece was, the more important it was. Amanda's refusal to research anything and her lofty disregard for libel were dubbed by Janice 'first impressions journalism', art in words, unique to her magazine.

This argument, ingenious as it was, had never washed with Alice. Nor had it, as Brant now explained, washed with Amanda's latest victim, a celebrated actor. Who was, it seemed, threatening to sue *Style* on ten different counts.

'How come it got this far?' Alice demanded. As Brant's deputy, she was entitled to get cross with him on occasion. 'Did no one up here have a look at the piece?' Even as she spoke, she knew that Janice, with her trademark pig-headed irresponsibility, would have rushed the interview to print without letting Legal see it at all. And not for the first time.

Brant shrugged. 'Look, Alice, it's in your hands, OK? If anyone can get us off this hook, you can. You've done it before.'

Alice rubbed her tired eyes. Yes, she bloody well had. A

great deal of her time, energy and expertise had, infuriatingly, been spent saving Amanda Hardwick's neck. Yet, thanks to her efforts, and despite the proximity of Amanda's interviews to the wind and knuckle, the only retribution so far were some strongly worded warning shots from affronted celebrities' lawyers.

Alice worked on the Hardwick piece for the rest of the morning. It was, as Brant had said, a disaster. *Style* really had done it this time. Alice had arranged to see its most notorious contributor that afternoon in order to find out what was true and what wasn't. She was not looking forward to the meeting. On her every previous encounter with Amanda Hardwick, the journalist had exceeded her reputation for arrogant unpleasantness.

Shoving the offending documents in her desk, Alice dragged herself out for coffee and a bagel.

In the café, she carried her cardboard tray over to a table by the window. Lying on it was a copy of the *New York Times*, open at the Weddings/Celebrations page.

Alice flicked an eye over it as she ate. Among the flotsam and jetsam washed up on this week's matrimonial shores was a bride who had founded 'a humor Website for people with one Jewish parent'. Two male doctors were 'celebrating their partnership'. A voice-over artist was marrying a trumpet player and a cardiologist was marrying a 'hematologist-oncologist'. Whatever that was. The most interesting union, Alice thought, was the New Haven automobile princess who, in a classic 'Uptown Girl' scenario, had married a local carpenter, son of a builder and a supermarket worker. Alice wondered what the bride's fearsome-sounding parents, clearly East Coast royalty, made of it all. And especially what they made of the bridegroom's mother and father.

She chewed a fingernail contemplatively and imagined her own entry on the page: 'Miss Alice Lamorna Duffield, daughter of Mrs and Mrs James Duffield of Madron, Cornwall and deputy chief legal adviser to the Intercorp Magazine Company, was married last evening to . . .'

Who? Someone who sounded like a firm of solicitors, if the men on the rest of the page were anything to go by. Grayling Hotchkiss. Bradford Todd. Pulling a face, Alice got up to go back to work.

Later that afternoon, a short blonde strutted into her office. Her head seemed to rise straight out of a large white cleavage and her red-lipsticked mouth wore a sulky, defensive expression.

'Would you like some coffee?' Alice offered. No harm, she thought, in being civil.

Amanda Hardwick clearly thought otherwise. She put both hands on a pair of plump hips. 'Just how long is this going to take?'

'Long enough for coffee.'

'Oh, for Christ's sake. I'll have a skinny latte,' the blonde huffed.

'Sorry,' Sherry said. 'The machine only does filter.'

Amanda Hardwick fixed her with a cold eye. 'So you'll just have to go down to Dean & Deluca and get me a latte, won't you?'

Sherry gaped. The coffee bar, as everyone present knew, was seventy-four floors down and two street crossings away. 'I'm, like, six months *pregnant*?' Sherry said, pointing with both hands at her bump.

Amanda stared coolly back. 'I think,' she said witheringly, 'that you're confusing me with somebody who gives a shit.'

'Sherry hasn't got time to go and fetch one,' Alice cut in hastily. 'It's filter or nothing, I'm afraid.'

After some pouting and protests, filter was accepted. The meeting began.

'I'll run through the contested items,' Alice gestured at the article, which she had highlighted in various places. 'The first concerns your claim that your subject dyes his hair and has had several facelifts.'

'He does,' snapped Amanda Hardwick. 'He has.'

'Do you have proof?'

'Yes.'

This answer was a pleasant surprise. Hope rose in Alice that the case was salvageable after all. 'Great. So what's your proof?'

Amanda Hardwick pressed her thin red lips together. 'I don't need *proof* proof. You've only got to look at him.'

Alice flexed her fingers. 'I see. Well, *he* says his hair isn't dyed and his face is the one he was born with. So the onus is on you to prove otherwise.'

'*What?* This is pathetic. I can't believe you've dragged me up here to tell me this.'

'So that's a no then, is it?' Alice enquired calmly. 'You have no evidence on that point?'

Furious silence greeted this.

'And then,' Alice moved her finger down the page, 'there's your allegation that he suffers from a sex addiction and takes recreational drugs.'

Amanda jumped up and clamped a hand melodramatically to her forehead. 'Oh, please. I can't believe I'm hearing this. Get with the programme, will you? All Hollywood knows *that's* true.'

'I'm afraid that won't stand up as evidence in a court of law,' Alice said gravely. 'Or will all Hollywood come into the witness box?'

'He sniffed all the way through the interview. What more proof do you want?'

'That could have been a cold. Did he admit to you in the interview that he was a drug-taking sex addict? Or . . .' Alice ran her digit down several more paragraphs, 'that his two young children aren't his at all and their father is actually Brad Pitt?'

Christ. The more you read, the more unbelievable this interview was.

'All Hollywood knows that as well,' Amanda said defiantly.

Alice propped her chin up on one hand and stared wearily at Amanda. 'Quite apart from any immediate legal implications, have you any idea of the devastating effect this sort of rumour can have on a family? Those are *children* you're talking about. Little kids. But old enough to understand. This sort of thing can ruin lives.'

Amanda looked scornful. 'What is this obsession with kids round here?' she snarled. 'What are you, the fucking Mothers' Union?'

'I'm just pointing out,' Alice said calmly, 'that these are vulnerable youngsters you're writing about. The courts won't like it.'

'What do I care about some effing celebrity kids?' Amanda snarled. 'Or any kids, come to that? Kids, schmids. Anyone who has them deserves all they've got coming to them.'

Alice regarded her levelly. The baby-hating career bitch personified, she thought. Shame Sherry wasn't here to see the real thing in action.

Amanda leant over the table, giving Alice a grandstand view of her cleavage. 'Look, baby,' she spat, 'you do realise who you're dealing with here? I'm Intercorp's star writer, OK? And who the hell are you? Some jumped-up goody-goody drone pen-pusher in the effing legal department, that's what.'

Who just happens to have saved your skin more times than you've had hot dinners, Alice thought savagely. She restrained the urge to fling her desklamp, keyboard and computer screen at the woman in front of her and instead folded her hands composedly. 'These are serious allegations and he's going to sue. All I'm trying to do is establish what evidence you have. So far, to be honest, it doesn't look like much.'

It was at this charged point that Sherry came in bearing a tray of freshly brewed filter coffee. As she put a cup and saucer down by Amanda's elbow, the elbow shot out. The cup and its contents were propelled all over Sherry's maternity mini skirt, maternity fishnet tights and maternity knee-length suede boots. Alice gasped. She had no doubt that the action was deliberate. Sherry, meanwhile, looked as if she were about to give birth on the spot.

'So sorry,' purred Amanda, eyes wide in mock shock. 'So clumsy of me. But that's the problem with these cups, isn't it? No lids! Would have been so much better if you'd got the latte after all.'

She got up, seized her handbag and strode out.

'You OK?' asked Alice.

Sherry was scrubbing frantically at her skirt with a handful of tissues.

'You should send her the cleaning bill for that,' Alice suggested.

'Why don't I just sue her?' Sherry's large eyes flashed with fury.

'Why not. Join the club. Everyone else is suing her at the moment.' Alice banged her head against her desk in frustration. 'Jesus. Who'd be a magazine lawyer?'

Sherry stared at her in concern. 'You know, you need a break. You've been working your ass off lately.'

'I know I have,' Alice muttered. 'But where would I go for a break? I haven't the energy to organise anything. And it's not,' she added miserably, 'as if I've got anyone to go with, either.'

'You should get out more,' Sherry advised. 'Meet people.'

'No time.' Alice rubbed her eyes. But she knew, and knew Sherry knew too, that this was an excuse. She had, in fact, opted out of the New York dating scene. It was too competitive, too serious. Dates here were like job interviews, usually for jobs one wasn't certain one wanted.

Moreover, Manhattan Man seemed completely to believe the publicity about his scarcity value. Even the ugly ones with rampant halitosis were convinced that somewhere in the city were at least ten stunning women desperate to marry them.

Alice's gaze lowered to the papers Sherry was scrubbing her skirt with. What she had assumed to be tissue now looked suspiciously like the advice the outside attorney had sent for the whisky cake case.

'Gee, sorry,' Sherry grinned. 'My brain's just all over at the moment. Pregnancy, eh?'

'Pregnancy.' Alice gave her a thin smile.

The telephone rang. Sherry disappeared off to answer it. 'Your mother,' she announced over the intercom.

Alice snatched the receiver up gratefully. Her mother. One shard of sanity in a mad, fractured world. 'Hi, Mum.'

'Hello, darling. Now listen. I've got some news for you.'

Alice listened. Her stomach twisted with dismay. 'But, Mum, I can't just drop everything because Sally's getting married.'

'But she's your cousin, darling. You used to be very close.'

'Yes, but I haven't really seen her since the Bay City Rollers were in the charts.'

'Who?'

'Never mind, Mum. I just mean the last time Sally and I got together we were wearing flares and platform shoes.'

'That sounds,' her mother said briskly, 'a vast improvement on what Sally wears now. Her hair is blue, apparently.'

Alice smiled. Sally's recent career, to the reported despair of Alice's Aunt Frances, had featured stints as a face-painter and community juggler, the latter post, to Sally's Tory-voting father's disgust, being sponsored by a liberal-minded local council. Who she might be marrying defied speculation.

But speculate, Alice decided, was the most she planned to do.

'I'm sorry, Mum,' she said resolutely. 'Too busy.'

But Alice's mother was not going to give up easily. 'Come *on*, darling. Time you took a break from that high-flying career of yours. The family would love to see you.' The command, for so it undoubtedly was, rolled from Cornwall, under the Atlantic and up to Alice's seventy-fourth-floor Madison Avenue office. 'You could do with a holiday, I'm sure.'

Alice hesitated. High-flying career? Never, thanks to Amanda Hardwick, had she felt quite so professionally low. Or quite so in need of time off. But was this the pick-up she needed?

'Do come, darling.' Her mother had changed tack and was now wheedling. 'Aunt Frances particularly wants you to. She's really rather devastated about the wedding, you know. The groom's called Bo and he's in an anarchist circus.'

Alice smothered a snigger. 'What's an anarchist circus?'

'They do things with dustbin lids and old car engines.'

28

'What's wrong with that?' Alice was teasing her mother. But on principle, as an extremely fair person and a lawyer to boot, she deplored condemnation without proper trial. 'Those sorts of circuses are very trendy. They make a fortune, some of them.'

'Not this one, I can assure you. Still, at least his father was a vice admiral. That, and the fact she's persuaded them to marry in church is about the only thing that's keeping Frances going.'

Alice scrunched her free hand into her mouth. She mustn't laugh. The situation was obviously extremely serious.

'Because there's the baby as well, of course,' Alice's mother added.

'Baby? Sal's pregnant?'

'Darling, you just have to come,' her mother urged. 'Seeing Sally about to pop might make even *you* feel broody at last!'

Alice, irritated, did not reply.

'Well?' The Cornwall end clearly wanted closure.

'I don't know, Mum.' But Alice felt her resolve cracking. Apart from anything else, the wedding had definite comic potential. 'Sally's timing could hardly be worse,' she demurred, as a feeble last stand at resistance.

'Frances's sentiments exactly, darling. Now when can we expect you at the airport?'

Chapter 3

Armani-ed and Manolo-ed outside the church on the wedding day, Alice felt glad she had come home. She had forgotten just how beautiful England could be. And the West Country in particular. Today was a picture postcard from Somerset: blue skies, snowdrops, glossily new-leaved hedges and a lovely old village of fudge-coloured stone.

Adding to her good mood was the unusual, agreeable sensation of standing out rather glamorously from the crowd. Generally, Alice had little interest in fashion, yet, working where she did, she disregarded it at her peril. She had settled on a style that was less dressing to impress than dressing to pass muster; fortunately her long body, thoughtful oval face, blonde hair cropped neatly to chin length and straight-backed, authoritative walk were sartorial short cuts in themselves. Although her tailored cream suit and sharp heels wouldn't have raised a postboy's eyebrow at Intercorp, they looked quite dazzlingly chic here. Admittedly, there was little competition.

The bridal party had clearly barely bothered. Aunt Frances's one concession towards occasionwear was an unflattering fuchsia flowered hat that clashed with her veiny nose. Her boxy tweed suit emphasised a figure straight out of an Edwardian cartoon; from small and surprisingly slender ankles her body swung upwards and outwards like the bow of a ship. Her expression was grim, conveying that today, so far as she was concerned, was no cause for rejoicing.

Sally's father, Uncle Tommy, looked even less festive. He was red-faced, wild-eyed and had the air of a bomb about to detonate. He greeted Alice more brusquely even than usual: 'Still not married?'

'No,' Alice suppressed her annoyance. Doubtless there would be many such enquiries that afternoon.

'Still no kids?'

Alice shook her head.

Uncle Tommy looked her fiercely in the eye. 'Well, I'm *bloody* glad to hear it,' he exploded, before turning on his heel and stomping off.

Alice filed into the cool gloom of the church and took a pew next to her parents. In front was Aunt Frances. Her fuchsia foliage shook violently from time to time as emotion threatened to overwhelm her.

Alice had been looking forward to seeing Bo, the contro-versial groom. But he was not, as expected, nervously ring-twisting at the front of the church.

'It's ridiculous,' Aunt Frances snarled over her shoulder

to Alice's mother. 'It's the *bride* that should be late.'

'Look on the bright side,' Alice's mother whispered back. 'He might have had second thoughts.'

The hat stopped shaking. Aunt Frances turned round with the wondering look of someone reprieved at the last minute from a death sentence.

The murmur of conversation was by now loud enough to drown the stumbling fingers of the village organist. Then came a silence so sharp it was as if everyone had been turned off at the mains. This was followed by a strange, unsteady, clunking noise.

Alice, glancing over her shoulder, saw a man with dreadlocks, a patchwork waistcoat and an insane grin coming up the aisle on stilts. There was a strangled gasp from the pew in front. When Alice looked in her aunt's direction, the fuchsia flowers were once again shaking furiously.

'Here Comes The Bride' suddenly struck up, and a beaming Sally appeared in the aisle. She wore a pointy hat swathed in chiffon and a long green gown which gathered in at the breast and flowed outward and over a vast pregnancy bump.

Aunt Frances now seemed beyond emotion. She stared, lost, at Uncle Tommy, on whose arm Sally was draped. Uncle Tommy, dwarfed on the one side by the stilted Bo, and on the other by his daughter's wimple, looked desolately back at his wife.

The vicar stepped forward, cleared his throat and stretched upward on tiptoe with the loudly whispered request that Bo lower himself.

'Not as easy as it looks, mate,' was Bo's cheerful reply. 'But bring us over that table and I'll see what I can do.' 'That table' being the altar in the antechapel, the vicar, eyes bulging, looked elsewhere for a dismounting block. After some moments, he found one in the shape of the organist's stool and the bridegroom was returned to earth. The organist played on, standing up throughout, and in noticeably improved fashion.

'Dearly beloved,' the vicar said.

The congregation composed themselves. The event was following the usual script at last.

'We are gathered together here in the sight of God—'

'Whoa,' said Bo, holding up his hand. 'Like . . . whoa!'

The vicar paused and looked at him over metal-rimmed half-moon spectacles. 'I'm sorry?'

'When you say God, man,' Bo said in his rapid, sing-song voice, 'we're talking about *any* god, yeah? Not just the one in the Bible, right? We're including, like, nature gods and that?'

'Oh, for God's sake,' muttered Aunt Frances viciously, if appropriately, in the front pew.

This ecclesiastical nicety – or essential, Alice supposed, depending on one's viewpoint – took some time to settle to Bo's satisfaction. When it eventually was, the service proceeded to its usual conclusion – both Frances and Tommy visibly restraining themselves during the 'just cause or impediment' section. Bo and Sally issued forth from the church beneath a guard of honour of fire-eaters drawn, Alice assumed, from the ranks of the anarchist circus.

Once outside, everyone revolved in the usual chattering mêlée. The fire-eaters sat down in a circle on the churchyard grass and began opening cider. Alice watched with trepidation as one held out a bottle to Aunt Frances and invited her to 'take a slug, man'. To her amazement, Aunt Frances, having clearly passed the point of no return, accepted the offer.

The reception was held in a field and featured a marquee bar, jugglers, more fire-eaters and, a discreet distance from the main attractions, a 'head tent', which Aunt Frances had been persuaded was a hospital facility for those who had drunk too much.

The bar was chaos, and a mutinous atmosphere prevailed. This was caused by Uncle Tommy's operating a two-tier drinks system: champagne for those – mostly family – he considered worthy, beer and scrumpy for those – mostly friends of his daughter – he did not. Predictably, the deemed unworthies were as keen to get their hands on Uncle Tommy's Pol Roger as he was to keep them off it.

As a respectable member of the family, Alice had no difficulty obtaining a bubbling glass. Tactfully, she took it away from the bar, sat down on a hay bale and sniffed the grass-scented air.

'Great, isn't it?' a man's voice next to her said softly.

Alice jumped. She squinted at the person who had spoken. It was difficult to see what he looked like, his head being between her and the lowering sun. She could, however, make out broad, muscular shoulders, longish dark hair and a wide, white smile.

As he moved his head, the sun struck at a different angle. It revealed a face straight from an Old Master drawing: fine nose, full lips, sharp cheekbones.

'Hello,' Alice forced out through her suddenly dry throat.

His eyes, thick-fringed by black lashes, were narrow, green and piercing. She felt held in their beam, and that the beam was sweeping the ocean bottom of her soul.

'Hello.'

His wide-lapelled brown pinstripe suit set off his wild hair to glamorous effect. He looked, Alice thought, like a rock star meeting his accountant. Or was he a model? It seemed unlikely that Sally, being a crusty, had friends in the fashion business. But you never knew.

'Versace?' She nodded at the suit. She was on shaky ground with designers, but prepared to give it a try.

His teeth flashed. 'Scope.'

'Scope?' Some happening new English design team, no doubt.

'Second-hand shop. It's the disability charity.' He held out a large brown hand. 'I'm Jake, by the way.' His eyes danced as he looked at her.

'I'm, um . . . Alice.'

'And what do you do . . . Alice?' As his tongue caressed the 'l', she saw its red tip flick out from between his lips.

She tore her eyes away. 'Company lawyer in a glossy magazine firm.'

'What does that mean?'

Alice wasn't sure it meant anything. It was meaning

increasingly less to her. Reluctantly, she explained.

He rubbed his chin with a forefinger. 'So, to sum up, your job's about making sure some celeb doesn't get a payout because someone from Intercorp's papped their penis?'

'Basically, yes.'

'Or about trying to save some flaky journalist who can't be bothered to check her facts?'

'That's about the size of it.' Perhaps, Alice thought, Amanda Hardwick had not been the best example to cite. The libel action being brought against *Style* had every prospect of success for the actor. The payout, when it was awarded, would be huge. As would her own sense of professional failure, despite the efforts she had made. She had never lost a case before. Ever.

And Amanda Hardwick, of course, would escape free of any blame or responsibility. She would sail on like a leaking tanker, leaving others to clear up the mess.

'It sounds an awful thing to do for a living,' Jake said baldly.

'It is.' She twiddled her empty champagne glass unhappily.

'So what are you doing it for then?'

'You tell me,' Alice said gloomily.

'I'd rather get another drink.'

Champagne, they found, was flowing freely now. Uncle Tommy had apparently admitted defeat and stomped off home.

Jake took a bottle from the bar and led Alice outside. A bonfire had been lit and rippled against the gathering dusk like a ragged red flag. He drew her some distance from the crowd and the tents, to a group of trees whose branches hung low and screening.

He took off his jacket and spread it on the grass. Alice, mindful of her cream suit, was grateful for this. She smiled at Jake and held out her glass. But the hand holding the bottle hesitated. 'Don't you feel wasted?' he asked her.

'I'm definitely starting to feel woozy,' she confessed as he filled the glass. She took a mouthful. The calming, thickening sensation in her head increased as the fizzy liquid flooded her stomach.

'Not that sort of wasted.' His tone was serious. 'I mean what you were saying about your job. Don't you want to do something more worthwhile with your time?'

'Like what?' Alice said defensively. 'What do you do?'

'I run a recycling magazine.'

'Do you? I thought you were a model. Something in fashion, anyway.' Too late, blushing, Alice realised this was as good as admitting she considered him drop-dead gorgeous. But Jake, snorting, didn't seem to have registered a compliment.

'All those glossies have affected your brain,' he told her.

'Probably. But – a recycling magazine? That's, um, *great*.'

He shot her a swift, speculative look. 'Interested in recycling, are you?'

Alice wasn't sure that 'interested' was quite the word. Certainly, she recycled her wine bottles whenever she remembered, but did not find the process particularly fascinating. But she sensed that to say so would offend. 'Well, it's important, isn't it?' she hedged.

'You bet it is. But not enough people think so.' He grinned ruefully into the fire. 'It's slowly catching on, but there's a long way to go.' He shrugged. 'We'll get there, though. We have to. For everyone's sake.'

'It must be great,' Alice said enviously, 'to do something you really believe in for a living.'

He looked at her through long fire-lit eyes. 'Well, you could too, you know. You're a free agent. A single girl – am I right?'

'Is it that obvious?'

'Not in the least. As soon as I saw you I was looking around for the lucky guy.'

'You're too kind.'

Jake ignored her ironic tone. 'So what I'm saying is, you can do what you like. You're, ahem, unattached. Earning big bucks, I bet . . .' He looked at her for confirmation. Alice did not bother to deny it. The fact her salary was large had somehow lost its excitement. Along with everything else concerning work.

'With nothing to spend it on but,' he glanced at her spike heels, 'shoes.'

Alice laughed.

'So, come on. You've got dosh galore. You could easily afford to take some time out. Think about what you really want to do with your life.'

'You seem to have it all worked out for me,' she teased. 'What if this isn't the right time?'

'We never recognise the right time until it's too late,' Jake said gravely. 'What you need to do is live more in the moment.'

He topped up her glass again. Alice felt her brain start to thump. She tipped back her head, absorbing the sounds and scents of the spring evening and the increasingly raucous whoops coming from the wedding party.

'And kids?' Jake asked lightly. 'Where do they fit in? Oh, don't tell me.' His voice was mocking. 'Let me guess. There's no room in your busy, kick-ass, work-obsessed life. You're one of those typical career—'

'No I'm *not*,' Alice snapped, sitting up angrily. 'And you know what? I'm sick of people thinking that I am. I've always wanted children. *Always*.'

'So what are you waiting for?'

Alice stared crossly at her hands. 'Oh God. I don't know. Nothing in particular. Or lots of things. Like the right man. It's not simple.' She looked despairingly back towards the bonfire.

Some of the more uninhibited guests were now dancing around it naked. They did not, needless to say, include Alice's parents, who had gone back to their hotel long ago. Nor did they include Aunt Frances, who had taken one look inside the head tent and had not been seen since. Some rumours held that she had exited in hysterics. Others, still more dramatic, claimed she remained inside.

Alice realised that Jake was watching her. The ridges of his cheekbones reflected the flickering firelight. His eyes glowed wolfishly.

'Don't you ever think about giving New York up?' he asked softly. 'Coming home?'

'Why are you so interested?'

He grinned. 'Selfish reasons. Because you're gorgeous and I fancy you rotten.'

Alice's mouth dropped open.

He refilled her glass. At the touch of his hand she felt a current, faint but definite, pass between them. She jerked her hand away in panic.

'Did you feel that?' he whispered.

Alice's heart was speeding. She looked accusingly at the glass.

'It's nothing to do with *that*,' Jake said with a throaty laugh. 'Look at me.'

Alice looked. There was no mistaking the message in those eyes. It was the oldest in the world, designed through centuries of evolution to be impossible to misunderstand. She forced herself to look away. This couldn't be happening.

He moved his face towards hers. She could almost taste his breath. Her eyes started to close of their own volition and she felt her tongue tingle, her mouth water and her lips twitch to be kissed. So this was what pure animal attraction was like. She'd never believed it existed outside the movies.

'Enjoyed that, didn't you?' he murmured as they both came up for air. She nodded. His eyes, close to hers, narrowed with satisfaction.

'So did I. I don't see the point of beating about the bush. If you like someone, you should tell them. We don't have time

41

on this planet to mess about. It's a waste to do otherwise and I hate waste. Of all descriptions.'

As his face approached hers again Alice felt herself pulled towards him, a helpless iron filing before a powerful and very sexy magnet.

He pressed her hard into the grass with his kiss. 'Don't go back to bloody New York,' he growled.

Alice did go back, however. As she had always intended and as her ticket dictated, she returned to New York the very next day. She had, after all, a life and career there; which, despite their shortcomings, were not going to be knocked off course by a wedding reception snog, however pleasant. And the snog with Jake had been very pleasant. The best ever, in fact. And, in fact, rather more than a snog.

Her face warmed at the memory. He'd lain on the grass watching her as, repeatedly, she'd got dressed. Then, just as she fixed the last button and crease, he would pull her down, kiss off her lipstick and push up her skirt.

Night after New York night, Alice relived their encounter. At odd moments during the day his words would come back to her. 'You could easily afford to take some time out . . . think about what you really want to do with your life . . . live more in the moment. And kids? Where do they fit in? What are you waiting for?'

Increasingly, in the office, Alice found herself gazing at Sherry's burgeoning belly. Outside, too, babies suddenly seemed to be everywhere. Had Fifth Avenue always been full of fashionable mothers pushing offspring in designer infantwear? Every magazine she looked through seemed alive with beautiful families. Even the billboards bounced with babies.

And as if to ram the point home Alice's walk to work through Central Park had recently become enlivened, if that was the word, by the Buggycisers, a group of stressed-looking mothers with black smudges under their eyes, who gathered each morning to perform a series of violent exercises whilst holding on to the handles of their baby strollers. 'Buggycise,' proclaimed the portable sign next to the group. 'Rapidly Reclaim Your Pre-Birth Figure.'

The buggies involved, Alice guessed, were the Maseratis of their kind. Covered in sheeny mountaineering fabrics in grey and khaki, they bristled with black rubber trim and sported takeaway caffè-latte holders and broad-tyred wheels crowded with chrome spokes. They looked as if they could tackle Everest with ease. As did the Buggycise instructor, a frowning female in hi-tech sportswear barking orders into a headset.

Buggycise looked hard work to Alice. She felt sorry for the mothers, but sorriest of all for the babies who, straitjacketed in their strollers, were obliged to witness the exertions of their gasping parents. Some babies were crying, which seemed a natural enough reaction to what must be, at that age and from that angle, a terrifying sight. And those not already roaring invariably did so at the point in the class where the women seized the stroller handles and jogged off at top speed down the central artery of the park.

It made Alice shudder. Surely childbirth was traumatic enough without rushing about in leggings immediately afterwards? Some of the babies looked only weeks out of the womb. But perhaps this was just the New York way. FAO Schwarz, after all, stocked serried ranks of Baby Mozart, Baby Bach and Baby Einstein DVDs, which promised to light the flame of genius in the tiniest of brains. No doubt it was this the Buggycise babies had to look forward to when they got back to their apartments.

But wasn't that preferable to what she had to look forward to when she got to work? The fallout from the Amanda Hardwick article showed no signs of letting up. Nor did Brant.

'You're slipping, Duffield,' he ungenerously observed one morning, waving the latest threatening missive from the actor's lawyers.

'I'm doing my best.'

'Well, do it better.'

Alice smarted. She *was* doing her best, goddammit. But why the hell, really, was she bothering? Where was the fun? Where was the bloody point? Did she really want this boss? This job? This city? That elegant little minimalist mortgageless flat, however enviable its position on Central Park? The train of thought Jake had started seemed as impossible to stop as the court case against *Style*.

Nor was this Alice's only preoccupation. Her period had been due within days of Sally's wedding. But she had been back almost a week and it had not yet arrived. There was, in addition, an unusual tenderness in her breasts. It was only when the nausea started that the impossible, the unthinkable seemed even vaguely probable. But how could it be? Jake had worn a condom.

When the line in the 'Pregnant' box showed triumphantly blue, Alice felt first of all a tremendous numbness. This was replaced almost immediately by a huge, near-heart-bursting surge of delight.

Admittedly, it would have been nice to have the choice. To have planned the pregnancy with the father. But frankly, given her age and her ovaries, that was just cavilling. Was she not unbelievably fortunate to have been given such a chance? Not until now, actually staring at the line that indicated her baby, did Alice realise how desperately she had wanted one. And how hard she had tried to repress what had seemed an impossible dream.

Although she could not yet feel the growing baby, knowledge of its presence glowed inside her. She surged with energy; even the prospect of coping alone with the different, difficult stages did not discourage her. She had money enough to cushion her from most things, while making decisions by herself was something she was used to. She would cope.

Only one thing really concerned her. This was a matter of conscience. Should she not let Jake know, at least? Did he not have a right to know? She cursed not having taken his contact details. But at the time there had seemed no point. Rather, that had been the point. Knowing she would never see him again had been what – combined with the champagne and his charm – had made her surrender in the first place.

* * *

'You say you met him at Sally's wedding?' From three thousand miles away, Alice's mother sounded uncertain. 'I don't remember him.'

'You might have gone by then,' Alice admitted. 'Or maybe you were somewhere else in the party.'

'And you didn't get his address at the time? Not like you, darling. You're normally so organised.'

Alice smiled wryly at her end. There had been nothing organised about the frenzied coupling behind the screening tree branches.

'What do you want him for, anyway?' her mother asked curiously.

Alice took a deep breath and tried to sound casual. 'Just a small, er, legal matter, Mum.' Hopefully the word 'legal' would forestall further questions until she was ready to supply the real answers. Keen as her mother was to have grandchildren, she would hardly view these circumstances as ideal.

'*Legal* matter?'

'Yes, but only a very small one. A very, very small one,' Alice said, with perfect truth. 'Anyway, Mum, the point is that I thought Aunt Frances might get his number or address for me. She could ask Sally and Bo.'

'They've gone to a vegan yoga camp in the Shetlands on honeymoon. Apparently it's got a birthing tent, whatever that is, for when Sally finally goes into labour. Can you imagine?'

'No,' said Alice. She was fervently trying not to. The labour aspect of having a baby sounded extremely unpleasant. 'But Aunt Frances can get in touch with them there, can't she?'

'I don't think impure elements from the outside world are allowed,' Alice's mother said. 'That's what they told Frances when she tried to ring. She was very offended.'

Alice racked her brains. 'Jake runs a recycling magazine. It'll be based in the West Country, although I'm not sure where. You might be able to track him down through the phone book.'

'I can try. What's this magazine called?'

'Ah.' Alice slapped her forehead in frustration. 'Forgot to ask.'

Her mother sighed. 'Really darling. I'll do my best.'

But Mrs Duffield's best, and Alice's own searches on the Internet, came to nothing.

Alice felt, on the whole, relief. She had done the decent thing. She had tried, failed and now her conscience was clear. The fact Jake knew nothing about it was probably a good thing. Less complicated, less messy.

So it was to be just the two of them together, her and the baby. Alice lay awake at nights and tried to imagine it. She was, after all, to be a mother. She would, after all, have a baby.

Chapter 4

'He's taking us to court?' Amanda Hardwick repeated at the London end of the phone.

'Yes,' Alice replied with a calmness she did not feel. 'You're going to have to go in the witness box.' She drove her nails into her palms with frustration. The last chance of salvation was gone. The actor had refused a generous out-of-court settlement. He was, Alice recognised, hellbent on making Intercorp suffer as publicly and humiliatingly as he presumably had himself. And, considering what had been written, she could hardly blame him.

'Fine,' trilled the person who had written it. 'I can wear my new black Dior.'

Alice struggled to control her annoyance. 'I'm not sure that's going to make any difference. His wife, as you know, will give evidence for the other side. She'll be going all out to get the glamour vote.'

'*Excuse* me,' Amanda Hardwick said acidly. 'Are you saying that I'm less glamorous than his wife?'

Alice paused. The question would be laughable were the situation not so serious. However worked-on her look, Amanda Hardwick could not hold a candle to the beautiful young blonde film star whose sexagenarian husband was bringing the libel action. 'She's very famous,' Alice gingerly pointed out, wondering why she was bothering to spare the Hardwick feelings. Actually, she did know. She was doing it for Intercorp's sake, to squeeze the best possible performance from the wretched writer during the trial. The better Amanda was on the witness stand, the better would be their chances of reducing the bill for damages. I still care, Alice thought, after all.

'I'm pretty bloody famous myself, actually,' Amanda thundered from the other end of the phone.

Alice groaned. Time, she decided, to bring this nonsense to an end. 'None of this matters. We're going to lose anyway. The only question is – how badly.'

'Lose? We're going to *lose*?'

'Yes. So what you and I need to do now is work out what you're going to say in order to get the damages down.'

'You're saying *I've* got to help *you* get the damages down?'

'That's right. It should be possible if—'

'Hang on a minute,' bawled Amanda. 'You're the fucking legal department. It's your job to sort this out, not mine. What sort of a useless shmuck are you?'

'Now look—' Alice prepared to present Amanda with a few

home truths. The first being that, had she not written a tissue of lies in the first place, they would not be in this situation.

'No, *you* look, Miss Goody Bloody Two-Shoes. Just because you're a shit lawyer about to lose a court case, don't expect *me* to bail you out.'

Click. Burr. Amanda's end had gone dead. Alice stared at the receiver in her hand. She was tempted to hurl it at the wall. Yet anger and stress was not good for the baby. Closing her eyes, Alice tilted her head back and gulped down several steadying mouthfuls of air instead.

'Hey there. Didn't realise you'd taken up transcendal breathing.'

Alice jerked her head violently up. She blinked away the tears of frustration still shining in her eyes. It was true. She was not imagining it. He really was there. Dazzlingly hand-some, dazzlingly smiling, so dazzlingly tall he filled the door frame, his arms blooming with dazzlingly red roses. Alice's mouth fell open. *Jake*.

'He says he knows you,' Sherry piped anxiously from behind. 'He just came in. I couldn't stop him.'

Alice half rose to her feet, then sank back in her chair. Her head whirled. 'It's OK. I do know him. Thanks, Sherry. Could you . . . er . . .'

'Shut the door? Sure.' As the huge bunch of flowers moved forward, Sherry retreated, grinning and making huge thumbs-up signs.

Alice looked at Jake. He looked back at her over the roses.

'What are you doing here?' she gasped. 'How did you find me?'

'I heard that you were looking for me. Through the grape-vine,' he said through the roses. 'Your aunt told some friends of Sally and Bo's, whom I happened to bump into. I had to come and make sure you weren't trying to sue me or anything.'

'*Sue* you?'

The eyes over the blooms were creased with amusement. 'Well, you never know. Apparently you wanted to talk about something legal. And you being a lawyer and all that. And considering what we got up to at the wedding . . .'

Alice reached hurriedly to switch off the intercom that connected her to Sherry. She hadn't the slightest doubt that her assistant was listening.

'So?' He was smiling expectantly at her. 'Go on. Shoot. What have I done? Sexual assault? Failure to keep your stomach lined with alcohol-absorbing sandwiches?'

'Sit down.' Alice felt suddenly nervous. It was no small thing to tell a virtual stranger they were linked to you for eternity by a cluster of cells.

The knuckles clutching the rose stems went white as she told him. His eyes widened with amazement. He did not, however, say anything. There was an awful silence. 'Well?' Alice whispered eventually. 'What do you think? Don't worry, I'm not after you for maintenance. I'll look after the baby myself . . .'

But he had tossed the flowers aside now and was dancing round the office, whooping, whirling, his hair streaming, with every appearance of delight.

'So you're pleased then?' Alice gasped, almost perspiring with relief.

His strong brown hand slapped the table for emphasis. 'Pleased? Christ, it's not every day you find out you're going to be a father.'

Then, much to the frustration of Sherry, who had crossed from her desk to see what the noise was, he winked at her, locked the door, pulled down the blinds and pulled Alice towards him.

'We can't!' Alice gasped, as he pushed her floorwards. 'Not *here*.' But, it turned out, they could. And did.

Afterwards, he pushed the hair back from her forehead and smiled into her eyes.

'Alice. Look, this is it. You've got to come back now.'

'What?'

'Come back with me. Home. To England. Have the baby and think about the rest of your life.'

'Did you say *with* you?'

'Sure. Why the hell not? Why should you look after it yourself? It's my baby you're carrying.' He kissed her naked stomach and smiled into her eyes. Alice felt herself melting again.

That night, he took her to the Rainbow Room, her favourite bar in the city. Sixty-four floors up, sipping champagne – 'just the one, OK,' Jake warned – and looking with a full heart over Manhattan, Alice felt she had never been so happy.

'To us,' Jake said, and she clinked her glass hard against his.

'To us all,' she giggled, rubbing her stomach.

'To us all at home in England,' he added, raising his glass again. 'You'll love it,' he assured her. 'The cottage is straight from central casting. Beams, huge fireplaces, garden. Peace and quiet.'

'I don't think I'd want to be *too* quiet.' Alice smiled. 'I've lived here,' she swept an arm towards the vista outside the windows, 'for too long to want to be stuck in the middle of nowhere.'

'It's not in the middle of nowhere.' Jake sounded indignant. 'The village is just outside Bath.'

'Bath.' Alice remembered visiting it as a child. Jane Austen, Beau Brummell, sweeping crescents of porticoed houses. It was pretty and elegant. But did she really want to move there?

He stayed for a few more days. She took him sightseeing; Jake remaining unimpressed even by the view of Manhattan as seen from the Staten Island Ferry. 'Beautiful?' he echoed. 'Alice, I don't see beautiful. I see environmental disaster. I see profligate consumerism.' As Alice's face fell, he smiled at her. 'But then,' he added, squeezing her swiftly round the waist, 'I see the mother of my first child, and everything's wonderful again.'

As they walked through Greenwich Village, Jake waxed a good deal less lyrical about the historic house-fronts and bijou ambience than he did about his environmental magazine, *Get Trashed!*. Alice listened, half admiring, half scared as he outlined the fate awaiting the planet if people didn't get their recycling act together soon. So persuasive was he, so passionately committed to his cause, that she felt the first stir of outrage herself as she surveyed the urban landscape – every inch of it apparently rank with pollution – all around her. Listening to him talk, she felt like a churchgoer beneath the pulpit of a wildly charismatic priest.

And there were other ways his rants seemed to rouse him. Their lovemaking afterwards made fireworks burst in her head. It was as if he had to physically work off the tension he had built up in himself.

The more time they spent together, the more Alice realised that she had never met anyone who really believed in anything before. Let alone lived, as Jake so obviously did, by their principles.

'There's a reason for everything,' he had said about the baby. Had the reason she had become so unexpectedly pregnant been to save her from the meaningless life she was living and give her selfish, shallow existence some much-needed depth? As Jake's visit drew to an end, Alice became increasingly convinced that it was.

Jake proposed on his final day, on a boat in Central Park. Alice felt she was in an advert or a fashion shoot. The scene – a soft, sunny morning with a head-turningly handsome man staring besottedly at her against one of the world's most famous backgrounds – had an unreal edge. It was surely too romantic to be true.

'But you hardly know me,' she pointed out. 'It's all a bit whirlwind, isn't it?'

'Some things are, Alice. But that's because some things are just . . . right. Feel right.'

Alice stared at the water. 'It's a bit sudden.'

'And perhaps that's for a reason,' Jake said gently. 'You need to go with the flow, Alice.'

Alice trailed a hand in the lake. The flow felt cool and silky between her fingers.

What doubts, after all, did she have? He had flown over in a heartbeat without even knowing she was pregnant and had no qualms about taking full responsibility when he did. How many men would have done that?

And there was his ideological commitment. She loved him for his concern, his energy, his belief, the way he tossed back his hair and his eyes blazed. It kindled a dormant idealism she had not realised she possessed. Life with Jake – and the baby, of course – would have real meaning. It would be significant, useful, and a dramatic contrast to the trivial world of New York glossy magazine publishing. Not to mention that of New York legal back-stabbing. Perhaps it was time to get out of the writ race.

Last but not least, there was the matter of Jake's looks. How many men were as handsome or could bring her to the point of ecstasy with a few strokes of a sensitive, knowing hand?

What more, ultimately, did she want?

'I suppose it's all been a bit much,' she confessed eventually. 'All these surprises. It's very complicated.'

'It is if you want to look at it that way.' He reached for her face and lifted it to his. His eyes were radiant with sincerity. 'But as far as I'm concerned, the rest of my life is at the disposal of you and the baby. What's so complicated about that?'

'Nothing,' Alice admitted after a pause.

'So resign tomorrow.'

Through hooded, half-open eyes, the Head of Human Resources looked Alice up and down. She was a jowly, sour-faced trout in her mid-forties about whom a sense of disappointment clung like strong scent. At the moment, Alice knew, she was disappointed in her. But not half as much as Brant had been once he realised he was taking the Hardwick case into the courtroom himself.

'Sure is a shame you're going,' the HHR drawled. 'You were earmarked for great things here. Youngest deputy ever in the legal department and all that.'

Alice smiled politely. 'I know. But . . . well . . . I guess I want to do other things with my life now. I've got other responsibilities.' As she spoke, she felt a faint tug at the skirts of what used to be her ambition. She ignored it.

'Yeah?' The HHR tapped a pencil stamped with 'Intercorp Mags Mean Business' against her creased, plum-lipsticked mouth. 'That old last-chance-saloon scenario, huh?'

Alice looked steadily at her. 'What do you mean?'

The trout smiled. 'I think you know what I mean. Mid thirties, great career, but you forgot to have a baby, right? And now there's one on the way. You can't believe your luck, so you're gonna give everything up. Everything you've worked for. Tell me, honey,' she put her head on one side, 'you don't think that's a bit of a waste?'

'It's not exactly like that,' Alice said hotly. 'I've been less than motivated in my work for some time, as it happens.' She looked boldly at the trout. There. That would shock her. No one, ever, admitted to being unmotivated at Intercorp.

But the trout did not bat an eyelid. 'Sure. Who isn't, from time to time? It's natural. You've been working damn hard. But all you probably needed was a holiday. Six months off, whatever.' She leant forward. 'Honey, we can arrange it for you. All you have to do is ask.'

'No, thanks.' Alice swallowed, suddenly, wildly, tempted. But she must ignore the siren voice. It was too late. She had agreed to marry Jake. Agreed to go home to England.

'Well, I sure hope it works out for you.' The trout shook her head slowly from side to side. 'Kids, they're a big step. Harder than any job, oh boy.'

'I'm sure they are.' Alice smiled tightly, disbelieving. No work could possibly be harder than all-nighters at Intercorp. Motherhood, after that, would be a breeze. Especially with Jake to help her.

The HHR leant further across her vast walnut desk. 'You're sure you wanna pack it all in? Because we sure don't wanna lose you. We can fix you up with an apartment. Daycare. Whatever.'

Alice forcibly turned her head from side to side.

The trout raised an eyebrow. 'Well, honey, if it doesn't work out . . .'

'Doesn't work out?'

The trout opened her hands. 'Hey, you gotta face it. Motherhood might not be your thing. It ain't everyone's. And if it ain't yours, there's always a desk for you here. Remember that.'

'It's very generous of you,' Alice said stiffly. Of course motherhood was her thing. She was pregnant, wasn't she? It would have to be her thing, and for ever from now on.

'Generous!' The HHR snorted. 'You're joking, aren'tcha? We're not being generous. Just reflecting a proportion of what you save us every year in libel actions.' She paused judiciously before adding, 'Even if you don't win 'em all.'

Alice burned at this reminder of her one professional failure. 'Yes, well,' she snapped, 'I'm certainly not going to miss Amanda Hardwick.' Never seeing that wretched woman again was one of the greatest benefits of leaving New York. Her doubts about having made the right decision receded.

The trout raised an eyebrow. 'Hey, we're none of us gonna miss her, believe me. We're none of us sorry to see her go.'

'She's leaving?' Alice stared in amazement.

'Got the chop, didn't she? After her latest screw-up in *Style* magazine. That case you were working on – one too many for the guys upstairs.' The HHR stabbed a purple-tipped finger upwards in the direction of the executive floors. 'She's dead meat round here, let me tell ya.'

'No!' Alice felt a smile pull at the corners of her mouth. She had hated the fact Intercorp would lose the case. But if Amanda Hardwick went down with the ship, well, that was different. She had got what was coming to her at last. 'I hadn't heard that.'

'She only found out herself ten minutes ago.'

Chapter 5

Amanda reached for the small bottle of warm screw-top airline wine. Pouring it into her plastic glass, she tried not to reflect on the chilled champagne she knew was currently being served in First. She glanced at the screen set into the back of the seat in front. The small green plane marking the distance covered was barely over Newfoundland yet. She wriggled in her seat. Economy was torture. How did people stand it?

She closed her eyes, unwillingly reliving the events of the past few days. Never would she have thought it possible she would be sacked from Intercorp. What a sinecure she'd had there. First-class flights and five-star hotels all around the world to interview celebrities for Janice Kittenburgen. But no longer.

Amanda glugged back the wine and cursed that long-faced beanpole bitch of a lawyer who'd lost the case and killed the goose that laid the golden eggs. If she'd concentrated more on what she was supposed to be doing, done her bloody job properly in other words, I, Amanda thought, wouldn't be in this mess now. Damn her. Damn her to hell. She closed her eyes and indulged herself for a few minutes imagining a variety of lingering and painful deaths for the deputy head of the legal department. None seemed quite as bad as she deserved.

Amanda opened her eyes again. Thinking about the recent legal disaster was almost as much torture as Economy. She rummaged in a leather bag of modishly complex design – one of the many freebies she would no longer be receiving – dragged out a handful of glossy magazines and stared at the covers. This too, of course, was torture, reminding her of the cosseted world she had left behind. Everything was torture, basically.

Amanda gulped more wine and began to flick through the magazines. Her gut twisted with envy at the unrelenting display, page after page, of shiny-haired women with white teeth, fabulous figures, stunning homes and, presumably, wealth beyond the dreams of avarice. Many of them had beautiful children clasped in their arms, and were running happily with them about their gardens, or else bouncing up and down with them on one of those vast, round trampolines that were obviously this year's must-have accessory.

As were the children themselves, of course. Amanda narrowed her eyes in thought. It was obvious from the pages before her that children were more fashionable even than trampolines at the moment. At a subconscious level she knew this already; she'd been in enough *Style* features meetings when it was discussed, after all. Not that she had listened. Babies, shmabies, or so she had always thought. Boring, noisy, smelly and sick all over your Marc Jacobs. As for pregnancy, it not only prevented you having fun, but interfered with your career and lost you power and money. Basically, motherhood was for losers.

But was it? Had she been too hasty? Three of the five glossy magazines she had brought with her contained celebrity mother-and-baby supplements packed with famous parents gambolling with photogenic offspring. None of them looked powerless or poor. The ads were full of children as well. Everyone from Burberry to Gucci seemed to have decided that infants were It.

From the evidence of these glossies, Amanda concluded, babies looked more than bearable. They didn't, after all, stop you having fun – the world apparently abounded with luxury hotels complete with nannies to mind kids while parents hit the swim-up champagne bar. Nor did babies stop you having nice things – on the contrary. The baby gifts a certain pregnant supermodel had received from celebrity friends included Baby Dior outfits, a monogrammed bathrobe, Pucci print Babygros, pink suede moccasins, a Ralph Lauren hat and mitts in lavender merino wool. Plus a pair of baby Tod's driving shoes in sky blue!

Feeling panicky now, Amanda read how a pram called Bugaboo Frog was 'every hip new mum's accessory of choice'. Terror rose within her. Motherhood was officially glamorous. Everyone who was anyone was beating a path to the birthing centre. But without the least reduction in their status. In fact, downsizing – how she now chose to see that uncomfortable ten minutes in the HR department earlier – turned out to be positively fashionable.

Here, for example, was a piece about how former top female fund managers were opting out of the rat race for a life of domestic bliss at home with the children and cookie cutters. Amanda absorbed through widened eyes how a White House speechwriter's formerly high-powered wife had written a bestselling novel on the housekeeping life. It might be made into a *film*.

That settled it.

Amanda, who saw the world as a chocolate box from which she always got first pick, hated to think she was missing out on anything. She needed to get in on this one. And fast.

She thrust a shaking hand in the air as a harassed hostess trundled past. 'More wine,' she barked.

The bottle was even warmer than the one before. But Amanda hardly noticed as she sloshed it into her glass. Her thoughts now concentrated on her husband. Was Hugo, she wondered, father material?

All the basics were there, she supposed. He was good-looking in just the way she liked – tall, neat-featured and with luxuriant dark hair. He kept middle-age spread at arm's length with energetic squash sessions and as a consequence had the type of lean, muscled torso that rose without a shred of spare fat from the waistbands of his tailored pinstriped trousers. It also looked very good against white sheets on Sunday mornings.

He was an efficient bread winner too, she had to give him that. He was the most successful employee of the estate agents he worked for. Amanda could almost overlook the company's embarrassing name – J. Bond, Special (Estate) Agent, 007 Islington High Street, for God's sake – because of the constant stream of champagne cases, complimentary weekends away and sports cars on loan as rewards for Hugo's excelling performance targets. There were bonuses too.

But the money did not go far. Occasionally it went as far as Portofino, the Maldives or whatever other luxury retreat Hugo had hit on. Usually, however, it went only as far as the designer emporia of Bond Street. Hugo, who enjoyed living up to his firm's image of tongue-in-cheek suave, had a soft spot for Savile Row suits and hand-made Jermyn Street shoes. He had almost as many costly designer face products in the bathroom cabinet as she did. Then there were all his gadgets – the mobile phone you could make an entire movie on, the new edition ironic-retro iPod . . .

Amanda finished the wine and plonked her plastic cup down decisively. Well, that would all have to stop now there was a baby on the way. How else were those junior J. P. Tod's to be paid for?

Particularly given their other debts, notably those for last year's wedding in a fashionable London club. Amanda still had no idea how something involving so many freebies had been so expensive. She'd cut every corner possible; had waited until the last minute to choose between (free) Manolo and Gina and kept several (non-charging) dress designers in nail-biting suspense. The bills had been astronomical, even so.

The baby, Amanda realised, also raised the question of the house. The house they did not have, as opposed to the flat that they did. Despite Hugo's access to the best and the brightest properties in London, their own place was crap, frankly. Their third-floor apartment was all wrong for a child. You couldn't swing a kitten round it, let alone a baby. There was one bedroom, no hi-tech family media-room-cum-cinema and, worst of all, nowhere whatsoever to pitch a huge circular trampoline. Basically, they'd have to move.

But not south of the river to some Nappy Valley ghetto. And Amanda had no intention of going out east. She still had nightmares about the area she'd lived in when she first came to London; the road lined with graffiti-festooned front doors, neighbours who dumped three-piece suites outside their houses and a postcode that meant bank cards had to be collected in person from a branch two buses away.

So where should they live? Amanda's gaze dropped to the magazines again. Most of the pictured happy families dwelt in rural, parklanded splendour without a tower block or overhead cable in sight. The family in *Harpers & Queen* stood before a vast cream-painted mansion against which, with their white clothes and gleaming blond hair, they were actually barely visible. 'The countryside!' enthused the father, a Lord Fairbourne, who was the best-looking aristocrat Amanda had ever seen. His wife, she noted sourly, was possibly the second best-looking. 'The country's the only place for children if you ask me,' Lord Fairbourne went on.

'Clean air, lots of space and a better quality of life. We're really awfully lucky.'

Lord Fairbourne had a point, Amanda knew. He was lucky to be living in the countryside. Not only was it apparently nice, much more importantly, it was fashionable. *Style* had run features about it being stuffed with celebrities. Madonna. Claudia Schiffer. Kate Winslet. Jordan – well, perhaps she wasn't the best example. The point was, the sticks were currently chic. Particularly if you had children; an extraordinary number of stars, for example, were currently putting the cot in Cotswolds.

Amanda had never, up until now, imagined herself more than a storecard's toss from Selfridges. But the country had its own style advantages, including removing her far from the London magazine industry tom-toms. Being what they were, they would even now be beating out the news that Amanda Hardwick had come a spectacular cropper and that her career was over. Well, they could all eff off, frankly. Careers were pretty over themselves. The smart money was on motherhood and nesting.

Amanda stretched – as best she could, given the space restrictions – and congratulated herself on sorting out the whole of their future in fifteen minutes or less. She could hardly wait to tell Hugo about it all.

That very moment, in the offices of J. Bond, Special (Estate) Agent, 007 Islington High Street, the champagne corks were popping. The James Bond theme tune, as always on triumphal occasions, was roaring from the corporate ghettoblaster.

'Congratulations, old boy.' Toby from Leases and Lettings raised a glass of warmish yellow fizz in Hugo's direction. 'The supersalesman triumphs yet again. So the Aston stays *chez toi*, I take it.'

It was a standing joke within the office that the Aston Martin awarded each month, for a month, to whoever had exceeded their sales targets, had been parked outside Hugo's flat since the incentive had been introduced. Or perhaps standing joke was not quite the phrase, especially among Bond staff who relied on public transport.

'Yes, well done, Hugo,' offered Charlie the sales secretary, shimmying unsteadily to the music in her high heels.

'Easy when you know how.' Hugo eyed Charlie's ample cleavage as he knocked back the rest of his champagne. Lanson was not his favourite – personally he preferred Laurent Perrier – but it did the trick. Wellbeing was coursing through his veins.

The sale had been a triumph, there was no doubt about it. His reputation as Bond's most dynamic salesman was not only assured, but enhanced. No one could have sold that place but him. It had taken every trick in the book, gone to both the bridge and the wire, pushed the envelope and any other metaphor that one cared to employ to convince the portly, young and pompous barrister that the unconverted former office, complete with abandoned furniture was the dream home he wanted to spend the best part of a million pounds on.

'You can't afford not to buy it really,' Hugo had argued, the double commission the vendor had promised if he could 'offload that shit on to some mug with more money than sense' looming large in his imagination. 'Frankly, once the new Channel Tunnel extension opens at St Pancras there's going to be a gold rush for property round here. You'll be quids in.'

This was to an extent undeniably true. The forthcoming opening of St Pancras International and the associated redevelopment of the King's Cross area had heralded a boom time for J. Bond, Special (Estate) Agents. It had also brought about its rebranding. Seeing the biggest potential for property since Docklands in the Nineties, Hugo had racked his brains for a gimmick to make the film appeal to the young, monied and hip flocking to the area. What had formerly been the old family firm of Jeremiah Bond Ltd, Property Agents, had, therefore, at his suggestion, become something altogether wittier, more memorable and snappy. Who cared if people like Amanda thought it naff? Naff was big, as evidenced by some of the properties they were selling.

And none was naffer than the striplit wasteland on the Holborn border that the barrister had enquired about, and which Hugo had, against all odds, succeeded in selling to him.

He took another swig of champagne and smirked at Charlie. 'I'll give you a lift to the Tube in the Aston if you like.'

Charlie batted her long eyelashes. 'You can take me home. It's on your way.'

Hugo hesitated, tempted. His glance lingered on the round outline of breasts beneath her tightly buttoned shirt. Then he smiled and shook his head. 'You forget I'm a married man.'

'No I don't.' Charlie sidled up closer to him. 'So come on. Tell me more about the sale.'

Hugo raised his cup to his lips and recalled the scene of his triumph. Not that that had seemed the likely outcome at first.

'There's an underground car park, of course,' he had said encouragingly as the barrister examined the tumbleweed under a clapped-out desk. Hugo hoped he wouldn't be asked too many questions about the car park. The prospect of descending to the building's damp bowels to inspect it had not been attractive. Hugo consequently hadn't bothered. Nor had he inspected the 'flat' itself particularly thoroughly. But details weren't his thing. He was a big picture man, one who liked to get clients warmed up to the potential of a building, excited about their vision for the place. His selling technique was dazzling, seat-of-the-pants stuff. It was smoke and mirrors, not plumbing systems and septic tanks.

'Underground car park? Won't need it,' the barrister said, straightening up. 'I get about by tricycle.' He rubbed his hands together as if knocking the dust off. Everything about him suggested he was on the point of leaving.

Hugo looked around him in desperation. The barrister had been the only person to request a viewing. If he couldn't sell this place to *this* sucker, the commission would be down the toilet. Wherever that was.

He tried another tack. 'The photocopier is included in the

sale,' he said, gesturing towards the vast grey plastic behemoth from the dawn of Xerox time.

The barrister squinted at it through thick spectacles. 'What would I want a photocopier for at home? I've got one at work. And this one's prehistoric anyway.'

Hugo grinned. He had an answer for this. 'All the more reason why it makes a perfect conversation island.'

The barrister's glasses flashed doubtfully. 'What's a conversation island?'

'They're more usually in kitchens,' Hugo said rapidly. 'Those big blocks that groups of glamorous people stand around and chop things up on in a companionable sort of way? Or have drinks off? They've usually got tiles on the top, or wood? But an authentic seventies photocopier would be something else altogether. You'd have a retro-ironic conversation island, no less. And let me tell you, no Manhattan loft apartment's complete without one of *those* these days.'

The barrister seemed impressed. Hugo made a mental note to find out what chambers he worked for and make sure that, in the event of any legal difficulty, he avoided them like the plague.

'The stationery cupboard's in the sale as well,' he added, gesturing at a huge and hideous grey metal box. 'Fantastic ice-breaker – a *real* stationery cupboard! Think of all those *The Office* theme parties you'll be able to have.'

The barrister nodded. '*The Office*,' he repeated tonelessly. 'Yeah. Hilarious.' His face was entirely straight.

'And look at the walls. Those tag ends of last year's Christmas decorations stuck on with Sellotape – kitsch-ironic or what?' Hugo was more than warming to his theme; he was positively smoking. 'And the photocopier could really come into its own at parties, if you get my meaning.' Deciding to go for broke, Hugo tapped his bottom and grinned.

The barrister was looking excited now. He licked his shiny red lips. 'Yeah. Fantastic.'

'So,' Hugo smiled, striking, as always, while the iron was hot. 'Do we have a deal?'

They did.

Afterwards, they went outside; Hugo to hail a taxi, the barrister to return to Gray's Inn on his tricycle. Once he had trundled a safe distance down the road, Hugo punched the air in triumph. What other estate agent in London – the world, even – could seal a million-quid deal with a clapped-out seventies photocopier? He wished Amanda was not still in New York. He could hardly wait to tell her. Of course, he could always call her. But that wasn't the same.

He needed to see her. They really had to spend more time together; make solid what was starting to feel worryingly impermanent. Her Stateside commitments meant they had been apart even more than usual lately, giving him unwelcome opportunities to consider their relationship. Without her forceful physical presence to remind him, it was, for example, disturbingly easy to start wondering why they had got married at all.

Their affair had been hasty and scattered, fitted in between her trips round the world for *Style* magazine. He had fallen for her flashy glamour, and she, he suspected, for what women usually fell for in him; his honed-to-perfection brand of floppy-haired, chisel-featured, slightly sleazy patrician charm.

The sex, on the whole, had ticked the 'experimental' box. Usually after Amanda had read or been told something about the erotic predilections of someone famous she admired. This was not always a success; Hugo had forgotten who it was who enjoyed Viagra-spiked oysters. But he remembered the blinding headache it had given him. As for whoever it was who liked sea-fresh sashimi eaten from each other's naked flesh, the feel of raw tuna on one's skin was vile and the fishy aroma lingered unpleasantly afterwards. But balanced against this had been plenty of more successful encounters.

The result of one had been his drunken Valentine's Day proposal in the whirlpool bath of a country house hotel he couldn't now remember the name of. But there had been no doubts on the wedding day. He had been happy enough to walk Amanda down between the two banks of chairs in the restaurant of the fashionable London club that had been converted into a chapel for the occasion. She had looked wonderful, her brass-bright hair caught up with summer flowers, her dress a heavy satin Empire-line number straight out of *My Fair Lady*. Her something old had been some antique earrings he had given her, her something new some crazily expensive underwear. The something borrowed, he recalled, had been a friend's pearl necklace, which had later in the evening become something lost, and the friend an ex-friend. He couldn't remember the something blue. Unless it was how he felt now.

A soft voice broke into his thoughts. 'You're sure you don't want to give me that lift?' Charlie was gazing at him with melting eyes. Most of the rest of the staff, Hugo saw, had gone. No one would know. He paused, then reluctantly shook his head. 'Why not?' Charlie pressed. 'Your wife's away.' Hugo nodded. But Charlie, he knew, was not the answer to his and Amanda's problems.

The Heathrow arrivals door sprung open. Amanda, laden with luggage, stomped crossly through. For the first time in years there would be no Intercorp-financed driver holding her misspelt name up on a card.

She watched enviously as a glamorous mother and baby she had seen descend from Upper Class were greeted by a uniformed chauffeur who bore them efficiently off. Making an immediate resolution that, whenever she and their baby flew transatlantic, they would have the same treatment, Amanda headed reluctantly to the Heathrow Express.

She checked her mobile. The only message was from Anne Dexter of *Class* magazine, famously one of the snootiest editors in London. 'Amahndah? It's Ee-ann Dextah here. Just wondered if you could give me a tinkle.' Like hell, Amanda thought. The old bat would be ringing to crow, to get some juicy first-hand quotes. It was easy to imagine the what-are-your-plans-now, anything-lined-up interrogation that would be all over the West End by close of play that afternoon. The reason it was easy to imagine was because Amanda had done it so many times to others.

Gritting her teeth, Amanda stuck her bags on the escalator going down to the Heathrow Express. No point dwelling on the past, she told herself firmly. There was the future to consider. By now she had thought through the baby scenario so often she could practically feel the foetus move. One slight problem, of course, was that Hugo had not thought about the baby scenario at all. He therefore had some significant catching-up to do before he shared her point of view. But that was nothing new.

She planned to speed up the process with a little subtle persuasion. Surprise was to be her weapon. He had no idea she was coming home, largely because, between HR department interviews and the rush to JFK, she had no time – or indeed inclination – to tell him of the ignominious way her Intercorp career had ended.

By the end of the afternoon, she was ready. Courtesy of her not-yet-cancelled corporate credit card she had had a facial, a seaweed body wrap, a Dead Sea scrub, her hair and nails done and her teeth bleached.

Then she had hit the shops. To one used to summoning direct from the designers whatever she wanted to wear and then conveniently forgetting to return it, this had obviously been a comedown. But Amanda, magnificently overcoming the humiliation, had tracked down the highest pair of heels ever seen and descended with a growl of triumph on a plunging red sequinned gown with tight waist and slits up the sides.

Now, from the top floor window of the flat, Amanda saw Hugo's Aston Martin draw to a halt outside. She checked herself in the mirror and draped herself across the sofa. What a surprise for him this would be.

Hearing his key scrabble at the door, Amanda stretched her mouth and rolled her eyes to rid herself of any set facial expressions. This was her moment.

Hugo, entering the flat, was regretting not having given Charlie a ride. And not just in the going-home sense; the alcohol, plus the testosterone rush of the office-apartment sale, had produced a degree of sexual excitement that urgently required relief. Especially when one added to it the stress of having his homeward progress in the Aston Martin impeded by some twenty-mile-an-hour arsehole whose back window sported one of those infuriating 'Baby On Board' stickers. The way the moral high ground was routinely commandeered by the infant-owning classes never failed to irritate him. Especially as people with babies were, as everyone knew, the world's worst drivers. Those Islington mothers doing the prep school rat run to Hampstead in their Challenger tank-sized four-wheel drives, for instance . . .

He opened the sitting-room door. The first thing he saw was a shapely leg in a cartoonishly high heel extend upwards from the back of the sofa. 'Daaaaarling!' drawled Amanda's voice.

'*Bloody hell*. When did *you* get back?'

As he approached the sofa, Amanda slid him a sluttish look from under her lashes. Then, fiddling with her hair with one hand, she ran the other down what, thanks to the heels, appeared impossibly long legs.

'You never said you were coming . . .' Hugo swallowed and stopped. Her cleavage was nothing less than a chasm. Pale, creamy and faintly shaking, it looked as if a man could fall down it and be lost for ever. Hugo, looking at it and licking his lips, felt he would like to be that man.

As Amanda slowly parted her legs and flicked aside the red sequins to reveal a complete absence of underwear, Hugo felt his head spin. 'God, I've missed you,' he growled.

A strap tumbled down one creamy shoulder. One fore-finger circling an exposed nipple, Amanda stretched red and shining lips in a lazy smile. 'And I you. And I've got the best news. Darling, something's going to happen to make our marriage complete. To draw us together, closer than we've ever been before.'

'Great,' said Hugo, who was intending to get close at the earliest possible moment. 'What's going to happen?'

Amanda clasped her hands together and summoned a dewy look to her eyes. 'Darling. Hugo. We're going to have . . . a baby.'

'A *baby?*' Hugo echoed. Gone were the fuzzy effects of drink. His head, suddenly, was as clear as a bell. His vision was so sharp he could have flown a night fighter. He stared at Amanda, frowning, trying to calculate; how long had it been since . . . 'But I had no idea . . . I mean . . . oh God.' He sank, shocked, to his knees in front of her, gobbling air as he searched for the right words. 'It's just that I didn't realise we were even trying—'

'We weren't,' Amanda cut in. 'But we are now.' She pulled him towards that chasm of a cleavage.

Hugo, disappearing into it, felt bewilderment mingle with lust. He had never suspected her to have a maternal bone in her body.

'Motherhood,' Amanda declared throatily, grinding her breasts into his mouth, 'is the one box on my life experience sheet that I haven't ticked yet.'

She pushed him back and stood up. As he remained kneeling, she placed one of her stilettos in the centre of his chest. She forced him down, down against the polished wooden floor of the sitting room and began to unzip his trousers.

'After all,' she added, 'I've been there, done it, stayed in the same celebrity compound as Bruce Willis at the Turks and Caicos spa resort and got the Stella McCartney T-shirt.'

'Eh?' said Hugo.

'Never mind,' said Amanda, lowering her head, 'I mean that now I want *more*.'

Hugo wanted more too.

'I've had all the excitement,' Amanda growled, as, with a matador flick of her side-slit skirt, she lowered herself on to him.

Hugo snapped his eyes open indignantly, 'What do you mean you've had all the excitement? We've been married less than a year. What about the best being yet to come and all that?'

'I mean,' Amanda gasped, her voice leaping several octaves, 'I've had all the great life experiences. I've stayed at Sandy Lane, flown Concorde, dined with Tony Blair.'

'Tony Blair?' Hugo yelped. He had not realised dinner

with Tony Blair was a great life experience, particularly the dinner Amanda had attended. Prawn cocktail and rubber chicken as one of a cast of media thousands, from what he'd gathered.

'The point is,' Amanda threw her head back as she rode him, 'that what I want now is the greatest life experience of all. Babies.'

As he thrust upwards beneath her, Hugo tried not to think about babies. Or, rather, think about what he thought about them. That they were sick on you and cried. That they stopped you going out at night and kept you up instead. That if he ever wanted to sing 'The Wheels on the Bus' to some two-year-old, he had plenty of godchildren. He presided at fonts these days with the same regularity he had appeared as best man a decade ago.

'You see,' Amanda panted, lashing her head from side to side now, 'it's all very well for you. Men,' she added, with an expert jerk of her pelvis, 'can wait.'

No they can't, Hugo thought wildly, his need rising swiftly and unstoppably.

'But I don't have that luxury. I'm thirty-five. A few years from now I'll have ovaries like walnuts. Do you want to be fifty and childless?' She raised herself slightly, as if to clamber off him. Damn her, he thought, squirming with frustration, recognising her cruelest trick. She'd developed to an art form stopping just before the crucial moment. No end of treats and presents had been quite literally screwed out of him this way.

Beneath her, Hugo moaned. He had no idea about being fifty and childless. He knew that he liked being thirty-six and childless, but he was prepared to believe this might change. As Amanda lowered herself once more, he wondered what exactly he was letting himself in for. Fatherhood. It was a big question. And one to which he was unsure he had the answer.

Chapter 6

Hugo shifted in his seat. The chairs were hard, the room was hot and these antenatal classes always seemed to last for ever. Tonight seemed the longest yet.

It had kicked off with Lotti asking all the women present to stand up and point out the location of their pubic bone. Matters had not improved since.

The worst moment was when Lotti demonstrated the deep breathing exercises. She had sounded so embarrassingly orgasmic that the effort of keeping his face straight had given Hugo a stitch.

Now Lotti was giving a general talk about pregnancy, which clearly assumed that none of them had the faintest idea what it was. It was illustrated with a large and lurid card-mounted cross-section of the pregnant female body, propped up on an easel. Hugo shuddered at the shiny purple kidneys and the tubes and twisted muscles of the heart. He stared with queasy concern at the large, pink inverted baby in the illustrated womb. He hadn't realised babies grew upside down. It couldn't do them any good, surely. Amanda constantly complained about the design faults of pregnancy. He'd thought she meant the clothes.

Next, Lotti showed the class a plastic oblong pierced with different-sized holes. It looked just like a giant pasta measurer to Hugo until the midwife explained that the smallest, barely visible hole was the normal size of the opening of the cervix. 'And this,' she added, rotating her forefinger within the biggest circle, 'is the ten centimetres Mum needs to dilate to before Baby can be born.'

There were a few gasps at this. Hugo leant forward in horror. 'It's not humanly possible!' he exclaimed, realising too late that he had spoken aloud.

'Evidence that it is is all around you,' Jake remarked smartly.

Hugo glared at him. His first impression of Jake as smug and objectionable had only increased with subsequent meetings. And then there was that ghastly, simpering wife looking adoringly up at him. From what Amanda – frothing with rage – had told him about Alice since the first class, he realised that his initial view of her as scrubbed and innocent-looking had been wrong. Her serene expression, it seemed, was a veneer beneath which lurked a skilled plotter and vicious back-stabber.

A hand went up on the left-hand side of the horseshoe. 'Excuse me,' asked a woman called Martha, who habitually took copious notes. 'But are we going to learn anything about what to do with the baby once it gets out? Nappy-changing and all that sort of thing?'

There was a murmur of agreement at this. The expression on Lotti's face, however, was pure incomprehension. 'The mitwifes show you that,' she said.

'But aren't you a midwife?' asked Martha.

'Yesh.'

'So why don't you show us?'

'Because this is antenatal class,' Lotti explained with elaborate patience. 'We are here concerned with the birth only. That stuff you talk about, it's postnatal. After birth.'

'I understand,' said Martha. 'But it would still help us all to know in advance.' She looked round the class for agreement.

'Speak for yourself,' Amanda said haughtily. 'I'm having a maternity nurse.'

There was a disgusted snort from Jake. Laura, meanwhile, looked envious. 'Lucky you!' she exclaimed.

Amanda preened. 'Great, isn't it? She'll be coming for six weeks from when the baby is born.'

'That'll cost,' remarked Jim from St Helens.

It would indeed, Hugo reflected. Yet, the admittedly vast expense aside, he was reasonably happy with the maternity nurse idea. All he knew about theirs was that she was called Nurse Harris. But his imagination filled in the gaps, summoning an image of a sexy *Carry On* blonde in a uniform and black stockings. It was the part of fatherhood he was most looking forward to. The rest hardly bore thinking about.

'Now, class.' Lotti reached behind the easel and produced a bulging pillowcase. 'Everything in this bag relates to the birthing process, yes?'

All eyes swivelled warily to the pillowcase. 'You might come across some of dese things in the hospital,' Lotti explained. 'So you will want to know what they are.' Hanging out of the top of the pillowcase was a mass of plastic tubing and various offputting metal objects. Hugo had no desire to know what any of them were.

Lotti rattled the pillowcase. 'We make this like a party game, yes? We pass the bag along and when the music stops, the person who is holding it pulls something out, yes?'

Hugo looked round for a ghettoblaster but couldn't see one. He wondered where the music was going to come from.

'Like Pass the Package, yes?' Lotti urged.

'Parcel,' Amanda said testily. 'Pass the Parcel.'

'Pass the Parcel,' Lotti repeated, nodding thoughtfully. She proffered the pillowcase to Hugo. 'Off you go, Yogi.'

Hugo seized the pillowcase's cotton edges and stared into its contents. He looked up in alarm as a strange, high-pitched wail began to fill the room. The noise was coming from Lotti, who was rocking from foot to foot, head on one side, humming tonelessly. Just as Hugo was wondering whether she was ill or not she stopped, snapped her head up and stared at him.

'You still have the bag, Yogi,' she chided.

'Oh, I see. That was the music?'

'Yes. You can pull out of the bag now.'

Hugo slid an unwilling hand into the pillowcase. It closed

around something thin, hard and cold. As it reappeared, Hugo found himself looking at a metal object like a large salad server.

Lotti beamed. 'Forceps,' she explained. 'To drag Baby out if she gets stuck,' she added cheerfully.

'Baby won't be getting stuck,' Amanda said tartly. 'I'm having an elective Caesarean. At the Cavendish,' she added, with emphasis.

Hugo's heart sank. He had been trying not to think about the Cavendish. He could understand the maternity nurse. He could understand Amanda buying designer satin maternity bras – the standard sort were, as she said, too repellent for words. He had even been prepared to indulge her 'nesting' instinct; too late had he realised this was a euphemism for ordering all the most expensive home furnishings she could lay her computer mouse on. Number Four Fitzherbert Place must, Hugo thought despairingly, be the priciest nest ever built.

But he had always disputed, and still did, that she needed to have the baby at a private maternity hospital like the Cavendish. In vain had he explained it was the last straw – well, more of a bale, really – that would break the back of their bank balance.

'Elective Caesarean?' Lotti was regarding Amanda as a vicar might regard a lost soul. 'Well, of course it is your choice not to have a natural birth,' she said sorrowfully.

'You bet it is,' Amanda retorted. 'I don't fancy being doubly incontinent and I've found my pelvic floor quite useful over the years.'

Lotti looked hurt.

The bag's next stop was Jake, who pulled out a thin length of tubing.

'For epidural,' Lotti told him.

Jake smiled pityingly, pulling the tube through his fingers. 'Alice and I won't be needing that. We've put on our birth plan that we're having the baby naturally. At home.'

Lotti nodded delightedly.

Hugo winced. Home births sounded hideously messy. On the other hand, they probably had certain cost advantages over the Cavendish.

'So you're having no pain relief *at all*?' The gap-toothed Laura peered round at Alice. She had an even more revealing top on this week. Her husband, Hugo had noticed, remained absent.

'Research has shown that it's bad for the baby,' Jake told her swiftly.

Laura eyed him. 'I was asking Alice. She's the one who's pregnant.'

'We don't see it like that,' Jake said calmly. 'We're taking equal responsibility throughout, so we think of it as us both being pregnant.'

Christ Jesus, Hugo thought. If there were such a thing as an earnestometer, it would go right off the dial at this point.

Alice smiled at Laura. 'No, I'm not having pain relief. Not if I can help it.'

'Well, the best of bleeding British to you in that case. As it were.' Laura sat back in her seat. 'Personally, I'm having every form of pain relief going.'

'Good for you,' applauded Amanda.

Lotti looked anxiously at Laura. 'You're sure about this? You might not need it,' she cautioned. 'Breathing exshershises can be really very useful in reducing pain . . .'

'Is that right?' asked Laura in tones of withering disbelief.

Lotti shrugged and looked at her watch. 'We have fifteen minutes left,' she announced, beaming toothily again. She flung out a pair of sinewy forearms. 'Over to you. This is the point in the class in which we exchange ideas.'

Hugo stiffened. This sounded dangerous.

'What sort of ideas?' Amanda asked suspiciously.

'Worries,' Lotti smiled.

Hugo flinched. Worries? Was it that obvious?

'Everyone,' said Lotti, 'is now free to tell the rest of the class about any aspect of birthing they are concerned about. Air their anxieties, you know? It's all perfectly natural. And goot to do it in this situation, where we are all in the same ship together.'

'Boat,' snapped Amanda.

Lotti's good nature came Teflon-coated. She was impervious to insult. She smiled at Amanda. 'Boat, yes. You are right. So.' She looked expectantly at the class. 'You tell me your concerns and I try to give you honest answers.'

Hugo wondered which aspect was more terrifying: his worries, or Lotti's honest answers.

Thick silence fell on the class.

Lotti pulled a quizzical face. 'There is no one here with consherns they would like to share with the class in a relashed, intimate and trushting environment?'

Further silence.

Then someone broke it. 'Sex,' drawled a voice. It was Laura who had spoken. There was a titter.

'Sexsh?' Lotti repeated doubtfully.

Hugo eyed Laura warily. If only she and Amanda had not got on quite so well after the first antenatal class. Subsequent sessions had revealed Laura to be a rampant attention-seeker who clearly got no attention from her ever-absent husband. There was, Hugo felt, something unstable and rather desperate about her. She slid him nakedly provocative looks at every opportunity and, though a natural flirt himself, he felt uncomfortable around her. Amanda, on the other hand, clearly felt the opposite. In Laura she had found the perfect accomplice for long afternoons having prenatal spa treatments at Bath's leading health club. During which, it seemed, sex was high on Laura's conversational agenda.

'Laura told me,' Amanda revealed after one such afternoon, 'that it took her ages to get pregnant because Fergus's sperm count was so low.'

'That's awful,' Hugo said.

'Embarrassing, you mean. But apparently it's a very common problem.'

'I mean it's awful that she told you.' Hugo felt a reluctant male camaraderie with the ever-absent Fergus. 'Bit private, isn't it?'

'Whatever.' Amanda shrugged. 'Anyway, in the end, Laura had to send him to *sperm camp*!'

'Sperm camp?' Hugo frowned. 'What the hell's that?'

'The latest thing among thirtysomethings struggling to conceive,' Amanda grinned. 'It's like *The Krypton Factor* for willies. They're based in former army camps and the idea is to do lots of exercise.'

'What difference does that make?' Hugo was unconvinced.

'Gets the testosterone levels up,' Amanda supplied. 'And you can't drink or take drugs but there's lots of phallocentric stimulation. They hug trees – phallic symbols, you see – and eat nothing but sausages. And the whole place is covered in Jordan calendars. Apparently when Fergus came back he wanted it ten times a day.'

Hugo wasn't sure he wanted to know.

'There's only one in this country so far,' Amanda rattled on. 'Somewhere in Devon, I think. It costs a fortune, apparently.'

Hugo nodded. That figured. Everything connected with childbirth cost a fortune.

'It's a shame in a way that *you* didn't go,' Amanda mused.

'*Shame?*' Hugo spluttered.

'Yes. I could have written about it for *Vanity Fair*. Graydon would've loved it.'

Hugo had no idea who Graydon was. But he knew, on this evidence alone, that he didn't like him. 'I thought you weren't writing any more,' he challenged. 'You said you'd given up your career for the greatest career of all – motherhood.'

Amanda looked shifty. 'Yeah, well, I have. Sort of. But I might still do the odd piece from time to time. Keep my hand in, you know.'

'I mean, how soon can we have sex again?' Laura was asking Lotti as Hugo returned to the here and now.

Lotti beamed. 'Oh, I see. Well, I'm glad you asked me that question, Laura. Actually, intercourse can be resumed after several weeks if the birth is uncomplicated.'

'Several weeks!' gasped Martha.

'That's right!' beamed Lotti. 'The vagina can recover remarkably quickly.'

The man beside Martha visibly brightened at this. Laura, too, looked pleased. She nodded and looked laughingly around. Hugo studiously avoided catching her eye.

Silence again. 'Anything else?' Lotti paused. Then she smiled. 'Well, how about it if I ask you all some questions?'

Hugo riveted his gaze to his shoes.

'How do you feel about becoming a daddy?' she asked someone.

Him. With horror, Hugo realised she was asking *him*. The sixty-four-thousand-dollar question, coming straight out of left field. His heart thundered. His hands were twisting together. He opened his mouth and closed it. Then opened it again.

'Er . . . being a daddy . . .' he said uncertainly. He paused for what seemed like hours. 'To be honest, I'm not sure,' he blurted.

'Not sure?'

He caught Jake's scornful eye and Amanda's furious one. Lotti was adjusting her glasses and peering at him as if he were a specimen in a laboratory. Fear swept him like wildfire. Why in God's name had he said that?

'I mean, not sure in a *great* way, obviously,' Hugo stammered, desperately clawing back what lost ground he could. And perhaps this *was* how he felt. Perhaps he *would* grow to love the baby after it was born and he could actually see it as a person, not just a lifestyle-cramping and expensive theory.

Lotti had moved swiftly on. She looked about for the next questionee. 'What about *you*, Jake? How do *you* feel?'

As if, Hugo thought sourly, we can't guess. He braced himself for the inevitable.

Jake beamed dazzlingly. 'There's nothing we're looking forward to more than parenthood. Is there, darling?' He squeezed Alice's slim hand, which was already linked in his. 'We can't wait to welcome our little one on to the planet. However appallingly exploited and abused that planet is at the moment.'

'Well, thanks a million,' Amanda snarled at Hugo once they got outside. 'Showing me up in front of the entire class.'

'Look, I'm sorry, OK?' Hugo pressed the automatic key fob in the direction of the Toyota with more force than was necessary. 'I didn't mean it to sound like that.'

'So what,' Amanda gnashed, '*did* you mean it to sound like?'

Hugo looked at her. Empathy had never been high on Amanda's list of virtues. But then, he supposed, in her line of work it couldn't be. The ability to imagine how other people felt was a positive handicap when penning the sort of hatchet jobs she had routinely filed to *Style*. To look to her for understanding about his baby doubts was, he knew, to look in the wrong place. It wasn't so much that Amanda refused to see things as he saw them. The plain fact was that she couldn't see anything from any point of view but her own.

Chapter 7

Alice loved Combe on sight. Jake's village consisted of a medieval church, thatched pub and tiny half-timbered cottages – of which his was one – dotted about the green.

It was, admittedly, rather further from Bath than she had imagined. Nor had she anticipated that, thanks to Jake's principled objection to all cars, the city would be reachable only by bus. Or buses; getting to the antenatal class involved two.

There were other surprises as well. Such as the extent to which Jake lived and breathed his environmentalist beliefs at home. Alice was amazed at the ingenious uses to which Jake put the many articles he picked up from tips, skips or his own household rubbish.

Yet, eager to support him and anxious to show herself a worthy ideological consort, she was swift to agree that old colanders screwed to the ceiling made attractive and effective lightshades. Although she privately considered the metal variety prettier than the plastic. Records with the middles knocked out and made into picture frames looked very striking too, and the ex-television in the sitting room made, as he said, an excellent aquarium. As Jake pointed out, 'There's always something on the telly in this house and we don't even need a licence.'

Despite such excitements, Alice found country life quieter than expected. While she wouldn't have objected to the odd glass of wine, Jake was now worried about possible foetal alcohol syndrome, and so the pub, which offered the village's only social stimulus, was more or less out of bounds. There was, however, always plenty to do at home. Checking the *Get Trashed!* page proofs before they went to the printers, for example. The International Letters section particularly made fascinating reading.

'Listen to this,' she urged Jake as they sat over the proofs one evening. ' "In my part of China, we only get about twenty-five days of true blue sky a year. Blue sky good for laundry, so when grey takes over, I think: these pants won't dry by sundown, I'll have to wait till tomorrow to do wash. I feel degradation of environment through my pants." ' Alice giggled.

Jake's face, however, remained utterly straight. 'What's so funny?' he asked. 'He's concerned about the changing weather patterns. As we all should be, if we had any sense.'

The evenings there was no proofreading were filled with other pursuits. Writing letters to multinationals demanding earth-friendly practices or less wasteful packaging was one at which Alice, with her lawyer's flair for menacing paragraphs, proved particularly adept.

Or she and Jake would sit at the kitchen table recycling salvaged items. His quest for ever more inventive uses for household waste – it was his proud boast they put out only one black rubbish bag a month – was, Alice found, an absorbing way to pass the peaceful country evenings. They made keyrings out of old shower curtain rings, or twisted the wire from used spiral-bound notebooks into coathangers.

'The wire from an average notebook is up to nine feet long,' Jake would tell her as they worked. 'Just think about it, Al.'

Alice gazed into his impassioned, handsome face and thought about it. She also thought about him and the nobility of his cause. Her conviction that he brought meaning to her existence was one of the many reasons why she loved him. And, of course, he had brought meaning to her body too. Preparing to produce a child, it was finally fulfilling its potential as well.

The only serpent in Alice's Eden was that her mother and Jake not only did not hit it off, but would probably like to hit each other. Mrs Duffield's first visit to Combe was not a success.

Her first shock was to find that Jake's cottage, instead of being called Honeysuckle, Apple Blossom or something similarly picturesque, went by the more striking name of the Old Morgue.

'You mean . . . they stored dead bodies here?' she gasped to her daughter.

Alice shrugged. 'So what? It's reusing an old building in a way that makes sense. And the rent for this cottage is cheaper than any of the others.'

Her mother looked at her in concern. 'Surely money's not an issue with you, darling? You must have lots of savings, especially now you've sold the New York flat.'

Alice paused. It was true that the flat sale had left her with a sizeable sum that her share of the Old Morgue rent barely dented. But the loan she had given Jake to prop up the eternally cash-strapped *Get Trashed!* had made a small hole. Not that she minded; it was she who had pressed the money on him once the extent to which the magazine was struggling was revealed. While in theory it survived on subscribers, at the moment they seemed thin on the ground.

Of course, as expected, he had resisted her money at first. 'I can't accept it,' he insisted.

'But I want to give it to you. I want to do something useful with it at last.'

Jake's face had lit up in an ecstatic beam of acceptance. 'Al, you're an angel.'

'Don't be silly. It's just sitting there otherwise. And it's not just my money, anyway. We're married now, remember.'

Yet the double-quick Manhattan register-office service had been over in the blinking of an eye and was in fact quite hard to remember. Rather more unforgettable had been the hurt in her mother's voice when she was told. Fortunately, the additional news about the impending grandchild had taken away some of the sting, as had the revelation that Alice was returning to England.

But, as Mrs Duffield's visit proved, this new proximity was not without its problems.

'Darling,' her mother exclaimed now, coming in from examining the Old Morgue's garden. 'There's the most ghastly pile of festering rubbish on your lawn. It's just by the back door and it's absolutely covered in flies. Don't you think you should move it?'

Alice took a deep breath. 'Actually, Mum, it's not a pile of rubbish. It's Jake's, erm, wormery.'

'Wormery?' Her mother looked appalled. 'You mean . . . there are *worms* under there?'

'Yes. About three thousand of them. They came by post . . .'

'Post!'

'. . . and they eat our kitchen waste. Recycling organic matter by feeding kitchen waste to worms is one of the most ecologically sound things you can do.'

'I see.' Mrs Duffield swallowed hard. 'Well. If you don't mind me saying so, darling, they don't seem to have eaten very much of it.'

'It takes about six months for a wormery to really get going,' Alice said defensively. 'They like their food to be slightly rotten before they tackle it. We have to give them plenty of worm treat as well.'

She did not add that they themselves had been so concerned at the worms' apparent lack of appetite that Jake had called the Worm Hotline to investigate the problem. She doubted her mother was ready to discover a worm hotline existed. She was still getting over it herself.

'Six months! Mrs Duffield's face was a mask of horror. 'But won't they escape and wriggle into the kitchen? Won't they attract vermin? Won't they *smell*? And, darling, what about the *baby*? It won't be good for it, surely, having them all wriggling around.' She screwed up her face.

'Jake says it will be very educational for the baby,' Alice said firmly. 'He wants to make the garden a biodiversity haven for wildlife.'

The next crisis concerned tableware.

'What's this doing on the table, darling?' Mrs Duffield whispered at dinner-time when Jake was out of the room. She was waving half of the cardboard centre of a toilet roll at her daughter.

'It's a napkin ring, Mum.' Alice looked brightly at her mother over her lentil soup. 'It's Tip of the Month – in the sense of helpful hint, rather than landfill site, of course – in *Get Trashed!* Great, isn't it?' She tore a piece of bread from the tubular loaves Jake baked by pushing the dough in erstwhile bean cans.

Alice's mother turned her attention to the former cottage cheese containers serving as soup dishes. 'I suppose those are Jake's idea as well.'

Alice felt irritated. 'Come on, Mum. You don't need bone china. Wouldn't you rather save the planet?'

Yet a planet where rinsed-out plastic milk containers became on-table water jugs was not, she knew, a planet her mother had any interest in saving. Mrs Duffield liked her creature comforts. She did not like sleeping on mattresses on the floor so the earth's timber could be spared from making a bedframe. Nor did she enjoy sitting about on 'chairs' made of recycled peach boxes. Least of all she appreciated having to bathe after Jake in his 'gravy' because the cottage rules forbade wasting water.

'He's rationing it extra sternly at the moment,' Alice explained, 'because of the birthing pool.'

Mrs Duffield's face tightened. 'Birthing pool?'

'That's right,' Jake said. He was now back at the table and buried in a copy of *Complete Rubbish*, *Get Trashed!*'s bitter rival. 'It's in the birth plan.'

'Birth plan?'

'You write down how you want the birth to be and show it to the hospital,' Alice enlightened her.

'I'm not sure they had such things in my day,' Mrs Duffield said. 'The only plan, as I remember it, was that you went into hospital and the baby came out.'

'Would you like to see it?' Jake asked. Alice stared at him in anguish. She had been hoping this subject would never come up. Her mother was sure to disapprove, especially as the plan was mainly Jake's. In the end, given his clearly strong feelings on how their baby should arrive, it had seemed easiest if he drew it up himself.

'I'll get it for you, Mum,' she said reluctantly. She went to a corner of the room and rummaged in the cardboard box that served her as both desk and filing cabinet. She passed the sheet of A4 to her mother.

' "Our wish is for a home birth, and one as natural as possible," ' Mrs Duffield read aloud. She looked up at Alice, 'Darling, are you sure? First births can be tricky, you know.'

'We're sure,' Jake answered.

Mrs Duffield lowered her head over the paper again. ' "We will listen to Alice's body and respond to its needs." ' She adjusted her bifocals. ' "We do not require gas and air, pethidine and, above all, no epidural. Alice will spend the early stages of labour in her own bed, then, as delivery gets closer, transfer to the shower curtain . . ." *Shower curtain?*' She looked up in horror. 'Darling, you're not having the baby standing up in the bath. Surely?'

'Of course not,' Jake said impatiently. 'The shower curtain will be taped to the floor to catch any—'

'I see,' Mrs Duffield hastily interrupted. She returned to the birthing plan. ' "Soothing whale music will create a cocooning atmosphere and throughout the labour Alice will enjoy the facility of a birthing pool . . ." '

'And there it is,' Jake said triumphantly, pointing to where the box containing the apparatus, hired from an earth-friendly lifestyle centre some weeks ago, stood against the wall of the sitting room.

As the visit dragged by, her mother's obvious reservations about her husband and father of her child became harder for Alice to bear. Could she not see that Jake was right to have the concerns that he did? Misuse of the planet was selfish in the extreme; a disaster that would eventually engulf them all.

'Yes, darling, I agree,' her mother said unexpectedly at the railway station where, after a long and arduous bus journey, they finally said goodbye. 'I just wonder if the way to save it is to drink out of old yoghurt pots, that's all.'

Hugo could see at a glance why this was a tough property to sell. The reasons that it had sat, unmoving, on the books of Dunn and Dustard for the best part of a year were horribly obvious.

'This'll test your mettle, London boy,' Neil had grinned, waving the house's details at him. 'If you can shift this, I'll believe everything you say about being the hottest salesman in the South-East.'

Hugo had taken the sheets of A4 with a smooth confidence that completely concealed his irritation. How dare the bastard cast doubt on his brilliant sales record? He didn't just have to take Hugo's word for it: his written references were so glowing you could practically see them in the dark.

'Leave it to me,' Hugo said confidently.

He felt less bullish now, looking up at the rotting station house on the old branch line now reserved for nuclear waste or some such spoil of industry. The buyer he was supposed to be meeting here was the first for months, and the heat was on to sucker him in. Neil wanted the place out of the shop window and out of all their lives. Achieving this would, Hugo could see, require every trick, dirty or otherwise, he had learnt during his days at J. Bond, Special (Estate) Agent, 007 Islington High Street. But he *had* been the hottest salesman in the South-East and he *would* show Neil, damn him. Even if Neil had, so far, been deaf to all his suggestions for improving Dunn and Dustard, including that it be renamed Darcy and Dustard to cash in on Bath's Austen connection.

How, he would show Neil, he was not quite sure. Looking round the station house initially, he had assumed the bedroom walls to be a rich, deep brown. Until, that was, a light fitting fell off revealing pristine whiteness beneath. The brown was nicotine and, when he looked at it closely, he made out two large, brown ghostly shadows on the wall where the previous residents had apparently sat in bed smoking. The carpets were the sort that needed mowing rather than hoovering and, to judge from the small stinging itches all over his calves, the whole place was full of fleas. It would, Hugo realised gloomily, need a true romantic, not to say a Rentokil man of arms, to see the potential in a place like this.

The client arrived. He was a small, weaselly man in his sixties in whom the romantic urge did not look strong. Five minutes later, Hugo's sales pitch – original features, atmosphere, historic interest – was in trouble. The potential buyer did not look impressed. In fact, he looked increasingly less like a potential buyer.

'I was after an investment property really,' he said, looking doubtfully round. 'Something I could rent out for a lot of money.'

'And you couldn't have come to a better place,' Hugo assured him with chocolate smoothness. Desperation always kick-started his powers of greatest persuasion. He tapped the nearest wall and affected not to notice the shower of damp plaster that resulted. 'This has enormous rental potential. Huge.'

The weaselly man's eyes fixed on the broken windows and crusty ridges of damp on the walls. 'Who'd want to rent this place? No, sorry, I don't think I'm interested.'

'Such a shame.' Hugo gave him a pitying smile, the kind a teacher might give a not-terribly-bright child. 'Especially considering the huge trainspotting market,' he said lightly.

'The trainspotting market?'

'That's the one.' Hugo flicked an imaginary piece of fluff off his sleeve. 'Do this place up a bit and you'll be renting it out all year round, no problem.'

The man looked speculatively at Hugo. A light – small but definite – had kindled in his eyes. 'The trainspotting market,' he repeated. 'You mean . . . ?'

'Rail enthusiasts.' Pressing home his advantage, Hugo maintained his laid-back drawl and air of faint amusement. It was vital that people didn't think they were being pressured. Otherwise you got the dreaded pushy-assistant-in-a-shoeshop effect and clients voted with their feet. 'You know how some people are about the old choo-choos,' Hugo smiled. 'They get trains on the brains. Make this place into a luxury holiday let and you'll coin it in.'

The weaselly man's eyes were shining with excitement.

'You're right. The trainspotting market. Bloody hell. I hadn't thought about that.' He rubbed his hands together. 'You could make a fortune.' He beamed at Hugo.

'*Ye-es*. But you'd better move fast if *you're* going to,' Hugo replied casually. 'There's quite a lot of interest in this place, as you might imagine.' No need to tell him that the form the interest took was the agency's wish to get rid of it.

'Is there? Yes, I bet there is.' The weasely man looked panicked. 'It's a deal,' he said suddenly. 'I want to buy it.'

Hugo drove away chuckling. He hadn't lost his touch after all. Unbelievable that poor sap had fallen for the train-spotting line, though. A luxury let for rail enthusiasts, *his arse*. Trainspotters did not tend to be of the high-spending, luxury-living persuasion. Rather, they tended to be of the hanging-round-freezing-stations-in-anoraks persuasion. None looked as if they had twopence to rub together. Still, that wasn't his problem now.

Hugo swung on to the motorway and cruised down the fast lane in the Toyota. This damned family four-wheel-drive Amanda had made him buy felt like a tank in comparison to the Aston Martin. Which, in the medium term, he was unlikely to be enjoying again; Neil didn't go in for metropolitan-style sales incentives. 'We don't pay London salaries here, you know,' he had warned. Except to yourself, Hugo had thought.

God, he missed London. But it would be almost worth having left it to see Neil's face when he told him he'd sold the station house.

As he re-entered the city, his mobile began to shriek with missed call warnings. No one had left a message, however; something and nothing, Hugo assumed. There would probably be a message at the office, but that was his second stop. First was a café and a takeaway bacon sandwich.

Hugo was starving, but then he always was these days. Strange food cravings assailed him at even stranger times. It was, he supposed, nerves as the baby's arrival grew more imminent. During the last few weeks it had been him, rather than Amanda, who got up in the middle of the night for peanut butter and banana sandwiches, washed down with full-cream milk. It was having an expansive effect on his normally lanky six-foot-two frame.

Hugo got to the café to find the lunchtime queue in full swing. It was a full twenty minutes later that, reeking of frying bacon, he reached Dunn and Dustard. No sooner had he entered than a pinstriped explosion burst from Neil's office.

'Where the fuck have you been?' demanded the managing director.

Hugo, now arrived at his desk and tearing into his bacon sandwich, looked up, unsurprised. Investing every minute of the day with as much drama as possible was all part of Neil's self-importance. Hugo smiled at his boss. What he was about to tell him should prick that self-importance right where it hurt.

'We rang you about four hundred times on your mobile,' Neil ranted. 'You never picked up.'

'Couldn't. Miles out of range. Selling that station house,

remember?' Hugo spoke through a savoury mouthful of bacon and tomato. He felt deep satisfaction. Was there a better flavour combination in the world? He grinned at Neil, preparing to reveal the great news. Surely his use of the word 'selling' had been a clue.

'You won't be smiling in a minute,' Neil said grimly. 'The West Country General rang. They say Amanda's gone into labour.'

Somewhere far below, Hugo heard a soft thump. It was the bacon sandwich falling out of his hand on to his desk.

'Labour?' he repeated. 'Amanda? She can't be. She's at home. The new kitchen's being fitted today.' He paled. The thought of the new kitchen was almost as frightening as the birth, frankly. Amanda had insisted on the most expensive kitchen known to man, complete with hand-carved units and chandeliers. What was incredible – apart from the price – was the fact that she had no interest whatsoever in cooking.

'They definitely said it was Amanda.' Neil was obviously delighted at the impact his words were having. He handed Hugo a Post-it note on which the hospital's telephone number was scrawled.

'Can't be. She's having an elective Caesarean at the Cavendish in a fortnight.' Hugo fought to sound firm and remain calm.

Neil shrugged. Hugo seized the phone – on which the bacon sandwich had partly fallen – and dialled the hospital. Getting through to the necessary department took some time. A midwife eventually answered, said that she would check, then put the receiver down. Hugo heard her footsteps dying into the distance. After what seemed hours, during which he anxiously picked bits of tomato off the receiver, the footsteps returned.

'Your wife is currently three centimetres dilated.'

Hugo remembered Lotti's pasta measurer and winced. 'No, there's been a mistake,' he insisted. 'You've got the wrong person.'

'Is your wife's name Amanda Hardwick?'

A warm surge of blood filled Hugo's face. 'Er, yes. Yes, it is.'

'Well, she was brought here late this morning. In labour.'

'But the baby's not supposed to be born yet,' Hugo wailed.

There came from the other end what sounded like a snigger. 'Babies don't always do what they're supposed to,' said the midwife. 'As you may be about to find out.'

'Ow,' bellowed Amanda. 'Ow. Ow. OW!'

The pain she was in was unbelievable. No one had warned her it would be as bad as this. It was so bad that she'd had to abandon making notes for a first-person, as-it-happens piece about giving birth. *Vogue*, she had thought, were bound to be interested.

She had intended the piece to be amusing and had managed the first few lines. 'Considering the comfort-challenging design faults of pregnancy – bowels below baby, stomach in throat and so on – it's quite incredible the human race has survived as long as it has . . . Ow!'

The exclamation marked the point at which Amanda ceased to see anything amusing about it.

Wendy Holden

Almost as unbelievable and unamusing as the pain was the fact Carinthia was arriving two weeks early. Amanda loathed people who came early. It was rude, unfashionable, caught you on the hop and, worst of all, implied they had nothing better to do. The sort of people Amanda prized always had something better to do. They were powerful and busy, with lots of calls on their time. If, as was intended, Carinthia was going to grow up to be one of them, she had better start mending her ways.

'OW!!!' yelled Amanda, as another mighty spasm crushed her pelvis. It was like the worst period in the world, or, rather, all the periods she had ever had occurring simultaneously. 'Look,' she gasped at the midwife through watering eyes. 'Get me a fucking epidural, will you? Now. This minute.'

The placid and pretty Chinese midwife was checking the print-out of the baby's heartbeat. She looked calmly at Amanda. 'You have to dilate to four centimetres. So far you are three.'

'THREE?' yelled Amanda. 'But I've been at it for *hours*. I'm being split in fucking half here. What are you, some sort of sadist?'

'We can't give epidural before four centimetres dilated,' said the midwife, whose name, according to her badge, was Una.

'Well, I *might* be four now,' bellowed Amanda, as another spasm gripped her. 'If you could be arsed to look. As it were.'

Una checked her watch. 'I looked thirty seconds ago.' She walked towards the door.

'Where are you going?' Amanda lunged towards her in a vaguely preventative gesture and almost fell off the bed. 'What about my bloody Caesarean?'

Una folded her neat arms. 'Doctor say Caesarean not needed.'

Amanda sat as bolt upright as her condition would allow. '*Not needed?*' she bellowed, aghast. 'But I'm too posh to push.'

This powerful argument left Una unmoved. 'Is dangerous operation. Only do if medical necessity.'

'But this is a medical necessity,' shrieked Amanda. Was that great lump in her stomach really going to come out of her front bottom? It was impossible. It would kill her. 'I'm in *agony*.'

Una nodded. 'But you not dilated enough. I back in ten minutes. You ready for epidural by then.'

As the door closed, Amanda let out a scream of frustration that wasn't entirely due to the pain. It was due to the Cavendish maternity hospital too.

Amanda had been in the hallway at Fitzherbert Place, shouting at the workmen fitting her new luxury kitchen, when the first twinges struck. As the twinges deepened and lengthened to cramps, she fled to the phone and called Hugo. When, to her apoplectic fury, his mobile did not pick up, she dialled the Cavendish.

All of their operators were busy. After listening to the whole of Vivaldi's *Four Seasons* apparently performed on a stylophone at the bottom of a dustbin, Amanda was still glaring at the telephone keypad. Halfway through *Music for the Royal Fireworks*, an operator came on the line. Sixty seconds later Amanda began a firework display of her own.

'What do you mean you can't admit me today?' she yelled. 'I'm coming in for a fucking elective Caesarean.'

'Yes, madam, indeed you are. But the operation is booked for two weeks' time.'

'So?' raged Amanda. 'The baby's early. You're just going to have to do it today, that's all.'

'I'm afraid that's impossible, madam.'

'So what the fuck am I supposed to do?' bellowed Amanda. 'Do it myself with the bloody kitchen scissors?'

'Madam, if you could just calm down and stop swearing . . .'

'*Calm down?*'

'Madam, I must ask you to remember that stress and over-excitement are inadvisable in pregnant mothers,' said the receptionist in her unengaged monotone. 'It may precipitate the birth.'

'Well, it's a bit late for that now,' Amanda snarled, thinking longingly of the glossy brochure photographs of the hospital's private suites. The four-poster beds, whose damask curtains and magnificent carving concealed touch-of-a-button adjustable mattresses and more state-of-the-art equipment than NASA could dream of. The vintage-champagne-filled minibars. The huge, luxury-hotel-style bathrooms with hot tubs and miles of marble. 'Look,' she gasped urgently as the cramps struck again, 'you've got to get an ambulance here – I mean, one of your chauffeurs. You send chauffeurs, don't you? That's part of the deal, isn't it? A luxury limo with medical assistance on board?'

'Indeed it is, madam, for those with the right coverage.'

'Coverage?' Amanda said suspiciously. 'What do you mean?'

'Madam, can I ask you if you took out the Cavendish Hospital's Early Bird Insurance Package?'

'The what?' yelped Amanda in mid-spasm.

'I've got your details up on the screen now, madam,' went the monotonous singsong, 'but you only seem to have taken out the Standard Delivery Package.'

Amanda vaguely remembered arguing with Hugo about this. He had pointed out that the Early Bird cover would more than double the cost of her Cavendish care. And as it was obviously quite impossible a child of hers would be early, Amanda had dropped the idea. *Sod* Hugo, she now thought vehemently. She might have known it would be all his bloody fault.

'So you're saying that, despite the fact I'm booked into your hospital and I've paid an effing fortune for it, you can't – won't, rather – give me any treatment at all?' she said slowly.

'The Basic Delivery Package does not cover a patient for early arrivals,' the receptionist confirmed. 'Have you got the number of your local hospital?'

Amanda, now lying grumpily on the damask-free NHS hospital bed, succumbed to another spasm and tried not to remember what happened next. The journey to West Country General in the kitchen fitters' van. Asking them to take her, just after she'd accused them of bodging, incompetence and fraud, was bad enough. But the bumpy ride on the grubby van seat was another dimension of discomfort altogether. Hardly the limousine arrival she had imagined. And paid for, dammit.

'Ow!!!' she screamed, as the worst pain so far gripped her body. 'OOWWWW!! AAAARRGGHH!!'

Hugo rushed frantically about in the bowels of the West Country General, clutching an increasingly wilted bunch of petrol-station flowers. He was unable to understand why Amanda wasn't in the Cavendish. She'd made enough fuss about the place. That she'd had a last-minute economy drive seemed unlikely.

The grey lino corridors were familiar, yet unfamiliar. He had long since left behind the last of the signs for the birthing centre.

'Ooof!' Hugo was suddenly, conclusively, winded. He opened his eyes to realise that the person he had run into was the beautiful paediatrician, Dr Watson.

'You again,' she said icily.

Hugo stared back desperately. 'Birthing centre?' he gasped.

The doctor was instantly all professional solicitude. She pointed an elegant finger. 'That way. Up the stairs and round to the right. Your baby, is it?'

Hugo nodded.

Dr Watson smiled. 'Good luck. I'll probably see you later. I check all the newborns.'

Hugo felt suddenly, wildly glad that she was checking the newborns. Rushing in the direction indicated, he turned yet another blazingly striplit corner to find – at last, at glorious last – the words 'Jane Austen Birthing Suite' on a sign above a double door. Dashing towards it, Hugo desperately hoped he had not Missed It. But only because Amanda would be cross if he had. In his heart, Hugo had no desire to watch the birth. Least of all from the batting end, as Neil insisted on calling it. 'Stick to the bowling end, that's my advice,' he had yelled as Hugo left the office.

Hugo intended to do just that. The last antenatal class had featured videos of actual births: large hairy women screaming in agony whilst holding on to men with huge beards. One of the women – the Home Office pathologist, interestingly – had cried at seeing what lay in store for her. Hugo had felt like doing the same. Frankly, giving birth looked horrible and ugly. Not only that, it looked dangerous as well.

As now, finally, he had got to where the action was, Hugo felt tight with anxiety. Please God, he prayed, as he rarely did, let everything be all right with Amanda and the baby.

He cannoned through the double doors of the Jane Austen Birthing Suite. The dull-eyed security guard on the other side looked up, startled, as something tall, pinstriped and agitated appeared in his midst.

'I've come to see my wife,' Hugo squeaked through a throat dry with tension. 'She's called Amanda Hardwick. She's in here having a baby.' He looked expectantly at the guard, but congratulations, recognition even, came there none.

The guard, whose twelve-hour shift was finally coming to an end, yawned. He ran his finger slowly down a clipboard. 'Oh yeah,' he drawled eventually, without looking up. 'You in the wrong place. You expected in Bereavement Suite.'

There was a gasp of horror from Hugo.

The guard looked up to see the tall, pinstriped man seem to hang briefly in the air before crashing down like a felled tree.

Chapter 8

It was dark when Alice woke. She knew immediately and instinctively that the dull, period-like pains were the baby coming. A day or two early, but clearly on its way. She felt a surge of excitement, followed by dread. This was it.

As, slowly, the pain faded, she wondered what the time was. In New York, one could tell by the traffic. It rushed and roared until about two in the morning, died off gradually for about an hour, after which there followed almost complete silence between three and half-past four. That the city never slept was a myth. Then, from four thirty onwards, the traffic built up again in a steady crescendo and the day began. In this village, however, it was as silent at nine p.m. as it was twelve hours later. It was one of the aspects of country life she'd found most difficult to get used to.

She lay there, deliberating. Should she wake Jake? She turned her head and looked lovingly at his handsome profile, reluctant to acquaint him with his coming responsibilities. Let him dream on for a little while longer.

The pains were, anyway, faint and widely spaced. The real action, Alice recalled from the antenatal class, began only when they were strong and frequent. She hoped that strong was not a euphemism for painful. It was not that she was faint-hearted. She agreed wholeheartedly with Jake that pain relief was selfish as, though it might make her feel better, it could also harm the baby. But now the actual, raw, medically unaided moment was on her, she flinched at the prospect of hours of unending agony.

Think Your Way To Pain-Free Delivery, the second-hand manual given to her by Jake as an alternative to all the 'useless waste of trees' she might otherwise have bought, had not really been much practical use. She had found it impossible to, as the book urged, close her eyes and imagine her vagina to be the size of the Milky Way. The size of *a* Milky Way, perhaps. As the birth approached, Alice was growing ever more conscious of the tiny hole the baby had to come out of. She tried not to think about Lotti's dilation gauge.

Ouch. That was a sharp one. Alice's eyes watered with the sudden pain. Were the contractions coming slightly more quickly now?

'Jake!' she whispered. 'I think the baby's on its way.'

'Uh?' Jake shot up in bed. 'It can't be. It's not due yet.'

'Well, it's coming, ready or not,' Alice replied, more calmly than she felt. The contractions were faster now. And stronger, which, unfortunately, did mean painful.

'Shit.' Jake ran two hands through his bed-tousled hair. 'I haven't got the birthing pool built yet. But don't worry. I'll sort it.' He was now bounding about the room stark naked. His penis and testicles were swinging agitatedly. 'Stay there,' he urged her. 'It'll all be OK, I promise.'

'I know.' Alice smiled up at him as he pulled on a T-shirt and bounded down the rickety stair.

Five minutes later, she was struggling to her feet. It had occurred to her that Jake might need help with constructing the birthing pool. It had looked very complicated on the box. She levered herself up and made her way down to the sitting room where, in the quarter-light of the coming dawn, she found Jake looking cross amid a sea of cardboard, Styrofoam and shiny plastic slabs.

'Is it tricky?' she asked fearfully.

'Not just that,' Jake huffed. 'It's supposed to be ecologically friendly – and look at this.' He held up one of the pieces of Styrofoam. 'How rainforest-destroying can you get?'

As the pain gripped her in its vice and squeezed mightily, Alice closed her eyes. She arched her back and let the long, low moan of agony escape. Then she felt Jake's twitching, sweating hand on her brow.

'Oh, Al, sweet, don't worry . . .'

'Have you called the midwives?' she gasped. 'I think it's probably time they came round.'

He leapt to his feet, alarm in his eyes, and rushed to the phone. Alice, meanwhile, tried to ease the pain with a turn around the tiny kitchen. The sink was full of unwashed jars and tins destined for a new recycled identity, presumably somewhere within the household. Alice squirted some Fairy over them and began to run the hot tap, only to discover that no hot water came out of it. Horror clutched her. Surely the heater hadn't picked this morning of all mornings to pack up again. Didn't it realise there was a birthing pool to fill?

'The midwives are calling back,' Jake announced when she returned to the sitting room. He was hulking over the birthing pool pieces again.

'How are you feeling?' he asked.

Alice forced a smile. 'Better,' she croaked, breathing more calmly as the contraction eased.

'You're sure?'

'Yes. Can I do anything to help?'

She was determined not to appear to be wallowing in her pain. That would be selfish and, as Jake repeatedly said, neither he nor the planet had time for selfish people.

She plucked the birthing pool leaflet gently out of his hand and looked at it. It was full of complicated line drawings of panels, arrows and bolts. In the final one a huge-stomached woman, sitting in the completed hexagonal construction, contemplated the head of an infant emerging from between her wide-open thighs.

'Well, if you *really* want to make a start on that,' Jake said, evidently relieved, 'I'll go and find the garden hose.'

'Garden hose?'

'To fill the pool.'

'Er, Jake, the water . . .'

But he had left the room. The telephone rang. Clutching her stomach, Alice clumsily made her way towards it.

'This is the Jane Austen Birthing Centre at West Country General Hospital.'

There followed a minute or two of explanation.

'I see,' Alice said slowly. 'And you're quite sure about this? The situation's not likely to change?'

'I'm afraid not,' the other end confirmed.

Alice sank despairingly to the floor. Tears of terror swelled in her eyes. Oh God. Could this nightmare really be happening?

Then an idea struck her.

'Are you all right, madam?' the other end asked anxiously.

Alice was silent. She was busy processing the astonishing, wonderful, rescuing possibility that had just occurred to her. 'Er, hang on a moment,' she murmured. Could her calculations be right? Please God, let them be right. No, she was sure she was right.

Frankly, she'd better be. 'Actually,' Alice told the hospital, 'don't worry. I've got another plan.' She rang off and dialled a number before another contraction kicked in.

A few minutes later, Jake re-entered the sitting room, brandishing a dusty garden hose. 'Found the whale music as well,' he added, triumphantly waving a cassette.

'That's fantastic,' Alice told him. 'But,' she added gently, 'we won't be needing it.'

He looked appalled. 'Why not? Do you want to listen to something else?'

'I won't need it because I'm going to hospital.'

Jake's broad, handsome face creased with annoyance. 'But, Al, we agreed. Home birth. The midwives come here. We're going to listen to your body and take it all from there.'

'But my body,' Alice groaned, 'is saying it needs to be in a hospital. Now.'

'A hospital's not in the birth plan,' Jake said stubbornly.

'Fuck the birth plan!' Alice shrieked suddenly, finding being reasonable whilst in torture-chamber-level pain finally beyond her. She closed her eyes to shut out Jake's shocked expression. 'The hospital can't send any midwives,' she muttered.

Jake's face darkened with fury. 'What do you mean they can't send any bloody midwives? They're a fucking hospital, aren't they?' He leapt for the phone, which lay on Alice's thighs.

Her hand tightened over the receiver. 'Look, there's no point arguing with them,' she gasped, feeling the sweat trickling down her forehead. 'The problem is that you need two midwives for a home birth, and they can't spare two tonight. They're all busy. So I'm going to hospital.'

'To the West Country General?'

'Well I could go there, but I'm not,' Alice yelped as the agony struck again. 'They're obviously run off their feet at the moment.'

'Where, then?'

'Somewhere . . . ow . . . called the Cavendish.'

Jake's face drained of all its ruddy outdoor colour. 'The private hospital? The one where that arse of an estate agent and his stuck-up wife are going?'

Alice, fists clenched tightly, looked at Jake incomprehendingly. She vaguely remembered Amanda Hardwick saying something about the Cavendish, but she was now in too much pain to care.

'It's like this,' groaned Alice, gearing up to one final, huge effort at explanation. 'My Intercorp private health insurance is valid to the end of the year. It covers everything. I rang them and they recommended I went to the Cavendish. It's the nearest, the newest and the best-equipped maternity hospital around and they'll take me immediately. My policy even covers me for this package they have called Early Bird, for people whose babies come before they're supposed to.' She flopped back, exhausted by the effort of speech, before rallying for one last time. 'They're sending a limo-ambulance for me now.'

The birth, Amanda thought, had hardly been pleasant, although matters had dramatically picked up following the epidural. Carinthia had appeared soon afterwards. In textbook fashion too, give or take a couple of stitches. She hated to admit it, but Una was right. A Caesarean had not been necessary.

The only non-textbook aspect of Carinthia's birth was that the baby was not, after all, Carinthia. That small, beautiful, flattering version of herself conclusively failed to materialise.

'Baby boy,' Una had said, plonking a gory lump on Amanda's stomach. Amanda stared at it.

It wasn't the blonde cherub she had imagined. It was dark, wizened, and with unpleasant purple-red skin. In addition, something about its slimily bent angles reminded her of giblets and she was glad when Una took it away to clean it up.

Amanda was not unduly worried about her reaction. Maternal feelings came later, all the books said so. She therefore gave free rein to the fact her main emotion as a new mother was disgust. The postnatal ward was disgusting as well, the walls a plaster pink and the ugly curtains round the beds suggestive of a Transylvanian youth hostel from hell. And the noise! The other mothers, health tourists to a woman, Amanda suspected, yelped and keened even more than their squawling babies. In the end it had been well-nigh unbearable.

Amanda had tried at an earlier stage to bag one of the few private recovery rooms, but they were allocated on a first-born-first-served basis. Amanda's labour having been twelve hours at the final count, she'd been conclusively pipped at the post. But in the end, she'd had the last laugh. She'd kicked up such a fuss that the hospital had allotted her the only private vacant room they had available. Which strictly speaking had another use altogether.

'It was a bit of a shock, that's all, being told to go to the Bereavement Suite,' Hugo bleated as Una ministered some hot sweet tea.

'Well, so what?' Amanda snapped back. 'I'm lucky to be here, let me tell you. I had to do a lot of persuading before they'd open it for me.'

Amanda was far from pleased. The fact that Hugo had

not made it for the birth was infuriating. To give birth alone was frankly embarrassing. As if one was a single mother or something. But then, Amanda thought bitterly, perhaps that was preferable to having a husband who turned up in the state that Hugo had. In a wheelchair, with his head bandaged and an aluminium vomit bowl on his knee.

One heard of husbands getting squeamish in delivery rooms, but Hugo was the first she'd known to collapse before he even got there.

'But I thought you were both dead.' Slumped in his wheelchair, Hugo relived the horror of the moment.

'Well, we're not,' Amanda had briskly pointed out. 'Now pass me my mobile, will you? I'm phoning the Cavendish.'

'You're not supposed to use mobiles in hospitals . . .' Hugo's voice trailed away. There was no point arguing with Amanda in this mood. In any mood, come to that.

Hours later Amanda stared up, satisfied, into the canopy of a Cavendish four-poster. The phone call it had taken to achieve this was admittedly long and terse. She had threatened the Cavendish's director with an unfavourable mention in the first-person birthing piece she was writing for *Vogue* if he didn't allow her to convalesce there, at least. She could not imagine why this obvious and simple route hadn't occurred to her before. Pregnancy clearly fuddled the brain. Thank God she wasn't pregnant any more.

As Amanda sighed happily and tapped away on the Internet-connected laptop that was all part of the Cavendish service, Hugo, sitting in a tapestry-patterned wing chair in the huge bay window, lowered his copy of *The Times*.

'What are you doing?' he asked. 'You're not working, surely? You've just had a baby. What about quality time dandling angelic infants in the dappled sunlight under the apple blossom?'

'Oh, for Christ's sake, it's hardly the weather for it.' Amanda threw an impatient hand in the direction of the sleet outside. 'Look, I'm just checking my e-mail, OK? I sent the sperm camp idea to Graydon, but, ah, here's my inbox, um, no, sod him, he's not come back to me yet. And *Vogue* still haven't made their minds up about that first-person birthing piece either.' She frowned. 'But while I'm at it, I'll firm up Nurse Harris's arrival time. She's due tomorrow. Mary-poppins. co.uk,' she muttered to herself, typing in the maternity nurse agency's e-mail address.

Hugo glanced apprehensively at the cot. The baby was asleep, although he had little faith in this state of affairs continuing. A mere few hours' acquaintance had revealed in the child a tendency to go off like a bomb at any moment. Like mother, like son, Hugo supposed. He wondered in what way, if any, the child resembled him. Not in looks, or at least not so far. The baby was scrunched, purple and terrifyingly fragile-looking. The only remarkable resemblance it bore, so far as Hugo could see, was to a baby.

Hugo knew that to think this was a terrible failing. Becoming a father was famously one of the great life experiences. Men burst into tears when they first saw their offspring and were filled with an overwhelming sense of wonder. Yet Hugo's main sensation in the hours that followed the birth was that of terminal uselessness.

There seemed nothing he could do, no role he could play. When the baby was awake, Amanda and her two assigned Cavendish nurses were occupied with it to such an extent that Hugo never got a look-in, and hardly a look. The only time he had tried to bond with his son had been in the full public glare of these ancillary personnel and he had not known what to do or to say. The baby had screamed the whole time he had held it, which had not helped. The mewling, cat-like cries upset Hugo and made him want to wail too.

So now he sat in the chair pretending to read the paper, but in reality scouring the corners of his heart for some trace of fatherly feeling. Any joy, so far, was mainly attributable to the fact that the baby was not called Carinthia. Amanda had apparently once known someone glamorous with this name, but it was none the less that of a province of Austria and a ridiculous thing to call a child. You wouldn't get Austrians calling their offspring Humberside. Fortunately the baby had provided the solution by being a boy.

But this still left the question of what he would be called. Amanda was working on the answer with the help of *Names for Leaders*, a smartly bound and complimentary volume provided as another part of the Cavendish service. The names all seemed impossibly elaborate and were, Hugo suspected, pitched with deliberation and cringeworthy accuracy at the aspirations of Cavendish clients. The boys' section, for example, included such horrors as Merlin, Vercingetorix and Ezekiel, all of which Amanda loved. Plain English names like James and John, which Hugo liked, were nowhere to be seen.

The baby stirred. Contrary to expectations, it did not erupt in a yell. It snuffled a bit then seemed to go back to sleep.

'Thank God,' Amanda muttered from the bed. 'He's chewing my nipples to shreds.' She already hated breastfeeding. There had been a sharp exchange of words when one of the nurses, instructing Amanda in the proper procedure, had advised her to 'get into a comfortable position'.

'Comfortable position?' Amanda had yelled, outraged. 'I've had my arse ripped open and my tits feel like rugby balls. There's no such thing as a comfortable position.'

Hugo raised the battered paper again and ruminated once more on his lack of feeling. Although there was, actually, one overwhelming feeling he'd had constantly since the birth. Apart from the ache where his jaw had met hard hospital lino, that was. This was the feeling of needing a stiff drink.

He knew that a free bar was all part of the Cavendish service. He had seen the large lounge downstairs when they arrived. He recalled the flickering fire, beams, squashy leather sofas and, no doubt, as many cut-glass tumblers of whisky and soda as you could force down your gullet.

He silently folded the newspaper and contemplated the scene before him. Amanda was nodding over her laptop and Merlin-Vercingetorix-Ezekiel was sleeping – well – like a baby.

Hugo rose gently from his easy chair. He'd only be ten minutes. It wasn't as if anyone would miss him.

He made his way down the sweeping baronial staircase and into the lounge. The faint smell of antiseptic could be detected amongst the pot pourri and cigars. The cigars were free too, Hugo realised, helping himself to a fine-looking Romeo y Julieta. How did the saying go? A baby was only a baby. But a good cigar was a smoke.

He perched on a swivel stool, placed his elbows on the polished copper surface of the cocktail bar and stared at the drinks menu. There was a theme here, he realised, although he was not sure that it was appropriate.

C-Breeze was top of the list, followed by Puerpal Haze, Forceps Flip, Dr Tom Collins and Twin Martini. Perhaps worse were the cocktails whose names had not been tampered with, but to which the context of the clinic lent hideous new meaning. Slow Comfortable Screw and Screaming Orgasm, for example, both of which, judging from the frank gynae-cological details of the birth Amanda had supplied him with, seemed some distance away at the moment. As for Bloody Mary . . . grimacing, Hugo put the menu down and asked the barman for a stiff whisky and soda.

As, with grateful reverence, he took the first mouthful, he was aware of another pair of elbows arriving next to him. Checked, lumberjack-shirted elbows.

'Champagne, zurr?' slurred the barman in what struck Hugo as a highly bogus Continental accent. 'Cocktail, zurr?'

'No, thanks. Got any, like, organic carrot juice?' asked a

voice Hugo recognised. His insides shrank. It *couldn't* be. They were having a bloody home birth, weren't they? What the hell was he doing here? Hugo stared fiercely at the cut-crystal bottom of his whisky tumbler.

'Carrot juice?' repeated the barman, surprised. 'I don't theenk so, zurr.'

'Well, water then?' The customer was evidently put out. 'Reverse-filtered, obviously.'

'I theenk we might have a bottle of water somewhere,' the barman said doubtfully. After bending and burrowing under the bar, he re-emerged empty-handed. 'Sorry, zurr. Most of the gentlemen who come down here, zey are wanting alcohol. Cigars. You know, for celebration.'

The newcomer waved his arms energetically to rid the air of Hugo's cigar smoke. 'Well, not all of us want to celebrate by poisoning our livers and igniting phallic symbols to the detriment of the atmosphere.'

Hugo sensed that his neighbour had now turned and was looking at him. 'Hey,' he said. 'If it isn't Yogi!'

'Hello, Jake,' Hugo forced out through a face rigid with dislike. 'Didn't realise you were here. What happened to the home birth?'

'Baby came day before yesterday. Slightly before schedule.' Jake looked momentarily irritated. 'But hey, that's Mother Nature for you, no?' he added, recovering his customary jauntiness.

'How do you mean, "slightly before schedule"?' Hugo sensed something Jake didn't especially want to talk about.

'Er . . . emergency Caesarean. Things got a bit complicated.'

'Emergency Caesarean!' Hugo exclaimed. So the all-natural organic couple had had the most hi-tech, unnatural delivery imaginable.

'You were having a Caesarean too, right?' Jake hit back defensively.

'No, actually Amanda had a vaginal delivery.' Hugo savoured the sensation of having scored a point.

'You wan' tomato juice, sir?' interrupted the barman, hopefully brandishing a small red bottle at Jake.

Jake looked at him suspiciously. 'Is it GM?'

'Sorry, no. Ees Schweppes.'

Jake settled on a glass of milk. The barman handed it over in an elaborately tall glass decorated like a carnival float with so many pink paper umbrellas, cherries and swizzle sticks that Jake's face was invisible behind it. Hugo doubted this was accidental.

'So. Congratulations.' Jake lifted his over-burdened glass.

'Thanks. Congratulations to you too.'

'Fantastic, isn't it, fatherhood?' Jake smacked his lips after draining some of the milk and punched the air with one of his sinewy brown forearms. Hugo nodded briefly, uncomfortably reminded of that last, cataclysmic ante-natal class.

'Best feeling in the world,' Jake added.

'Yes.'

'Nothing like it, eh?' Jake disappeared behind the cocktail umbrellas as he took a sip. 'Just – incredible. So – moving. So – amazing.'

Hugo said nothing. Why hadn't he felt like that? The only excuse he could think of was that the knockout blow to his chin had temporarily suspended all normal emotion.

'I mean, the moment the baby came out . . .' Jake shook his locks in wonder, '. . . just the best moment of my life. You were there, yeah?'

'Didn't quite make it,' Hugo muttered into his whisky and soda. Directly he had admitted this he wondered why he had. It would have been so easy to lie, to have not presented Jake with such an easy target.

'Didn't make it?' Jake's voice was a shout of triumphant amazement. 'God, I wouldn't have missed it for the world. I was there *every minute.*'

Hugo felt the overwhelming urge to knock Jake off his swivel stool. Instead, he pushed his empty glass towards the barman again. 'Comfortable here, isn't it?' he observed.

'Can't wait to see the back of the place myself. We're going home today.'

'Today? Bit early, isn't it, if Alice only had her Caesarean the day before yesterday?'

Jake shrugged. 'We want to get Baby home, get on with family living, all of us together.'

Hugo tried and failed to imagine home life with Amanda and Merlin-Vercingetorix.

'Anyway,' Jake added disapprovingly, 'this place is a bit restrictive, don't you think?'

'In what way?'

'Well, the placenta for one thing.'

'What about it?' Hugo asked.

'I was going to make it into pâté. Found a great recipe on-line. But when I asked for it they said it was too late, they'd got rid of it.' He frowned. 'I mean, I'm the father. I've got rights over that placenta.'

'I suppose so.' Hugo had been all too happy to waive his.

'Anyway.' Jake drained the milk, slipped off the stool and punched Hugo playfully on the shoulder. 'Gotta get going. See you around, Yogi.'

'The name's Hugo,' Hugo winced at the force of the blow. 'And not if I see you first,' he muttered through gritted teeth.

Chapter 9

Alice adored her new daughter. From the first minute she held Rosa, a wave of emotion crashed through her in which swirled love, relief, awe and a determination to protect this tiny creature for whose existence she, with Jake, was entirely responsible. Her first impressions of motherhood were that it was everything she had imagined, but more so. All the clichés were true. She had never thought it possible to love anything this much.

'Now you know how I feel about recycling,' Jake grinned from the bedside when she told him this.

Alice laughed. How could she have thought, as she occasionally did, that Jake might lack a sense of humour? She felt she was drowning in happiness. 'I can't believe it,' she sighed ecstatically to Jake, clutching the warm bundle of baby close. 'Just think, I almost missed out on this altogether.'

'Like I said, Al, it happened for a reason,' Jake assured her with a gentle smile.

'Darling!' The door of Alice's private room flew open to admit her parents.

'Did you get my roses, darling?' Mrs Duffield asked, after exclaiming delightedly over her new granddaughter. 'Frances sent some too.'

Alice was surprised. She had not received any flowers. 'What a shame,' she lamented. 'Roses are my favourites.' And the reason, moreover, that Rosa was called Rosa. Or Ro, as Jake shortened it to, just as he abbreviated Alice herself to Al. This, she knew, irritated her mother.

'I know you like roses, darling. Why do you think I sent them?' Her mother darted a loaded look at Jake, who was perusing the latest issue of *Get Trashed!* at the bedside. The sight of him admiring his own publication with his newborn daughter mere feet away did not impress Mrs Duffield. Who cared if he was 'checking for mistakes', as Alice hurriedly whispered.

Underlying her indignation was her suspicion that Jake had not only failed to give Alice any flowers, but also any other token marking the arrival of the baby. She was wrong in this assumption, but only because Alice had, reluctantly, judged it best not to show her mother the recycled toothbrush, which, stripped of its bristles, bent with the aid of hot water and painted with rather shaky stars, made what Jake, presenting it to her, had described as a 'birthing bracelet'.

Alice's mother decided not to dwell on the matter of the flowers. There were other issues to address. 'About Rosa's christening,' she said briskly. 'If you would like to, you could use our garden. It's perfect in the summer – we could have a champagne reception. A marquee. The lot.'

'Your mother's dying to buy a hat,' Alice's father chuckled.

His wife tapped his hand playfully. 'Shush. But seriously,' she looked at Jake and Alice, 'I'm sure the vicar at St Enodoc's would love to do the service. Alice was christened there, after all.'

The offer, Alice knew, was a very attractive one. A party in her parents' vast and pretty Cornish garden, tumbling with honeysuckle, orange blossom and general summer glory. Plus a service at the grey stone church in their village, where to walk out of the porch was to enjoy a breathtaking view over fields to the sea. Her mother, Alice knew, had cherished hopes that she would be married there some day. Hopes that she had evidently now transferred to the next best thing.

And hopes that, Alice feared, would unfortunately have to be dashed. 'Er, the thing is, Mum,' she began uncomfortably.

'We're not planning a christening as such,' Jake interrupted.

'You're not?' Mrs Duffield blinked.

'Although we haven't ruled out some form of humanist ceremony,' Jake added brightly.

Alice's parents looked nonplussed. 'Humanist?' echoed Mr Duffield. 'Isn't she C of E?'

'Actually,' Alice explained gently, 'when we filled in Rosa's religion on the hospital form, we didn't put C of E.'

'Oh.' Her mother, while disappointed, was trying her best to look bright and interested. 'So what *did* you put?'

'Pagan,' said Jake proudly.

The conversation quickly switched to the weather, giving Jake an opportunity to share the latest depressing intelligence concerning greenhouse emissions.

'Funny, isn't it?' Alice mused after her parents had gone.

'What is?' There was, so far as Jake was concerned, nothing remotely amusing about the Duffields.

'The flowers. Funny that she sent them and they never got delivered.'

Jake lowered *Get Trashed!* which bore the legend 'Do NOT Throw Away. Use As Cat Litter' on the back. Alice wondered what people without cats were supposed to do with it.

'Actually,' he said lightly, 'they did get delivered.'

'They did?'

'But you were asleep when they came so I thought I'd take them down to the local Action on Addiction drop-in centre.'

Alice blinked. '*Where?* Why? Why did you do that?'

'Because they would have meant nothing to you and everything to them.'

Flowers from her mother for becoming a mother herself? 'They would have meant something to me,' Alice said quietly. How could Jake have given them away? She wondered what bouquets of roses would mean to recovering drug addicts anyway. Or perhaps not so recovering drug addicts, who knew?

Jake gave her his most dazzling smile. 'Come on, Al. You're

in the lap of luxury here and what have they got? Nothing. It would have been selfish to do anything else.'

Alice felt guilty. She could see he had a point. Jake was so much greater and more generous a spirit than she was. Feeling unworthy in comparison was becoming a familiar sensation.

But still, secretly, she regretted the loss of the roses. Alice loved flowers and wished they could grow some in their own garden, but all horticultural efforts had been restricted to Jake's organic vegetable-raising. This had not been successful so far. No more successful than the wormery which, for all the Hotline's assurances, did not seem in the least to be settling down and eating. Had they, Alice wondered, been sold the world's only known colony of anorexic earthworms?

As Amanda showed no inclination to leave the Cavendish, it fell to Hugo to welcome Nurse Harris to Fitzherbert Place on the day set for her arrival. He drove from the hospital in a state which, as he guiltily recognised, involved more excitement and anticipation than he had managed to summon for the baby's birth.

The woman waiting outside Number Four's as-yet-un-painted front door, however, bore little resemblance to the *Carry On* blonde of Hugo's imagination. Tight of uniform, black of stocking and rearing of cleavage she was not. Rather, she was solid, foursquare, tall and broad, with thick calves, big hands, and a face, Hugo thought, straight out of some particularly bleak period drama.

'You must be Nurse Harris,' he said, hoping she would

contradict him and turn out to be someone from the council or the local Methodist church. To his disappointment she nodded a brisk affirmative.

Nurse Harris's chest was certainly huge, but had the shapeless, bulky appearance of the arm of a sofa. Otherwise, in descending order of how they struck the viewer, came large teeth, round bulging eyes, straight grey hair and fleshy putty-coloured cheeks.

Only in the fact that she wore a uniform did Nurse Harris resemble the *Carry On* stereotype. But there was nothing remotely titillating about it. The dress was mid-calf length and grey, the belt black, the stockings flesh-coloured, and the collar and cap white. Stern though it was, Hugo was already finding it impossible to imagine her in anything else. Nurse Harris had the air of having been born in uniform.

She also had the air of being accustomed to better things. On first seeing her bedroom at Fitzherbert Place, with the deep crack on one wall and the damp stain on the other, Nurse Harris looked round wordlessly, gave a deep, disapproving sniff and remarked, 'It wasn't like this at Lord Fairbourne's.'

Asking what it was like would, Hugo realised, be folly of the highest order. But asking was not necessary. Ten minutes after Nurse Harris's arrival he knew that it was like a luxurious, self-contained flat in the east wing of Fairbourne Hall. And what Fairbourne Hall was like was a large cream-painted stately home set amid rolling parkland. A structurally iffy terrace house it was not. Albeit, thanks to Amanda, a terrace house with a Hollywood kitchen installed by Bath's most expensive fitters.

Just who the hell, Hugo wondered, was Lord Fairbourne, anyway? Amanda, he recalled, had read about him in some magazine or other and been profoundly impressed. She had been determined to track down the very maternity nurse he had used. Not for the first time Hugo cursed his wife's reading habits.

'Not dark enough,' was Nurse Harris's verdict on the nursery. 'You must install blackout blinds and curtains with lightproof linings *immediately* if Baby is to get the sleep he needs.'

'Oh, right,' said Hugo, wondering where all this equipment was going to come from. It was clearly required on the double.

'I don't mind telling you . . .' Nurse Harris offered in what unexpectedly promised to be a moment of constructive suggestion.

'What?' asked Hugo.

'I had *exactly* the same problem when I arrived at the home of, *ahem* . . .' In hushed tones, Nurse Harris spoke the name of a very famous rock star. '*He* hadn't got blackout blinds either.'

Hugo felt encouraged to be in such glamorous blind-less company. 'So what did he do?'

'Called Harrods *immediately* and got someone to come round and put it all up. It was no expense spared in *their* house.' Nurse Harris's rather boiled-looking eyes swivelled disapprovingly about. They settled on the largely exposed bottom of Gary, the painter recently engaged by Amanda to paint the upstairs in heritage colours. Hugo disliked the dull blue currently being applied to the landing. It was, he had realised after considerable effort of memory, the exact shade of the covers of maths exercise books at school.

Hugo nervously rubbed his hands. 'Harrods.' That sounded expensive.

'Don't worry,' said Gary, looking up. 'I've got the answer, squire.'

Hugo was surprised that Gary had been listening. He certainly never seemed to when being given instructions.

'What if,' Gary offered in his oddly high squeaky voice, 'I just paint all the kiddo's windows black? A coat of black on the outside and you won't be able to see a thing, squire. No need for blackout whatsits.'

Hugo looked at him in amazement. 'That's a very good idea, Gary.' He turned to the maternity nurse. 'What do you think, Nurse Harris?' He accompanied the query with his most dazzling smile. Battleaxe she may be, but he'd crack her. No woman he had yet met was impervious to the famous Fine charm. Apart from Dr Watson, the paediatrician, but even she had been friendlier when they last met.

Nurse Harris, however, seemed unmoved. 'Well, it's certainly unorthodox. But if it's really the best you can do . . .' She pursed her lips. It went without saying that such a thing would never have happened at Lord Fairbourne's.

'Now, on another matter, Mr Fine,' Nurse Harris said sternly. 'I'm going to explain my routines to you. It's vitally important that they are adhered to. There are specific times for sleeping, eating—'

'Sounds great,' Hugo interrupted encouragingly, turning the charm up as far as it would go. He wasn't beaten yet, not by a long chalk. 'We all need some discipline round here.'

Nurse Harris frowned. 'Mr Fine, the routine of which I am speaking applies to Mrs Fine and Baby. I am not proposing to supervise anyone else in the family.'

Nurse Harris's routines, pinned up with great speed all over the baby's nursery walls, made Hugo's head spin whenever he looked at them. His son was supposed to wake on the dot at 6.45, bath, dress, be breastfed by Amanda, spend two hours playing and then return to bed for forty-five minutes. His next feed was at 10.30, after which he would be engaged in a variety of activities until his lunchtime sleep. Given his commitments, it seemed to Hugo surprising that the baby didn't have his own PA. Perhaps it was no bad thing he was still in the Cavendish with his mother. With a schedule like that awaiting him when he came out, he needed to rest while he could.

Alice didn't want to leave the Cavendish any more than Amanda. She adored being warm and comfortable, in a proper bed that was not on the floor, drinking out of proper glassware and eating from china plates. She hadn't realised how much she had missed these things, yet resisted letting Jake know this. He was sure to deplore such self-indulgence – and with good reason.

Personally, she could have used another few days of luxurious rest. But Jake had hated the place and was determined to get her home. The hospital was, he had made clear, against all his principles.

Back in the Old Morgue, Alice tried not to notice the contrast. Or the heaps of detritus in the kitchen, the latest results of Jake's 'foraging'. She tried desperately not to mind when, as she opened her underwear drawer, a group of fruit flies, refugees from the ever-more-rotting wormery, flew out.

Instead, she concentrated on the positive. Such as the changing table made by Jake from recycled milk crates. Whenever Alice was tempted to think it was a bit wobbly and slightly too low, she immediately asked herself how many fathers would bother to build their firstborn such a thing. It was hard to think of a more touching expression of paternal devotion, combined, of course, with commitment to the planet.

'The most environmentally friendly one on the market,' Jake grinned at the table's ceremonial unveiling, whisking aside a towel to reveal his masterpiece. 'The inside of the mat's made of hemp. This whole changing station is a miracle of sustainability!'

Another such miracle was Rosa's sleeping hammock, constructed along authentic American Indian lines from sacking, rope and some old clothes props Jake had found in the cottage garden. Alice's secret worry, that it was a rather tenuous construction, was one she kept to herself.

Despite such conscience-calming equipment, Rosa proved a restless sleeper. Night after night Alice lay in the dark and listened to her mewling before finally bursting out into a full-blown, nerve-shattering bawl. Dragging herself out of bed, Alice would wince at the still-tender Caesarean scar.

'Everything OK?' Jake said sleepily, as tonight, as usual, Alice crossed the bedroom to the hammock.

'Fine. She just needs changing.' Alice held her daughter close and took her into the bathroom where she laid her gingerly down on the recycled milk crates.

As she set about the pins and undoing the nappy, Jake appeared at the door. 'Just watch her while I rinse this out, would you?' Alice asked.

She had accepted without question Jake's suggestion that they use terry nappies instead of disposable ones. She agreed that any other course would be monumentally self-indulgent. Terries were fiddly, they were difficult, they were bulky and they involved three rather unpleasant buckets (or recycled catering-size margarine tubs) standing around at all times in the kitchen. But at least they weren't adding to a landfill mountain comprising four per cent of the total household waste in the whole of Britain.

These statistics Alice would repeat like a mantra as she stood, as now, with the freezing water from the toilet flush streaming over her reddened hands, watching the green effluvia dislodge from the sodden material she held. Sometimes, as now, it took more than two flushes, and long minutes' waiting in between while the temperamental cistern filled. Eventually, Alice handed Jake the partially clean nappy to take downstairs and add to the soaking bucket while she began the thankless task of putting a new one on the still yelling baby.

Despite the nappy change, Rosa's roars were harder and more urgent than ever. It was clear that something else was wrong.

'I think she's hungry,' Alice guessed. 'I'll just take her downstairs and feed her. Shush, darling,' she whispered into the baby's warm head.

'I'll come down with you,' Jake offered.

'Really, you don't have to. No point us both being up. Better if you go back to bed.'

'No, I'm coming too. I'll make you a cup of tea.'

She smiled at him. Had any new father ever been so considerate?

Downstairs, Jake guided Alice towards an orange-box armchair. She lowered herself carefully and began the struggle to unite baby to nipple.

'Has she latched on yet?' Jake called from the kitchen. Alice felt her heart swell with loving pride. How many other fathers not only knew but used the correct terminology? 'Yes,' she called softly back, trying to keep the wince out of her voice.

The main thing was that the crying had stopped, even if the agony in her breasts had started. It sometimes seemed to Alice that childbirth – its immediate aftermath, at least – was the constant swapping of one uncomfortable experience for another.

'Damn, we've run out of milk,' she heard Jake mutter under his breath.

Alice looked down at Rosa and hoped she hadn't done

the same. That was the problem with breastfeeding; it was impossible to tell. Even after Rosa had fed for hours, or what seemed like hours, she often spent the rest of the night screaming, apparently starving. Alice hoped this would not be the case tonight.

'You know,' she said conversationally to Jake as he came into the sitting room with two cups of milkless greenish water, 'I'm beginning to wonder whether bottle-feeding Rosa might not be an idea.'

'Bottle-feeding?' Jake repeated. Alice detected an ominous note in his voice.

'Oh, not with formula, obviously,' she said hurriedly. 'I mean breast milk. You can express it into bottles with a breast pump, so it wouldn't make any difference to Rosa. And my poor old savaged dugs could recover,' she added, grinning.

Jake dropped on his hunkers before her and took her hands. 'Al,' he said persuasively, 'don't you see it's the thin end of the wedge? If you start giving Ro one bottle, it'll be five a day of formula before you know it.'

Alice gave a surprised laugh. 'Of course it won't. It's just that one of the midwives mentioned that it was a good idea to introduce bottles at the end of the fourth week. Any later and Rosa might reject them.'

'Midwives!' Jake scoffed. 'They're all in the pay of the baby milk companies.'

'Oh, Jake. I'm sure that's not true. And surely the occasional bottle won't do any harm? At least then I'd know what she was getting.'

His smile was gentle but his eyes had a steely glint. 'Don't you think it's a bit selfish to put your comfort above what's best for Ro?'

Alice sighed. He was right, of course. The fault was obviously hers. She must try more and complain less.

'Breast is best.' Jake bent his head forward and kissed her bosom. She gasped softly. It was amazing, after the battering her body had received, how he could still set it jangling with desire. With the lightest of touches. Of looks, even.

'Go back to bed,' Alice murmured.

He pulled at her hand. 'Only if you come with me.' He had, she saw, that New York look in his eye. Smouldering, suggestive and thoroughly thrilling.

'I can't.' Alice gestured at Rosa with her free hand. 'She's not finished yet.'

'OK,' Jake nuzzled her neck. She shuddered with pleasure. 'All I'm trying to do is support you. You do know that, don't you?'

Alice nodded, the tears springing to her tired and heavy eyes.

'You are happy, aren't you, darling?' He was looking at her intently.

'Of course I'm happy.'

'You don't regret giving up the rat race? Coming here to live with me?' A hank of long dark hair had dropped fetchingly into his eyes, its end touching his lips and making her stomach twist with longing.

She shook her head, sniffed again and smiled. ''Course

not.' She gathered the contentedly suckling Rosa closer to her. 'How could I?'

'Good. I'm happy too, darling.' He kissed her lingeringly on the lips. 'And if you try harder with the breastfeeding, I'll be happier still.'

In Fitzherbert Place, Hugo opened an eye. In the midnight dark, something was stirring. It was the baby. Or Theo, as they – or rather Amanda – had finally decided to call him. In vain had Hugo pointed out that he had been at school with a Theo, who, thanks to his lack of academic distinction, was widely known as Thicko. Hugo, who had hardly set the examiners on fire himself, feared the same fate for his son.

His ear strained into nothingness. Theo seemed to have gone back to sleep. Hugo, intending to do the same, burrowed thankfully back beneath the duvet.

Beside him, Amanda was sleeping like the proverbial log. He, rather than she, was always the one to wake up when the baby did. Amanda, these days, always slept with earplugs.

'But you won't be able to hear Theo crying,' Hugo had objected.

'Exactly,' said Amanda, squishing the foam rubber cylinders into her ears. 'That's the point.'

'But you're his mother.'

'Yes, and you're his father. And Nurse Harris is his maternity nurse.' With that, Amanda had turned over and pulled the duvet over her head.

Waaaaahhh! The high-pitched, indignant roar had begun

again. Hugo never failed to be amazed that something as small as a baby could make such a huge noise. He jerked upright and looked at the clock: 2.37 a.m. He nudged Amanda.

She fiddled in her ear and removed one of the grubby plugs he was growing accustomed, but disgusted, to finding in the bed. 'What's up?' she snarled.

'Theo. He's crying.'

'Oh, for fuck's sake,' Amanda snapped. 'What the fuck's the fucking matter with him *now*?'

'He's a fucking baby, Amanda. That's what's the fucking matter with him.'

'What's that fucking old bat doing then?' Amanda demanded furiously. 'She's supposed to fucking see to him in the fucking night.'

'Fuck knows,' groaned Hugo.

Had the old bat even heard Theo? She usually did, it had to be said. Whenever Theo had gone off, as Hugo thought of it, in the past, the cries almost immediately subsided amid the efficient sounds of doors softly opening and closing. But perhaps Nurse Harris was in a particularly deep sleep.

Bugger it. 2.38 a.m. was a sod of an hour to be getting up. And as Amanda clearly wasn't, he obviously was. Cringing, Hugo peeled back the covers, the chill of the bedroom sweeping across his chest, which was bare like the rest of him. Hugo had always slept in the nude, the better to be ready for action, as he had joked to various girlfriends through the years. Although now, practically celibate in the frozen depths of the country, he was beginning to wonder why he bothered. Lotti's assurances to Laura that sex could be resumed within weeks clearly did not apply in his case.

'I used to have a healthy sex life,' he had moaned to Amanda a couple of nights ago.

'Oh, yeah? Who with?' she had snapped back.

WAAAAHHHHHH!!! Hugo swung his legs out of bed. It was like submerging oneself in an agonisingly cold sea. Hugging his chest for warmth, he stumbled out of the bedroom and made his way upstairs to the third floor. At the nursery doorway, he grabbed the handle, pushed the door open, and froze. Froze even more than, in his completely naked state, he was doing already.

The nursery light was on. Bent over Theo's cot in the corner of the room was a familiar broad back. As Hugo stared, rooted in horror to the spot, the back turned. 'Mr Fine!' gasped Nurse Harris, a large hand flying to her chest.

Hugo turned and fled. But not before registering an astonishing fact. Nurse Harris, at quarter to three in the morning, was not wearing the candlewick and curlers one might have expected. She was wearing her uniform.

As Hugo skidded back down the stairs, he could hear Nurse Harris exclaiming to herself in tones of deep disgust. Quite what she was saying, he could not make out. But it seemed likely Lord Fairbourne came into it.

Chapter 10

Christmas was now approaching and Alice felt as excited as a child. She had always been moved by the festive season. But the first Christmas with their baby would be so special it made her eyes prick just to think about it.

Special was certainly one way of describing their Christmas decorations. The home-made, undyed, recyclable cardboard tree was hung with blown lightbulbs salvaged from a skip in which the stripped-out contents of an office had been thrown. 'Baubles!' Jake had announced triumphantly, arriving back with a bulging plastic bag. Alice had tried to be pleased for the sake of the planet. And anyway, when hung, they covered up some of the grease stains on the cardboard.

Alice's contribution to the cardboard tree was to cut out images from old Christmas cards salvaged from last year's rubbish. Alice dutifully threaded the various Santas, robins and bells with lengths of cotton unpicked from old clothes and tried to hang them on the slippery cardboard branches. As they worked, they sang recycling-friendly versions of traditional carols. 'While shepherds knitted socks by night/All from recycled yarn . . .'

Alice could not help contrasting this with the *King's College Christmas* tape and glasses of champagne traditionally accompanying her parents' tree-trimming. She dreaded them seeing Jake's. They wouldn't understand, she knew. Yet see it they would, for, despite her best efforts to discourage them, they were coming to stay over Christmas.

'We want to be with our new grandchild, darling,' Mrs Duffield had said, sounding hurt but determined as Alice tried yet again to put her off.

And if the tree was unlikely to impress them, the presents would still less. To Jake and herself the gifts were things of beauty, wrapped in line with the most rigid of recycling principles as expounded in the festive issue of *Get Trashed!*. Some were packed inside cereal boxes, and some stuffed into Jake's beloved toilet-roll tubes. All were wrapped around with toilet paper and decorated with ribbons made from the shiny insides of crisp bags.

But her parents *should* appreciate them, Alice thought crossly. Didn't they realise how selfish they were being, perpetuating an endless grasping materialist culture that was slowly strangling the planet to death?

She resolved that when the time came to unwrap her own presents she would give an ecstatic reception to the bracelet made from old shoelaces and the abstract sculpture Jake was making on the kitchen table from the entrails of some redundant machine. *That* would show them.

In the foyer of the Bath boutique hotel where they had stopped for a break in their Christmas shopping, Hugo and Amanda sat sipping cappuccinos. Both were staring, unseeing, at the gold-sprayed apples heaped in a gold-sprayed urn. Both were lost in their own thoughts.

Amanda was thinking how much better life was when Theo was safely at home with Nurse Harris. The novelty of motherhood had worn off weeks ago. If she were honest, it wore off the afternoon he was born.

What all the fuss was about, she could not imagine. As anticlimaxes went, being a mother was the biggest ever. Hanging around the house all day waiting for her nipples to be attacked was an intensely dull way to spend her time.

She had, she now accepted, been over-optimistic about babies. There was nothing particularly fascinating about them; two days after bringing Theo home she'd been bored out of her mind. Perhaps it would have been easier if he wasn't so ugly and had been closer to the blond, blue-eyed cherub of her imagination. But Theo was skinny and dark like a monkey. Even though, now, his hair was turning fairer, it had a worrying ginger tinge.

It wasn't just motherhood that was boring, either. Bath was boring as well. It had none of the glitz and glamour of the big city; Ayckbourn revivals starring Wendy Craig at the Theatre Royal couldn't really compare to first nights on Broadway with

Daniel Day Lewis. Or even the sad old South Bank. She'd never been much of a theatregoer, but it had always been there if she wanted it. Now, though, it wasn't. Provincial standards of journalism were, meanwhile, beyond belief – the local papers were full of wind-chime wars and front-page headlines such as 'Pensioner Dies In Fall Trying to Kill Spider with Slipper'.

Her own journalism was even more moribund. Motherhood and the provinces hadn't only been a personal cross to bear. It had been a professional one too. Her career had suffered, there was no doubt about it. All her recent efforts to interest people in features ideas had come to nothing. The impossible had happened: Amanda Hardwick had slipped below the radar.

It was almost a year since she had last written anything really big for anyone. Her last big piece, in fact, had been the one for Janice Kittenburgen which had caused all the trouble with Intercorp. She needed to get back on the scene, send out a few letters, apply for things, even. Get some irons in the fire.

What was stopping her, after all? Nurse Harris looked after Theo. She herself hardly needed to be there – despite being urged to cuddle her son more often, Amanda preferred to risk Theo's future emotional health rather than risk him possetting on any of her designer clothes. She hated, absolutely hated, no longer being able to wear black because Theo threw up all over her shoulder. The alternative – a wardrobe in all shades of the formula milk spectrum – did not appeal.

And she'd given up breastfeeding ages ago. She had been good at it and found it relatively simple, but loathed feeling like a Friesian. It seemed common to be so superabundant. Far more upmarket to struggle.

Nurse Harris did not share this view. 'A shame to stop when so many people have such trouble,' she had remarked. 'When I was with . . .' she dropped her voice to name a famous – and famously buxom – actress, 'she had, I might say, some difficulty.'

'Really?' Amanda's eyes had lit up. Nurse Harris's advice she could take or leave, but she was always ready to hear about her celebrity clients. 'You'd think with knockers that size she'd be producing pints.'

Sitting in the hotel bar drinking her coffee, Amanda ruefully remembered the glossy magazines she had read on the plane from New York. Those visions of glamorous parenthood to which she had responded with such high hopes. The vast houses. The endless gardens. The happy, carefree, fulfilled mothers clutching exquisite infants. She could see now that, at the very least, those women were richer than she, and had more help. Either that or the features had all been complete lies. But why was that a surprise? She of all people should have known that the lifestyles peddled by magazines were fantasies. What a bloody idiot she had been.

Hugo too was thinking about work. Neil was champing at the bit to have him back at Dunn and Dustard. His paternity leave was about to expire and he was needed. Things were busy; there had, apparently, been an unexpected pre-Christmas rush on houses.

Hugo was secretly relieved his time at home was nearly

over. Although he would never have admitted it to anyone, he felt no nearer to his son than he had when Theo was first born. This was due mostly to the fact that Nurse Harris seemed to dominate his every waking moment, ever ready to snatch her charge from inadequate parental hands. On one rare occasion, Hugo had taken Theo, bundled in a blanket, outside to show him the snow on the trees. Within seconds, Nurse Harris had shot out, grabbed the baby and disappeared back inside, muttering darkly about infant pneumonia.

'Come on. So much Christmas shopping, so little time!' Amanda poked Hugo painfully in the thigh with her high, sharp heel. 'Next stop's the spa. I'm booking some pre-Christmas postnatal de-stressers.'

Hugo wondered, with a maternity nurse to run everything, how stressful Amanda's postnatal period had actually been. And speaking of Nurse Harris, her wallet-punishing stay must be coming to an end soon. The sooner the better, particularly after that horrendous business in the nursery. He'd barely – as it were – been able to look the old boot in the eye ever since. Time, surely, for Amanda to take over and do her dandling angelic infants in the dappled sunlight bit. Her greatest-job-on-earth number.

He had noticed that Amanda had proved curiously difficult to pin down on the subject of Nurse Harris. But now, sitting opposite him in an armchair, she could hardly avoid it if he raised it, which he did.

'Nurse Harris is doing very well, I think,' Amanda returned with a warning flash of her eyes. 'If it ain't broke, don't fix it.'

'But *we'll* be broke soon, that's the point. Not only is the woman an absolute dragon, she's a dragon who costs six hundred a week.'

'Theo seems to like her. That's what's most important, surely?'

'Theo likes anyone who feeds him. His views aren't necessarily conclusive.'

Hugo was aware that he had lost her, however. Amanda's attention was now focused on a large-nosed woman in a tight fuchsia suit at the lobby reception desk. She stiffened with excitement and half stood up, one hand clamping her napkin to her knees and the other waving wildly. 'Laura! Over here!'

Laura whipped round on hearing her name. 'Well, if it isn't you two!' she declared in the ringing foghorn voice he remembered from the antenatal classes. Laura's cleavage, Hugo saw as she tottered over, was still her most distinguishing feature. Predatory as ever, it threatened to burst the moorings of her suit buttons.

Laura enveloped Amanda in a heavily scented hug. As her chin rested on Amanda's tailored shoulder, she gave Hugo an emphatic wink. 'Haven't seen you for a while,' she drawled through a thickly lipsticked smile. 'Where have you been hiding, handsome?'

'I've been busy,' Hugo said shortly.

'With the baby, I suppose.' Laura sat down, crossed her black-stockinged legs, produced a packet of cigarettes and lit one. 'Bloody hell, I envy you,' she said to Amanda. 'Fergus can't be arsed to do anything with Django.'

'Django?' Hugo repeated.

'What a wonderful name; you are clever,' Amanda exclaimed. 'Funnily enough, it was among the ones I was considering for Theo.'

Hugo stared. He hadn't realised things had been *that* close.

Laura shot a plume of smoke into the air. 'He's such a gentleman, Fergus,' she said with bitter irony. 'Told me the other day that having sex with a woman who's recently given birth is like throwing a banana down Oxford Street.'

'Charming,' said Amanda.

'He wants me to have a fanny tuck for Christmas.'

'Double charming.'

'Isn't it?' Laura looked glumly at her fuchsia-painted nails. Then she looked up, gave Hugo a smouldering smile and adjusted her bra strap. 'Anyway, at least I'm out of there for a few hours. Fergus's battleaxe of a mother is looking after Django.' She took a deep, scornful drag of her cigarette. 'You name it, I'm doing it wrong. How's Theo, anyway? Hair colour improved at all?'

Hugo stiffened indignantly. What had Amanda been saying about Theo's hair? It looked perfectly all right to him.

'Still a bit ginger,' Amanda confessed. 'But I've got Charles Worthington on standby in case it gets any worse.'

'There's nothing wrong with his h—' Hugo began, but Amanda cut in over him.

'So you've come Christmas shopping?' she asked Laura brightly.

'Um, not exactly.' Laura sat up, cigarette still in her mouth, and adjusted her cleavage still further. She smirked enigmatically. 'But I suppose you could say it's a Christmas treat.'

'That reminds me,' Amanda gushed. 'I'm going to book some postnatal pre-Christmas de-stressers at the spa. Shall I book you in too?'

'Yes . . . great.' Laura leant over and ground her cigarette out in the ashtray. 'Look, I'll give you a ring. I'd better go now. No, no, don't get up.' She swayed to her feet, tugging down the short, tight skirt and loudly kissed Amanda. 'See you around, gorgeous,' she murmured throatily to Hugo as, kissing him too, she bent so far over he could see the tips of her nipples.

As she clacked off across the marble, they gazed after her, Hugo with relief to see the back of her, Amanda with blazing curiosity.

'She's meeting someone,' she murmured, craning her neck to look. 'A man,' she added excitedly. 'Sort of blond and big. Very good-looking.' A largish crowd was now filling the previously empty lobby, so it was difficult to be sure, between the bodies, who Laura was disappearing with towards the lifts. But in the light of what she had just said, it seemed unlikely it was Fergus.

Hugo didn't care anyway. He had more pressing matters on his mind. 'Darling,' he ventured. 'As we were saying. About Nurse Harris . . .'

'*Nurse Harris?*' Amanda's eyes were wide with scornful amazement. 'God, Hugo, you're unbelievable. We witness a first-class, gold-plated, A-list piece of scandal like that and you want to talk about Nurse bloody *Harris*?'

'But we need to sort it out.'

'Not *now*,' snapped Amanda, signalling vigorously for the bill. 'We can't sit here all day. We've got Christmas shopping to do. There's a new boutique I want to look at. I need a new suit. Something smart.'

'New suit?' Hugo was surprised. Amanda was, or would be once Nurse Harris had gone, the full-time mother of a small baby. 'What for? Christmas Day?'

When, finally, Hugo cranked on the handbrake outside Fitzherbert Place, he felt unusually relieved to see it. The afternoon's shopping had been long, boring, crowded and alternately stifling hot and freezing cold as Amanda insisted on going in and out of what seemed like every single store. In the course of it, Hugo had decided that he hated Christmas, hated Bath and hated especially being Amanda's parcel-bearer, which meant attempting to walk along whilst laden like a gift-shop window and not fall over even though everyone he passed seemed to be trying to knock him off his feet.

In the kitchen, most unexpectedly, was a welcoming committee.

'Nurse Harris!' Amanda exclaimed, peeling her gloves off. 'Are you cold, or something?'

Nurse Harris, coat neatly belted over her uniform, was sitting on one of the Marie Antoinette chairs beneath the chandelier. The severity of her appearance only accentuated, Hugo thought, the room's ridiculous opulence. Kitchens were supposed to be functional places. Theirs looked like a ballroom with cookers.

A large brown suitcase, obviously packed, sat on the floor at Nurse Harris's side. 'No,' she said shortly. 'I'm not cold.'

'Well, it's very useful that you're here,' Amanda said briskly, trotting over the Indian stone floor in her heels. 'You can help Hugo carry the parcels in.'

Nurse Harris raised her chin in an affronted manner. 'I'm waiting for a taxi.'

Amanda stopped dead in her tracks. 'What?'

'A taxi?' Hugo echoed. 'Are you going somewhere, Nurse Harris?'

'I am leaving this establishment, Mr Fine.'

'Hang on, hang on.' Hugo held up both hands in panic. '*Why* are you leaving, Nurse Harris?'

Nurse Harris turned boiled, affronted eyes in his direction. 'I'd rather not say, Mr Fine. Not in front of Mrs Fine, anyway.'

'*Why* can't you say it in front of me?' Amanda demanded.

Hugo blushed to the roots of his hair. Oh God. He might have known Amanda would find out about the nursery incident sooner or later. He should have told her straight away. But the whole experience had been excruciating and he was sure she would only have laughed.

Nurse Harris said nothing, but stared accusingly at beetroot-faced Hugo.

As she did the calculations, the smile faded from Amanda's face. '*You?*' She looked aghast at Hugo. 'And . . . *her?*'

'It's not what you think,' Hugo assured her, panicked.

'No employer of mine,' Nurse Harris declared, 'has had

the extreme bad manners to show themselves *naked* to me before.'

'*Naked?!*' Amanda screeched.

'Look,' Hugo pleaded. 'I wasn't up to anything. You've got it wrong. What happened was a mistake.'

'The oldest fucking line in the book,' spat Amanda.

'I got up in the night to see to Theo,' Hugo persevered desperately. 'He was crying. I, um, couldn't find my pyjamas. I didn't know Nurse Harris was there.'

'A likely story,' yelled Amanda. '*Now* I see why you're so keen to get rid of her. Because she resisted your advances, that's why.'

Hugo ground his teeth in frustration. To tell the truth – that he'd sooner approach Gary the painter for sexual favours – would be rude. 'That's not what happened at all,' he protested. 'Please, darling. You've got to believe me.'

The rattling sound of a taxi could be heard coming up the road. Seconds later, the lights flashed through the window. Nurse Harris stood up.

'Is there nothing we can do to persuade you to stay?' Amanda's voice was hoarse with emotion. She was trying, Hugo realised, to appeal to Nurse Harris's soft side. He doubted this would work. Nurse Harris didn't have a soft side.

'Nothing whatsoever,' the nurse confirmed. 'This very lunchtime I accepted a post with,' she dropped her voice to name a member of the Royal Family. 'I'm a tolerant woman, Mrs Fine . . .'

'You'll have to be if everything one hears about *them* is true,' snapped Amanda furiously. She glowered at Hugo. '*Now* look what you've done,' she shouted. 'This is all your bloody fault.'

'But none the less,' Nurse Harris continued, looking disdainfully round the kitchen, 'this isn't at *all* the sort of thing I'm used to. I can tell you, it wouldn't have—'

'Happened at Lord Fairbourne's,' Hugo groaned as Nurse Harris picked up her suitcase, opened the door and stalked out into the night.

Chapter 11

'Happy Christmas, everyone.' Jake placed a large plastic bowl of steaming sprouts down on the lunch table.

The three people sitting at it exchanged strained smiles. There was a definite atmosphere, although not, as Alice had feared, because of the presents. These had not yet been opened.

The point at issue was that Alice's parents, on arrival at their Bath hotel, had discovered that their reserved suite had been cancelled and something smaller and cheaper booked in its place. It had then been discovered that Jake had done the rebooking.

'But why, Jake?' Alice remonstrated, her ear still hot from the angry telephone call from her mother.

'They didn't need a room that size.' Jake spoke without a hint of apology. 'And I gave the difference in price to the homeless.'

Alice sighed. 'Jake, I can see why you did it. For the best

reasons, I know. I just wish you'd discussed it with me first, that's all.'

'But you wouldn't have liked it and then the homeless would have lost out,' Jake pointed out, with some truth, Alice recognised. 'I didn't tell you for your sake, Al. You'd have been stopped from doing the right thing.'

Alice supposed she could see what he meant. But doing the right thing had moved on since then. On Christmas Day, it meant jollying everyone along and preventing any awkward moments. Fortunately, her parents seemed determined to make similar efforts.

'That's a very nice bowl,' Alice's mother remarked, looking at the sprouts.

Jake flashed all his teeth at Mrs Duffield. 'Glad you like it. It used to be the front of an old washing machine.'

'How terribly clever of you to think of doing that with your old machine!'

'Oh, it wasn't ours,' Jake said breezily. 'I found it on the tip and brought it home. It was a waste, leaving it where it was.'

'He made some amazing sculptures with the bits inside too,' Alice joined in.

'Not with the washing machine, Al,' Jake corrected her. 'The sculptures were from that smashed-up tape deck. But you're right, in a way – I brought the tape deck from the dump at the same time.'

'How interesting,' Mrs Duffield muttered into the napkin with which she was delicately dabbing the corners of her mouth and which, had she known it, was cut from one of Jake's old T-shirts.

There was a silence as the sprouts were ladled out using the cup from the top of an erstwhile Thermos. Everyone picked up the plastic knives and forks routinely collected by Jake from any fast food outlet he happened to be passing.

'Beer?' Jake offered Alice's father.

'Thank you.' Mr Duffield looked doubtfully at the former petrol container from which a weak brown stream of liquid was issuing into the jam jar by his plate. He picked up the jar and tasted it gingerly. 'Home brew, is it?'

Jake nodded vigorously. 'Best way to thwart the multi-nationals. Brew it in the bath.'

Alice's father made no comment. Particularly he made no comment about having worked in a legal capacity for a despised beer multinational for many years.

Alice slid him a grateful yet defensive glance. That her parents thought their son-in-law rude was obvious. And perhaps he was – a bit. But what they didn't understand was that Jake was an idealist. A visionary. A prophet, almost. And prophets and visionaries didn't have to be tactful. Generally speaking, they tended not to be. They operated on a higher, more important plane in which ordinary concerns such as manners were sacrificed for the greater good of mankind.

'In the bath?' Mrs Duffield echoed in horror. 'What do you use to wash poor Rosa if the bath's full of beer?'

'Not the *upstairs* bath.' Jake grinned at her. 'The one in the garden I got from the dump.'

Alice's mother looked puzzled. 'I didn't see a bath in the garden.'

'It's round the back,' Alice muttered.

'Although I must say you've got plenty of old loos and sinks outside the *front* door,' Mr Duffield remarked jovially. 'I counted about fifteen altogether. Are you storing them for someone? Or just planning five or six new bathrooms?'

'Jake's using some of the loos as planters,' Alice informed them.

The meal continued in silence.

'How's the magazine going?' Alice's father asked Jake presently. 'Booming, I should think. Everyone's very green these days.'

Alice felt tense. The magazine was a touchy subject at the moment.

'Nowhere near as green as they should be,' Jake said sourly. 'Which is why, since you ask, the mag's not doing as well as it should be. People have yet to catch up with the *Get Trashed!* take on eco responsibility.'

'I see.' Alice's father was nodding gravely. 'So you've got to water down the message to suit them, you mean? I can see that would be annoying.'

Jake's eyes flashed. 'Of course I'm not watering down the message. If anything, I'm doing the opposite. People need a kick up the arse about the planet. We've got to show the way, whether people want to hear about it or not.'

'But if your magazine's not selling . . .' Alice's mother faltered.

'. . . how are you managing to, um . . .' Alice's father faltered too.

'Pay myself?' Jake enquired archly. 'And the staff and the printers?'

'Well . . . yes.'

Jake dug a reclaimed plastic fork fiercely into a sprout. 'I'm managing, thanks.' The fork snapped.

Alice did not look at him. She thought of her gradually dwindling bank balance he was managing on and hoped her parents would change the subject.

'Delicious sprouts,' remarked Alice's mother.

'Sprouts? Glad you like them!' Jake, jauntiness restored, proffered some more. 'All home-grown and totally organic. We can't wait for Ro to get on to solids, can we, Al? She's going to have such fantastic food.'

'That's right.' Alice looked at the green spheres on her plate. Or, rather, the former frisbee which served as one. Picking them in the freezing cold had been ghastly, particularly when the means they grew by was taken into consideration.

'You grew them yourself? How clever of you,' Mrs Duffield made a determined effort at brightness. 'How *is* the garden these days? Worms getting on well, are they?'

Alice sighed. The worms were doing as badly as ever. The fact that Jake had another obsession in the garden – his vegetable patch – had, she hoped, been an opportunity to take them to the nearest bait shop. But he had rumbled her plans at the last minute.

She listened as Jake began to describe his Yin and Yang

vegetable patch. 'The Yin side's mostly white vegetables, turnips, onions and so on. Whereas the Yang is darker – beetroot, that kind of thing. And sprouts, of course.'

Mrs Duffield was nodding. Alice could almost see the hope rising within her that here, at last, was something she and her difficult son-in-law could have a conversation about.

'And what sort of fertiliser do you use?' she asked.

Under the table, Alice's toes curled.

'Fertiliser?' Jake grinned. 'The original and best fertiliser on the market.'

'Ooh, do tell,' urged Mrs Duffield. 'I'm always looking for good ones. Not blood, fish and bone, then?'

'Human sewage,' Jake beamed. 'Cheap, easy, accessible and frankly unbeatable. And planet-friendly, obviously.'

There was an exploding noise. Alice's father had spat out his Brussels into his napkin. His face was puce with disgust as he laid the bundle on the plastic surface of the shower curtain that, having failed to get a run-out at Rosa's birth, was now doing service as a festive tablecloth.

Alice's mother looked at her daughter in horror. 'Excuse me,' she muttered, pushing back her chair and thundering upstairs to the bathroom.

At Fitzherbert Place, Christmas for Hugo was going every bit as badly. Take this morning, for example. Amanda had come storming into the bathroom and let rip, Christmas or no Christmas.

'What the hell do you think you're doing?' she had demanded.

'Changing Theo's nappy,' Hugo said crossly. 'What does it look like?'

'It looks like my bloody face cream!' Amanda yelled, grabbing the small white tube out of Hugo's hand. She shook it at him. 'Have you any idea how much this costs?'

Hugo sighed. He had been unable to find normal nappy cream and was improvising. The cream he had found in Amanda's bedside drawer had seemed a reasonable enough substitute. He doubted it cost much anyway; Amanda, so long as he had known her, had never knowingly paid for beauty products. 'Paying is for little people,' he had heard her say more than once. 'People like me are given things.'

'This,' growled Amanda, still brandishing the tube, 'is a special skin treatment. It plumps out lines and adds radiance.'

'Well, if it's any comfort,' Hugo retorted, 'Theo's bottom looks very radiant.'

'You're useless,' exploded Amanda.

'Hello Pot, meet Kettle,' snapped back Hugo.

Nurse Harris's departure had revealed more than Hugo in the nude. It had also exposed the fact that neither he nor Amanda had the first idea about even basic babycare. Neither knew his or her way round a nappy, and were constantly losing count of the scoops when mixing the bottles of formula. But whether Theo was being under- or overfed seemed to make no difference. He cried all the same, all the time.

Christmas lunch, like all their food since neither could cook, was a microwaved ready-meal eaten to the accompaniment of a grinding, motor-like roar coming from upstairs.

'It's controlled crying,' Amanda snapped from over the rim of her several-times-already-filled wine glass. But it didn't sound very controlled to Hugo.

Following Amanda's nappy-changing attempts after lunch, Theo appeared looking traumatised in some lopsided Pampers and the present-opening began. Hugo received a book called *Brain Child – How Smart Parents Make Smart Kids* from his wife. She, meanwhile, received one from Laura, a novel called *Faux Pas*. 'It's about a girl with father issues, apparently,' she said, reading the blurb on the back. Hugo made a mental note to read it. He had a few father issues himself.

'Happy Christmas!' he said as the champagne cork exploded with a violence that made the baby jump almost out of his bouncer. His bottom lip trembled and he burst into tears.

'Oh, shit,' said Hugo impatiently, chiding himself for his clumsiness.

'Well, it's hardly his bloody fault,' Amanda pointed out savagely. 'Get his first Christmas Day off with a bang, why don't you?'

Hugo muttered self-conscious endearments at his infant son, who ignored him completely and continued to howl. Thank God, Hugo thought, he could escape back to the office after Christmas. Dunn and Dustard was admittedly far from being the most dynamic agency in the business. But at least – and actually for that reason – it was a haven of peace and quiet.

'I'm going to miss this.' Hugo grinned ironically at Amanda as Theo roared on.

She looked up from sloshing more wine in her glass. 'What do you mean?'

'When I get back into the hamster wheel.' Hugo rolled his eyes in mock despair. 'Back to the grindstone. Work.'

'Oh, that reminds me.' Amanda gave him a dazzling smile.

Hugo's insides twinged in warning.

'I've got a job,' she remarked casually.

Hugo blinked. He raised his hand. 'Hang on a minute . . .'

'Anne Dexter's been sacked from *Class* and they've asked me to step in. Temporarily at first, but they're going to see how it goes.' She punched the air with triumph. 'I'm an editor!'

'But you never told me about this!' Hugo exclaimed.

'Well, it's only just happened,' Amanda snapped. 'They asked me yesterday.'

Hugo shook his head in bewilderment. 'But if we're both working,' he said jumpily, 'who's going to look after Theo?'

Amanda opened wide astonished eyes. 'I hope you're not imagining that *I'm* staying out in the sticks changing nappies? A woman of my calibre? With the talents I've got to offer the world?'

'But you're Theo's mother!' Hugo could hardly keep pace. The world was unravelling around him. 'What about . . . ?' What about, he wanted to challenge, all the declarations about motherhood being the ultimate career and the best job satisfaction available? But he found himself speechless. The carpet had been whipped so utterly from under him that he felt almost physically winded.

'Yes, I *am* his mother.' Amanda's face had the appearance of a cornered rodent. '*And you're his bloody father. You* look after him.'

Hugo struggled to believe what he was hearing. While he realised that, in the week since Nurse Harris's departure, she had looked after Theo with a very bad grace, he had no idea his wife had been harbouring plots of this nature. How the hell was he supposed to take charge of Theo full time? He didn't know the first thing about him. Even down to the cream he had on his bottom.

'Tough,' Amanda said lightly when he explained this. She raised her champagne glass triumphantly. 'I've done my bit. I had him. Over to you, buddy.'

Meanwhile, at the Old Morgue, the gloom that had begun with the hotel bookings and deepened over the fertiliser showed no signs of lifting now everyone was gathering beside the recycled cardboard tree for the present-opening. This event had arrived sooner than it should have done, because lunch had been shorter than it should have been. A marked decline in Alice's parents' appetites had followed the revelation about the sprouts.

Alice watched tensely as her mother began to pick apart the toilet paper covering her gift. 'I suppose,' she said brightly, 'we should be grateful this hasn't been used before as well!'

As her father exploded with mirth, Alice did not dare look at Jake.

'It's made from an old computer keyboard,' she eagerly told her mother, who was releasing from its confines the chunky ring featuring her initials.

'How lovely,' said Mrs Duffield in strained tones. She slipped it on beside her Garrard diamonds and stretched her hand out to admire the effect.

Alice's father, meanwhile, who detested gardening, was staring nonplussed at his waterproof garden-kneeler made from strips of old wallpaper.

They had bought Jake some Umberto Eco novels. 'Joke, you see,' Alice's mother urged him. 'Eco – get it? You being an environmentalist and all that.'

But Jake was not smiling. His brow clenched as he examined the bleached paper the books were printed on; he was, Alice knew, calculating the exact amount of tree involved.

Alice had warned her parents not to bring too many presents for her. She saw now that they had circumvented this by buying a very small number of great value. She tried to suppress her thrilled excitement over her cashmere dressing gown for fear of offending Jake. But Jake was offended anyway over the flashing, talking Minnie Mouse Alice's parents had brought their granddaughter and which Rosa, now up after her lunchtime sleep, adored on sight.

He stormed into the kitchen muttering furiously about cultural imperialism and grandparental gifts that compromised parental values. Alice followed him and put a hand on his shoulder. 'Sweetheart, it's Christmas. Relax a bit, can't you?'

Jake looked at her with burning eyes. A muscle ticked in the plain of flesh below his high ridge of cheekbone. 'If we all relaxed, where would the planet be then?'

* * *

Later, in the bathroom, Alice was changing Rosa when her mother slipped in. 'Can I have a word, darling?'

Alice's heart sank. She had sensed this was coming and had been trying to avoid the word all afternoon. It was bound to be about Jake and uncomplimentary.

'Darling, I know he means well,' Mrs Duffield predictably began.

'He doesn't only mean well,' Alice attacked immediately. 'He does well too. He practises what he preaches.'

Alice's mother put a restraining hand – now minus the computer-key ring, Alice saw crossly – on her arm. 'No need to be so defensive. Honestly, darling, you're such a teenager sometimes. I only want to ask a question. You might be able to help me understand.'

'What's the question?' Alice grumpily pulled the terry over Rosa's leg rather tighter than was necessary. The baby squeaked in protest.

'Those baths, loos and sinks piled in the garden. And the washing machine. And all the rubbish inside the house as well.'

'Jake's waste transfer stations, you mean?' Alice conscientiously employed her husband's preferred euphemism.

'I was just wondering about them.'

'Wondering what about them?'

Mrs Duffield took a deep breath, 'Surely it's one thing, and one very laudable thing too, to recycle one's own household rubbish. Most people try and do it to a certain extent. But, darling, isn't it entirely another to go out, collect lots of rubbish from somewhere else and bring it all home?'

Alice rebutted the accusation immediately. 'You don't understand, Mum. Jake runs a recycling magazine and he's got to—'

'Yes, dear. Practise what he preaches, I know. But bringing all that junk in from elsewhere is a bit excessive, don't you think? I just wondered –' her mother continued gently – 'is Jake trying to recycle his own rubbish, or that of the entire world?'

Alice was silent.

'And some of the things he recycles, darling.' Mrs Duffield shook her immaculate pepper-and-salt head. 'That cake . . .'

Alice tensed. Admittedly, the uncertain, broken squiggles that, with the aid of a former toothpaste tube rinsed out and with its end cut off, Jake had piped over the wholemeal vegan Christmas cake were not particularly beautiful. 'It was the *Get Trashed!* top tip for December,' she said stubbornly.

'Yes, I can imagine. But, darling, how exactly is that going to save the planet? How many times a year, apart from Christmas, does one actually use a cake-icer, and isn't it worth investing in a nice metal one that would last and do a good job rather than—'

'Mother, that's enough.' Alice picked up Rosa and headed out of the bathroom. Before she could, Mrs Duffield caught her by the arm. Her smile had vanished.

'Alice, it's *not* enough.' The gentle tones had turned serious.

'And you can't just storm off in the middle of a discussion. Quite apart from being a grown-up, you're a lawyer. A professional logician. You're trained to listen to both sides of an argument. Why can't you hear me out?'

Alice looked at her mother resentfully. In her arms, Rosa began to mew and wriggle.

'Alice, your father and I are worried about you.'

'There's nothing to be worried about,' Alice said crossly. 'I've never been happier in my life.'

Her mother looked down, biting her lip. 'Darling, of course we're glad you're, er, so happy. It's just that some things make us – well – wonder. You know, you used to be such a career woman – high-powered, happy—'

'I wasn't happy,' Alice rebutted fiercely. 'At the time I met Jake I'd never been so miserable in my life. He rescued me from a pointless existence.'

Mrs Duffield sighed. 'But you were doing your own thing. And doing it very well—'

'I've got a different career now,' Alice snapped, jiggling Rosa in her arms. 'A *much* more important and rewarding one.'

'And that's great, darling, really it is. Rosa *is* adorable.' Her grandmother looked at her fondly.

'So what's the problem?' Alice demanded.

Mrs Duffield hesitated. She put out an arm and pulled at Rosa's nappy. 'Well, this sort of thing. I know terries are planet friendly, but they're not very life friendly. Believe me, I remember. And it's much worse for you, being restricted to only four.'

'Er, three actually,' mumbled Alice. Any more, Jake had decided, would be profligate.

Mrs Duffield rolled her eyes. 'You don't have to use terries, you know. Why make being a new mother even more difficult than it is? There are lots of convenient green whatsits around. I've been doing some research.' Rummaging in the pocket of her neat fawn slacks, she produced a catalogue and held it out to her daughter.

The thought of her mother researching – no doubt with enormous difficulty – the unfamiliar area of earth-friendly baby bottom products was touching. None the less, Alice let indignation get the better of her. She took the catalogue abruptly and laid it on the changing table. 'Terries are fine, Mum. They're not that difficult.'

'And then there's the breastfeeding thing.' Mrs Duffield looked pleadingly at her daughter. 'Darling, don't be offended at me saying this, but you're obviously struggling. The odd bottle would help *so* much. Formula's not poison, you know.'

'Jake thinks it is,' Alice muttered.

'Well, it isn't. You're living proof that it isn't. You were on it from two weeks old.'

Alice looked up in surprise. 'Was I?'

'Yes,' said her mother firmly. 'And what exactly did he mean about Rosa and solids? He's surely not going to have you slaving away making everything she eats out of the . . . *garden*?' She swallowed and edged a hand up her throat.

'Of course not.' In truth, Alice had no idea what Jake had meant. Or what solids might mean either. She'd been too tired to think about it. But they surely couldn't be worse than the endless agonising struggle with breastfeeding.

Her mother looked doubtful. 'Well, just remember, you can get jars of organic baby food now. You must do everything you can to make it easier for yourself, darling. You look exhausted.'

'I'm *not* exhausted.' Alice felt her eyeballs weighing heavy and aching in their sockets. But she was determined not to let slip a single word that was not loyal to Jake.

'There's no need to pretend,' her mother said gently. 'Believe it or not, I can see what you see in him. Jake is quite extraordinarily handsome.'

Alice gave her a faint, proud smile. 'He is, isn't he?'

'I think he's probably one of the best-looking men I've ever seen. And with a very powerful personality as well. But, darling, life with him seems a bit, well, spartan. Repressive, almost.'

Alice was stung. '*Repressive*? How can it be? Jake's one of the most advanced eco-thinkers of our time.'

'Yes, but look at your clothes.'

'What have they got to do with anything?'

'They're all second-hand. If not third.'

'That's not *repressive*,' Alice retorted. 'It's simply refusing to buy into the materialist culture.'

'Or buy anything new. You always used to wear such lovely things.' And you can buy super Fair Trade clothes now. They're very fashionable apparently. Gwyneth Paltrow wears them . . .'

Alice looked scornful.

Her mother pressed her lips together. 'Alice. Don't you

think your and Jake's lifestyle is, well, a bit extreme? I'm all for recycling – who isn't? But I really think Jake takes it too far. No one could live the way he wants them to, although you're trying your very best, admittedly.' She looked sadly at the milk crate changing table before meeting Alice's eyes again. 'I hate to say this, darling, but it's almost as if you've been brainwashed.'

Alice was white with anger. 'How dare you? How I live my life is no business of yours.'

Mrs Duffield had tears in her eyes. 'I know. And I wouldn't have said anything. Except that I love you, and your father loves you. Believe me, darling, I would much rather have said nothing. But we're both worried about what's happening to you.'

'Well don't. Worry about the planet instead.' Clutching Rosa closely to her, Alice marched out of the bathroom. If her mother was unable to understand the finer points of Jake's crusade against rubbish, the fault lay in her. Not him.

Chapter 12

'I don't know why you're screaming,' Hugo muttered, stumbling into the nursery at God only knew what hour of the night. As anticipated, the baby, lying on his back, was dancing up and down his cot in fury. His eyes were hard, black and relentlessly open.

Why, Hugo thought, was the one place he himself was so desperate to be – bed – such anathema to his son? What was so wrong with lying down and being warm and comfortable? This lack of logic seemed only to widen the gulf between them.

After half an hour of fruitless pacing up and down in the cold, the frustrated and exhausted Hugo decided to stick Theo back in his cot and ignore the wails as best he could. The baby, however, had other plans. Obviously sensing such a plot was afoot, he shot out a chubby arm and wrenched off Hugo's glasses.

This had become a favourite trick of Theo's of late, albeit one he could only employ when his father was not wearing his contact lenses. He was good at seizing his chances, however, and now, with his defences down, Hugo was easily outmanoeuvred. The glasses clattered to the floor and in the dim illumination of the night light Hugo was completely unable to see where they had gone. As he crawled around on all fours on the hard boards of the nursery floor, Theo, now back in his cot, roared triumphantly on.

It was all part of the unfairness of parenthood, Hugo reflected, finally reunited with his spectacles and tiptoeing away, that these midnight attentions, these most obvious and extreme demonstrations of fatherly sacrifice and devotion, were the ones Theo would have no memory of whatsoever in later life. He would, on the other hand, remember every awkward conversation verbatim, recall every difficult moment in excruciating detail and reconstruct his entire childhood accordingly. Just as Hugo did with his own parents. And there was another wrong he could not right: their both being dead meant there was no opportunity to tell them he knew now, for his sake, what they had gone through.

'Shit!'

The night light bulb pinged out. Thanks to Gary's black-painted windows, the way out was now impossible to see. Hugo stepped on a plastic turtle belonging to his son, shot across the floor at a terrifying velocity and crashed head first into Theo's chest of drawers. The shattering noise of impact and Hugo's howl of pain terrified the baby, who lay in pitch-blackness hearing what sounded like the world ending. His understandable response was piercing screams.

Head throbbing, Hugo crawled across the nursery floor, feeling his way through the booby traps formed by scattered toys. He yelped as he knelt heavily on a wooden brick and cursed as he collided with something large and plastic, which immediately began to flash with lights and perform a tinny electronic version of 'Daisy, Daisy'. Hugo recognised Theo's 'Silly Snail', a multi-function monstrosity someone – one of the few Amanda had not fallen out with, presumably – had sent from America.

The snail, Hugo thought, was ugly and vulgar, yet its obvious advantages, given his situation, now struck him. The illumination was activated by hitting a large button on the toy's top. And so Hugo progressed across the nursery floor, thwacking the snail at regular intervals to light his way and thinking longingly of bed.

Theo, however, screamed on. It was obvious that he wasn't going back to sleep. Hugo dragged his wrist towards him and saw that it was quarter to six. As the baby, quite clearly, had started his day, Hugo miserably accepted the inevitable. 'Time for bottle and bath, Theo,' he announced with all the cheer he could muster. Which, in point of fact, was not much.

Hugo hated bathing Theo. The baby was as slight and slippery as a fish and just as confident he could swim, trying constantly to twist from his father's grasp. Hugo hung on with a thundering heart, terrified of drowning him, terrified even of rubbing shampoo into the tiny, delicate cranium over which the bones had not yet formed.

Lifting Theo out of the water was almost worse; on contact with the air, the wet child set up a roar that continued earsplittingly throughout Hugo's attempts to dry him and apply baby oil to the thrashing, writhing body. By the end of this stage, soaked, greasy, limp and sweating with fear and effort, Hugo could have done with a bath himself. But there was no time.

Instead, there were nappies. Try as he might, aware as he was that millions of parents, some a great deal more stupid than him, negotiated them daily with complete success, Hugo simply could not get the hang of them. Of the two sticky tapes, one either side of the nappy, only one, thanks to Theo's constant wriggling, was ever attached. Hugo would stare at the nappy packet and study the illustration, trying in vain to work out how it was done. The only thing he knew for certain about nappies was that, just as soon as he had wrestled Theo into a new one, the baby would immediately fill it. Every time.

Dressing Theo was next. Hugo hated this stage most of all. The baby clearly viewed it as attempted murder and howled blood-curdlingly throughout. It seemed ironic to Hugo that Theo, who would happily roll off beds or attempt suicide in the bath, only considered himself genuinely in danger when his father was putting his clothes on.

Then came feeding. 'Breakfast, Theo,' Hugo panted, giving up the struggle with the poppers. He'd got about half attached; it would have to do.

Feeding Theo filled him with almost more dread than all the other rituals put together. The baby, now four months, had started on solids. Neither Amanda nor Nurse Harris had had to deal with Theo flinging baby rice about the kitchen in gloops that set almost instantly to a concrete-like consistency. Or screaming so much at being reined in to his high chair that Hugo, taking pity on him, loosened the straps only to turn round a few seconds later to see the food-plastered baby looking over the edge with the clear intention of throwing himself out.

Hugo had long since stopped looking to Amanda for help. Up at dawn and down the road shortly afterwards in the gleaming BMW supplied by the magazine company, his wife had neither time nor interest for anything other than her new job.

'Your turn now,' she would tell Hugo baldly. 'It's up to you to look after him. By yourself.'

Almost the first decision Hugo made by himself was that he absolutely could not look after Theo by himself. He needed professional back-up. He was also determined to return to work. But as, after the Nurse Harris experience, the idea of live-in help filled him with dread, he decided to seek it from a nursery.

Finding the right one had taken time. This was not because Hugo was looking for perfection. He was merely looking for somewhere that wasn't full. Chicklets was the only one in the whole of Bath that had places available for babies this side of Theo's twenty-first birthday, albeit only mornings.

This was a blow to Hugo's plans, not least because it meant working for Dunn and Dustard part time. If they would let him. Neil's dinosaur views on family matters had been aired more than once in the office. His best hope, Hugo calculated, was to schedule a meeting with his boss after one of his typically liquid lunches.

'He wouldn't have a free slot in the afternoon, would he?' Hugo wheedled Neil's secretary Shuna over the phone in as syrupy a voice as he could manage. He doubted this would have much effect, but he persevered. He had realised soon after starting at Dunn and Dustard that Shuna, whose contempt for the human race seemed general, reserved particular loathing for him. She was, like Nurse Harris and Dr Watson, yet another woman impervious to the famous Fine charm. Did it, Hugo wondered, exist any more? Had he left it behind in London, along with the rest of what made life worth living?

Shuna's hostility made sense after Neil let slip that her boyfriend had applied for Hugo's job. 'Chinless wonder,' Neil had guffawed. 'Mind you, she's got chin enough for both of them.' He had a point, Hugo thought.

'Neil's free at half past nine in the morning tomorrow,' Shuna snapped. 'But that's it. Take it or leave it.'

'I'll take it, thank you, Shuna,' Hugo said humbly. Inside he despaired. The optimum bear-with-a-sore-head slot was his.

Half past nine in the morning was, in addition, a time Theo was guaranteed to be awake. Very much awake;

bouncing-off-the-walls awake, in fact. Which was unfortunate, as Theo would have to come to the meeting. Hugo could hardly leave him in the house by himself.

Next day at nine thirty-five on the dot, Hugo arrived at his erstwhile and hopefully future part-time workplace with a wriggling baby under his arm and a number of smears on his lapel.

In his office, a predictably grumpy and bloodshot Neil looked at Theo with horror. 'He's not going to yell, is he? I've got a hell of a headache.'

'I don't think so.' Hugo spoke more confidently than he felt. Fortunately the baby, fascinated into silence by the sights and smells of the first office he had ever encountered, was less interested in making trouble than in the depressed weeping fig by Neil's desk. Hugo struggled to keep his keen-to-explore son in his lap while he outlined his plan for returning to work.

'So basically,' he finished, 'mornings only would be fantastic.'

Neil rubbed his red, bristly face and looked doubtful. 'I don't hold with part-timers,' he grumped. 'What's this all about anyway? I thought you were the shit-hot salesman with the lethal charm, not the househusband in the wholemeal jumper.' He stared at Theo, wriggling on Hugo's pinstriped knee. 'Didn't realise you were so politically correct,' he added disapprovingly.

Hugo sighed, grasping the baby round the waist to stop him lunging at the plant leaves he so clearly longed to rip off. 'It's nothing to do with political correctness,' he said loudly over the baby's protests. 'Or wholemeal jumpers. It's to do with the fact Theo can only go to nursery in the mornings. And the fact Amanda's in London all day every day.'

'That woman's wiping the floor with you. You should tell her, Fine.'

Hugo did not bother to say that he had, in fact, aired his concerns to Amanda. That she hadn't been interested in hearing them would not, he sensed, raise him in Neil's estimation. Besides, he was desperate to stop Theo making any more noise. He rummaged in his pocket for a dummy, praying he had remembered to put one in. He hadn't.

'I'll have to think about it,' said Neil.

'Well, can you think about it now? Otherwise I'm afraid I'll have to look elsewhere.' Desperation had made Hugo bold. His tired nerves, he knew, would not stand another interview elsewhere accompanied by Theo. Attracted by the glitter, the baby was now swiping in the direction of Neil's paperweight.

It was a gamble. Neil shot him a look. Hugo's ears filled with fizzing tension.

Theo, he realised, had stopped wriggling. His face was now bright red and his entire small being concentrated on some huge straining effort. Oh God, thought Hugo. Not here. Not now. But already wafting up into his nostrils was that familiar, pungent scent. Within seconds, he knew, the entire office would reek of it. For more reasons than just one he needed a quick decision out of Neil.

But Neil seemed in no hurry. He had got up and now

stood with his hands behind his back, looking out of the window on to the street. His vermilion features, when eventually they turned to Hugo, seemed oblivious to the building aroma of filling nappy. 'I *suppose* we could make an exception,' he said after what seemed to Hugo like hours. 'Not every firm would. Most wouldn't, in fact. But I *suppose* we could make it work.'

Hugo felt a powerful flood of relief. 'Thanks, Neil,' he said gratefully, repenting the unflattering thoughts he had entertained about this man in the past. Neil was decent after all. 'That's great.'

'At a lower hourly rate, of course. To reflect the lower overall commitment.' There was a sly look on his boss's face.

Hugo bit back his indignation. *Bastard.* In the time he'd been at Dunn and Dustard, he'd shifted more houses than you could shake a surveyor's report at. Lower commitment? How bloody *dare* Neil, the drunken, lazy . . .

He thanked his boss calmly, however. It seemed to him he had little choice. Apart from wanting to keep a toe in the water of adult existence – even if it was only *this* water – he needed whatever money could be brought in at the moment. The bills Amanda had racked up at Fitzherbert Place were horrendous, Nurse Harris had not yet been paid and the nursery fees, even for mornings only, were considerable. It would, in addition, be some time before Amanda's new salary reached the household. If it ever did.

'God,' said Neil, as Hugo and Theo prepared to leave his office. 'What's that awful stink? Drains or something?'

'Smells like it,' said Hugo, exiting hurriedly. 'I'd get them seen to if I were you.'

Changing Theo, with great difficulty, on the back seat of his car, Hugo resisted the temptation to drop the heavy nappy bag into the front seat of Shuna's nearby Audi convertible. She drove it top down in all weathers which accounted, he supposed, for the redness of her face.

Hugo sensed gloomily, as he struggled with his son's bottom, that his days of treating work lightly were over. The balance of power had shifted. Whereas before he had indeed been the super-salesman with the lethal charm, confident of his skills and value, able at any moment to leave Dunn and Dustard for whatever else might take his fancy, now he was under an obligation. Other firms, as Neil pointed out, might not be so inclined to accommodate Theo's nursery education.

'Bugger!' With a jerk of his strong little body, Theo had finally succeeded in escaping the nappy. As the bare-bottomed baby rolled triumphantly across the rubbish-strewn back seat of the car, his father lunged after him, managing to grab one plump little leg. Shrieking violently, Theo was thus hauled back to his original position.

'Hey, hey, *hey*, steady on, eh?' The familiar jaunty voice came floating from behind. 'Don't be too hard on Baby, huh?'

Hugo, now wrestling his son on to his back, shut his eyes tightly. Jake. The last person on earth he wanted to see just now. Or any time, come to that. 'I'm just changing him,' he forced through gritted teeth.

'So I see. Bit of a struggle, yeah? Disposable nappies aren't as convenient as you'd think, are they? Besides being the last word in eco-irresponsibility, of course. Alice and I use terries.'

Hugo wanted to say that it was amazing they didn't use recycled newspaper. Or grass. But his energy failed him. He kept his back turned and concentrated on Theo, hoping Jake would go away.

But Jake obviously had no intention of doing anything of the sort. Equally obviously, he was finding Hugo's discomfiture highly diverting.

'How's tricks?' he enquired in bantering terms. 'The world of shamelessly profiteering property agenting doing well, is it?'

'Never better.' One of Theo's fat little thighs fought free of the nappy. Hugo wrested it inside again. Theo, predictably, howled.

'Having fun with fatherhood, I see,' Jake remarked mockingly.

Hugo did not give him the satisfaction of an answer. But Jake did not seem to require one.

'Fantastic feeling, isn't it?' he enthused. 'Nothing like it in the world. It's literally impossible for Al and me to imagine life without Ro now. She's just made things complete between us. Isn't that how you feel? Complete?'

'Oh, absolutely,' answered Hugo. Complete is right, he

thought. A complete fucking disaster so far as he and Amanda were concerned. And actually, it was all too easy to imagine life without Theo. He could almost weep when he thought of the stimulating, financially stable and well-rested world he had once taken so utterly for granted.

Hugo turned his red and sweating face to Jake. Having anticipated a calm and well-behaved baby somewhere about Jake's person, he was surprised to see the world's most hands-on father out in Bath alone. Perhaps, Hugo thought sourly, that was the fantastic feeling Jake was referring to. He told him this, enjoying watching the other man's face tighten with irritation.

'As a matter of fact,' Jake said crossly, 'I'm here for an important meeting with an architect very keen on developing my ideas about eco-housing. Particularly the underground flat complex with grass roofs I've been working on.'

'You mean like the Teletubbies' house?' Hugo smiled, to Jake's obvious fury.

'No. Not like the Teletubbies' house. Whatever that's like. We don't watch television.'

Hugo had turned back to Theo and was now buckling him into his car seat. The baby began to yell.

'Hey, hey,' Jake said admonishingly. 'You're being a bit rough with him, aren't you? Gentle persuasion, that's what's needed.'

Something inside Hugo snapped at this. The urge to hit Jake hard in those persuasive teeth was almost unbearable, but teasing, while duller, was probably safer. 'Oh, Theo likes restraint really,' he said casually. 'He's had to. With us using the feeding-box method, and all that.'

Jake cocked his head. 'Feeding-box method?'

Hugo feigned surprise. 'You haven't got one? Just the best thing for getting the food down. Wooden box the size of a minibar with a hole in the door. You strap the baby inside, close the door so all you can see is its face sticking out through the hole and shove the food in its mouth.'

Jake's expression was contemptuous. 'That sounds disgusting.'

'Anything but,' Hugo explained earnestly. 'There's no slop or anything. No fuss, no mess. You should try it. And then there's our straitjacket cot. A bloody miracle, I tell you. Theo's not been able to get out of his blankets once . . .'

He found himself, however, addressing Jake's back. The other man was stalking rapidly away.

Theo's first day at Chicklets dawned a particularly wet one. Rain hammered on the windows of Fitzherbert Place. As he set off late despite all efforts not to be, Hugo thought thankfully of Chicklets's car park, adjacent to the nursery's front steps. They should at least escape a soaking.

His previous visits to Chicklets not having been this early in the morning, Hugo was unprepared for the volume of traffic about. In particular the Panzer division of vast, gleaming people carriers that greeted him as he turned into the nursery street. It was like encountering a military drive-past head on in the wrong direction.

Aggressively revving, hazard lights flashing, radios thumping, manned by wild-eyed women whose height seemed in inverse proportion to the hugeness of their vehicles, the Range Rovers, Land cruisers and SUVs of all other imaginable types blocked the road and the pavements for what seemed at least half a mile. The nursery car park was clearly out of the question.

Hugo looked doubtfully out at the streaming rain. Then, glancing at the dashboard clock, his doubts scattered. He was already fifteen minutes late for work. Like it or not, he and Theo would have to swim their way to Chicklets.

He remembered he had, some days ago in a fit of efficiency, put the fold-up baby buggy in the boot. He vaguely recalled seeing some rainproof plastics with it.

Leaving Theo where he was, looking wide-eyed out at the rain, Hugo jumped from the driver's seat and extracted the buggy. It was not a contraption he had much experience of and it took several minutes, rain pouring down his neck all the while, to work out how to detach the various levers and clips to persuade what initially looked like a small bag of golf clubs to unfold into a recognisable seat on wheels. This done, he fished Theo out of the car and shoved his squirming, yelping body under the buggy straps. Hugo paused for breath, wiping the faint film of sweat from his brow. All that remained now was the simple process of fixing on the plastic rainhood.

'Don't worry,' he assured the still-writhing Theo, now loudly protesting against the rain spattering his face. Dragging the plastics out of their protective covering, Hugo shook them out and stared at them. Contrary to his confident expectations, there was no indication as to which hook, tape or stud went where. Not for the first time he suspected the hand of a baby-hating sadist in the manufacture of child-related equipment.

As the rain intensified, so did Theo's howls. Kneeling down on the pavement, the wet soaking into his trousers, Hugo wanted to howl too as he struggled despairingly with the recalcitrant strips of Velcro and apparently mate-less studs and holes. To add insult to injury, the buggy's fold-out canopy, theoretically forming a weatherproof roof over the infant's head, kept falling off its side attachments and hanging drunkenly over Theo's face.

As he occupied part of the narrow pavement by the side of the car, a procession of state-of-the-art buggies, all pushed by tidy-looking mothers and all swathed, naturally, in efficiently attached plastic, were constantly shoving past and knocking him where he crouched.

Hugo imagined the uninspiring picture he must present to these mothers. Fumbling, crumpled, clueless, cruel, even, with Theo screaming like a banshee against the unaccustomed wet. The very essence of paternal uselessness. A *man*, for God's sake. Trying to care for a baby on his own. What the hell, they were no doubt wondering, did he think he was doing?

And it was, Hugo thought, tugging once more at the Velcro with the cold, raw hands of an Arctic fisherman, a good question.

'Can I help?' The voice, above his head, was as sonorous

as that of the Angel Gabriel. He looked up into the face of a red-haired woman with a handsome, if harassed, lean face. He registered with amazement that humour and sympathy, rather than contempt and disgust, were twitching about her mouth.

'I know what those plastics are like,' she said. 'They're buggers. I've got some myself.' She gestured at the polythene-swathed box on wheels she was pushing; the identical model to his own. 'Here,' she added. 'Let me.'

She crouched down. 'You slip these loops over the handles first. Then you stick the studs at the bottom through here. Then slip it over and . . . *voilà*!' Within seconds, it seemed, Theo was snugly encased in plastic. A flood of gratitude more substantial even than the shower swept over Hugo.

'You Chicklets?' the woman asked. 'Me too.' She stuck out a wet hand. 'I'm Barbara. I must say, it's great to see a man doing all this.'

'But not very well,' Hugo said apologetically.

'More than a lot of men bother doing, believe me.' Barbara flashed a rueful smile at him. 'Must dash, anyway. Work.' She rolled her eyes. 'Nice to meet you . . . er . . .'

'Hugo. And, er, thanks . . .' As he stammered his gratitude to her retreating back, he realised the rain was easing. Indeed, it had almost stopped. Ragged holes had appeared in the grey clouds, revealing more than enough to make a sailor a pair of trousers. He could even feel the sun on his back. The plastic had been fitted just in time to be removed.

With Theo now steaming up under his covering, Hugo pressed hurriedly on to Chicklets. The place was a hubbub of people; the corridor crammed with mothers rushing to drop off their children and race off to work before the nine o'clock deadline. Adding to the frantic, almost hysterical atmosphere was the fact everyone was expected to slip electric-blue plastic galoshes over their shoes before entering any of the children's rooms.

The idea, Hugo gathered from the information notices, was to safeguard the infants by keeping their surroundings clean. The much greater potential damage to the babies if their parents fell over while trying to snap galoshes on whilst holding them didn't seem to give rise for concern.

He waved at Barbara as she dashed past him on her way out. 'Can I give you a tip?' she gasped, skidding to a halt.

'Yes, please,' said Hugo humbly. 'As many as you like. As you see, I'm completely clueless.'

'I'd come either half an hour earlier or half an hour later if you're driving. Otherwise you've no chance. Not with the guerrilla mums out there in their battle wagons.' Barbara grinned and dashed off.

In the baby room, a capable-looking nursery assistant seized Theo from Hugo. 'Go now and don't make a fuss,' she instructed. 'Particularly on the first day.' With relief and an unexpected tug at his heart, Hugo turned his back and plunged out.

On the nursery steps, where he had left the buggy, he now faced the reverse struggle of folding it all up again. He was just congratulating himself on the remarkable speed with which he did this when he realised he had closed the handles round his ankle. He tugged, but to no avail. He lifted his knee and shook it, but the parental ball and chain held fast. The buggy was now immovably trapped around his leg, much to the amusement of the mothers dashing down the steps. 'Fuck it,' muttered Hugo. 'I'm the Mr bloody Bean of parenting.'

'*Hi*, handsome!'

Her. Complete with plunging cleavage and full make-up, despite the early hour.

'Hello, Laura,' Hugo said stiffly, jiggling his trapped leg agitatedly. 'How are you?'

'All the better for seeing *you*, sexy. It's been *ages*.' She wiggled her hips at him. 'So what's a gorgeous guy like you doing in a place like this?'

'Trying to get out of it,' Hugo said irritably, shaking his leg again.

Laura looked down and burst into loud laughter. 'Hugo! You're stuck!'

'I had noticed.'

She squatted down – with difficulty, given the tightness of her jeans. Amid a great deal of cleavage-heaving and what seemed rather unnecessary pressing of her face against his groin, she managed to un-concertina the back of the buggy and release him. She pouted up at him, batting her eyelashes.

'Thanks,' Hugo said, grasping the buggy handles. 'I'd better be off now.'

Laura, however, seemed determined to delay him. 'Didn't

know your boy had started *here*,' she grinned, smoothing her hot-pink tracksuit top over skin-tight denim hips. She had a talent, Hugo noticed, for making the most innocent remark appear a double entendre.

'He's starting today.' Hugo flinched as she started picking Weetabix crust off his collar. It was too intimate a gesture for that time in the morning – for any time, come to that.

'Django's here too,' she said. 'When he's not off with conjunctivitis.'

Hugo had no idea what conjuctivitis was. It sounded like an East European tennis player to him. He glanced at his watch. 'Look, Laura, much as I'd like to stay here all day talking—'

'You've got work to go to, sure.'

'Yes.'

He started to walk down the steps. Laura walked with him, twining her arm through his.

'Fancy a coffee?' she suggested. 'There's a good place just round the corner.'

'Er, like I just said, I've got to go to work. Sorry.'

'Oh, *go on*. Just a quick one.'

Hugo, looking into her eyes and about to refuse, saw something there that he was not expecting. Something beyond mere flirtation. Something begging and desperate. His surprise made him pause.

'Please?' Laura said, in a small voice.

'Oh, OK then.' The words were out before he could stop them. But what the hell? He was so late already he may as well be really late. Besides, he was under an obligation to her, thanks to that wretched bloody sabotage buggy. And having a coffee with her now would at least save him having to have one with her in the future. 'Just a very quick one, though. I've got to get to the office.'

'Have you gone back to the estate agents'?' Laura asked as they went down the nursery steps.

'Yes.'

'The same one? Dunn and whatsit?'

'Yes.'

'Only Amanda told me during our last spa session that you were going to be a househusband. We had quite a laugh, imagining you naked in a frilly pinny waving a feather duster.'

'Did you?' Hugo said stiffly. He could imagine the scene all too well. The spa one, that was. The other he preferred not to think about.

'Oh yes.' Laura dug him suggestively in the ribs. 'I could quite see you hoovering in the nude and knocking back the Baileys. I imagine,' she added, low and throaty, 'that you'd look rather gorgeous.'

Hugo now bitterly regretted the moment of compassionate madness that had led to him agreeing to this coffee. He resolved to get it over with as soon as possible.

'When's Amanda coming back?' Laura's elbows were spread out on the table and spread out on top of those was her cleavage. Quite a few of the male customers had slid sidelong glances at it already.

'Coming back? Er . . .' It was a good question. For how was he to know? Amanda had rung last night to say she'd been working so late at the office she was going to stay at the company's Soho flat. She might, she hinted, be doing the same tonight. And possibly tomorrow as well. 'But you'll be fine holding the fort with Theo, won't you?' she had trilled. 'Frankly, sweetie, you'd better be. You're going to have to get used to it. I might be going to New York next week.'

'But . . .' Hugo had protested, aghast. Too late. Click. Burr. Amanda had gone.

'Later this week,' he told Laura firmly. 'She's very busy with work.'

Laura's thickly mascara'd lashes fluttered downwards. 'Work! Lucky her. Must be nice.'

'Why must it be nice?' Hugo asked glumly, remembering how late he was.

'Having some sort of meaning to your life.' Laura's mood had switched abruptly. Her tone now was bitter.

Hugo wasn't sure what Laura meant, or that he necessarily wanted to know. Sensing dark, deep waters, he picked up his cup and drained as much coffee as he could, anxious to make his escape as quickly as possible.

Laura jerked her chin up and sniffed. Her eyes, Hugo saw, were swimming with tears.

'What's the matter?' he asked reluctantly.

She shook her head. 'Nothing.' He was tempted for a second to take her at her word. To say 'oh, okay then,' and get up and go. Instead, he found himself patting her hand and saying,

'Well it doesn't look like nothing. You're crying. Come on. Tell me what's wrong.'

'No one told me it would be like this,' Laura gulped.

'But I thought you liked it. I imagined you must come here a lot.'

She flung him an impatient look. 'Not the café, for Christ's sake. Having a fucking baby.' She bit her lip. Her face crumpled and reddened.

Sitting on the minimalist iron seat, Hugo clenched his buttocks with frustration. He'd been right about the deep waters. Oh why hadn't he escaped when he had the chance? 'How do you mean?' he hedged. 'Not that bad, is it?' Laura, after all, was a woman. She was bound to have a better grip on things than him.

Laura's head was now slumped on to her elbows. She spoke in a dreary monotone. 'Depends what you mean by not bad. Sitting in my bathrobe for days on end on my own. Too knackered to get dressed because the baby keeps me awake all night. Only ever seeing the milkman. Listening to shit plays on Radio Four about invisible housewives and Scottish submariners while I feed Django for hours and hours and *hours*. Stuffing myself with left-over Christmas chocolates and panicking whenever I lose the Gina Ford book. Feeling angry all the time. Going completely fucking mad, basically.' She slipped a hand round to her back pocket and pulled out a pack of cigarettes.

'But what about Fergus?' Hugo asked.

Laura cackled. 'What about him? *Got a big campaign on at*

the moment, yeah?' She imitated what was presumably his voice. Even from this Hugo gathered it was harsh, brusque and accustomed to getting its own way. She inhaled savagely on her cigarette.

'What campaigns does he work on?' The sooner they re-entered shallower, more general waters, the sooner he could get away.

Laura exhaled in a great angry rush. 'His main clients are anti dog-poo products for people's gardens. He sits in his office all day thinking up names like Doo Don't, Shit Happens and Piss Off My Lawn.'

Hugo let out an involuntary snort.

Laura looked at him levelly. 'Yeah. Ha ha. Except it's not that funny. His shitty work is apparently more rewarding than spending any time with his son or me. He didn't even take any fucking paternity leave.' Face twisted with anger, she ground the cigarette out in the ashtray. 'I may as well be a single parent. You know, I used to have a life once. A job. Friends. All that stuff.'

'Can't you get a nanny to help?' Hugo's eyes darted to his watch.

'Nannies?' Laura snorted. She touched the top of her head. 'Had them up to here already. The secret smokers, the ones who smash up the car, the ones who won't do laundry, the ones who get stroppy if Django's sick on them, the ones who shag Fergus, on the few occasions he's actually here . . .'

'Shag Fergus?'

Laura nodded, eyes screwed up against the smoke. 'Fergus is one of those men who think monogamy's some sort of wood.'

Hugo remembered the man Laura had been with in the hotel foyer at Christmas. He did not comment.

'So now I'm trying Chicklets,' Laura groaned. 'Sticking him in a nursery for a few hours so I can try and get my head together.'

'What do you think of it?' Hugo asked. 'Any good?'

She shrugged 'Too early to say. But at least those nursery nurses are someone else to talk to. Believe me, I need it. Now that I'm on first-name terms with the supermarket check-out staff and actually welcome cold calls from cable TV companies.' She scrubbed her nose with a paper napkin and gave him a bleary grin. Her mood, suddenly, had changed again. 'Hey. Enough of my moaning. Why don't you come round for a drink some time? We could have some fun.' An eyelid lowered in a lascivious wink.

Hugo's stomach tensed in alarm. He got up from the table, drained his cup and rummaged in his pocket for some change. 'Um, sure,' he said, sticking a five-pound note down on the table. 'But if you'll excuse me, I've really got to go to work now.'

Chapter 13

'It's wrong to see it as a chore, Al,' Jake said, giving her his most dazzlingly charming and persuasive smile. 'It's a privilege. A joy. You should want to give Ro the best possible nutritional start in life. Any good mother would.'

'And I do, of course I do,' Alice said, smiling bravely back while her heart sank into the mire.

How foolish she had been to imagine her feeding problems would be over once Rosa started on solids. Twenty ounces of breast milk a day were somehow still to be squeezed out. In addition Jake was now insisting Rosa must eat nothing but home-cooked baby food made with organic vegetables. Home-cooked by herself.

That this was entirely in line with her mother's prediction was maddening. But nowhere near as maddening as trying to make it. Alice, who had never been keen on cooking, hated every minute. She particularly hated the way that, following her labours, the kitchen looked like an explosion in a soup factory. Encrusted bits of the food mill piled up in the sink and there were peelings all over the floor and table. Pans with bits of courgette and carrot adhering to them crowded the cooker surface.

It was unrelenting. There had to be easier ways to ensure Rosa got her vitamins and minerals.

'Sure there are,' Jake said easily. 'You just need some good recipes, that's all. There's bound to be a good organic vegetarian or vegan baby cookbook. In fact, I'm sure I read about one in the *Guardian* the other week. *Ultimate Organic Baby Food Made Fun*, or something. Yeah, that was it. Had fantastic recipes for making bechamel sauce with breast milk.'

Alice gulped. 'I was thinking,' she ventured, remembering what her mother had said, 'more along the lines of organic jar food for babies.'

Jake looked disgusted. 'Ro isn't eating gloop from supermarkets.'

'I don't mean all the time,' Alice backtracked. 'I'm talking about *organic* gloop, anyway.'

Jake's beautiful face was stony. 'I don't see what the problem is,' he said. 'Why can't you make it yourself? You've got all the time in the world.'

'Actually,' Alice corrected him gently, 'I don't have *that* much time, as it happens.'

'Why not?'

'The breastfeeding, for a start,' Alice pointed out. 'That

still takes hours. And changing Rosa's terry nappies takes time. And then there's the proofreading for *Get Trashed!*. Not to mention that bit of book-keeping.'

'I didn't realise you didn't want to help,' Jake said huffily. 'I thought you believed in recycling as much as I do.'

'Of course I do, and, honestly, I don't mind helping,' Alice said earnestly. 'All I'm saying is that when I'm not doing any of that – which I am most of the day to be honest – I'd rather play with Rosa than slave over a hot food mill.'

Her voice softened as she spoke of her beloved daughter. Alice's idea of heaven was to stick her nose into the baby's warm, silken head and watch the serious little face with its swoop of nose and huge blue eyes as Rosa concentrated on whatever had caught her attention: Alice's house keys, a stray coin on the floor. Rarely, it had to be said, the washed-out former soya margarine tubs Jake thought for some reason would yield hours of playing pleasure. The flashing Minnie Mouse had long since disappeared; given away to the junkies or homeless, possibly. Alice had never dared ask.

'I just think,' she persisted, 'that it does no harm to give Rosa the occasional jar. Or make her something that doesn't involve redecorating the kitchen afterwards.'

'Such as?' Jake scoffed.

Alice shrugged. 'Boiled eggs and soldiers?'

'*Not* soldiers,' Jake chided. 'Leave militarism out of Ro's meals.'

Alice sighed. Only yesterday Jake had taught Rosa a version of 'This Little Piggy' in which the porkers went to the farmers' market and had nut rissoles instead of roast beef. It had struck her as a little excessive. 'Oh, Jake,' she had exclaimed. 'The Grand Old Duke of York will be having ten thousand conscientious objectors next.'

Jake had looked thoughtful. 'You know,' he had said, 'that's not such a bad idea.'

He wasn't looking thoughtful now, however. His gaze was accusing, mixed with just the right amount of guilt-inducing disappointment. Realising her laziness and lack of ethics, Alice felt her shoulders droop in defeat. 'OK. I'll go and get a cookbook.'

Looking on the bright side, a trip into town would probably do her good. Being stuck in the Old Morgue trying to concoct edible organic vegetarian baby food was making her stir crazy. In more senses than just one.

Neil, it was soon clear, intended to get his pound of flesh from the new part-time deal. What Hugo had once taken a day to do, he was now expected to achieve in a morning. Including, as before, all Dunn and Dustard's most challenging cases. Such as the delightful little castellated lodge which looked so appealing in the agency window. It was only when interested buyers physically visited the property that its position just inside the gates of a large cemetery was revealed. Stressing the quiet, flower-strewn nature of the neighbourhood, Hugo found, left most viewers of the place unmoved. It had eventually been bought at a knockdown price by a retired undertaker from Crewe to whom the lodge's location was nothing extraordinary.

'Tricky little number for you here, Fine,' Neil announced one day. 'Couple who want a property in Bath.'

'What's so tricky about that?' Hugo asked absently. He was trying to work out how, during the busy morning ahead, he could fit in a visit to a bookshop. Baby manuals, he was hoping, would lighten his childcare darkness.

Neil placed a piece of paper on Hugo's desk. 'They've sent through a few, um, *conditions*. They refuse to buy property from anyone who's been divorced, that has a number three in its address or has a front door any other colour than green.'

Hugo rubbed his tired eyes. 'Bloody ridiculous.'

Neil frowned. 'I'm not asking you for your opinion, Fine. I'm asking you to find it for them.'

Later that morning he showed an old lady round a bungalow called, incredibly, 'Osokozi'. Osougly, more like, Hugo thought, spotting the hideous brown-painted unicorns atop each gatepost. Despite its appearance and extortionate price, however, the client seemed genuinely interested in the property.

The old lady turned to him with rheumy, trusting eyes. 'Do you think you'd buy it, if you were me?'

Hugo hesitated. Coughing up for this place would clearly wipe out her life savings. On the other hand, what was that to him? There was no room for emotion in this business. Let it in and you were lost.

'You bet I would,' he said, flashing her his most persuasive grin. 'Matter of fact, I was thinking of putting an offer in myself.'

Lying to the old lady felt oddly difficult. At least, not as easy as it once would have been. But *caveat emptor*, and all that. Selling was his job. He could not allow himself to go soft on people at the very time his income was so unprecedentedly necessary. He had another mouth to feed now, although not a mouth that seemed particularly interested in being fed. He was definitely getting the mealtimes wrong. The sooner he got a childcare book, the better.

One of Osokozi's few virtues was its ease of access to the town centre. Hugo shot into the first bookshop he came across, where a Pre-Raphaelite assistant directed him towards the Baby and Toddler section. Hugo rounded the indicated corner and reeled at what he saw. He was, admittedly, looking for advice, but not quite in this quantity.

Advice stretched from floor to ceiling, shelf upon black ash shelf of doctors, psychologists and 'child care experts' of every hue. Literally. There was mile after mile of neon and pastel spines, none of which bore the title he wanted. *How to Put on Nappies, Feed and Other Basic Skills for the Terminally Clueless Parent* did not seem to be among the books on offer. They seemed concerned with more elevated issues: *Bringing up the Vegetarian Child*; *Raising a Child in Love, Justice and Truth* and *Raising a Child Responsibly in a Sexually Permissive Society*. Christ, Hugo thought, staring at the latter. Of all the problems facing himself and Theo, he hadn't even *thought* of that one.

At the other extreme, *Twenty Easy Games for Tinies* explained how to amuse infants by turning a napkin into a paper hat and an aeroplane sick bag into a puppet. Presumably before either had been used. Next to it was *365 Ways to Get Your Child Asleep*. Hugo gawped. There really *were* 365 ways? How come, in that case, he didn't know *one*?

Pulling out *What Happens During the First Year*, Hugo discovered that a baby of Theo's age 'should be able to pay attention to a raisin' and 'make a wet razzing sound'. His stomach rushed with panic. What was a wet razzing sound exactly? Had he ever even bothered presenting Theo with a raisin to pay attention to? Or any other piece of dried fruit for that matter? The hell he had. He was an appalling parent. The worst.

Miserably, he pulled out some books about feeding routines, threw himself down on the black plastic sofa and prepared to learn.

Hearing someone else come into the section, Hugo looked up. To his surprise, he recognised the newcomer.

He felt an initial jolt of dislike. It was Alice. Earnest, well-scrubbed Alice, wife of the unspeakable Jake, and the woman who had single-handedly ruined Amanda's American career. Although, admittedly, he didn't feel quite so indignant about that as he used to.

Alice did not look at the man in the book section. She turned her back quickly, hoping her red eyes had not been spotted. Quite unexpectedly, on the bus, she had burst into tears of frustration and exhaustion. And all because Jake had asked, as she left the Old Morgue, whether she could pick up some bicarbonate of soda.

'Why?' Alice had asked. 'I'm not baking anything.'

'No, but it's very versatile as a cleaning agent,' Jake had smiled. 'It's about time we took a more ethical approach to housework.'

Alice had looked back at him blankly.

'You can add it to white vinegar and it deodorises carpets, cleans drains and scrubs stainless steel, all without damaging the planet in the way conventional cleaning products do.' He'd pulled a face. 'Doesn't the thought of all that bleach swilling around in our sewers worry you?' Alice thought it worried her much less than trying to clean the bathroom with vinegar.

Because, of course, the doing of the housework with what basically amounted to a cruet set would obviously fall to her. It was this miserable prospect that had upset her on the bus. She was exhausted from a tiring night with Rosa, her bruised breasts flared with pain whenever she moved and her bones ached insistently as if she was coming down with flu which, given Jake's ever-more-restrictive approach to having the heating on, seemed probable. Alice, sitting at the bus's rear clutching a now peaceful Rosa, felt the tears slide silently down her cheeks. She had cried all the way into town. Only now, just outside the bookshop, had she succeeded in stopping.

Hugo watched Alice covertly. A baby in a sling, he noted, was sleeping peacefully on her chest. Whatever his reservations about Alice, it was hard not to be impressed with that.

Hugo could not now imagine the number of women – and men – with sling-mounted babies he must have passed in the street without any idea of the achievement he was witnessing. His early efforts even to put the wretched sling together, let alone get Theo into it, had left the baby screaming and he himself on the point of a stroke. The instructions were impossible to follow; his most successful effort had ended in Theo strapped upside down with his head sticking out of one of the legholes. In the end, Hugo had decided the entire Swedish-made contraption was yet another sick joke and had abandoned it in disgust.

But Alice had obviously managed it. And her baby, from what he could see, was not only clean and dummyless but had its hair brushed as well. This, too, struck Hugo as amazing. Never, before he had been in charge of a baby, had he regarded women with under-control infants as anything more than the way things should be. But now he knew the amount of effort involved in getting a child washed, dressed, changed, invariably changed again, fed, dressed again after the feed and finally ready to go out, not to mention sorting oneself out into the bargain.

But then, he reminded himself, if anyone was going to be triumphantly on top of things, it *would* be the ghastly, earnest Alice. The earnest Alice with a fist of steel too, if Amanda's venomous accounts held true of how this woman had held not only the entire Intercorp legal department but most of the company's writers in her pedantic, jobsworth, creativity-crushing thrall.

True, he thought, staring at her still profile, the megalomaniac aspect was not obvious. But, no doubt, all the more dangerous for that. Certainly, just like her execrable husband, she exuded an air of complete control, confidence and capability. Look at her now, leafing through – for God's sake – *Ultimate Organic Baby Food Made Fun*.

He felt a crushing sense of inadequacy. He himself, after all, could barely manage to heat up a baby food jar without burning the contents. Depressed, he looked down at the books spread across his knee.

Then, floating into his ears, came a soft sound. A sniff. He glanced immediately towards Alice. God, yes, her shoulders were shaking. Alice, earnest, goody-goody ghastly Alice, was *crying*. Weeping into *Ultimate Organic Baby Food Made Fun*.

Clearly not that much fun.

Books thumped to the floor as Hugo leapt to his feet in concern. 'Are you OK?' Stupid question. She would hardly be howling in a bookshop if she was.

'Here. Use this.' Hugo handed over a crumpled ball of linen formerly a smart monogrammed handkerchief presented to him by Amanda. 'It's clean,' he added. He'd now got the hang of the washing machine. But ironing was still some years off.

He looked politely away as Alice blew her nose. He was puzzled. Her behaviour was not at all consistent with what he knew about her. Evil people did not break down in tears. Nor did smug goody-goodies.

'Sit down,' he urged her, hurriedly scraping the rest of the books to the side of the squashy black sofa. She pushed some hair out of her face and glanced at him in bleary embarrassment.

'Excuse me saying so,' Hugo said, 'but I think we've met before. Weren't you in the antenatal classes at the West Country General?'

Alice nodded, surprised. She did not recognise him, and was amazed he recognised her. These days, she barely recognised herself. As she hadn't seen the inside of a hair salon for months, her blonde hair now sported long, mousy roots and spent most of its time in a ponytail. And it had been months since she had even seen her make-up bag; no doubt, by now, it had made its way to the drugs shelter. Bare-faced had felt strange at first. But after Jake insisted he loved her natural look best, there seemed little point bothering with full war paint.

'Hugo,' he said, shooting out a hand. 'Hugo Fine.'

'Oh, I remember,' Alice said, realising with dismay that this knight with the kind words and clean hanky was the estate agent husband of the unspeakable Amanda Hardwick. Surprise followed the dismay. He looked entirely different to the sharply dressed sophisticate she remembered. He needed a shave, his suit was crumpled and his eyes were bloodshot and swagged beneath large purple sacs of exhaustion. His skin was dry and stubbly, and he had a haunted, desperate look.

'Oily bastard,' she remembered Jake saying. He had, she recalled, loathed Hugo on the spot for reasons she didn't quite understand. He, after all, had not suffered at the hands of the Hardwick.

But the only oil in sight now was on Hugo's evidently unwashed hair. She noticed that his suit, as well as being creased, was stained; around the shoulders and lapels especially. A baby, obviously. She knew he and Amanda had had theirs; Jake had met up with him by accident, in the Cavendish hospital bar of all places. 'Drinking his own weight in whisky and smoking like a crematorium,' Jake had reported scornfully.

Recognising in Hugo all the signs of frazzled parenthood, Alice could not help a lurch of sympathy. She suppressed it immediately. The fact he was a harassed father didn't make him any less unpleasant. Which of course he was. Anyone who lived with Amanda Hardwick had to be.

The sooner she got away from him the better. Only – Alice looked at her bunched-up fist – the contents of her nose were in his handkerchief.

Lovely skin, Hugo was thinking. Great body, too; mother-hood had added no long-term surplus to the lithe frame clearly evident even under the bulky coat. And tears made those clear blue eyes bigger and clearer than ever. Close up, that long oval face had the serenity of a medieval angel. She didn't look evil, not in the least.

She did look suspicious, though. He supposed this was understandable. He was, after all, Mr Amanda Hardwick, and there was no reason to suppose Alice felt any differently about Amanda than Amanda felt about her. Or than he felt about Jake, and vice versa. He remembered with a flash of fury their last encounter over Theo's back-of-the-car changing session.

Yet even so, the wish that he and Alice could be friends was growing within him. Its root was not sympathy for her tears, nor even appreciation of her looks, but the fact that Alice clearly knew her way round a baby. He, on the other hand, didn't. Might she not be able to help him?

'I'd better be going,' Alice said. She placed a hand protectively over the baby in its sling.

Hugo racked his brains for a reason to detain her. 'So you had the baby,' he said conversationally.

'Yes.' Alice looked surprised.

Hugo felt himself reddening. What help was he going to ask for, anyway? Where did he start? 'Er . . . how old is he?'

'She,' Alice said abruptly, wanting to cut this conversation short. Unlike Hugo, she had no hidden agenda for wanting to stay and talk.

'Oh, sorry. Silly me. *Ahem.* So how old is *she*?'

'Four months.'

'Same age as mine. Mine's a *he* as it happens. Called, um, Theo.'

Her eyes slid to the pile of books beside him. 'I'm on a bit of a learning curve,' Hugo confessed sheepishly. 'My wife's ahem, away at the moment. I'm in charge, and not doing very well, to be honest.'

Damn it. What had made him mention Amanda? Alice's face tightened. 'I've got to go,' she said sharply.

'Me too.' Oh, well. He'd tried. But she plainly didn't want to be friends, and why should she? Given her relations with Amanda, it was surprising she still stood there.

He gestured at the books. 'Which of these would *you* buy? If you were an utterly hopeless, clueless, totally crap parent who did everything as badly as possible?'

As he finished the sentence, his smile was shaking. The misery, confusion, fear and sleeplessness of the past few days and nights had finally caught up with him, To his horror, Hugo felt his bottom lip tremble and his eyes well.

Alice, about to turn on her vegetarian-soled heel, now hesitated. It had been on the tip of her tongue to snap that what book he should buy wasn't her problem. But she'd already detected something in the way he'd said he was in charge of the baby. He'd sounded genuinely helpless. Now, unbelievably, he looked as if he was about to cry, which was not what one expected of anyone close to Amanda Hardwick. She stared at him, confused.

'Because,' Hugo sniffed, throwing himself completely on her mercy, 'I'm just lost, to be honest.' He snatched the top book off the pile and opened it at random. ' "Are we *really* listening to our children?" ' he read from it. He looked blearily up at her. 'Well, frankly, I am. Every night for hours on end.'

To his surprise, Alice giggled. It was a giggle utterly unlike Amanda's habitual titter. It was a warm, gurgling peal that made the world seem suddenly a better, brighter place. 'What problems are you having, exactly?' she asked.

'Um, well, it's difficult to be specific . . .'

'You mean everything's the problem?'

Hugo shifted in his seat. He hesitated to confess the full extent of his incompetence. 'You certainly could say that there are a few, er, challenges.'

'He's not sleeping?' Alice guessed.

The Wives of Bath

'Er, no.' Theo's near-insomnia was one of many problems, of course. But it would do for starters.

'The thing to do,' Alice said, 'is try and keep him awake as much as possible during the day. That's what I've been doing with this one,' she patted the back of her baby's sling, 'and it seems to work. They sleep at night then. It's obvious, really, I suppose.'

Hugo nodded. 'That makes sense. Theo does tend to snore all day and party all night. Although now he goes to nursery in the morning.'

'Well, that should help keep him awake.' Alice shoved *Ultimate Organic Baby Food Made Fun* under her arm. 'Good luck, anyway. I've got to go.'

He could think of no further questions to keep her.

221

Chapter 14

The novelty of coming to Chicklets had clearly worn off for Theo. This morning, like yesterday and the day before, the baby stiffened and whimpered as soon as he caught sight of the nursery building.

'Separation anxiety,' one of the nursery staff said briskly. 'He'll get over it.'

Hugo wished he could be so sure. Theo must really hate the nursery if he seriously wanted to stay with his father. It wasn't as if they had much fun together. Theo seemed to spend most of the time crying while he, in turn, tried to understand what he was crying about.

'Come on, darling,' he muttered now to his roaring son. 'Don't be like this. Not today of all days.'

An important meeting was scheduled for half an hour after he got in to work. Some clients selling a portfolio of Victorian brewery buildings were holding a beauty contest among local estate agencies. This morning was Dunn and Dustard's turn to audition. Neil, Hugo knew, was desperate for them to be appointed sole agent for the sale. Industrial heritage buildings of exactly this sort were in demand among the many young media and technology companies currently mushrooming in Bath. It wasn't exactly the King's Cross redevelopment pheno-menon, but probably the nearest Bath came to it. Hugo felt something of the old excitement in his loins at the prospect.

He couldn't afford to be late for the meeting. 'I'm depending on you to impress them,' Neil had warned. 'I've told them we'll get our best shit-hot ex-London supersalesman to screw the last sou out of any potential buyer. I've built up your charm and powers of persuasion. You've got to get in there and knock them dead.'

As, now, they mounted the nursery steps and Theo threw his body into a rigid block of screaming protest, Hugo groaned in despair. How the hell was anyone supposed to cope with this, let alone think about work at the same time?

He noticed one of the other mothers teetering towards the entrance. It was, he recognised, Sue. Barbara, who had helped him with the buggy raincover, had introduced them some days ago. The baby Sue carried was, like Theo, thrashing and screaming as if it was being murdered.

'Hello,' Hugo shouted over the row, noticing that Sue's normally cheerful features were drawn and had a distinct green tinge. 'You all right?' he added.

Sue shook her head. 'Stomach bug.' She nodded at the baby. 'Hamish gave it to me. He's fine now, don't worry,' she added hurriedly, glancing at Theo. 'But I've been throwing up all night.'

'You should be in bed,' Hugo told her as they entered the building.

Sue gave a hollow laugh. ''Course I should. But who'd take Hamish to nursery if I was? And I can't miss work. I've had so much time off recently with his various illnesses they're going to sack me if I'm off any more.'

'Poor old you,' said Hugo. Guiltily he realised that he wasn't the only parent with problems. Even Alice, for all her efficiency, had been crying about something. Many times since their meeting he had wondered what.

'Having a baby and holding a job down. It's a bloody nightmare,' Sue said as they reached the baby room entrance.

'Tell me about it,' Hugo agreed, sticking the still-thrashing Theo under one arm as he snapped on the regulation blue galoshes.

'Employers are so unsympathetic if you've got children,' Sue lamented as she handed Hamish over to an assistant. 'I ask myself all the time if it's worth it. The bloody job only just covers the fees anyway.'

'It's a struggle,' Hugo concurred. The camaraderie he felt with Chicklets' working mothers was not something he had ever anticipated. And yet there was something grimly enjoyable about it. They were all in the same boat, and a stormy boat at that. Sue, for one, was nauseous.

'I'd better go,' she said, gulping. 'If I'm lucky I'll make it to the loo before I'm sick again.'

* * *

Driving to work some twenty minutes later, Hugo rubbed his eyes. The nursery esprit de corps had faded and he felt exhausted and miserable. Theo's separation anxiety was a nightmare, exposing as it did the writhing pythons of guilt and general incompetence that lurked below the surface of his parenting attempts. What was he doing wrong? He wished he could ask Alice. Was there a way he could contrive to see her? There was so much he didn't know.

A sudden glance at the car clock was followed by the jerk of his foot on the accelerator pedal. He was going to be later than he'd thought for this bloody meeting.

'They started five minutes ago,' reported Shuna with satisfaction as he passed her desk.

Hugo ignored her, knocked on the closed door of Neil's office and went in. A woman in beige and a grey-suited man with a ratty, Oswald Mosley look sat side by side before Neil's desk.

Neil's red face glowed blue from the screen of the laptop into which he was peering, presumably to give an air of cutting-edge efficiency. He glared at Hugo as he entered.

'. . . depends entirely on the salesman,' Oswald Mosley was explaining in a grating voice. 'This is a very particular project requiring a very particular type of estate agent. Someone who'll be at ease with the sort of client we're hoping to attract – trendy London migrants, mostly. We're looking for some-one who combines knowledge and skill with charm, persuasion and sophistication. Appearance is of the utmost importance . . .'

'Look no further,' Neil boomed. 'Here he is, the man of the moment, right in the nick of time. Been out shaking up the property market already, eh, Hugo, even at this time in the morning?'

Hugo realised this was a prompt. 'Er, yes. Yes. Absolutely.'

'You see? This is your guy. The man never sleeps,' Neil grinned at the couple in front of him. 'Eats, breathes and even shits selling.'

The woman in beige looked startled. Neil, however, was on a roll. Hugo suspected he was also on the sauce already, despite the relatively early hour. 'Mr and Mrs Pinchett, meet Hugo Fine. Mr Legendary Charm and Sophistication himself,' Neil declared excitably. 'The best property salesman in the area, if not the entire country. The man whose services you are able to secure *only* by appointing Dunn and Dustard as your sole agents.'

Hugo summoned up his best, most confidence-inspiring and persuasive property-selling smile. He was aware, however, as he trained it on the Pinchetts, that they were not looking at his mouth. They were looking at his feet.

Neil was looking at his feet as well. A freezing feeling now crawled down Hugo's spine. Had he forgotten to clean his shoes?

Hugo, too, now looked at his feet to see that each of his size eleven Church's was partially concealed by a plastic cover of electric blue. He was still wearing the galoshes from the nursery.

'Thanks for telling me,' he growled at Shuna as he passed her desk after hurriedly exiting Neil's office.

Shuna flicked a glance at his feet. 'Oh, mistake, was it? Didn't realise. Thought it must be what all the shit-hot London salesmen were wearing at the moment.'

'Ha bloody ha,' Hugo tore off the plastic covers and shoved them in the bin. Shortly afterwards, the Pinchetts walked past his desk, neither meeting his eye. They were pursued by an apologising, pleading Neil, who directed at Hugo a furious glare before exiting the office himself, presumably to drown his sorrows in the pub.

At half past twelve Hugo looked at his watch. Neil had not returned, which was useful. A visit to Sainsbury's was urgently required before picking Theo up from Chicklets. There were no jars of baby food in the cupboard and the small cartons of ready-made formula milk – he'd long stopped trying to count the scoops of the powdered variety – had run out as well.

Oh, and God, there was the nursery cake to buy. As posters had been reminding everyone for weeks, Chicklets was about to hold a fund-raising cake stall to which all parents were expected to contribute. Hugo had got the strong impression that if he didn't, the baby would get it.

Rain spattered on the windscreen as he entered the super-market car park. The last space in the Parent and Child bays near the door had just been taken. He watched furiously as a large family of four exited their Escort, both enormously fat sons well into their twenties. Hugo thought of his tiny son being carried in the rain from the other side of the car park and saw boiling, furious red.

'*Excuse me!*' he shouted, winding down his window. 'That space is for people *with babies.*'

The mother, a round-faced woman in vast tracksuit bottoms, turned round. 'So what?' she blasted back. 'Oi've got my kids with me, haven't Oi?'

'Well, aren't you being a bit inconsiderate?' Hugo challenged. 'Those spaces are designed so people with babies in supermarket trolleys can unload them more easily. And they're nearer the shop door.'

For a moment, he could hardly believe what he was saying. Hugo Fine, former blade about town, now militant mouther-offer at supermarket parking space abusers. A parent with attitude, no less. But this sort of selfishness was simply intolerable. Especially if Theo had to suffer for it.

'Yeah, and so what's it to you?' yelled the woman's large, doughy husband. 'Oi don't see no kids in your car.'

Hugo whipped round to check Theo's car seat. It was empty. Sick panic surged within him until he remembered that of course it would be. Theo was still at Chicklets, waiting to be picked up.

As he drove off to find a space elsewhere, the fat family jeered and made gestures. Hugo hoped he wouldn't meet them in the supermarket. He'd just have to avoid the oven chip and cream cake sections, that was all.

Inside, Hugo stared at the wall of nappies, spirits sagging at the prospect of buying another large and expensive collection of the impossible-to-fit objects. This morning's attempt had, even by his own standards, been disgraceful. Theo had been impossibly squirmy and while Hugo had done his best, neither flap had stuck and he had been forced in the end to bundle Theo's trousers over the top and leave it at that.

He shoved some Pampers in his basket and moved on to the baby food. As usual, to save time choosing, he began to work his way along the shelf, piling every second jar into his basket.

As he reached the end of the row, a woman walked past. She was tall, slim and blonde, with a long, thoughtful face and wide eyes peering anxiously at a shopping list. A well-behaved baby peeped out of the sling around her neck.

'Alice!' Hugo exclaimed, in a rush of delight.

Her basket, he saw, was groaning with fresh vegetables. No doubt this was connected with *Ultimate Organic Baby Food Made Fun*. He looked at his own basket, groaning with jars, and gave her a guilty grin. 'You put me to shame.'

'What?' asked Alice distractedly.

'Cooking all those vegetables for your baby. I'm impressed.'

'They're not all for Rosa, actually. Some are for a dinner party tonight.'

Hugo stared at her in amazed admiration. Not only did this woman have her child under control, she entertained as well.

'A dinner party. What fun,' he said lamely. He could hardly remember the last one he had been to. It was somewhere back in the mists of time, when he had had some sort of life.

'Should be,' Alice smiled. 'Jake's asked a few of his *Get Trashed!* people round. His magazine,' she added, as Hugo looked blank.

Hugo remembered the ultra-worthy-sounding recycling organ. 'Great,' he nodded, hoping he sounded sincere.

He was, he realised, wasting an opportunity. Here in front of him was Alice, the most capable parent on earth and a positive fount of baby knowledge. And what was he talking to her about? Some boring eco-beanfeast involving her evangelist loon of a husband.

'Er . . .' He looked towards the café by the supermarket entrance. 'Would you . . . er . . . like a cup of coffee?' His tired mind suddenly fizzed with possibilities. He could ask her about the sleep issue again; maybe even move on to the nappy one.

'I'd love to,' Alice said politely. 'But I haven't really got time.'

'I can throw a cake in too,' Hugo pleaded.

Alice couldn't help grinning. 'Sorry.' She heaved her basket up to hip level.

Miserably, Hugo watched Alice walk away. There was, he knew, no point in pressing his case. Or asking for her phone number. She might suspect he was mad and possibly dangerous. And perhaps he was.

Then his heart soared as, unexpectedly, she stopped and turned. Had she changed her mind? Was the thought of a shot of caffeine before blanching all those mung beans more than she could resist, after all?

She walked back up the aisle towards him. 'Any idea where the organic miso is?' she asked.

'Sorry.' Hugo shook his head. And, as she glided off again, he was sorry. Sorry about resigning himself to years and years of not having the slightest clue what to do with Theo. To a lifetime of sleepless nights, separation anxiety and, of course, risible nappy-changing.

Then he noticed something small and brown lying on the lino floor in front of him. A purse, it looked like. Alice's purse?

He leapt on it like a starving man might leap on a plate of fish and chips. Surely it was Alice's purse. He must find her and give it back; thus demonstrating his honesty and good intent, he might be able to ask for her phone number.

He spotted Alice in the Baskets Only queue. She was standing beside a harvest festival pile of vegetables on the conveyor belt and slapping her pockets with panic. The checkout assistant, as was her privilege on such occasions, looked on with expressionless lack of sympathy.

'I think,' Hugo called as he approached, 'you're going to need this.' He held up the purse – which he was praying hard was Alice's – over the head of the person behind her.

'Do you mind not shouting,' snapped the woman queuing behind Alice. She was small and cross, and holding a basketful of cat food. 'It's very dangerous in a confined space, you know.'

Before Hugo could reply he felt a soft tug on his outstretched hand. Alice had taken the purse. Better even than this, she was beaming at him with tears in her eyes.

'Thanks,' she breathed, visibly drooping with relief as she handed her card to the assistant. 'You've saved my life.'

'My pleasure,' Hugo smiled. 'You look like you've had a bit of a shock. Still sure you don't want a coffee?'

Doubt flickered across Alice's face.

'Seeing as how I've saved your life,' Hugo prompted. He hated to twist her arm, but desperate times meant desperate measures.

Alice smiled at him. It was a no-holds-barred smile. Caught in its soft, full beam, Hugo felt a ripple in his groin. 'I'd love to,' Alice said. 'I can't now, though. But if you like I could meet you here in a couple of days. Friday?'

Chapter 15

'Is this reverse osmosis de-ionised water we're drinking?' The deputy editor of *Get Trashed!* was waving his jam jar in a demanding sort of way.

To her surprise Alice realised he was waving it at her. His tone was unexpectedly brusque; rather rude, in fact. Especially given he was a guest in her house and they had only just been introduced. As the editor's wife, she had anticipated more respect, but perhaps everyone was equal in the eco-community. She was determined not to seem offended, however. Her role, tonight, was to help Jake host the evening and make it a brilliant success.

'I'm not sure what you mean,' she said about the water. 'But it's out of the tap, if that helps.'

The deputy editor, whose name was Joss, raised his eyebrows in unimpressed fashion. 'Oh, well. If it isn't ROD, it isn't,' he said with bad grace. 'Is there any more in that tap, anyway?'

'Steady on,' joked a weaselly someone Alice remembered to be the layout person. 'Reservoir levels are dangerously low as it is.'

There were some guffaws at this. Alice laughed too, anxious to show willing. She wanted to enjoy the dinner party, despite her secret worries about her cooking and the ridiculously short notice Jake had given her to get the food together. Tofu kebabs, mung bean salad and chickpea flan had stretched her meagre culinary skills to the limit. She had her doubts about the flan, especially. But she would have doubted chickpea flan even if Delia Smith had made it.

A movement caught her eye. Jake was waving the ex-petrol container water pitcher at her. It was clear that she was expected to go and fill it up. She looked back, annoyed but trying not to show it. Why couldn't he be water monitor? She'd done her bit: the shopping and food. Now that the guests had arrived and were mingling in the sitting room, sipping organic mulled wine from jam jars and recycled mouthwash containers, she had been looking forward to a little social stimulation. Not yet more servitude.

She ignored him and smiled at Joss. 'Planning any holidays this year?' she asked, wheeling out an admittedly far from original conversational gambit. But one had to start somewhere.

'WOOF,' said Joss.

'Sorry?' She jumped, then collected herself. Perhaps dog impressions were his party piece.

'Worldwide Opportunities on Organic Farms,' Joss

elucidated impatiently in his nasal whine. 'I joined in 'ninety-five. I've been on working holidays in Bosnia, Tibet and Slovenia, as well as Wales and Albania. I can say "That couch grass needs to be got rid of" in seven different languages.'

'Gosh.' Alice tried hard to look impressed. 'But don't you, um, ever, you know, fancy something a little less . . . arduous? Flying off to some beach or something?'

Joss's already large nostrils flared with disgust. They now looked, Alice thought, big enough to crawl up.

'Did you know,' he asked her, 'that the carbon emissions from one transatlantic flight negate all the recycling you do?'

'Er . . .' began Alice, who didn't.

'Before WOOF,' Joss interrupted, 'I used to go on walking holidays. And even then, when I just took the train, I had to plant at least *one* tree in a sustainable forest afterwards to neutralise all the carbon I produced—'

'Excuse me,' Alice broke in. 'I think Jake's asking me to go and get some more water.'

'Yes, but can you ever be strong-willed enough to watch adverts on television without them subverting your shopping habits?' someone was saying to someone else as she passed them en route to the kitchen.

It seemed impossible that Jake's colleagues could always be so deadly serious about everything. Perhaps they just took time to warm up. Unsurprisingly, given the temperatures in the Old Morgue. And Jake had mentioned heat was rationed in the *Get Trashed!* office as well.

Besides Joss, the guests comprised the weaselly layout person and the chief sub-editor, an aubergine-haired beanpole called Jessamy.

Alice had been surprised when Jessamy shuffled in to the cottage. She had not realised Jake had women on his staff. Particularly ones as unusual as Jessamy.

It turned out that she supplemented her *Get Trashed!* paypacket by working as a goat psychologist.

'How *fascinating*,' Alice gushed, unsure what else to say.

Jessamy looked her up and down, obviously unmoved. 'So what do *you* do?' she demanded.

Alice realised this was the first time she had been asked this question since resigning from her job at Intercorp. 'I'm a mother,' she said proudly.

Jessamy's top lip lifted slightly in scorn. 'I know *that*, obviously. But Jake's a father, and he manages to be an editor too.' She shot him a glance that could only be described as adoring. Alice supposed she was not surprised at this. Of course Jessamy adored Jake. He was adorable, as well as off-the-scale good-looking. Which, reassuringly for Alice, Jessamy herself wasn't, not particularly.

'But what do you do besides *mothering*?' Jessamy pressed.

Alice kept calm. People were famously incapable of imagining what mothers did all day. Jake himself couldn't and he was Rosa's father. She smiled at Jessamy. 'Well, I do some odds and ends for *Get Trashed!*, obviously.'

'That can't take up all your time.'

Alice felt irritated – why the interrogation – but maintained her smile. 'You'd be surprised. There isn't time to do much else, to be honest.'

Jessamy lifted her chin. 'It's probably just bad organisation.'

Alice stared furiously at the floor. How dare this woman speak to her in this way? Was she aware she only had a job at her behest? Without the income from Alice's New York flat sale, now severely eroded, *Get Trashed!* wouldn't even exist. 'Excuse me,' she said in strangled tones. 'I thought I heard Rosa crying upstairs.'

She hadn't, of course. But she needed an opportunity to slip into the bathroom and collect herself. Closing the door behind her, she recoiled at the smell of the new vinegar and bicarb cleaning routine. The place stank like a fish and chip shop.

She took a deep breath and peered at her reflection.

The eco-friendly regime Jake insisted on was, she glumly concluded, doing absolutely nothing for her skin. Having feasted luxuriously on Clarins for years, it was objecting fiercely to its new diet of vegetable soap and water. Jake's recent ban on deodorant was another challenge; Alice hated to think that other people could smell her. But she rarely met other people these days so perhaps it didn't matter. And the crowd downstairs, anyway, were pretty whiffy themselves.

She looked at her clothes. She had worn her old jeans until they wore out and were replaced by tracksuit bottoms with holes in that Jake had foraged from some skip. Her mother's voice floated into her memory. 'You used to have such lovely clothes . . .'

When she returned to the sitting room it was to discover Jake's staff gathered about him in a tight knot. A debate about what *Get Trashed!* should feature as its next Tip of the Month was in full swing.

'Those underarm deodorant rollers,' Jessamy was saying. 'There's got to be a good use for those.'

Alice joined the group eagerly. A creative discussion was a luxury she had not enjoyed for some time. 'If you painted them, they'd make great skittles for a bowling alley,' she suggested. Really, the idea was rather brilliant when you thought about it. And much easier and more fun than most of the *Get Trashed!* tips she'd seen.

Joss looked at her from over the bridge of his nose. 'I don't think so.'

'Why not?' Alice smiled at Jake, expecting encouragement. But her husband's face, to her surprise, bore unmistakable signs of embarrassment. 'Al, I'm not sure you really get it,' he said.

'Get what?'

'*Get Trashed!*. You see, it's more than a magazine. It's a way of thinking.'

'A way of *life*,' Jessamy stressed.

'Look,' Joss said, in his nasal voice. 'Let's move on, shall we? The other thing we were going to discuss was whether or not we should go down the celebrity path. Have a star interview.'

Jessamy pulled a disgusted face. 'What, and be just like everybody else? We deal in real issues, you know. We live in the real world. We have real ethics. Real beliefs.'

'I agree with Jessamy,' Jake stated. For this, Alice noticed, he received another adoring look from his sub-editor. 'Having celebrities would just be lowering ourselves. We exist to heighten people's consciousness, not cater to the lowest common denominator.'

Joss looked annoyed. 'I'm not saying I *want* celebs,' he grumped. 'I'm just making the point that they help with circulation. Get sales up.'

'That's right,' Alice chipped in boldly. Why shouldn't she say what she thought? After all she almost entirely funded this magazine. She might not be allowed an opinion on Tip of the Month, but surely she was on this. 'It might help to have a famous face on the cover.'

'We need,' Joss said, 'some celebrity who's particularly associated with rubbish.'

'Easy!' Alice clapped her hands.

'Is it?' Jessamy asked frostily.

'Of course,' Alice beamed. 'There can't be a single celebrity who hasn't been up to their ears in complete rubbish at some time or other.'

The *Get Trashed!* editorial board looked at each other. 'This is no place for flippancy,' said Jessamy crossly.

'Look, Al, this is an editorial meeting we're holding here,' Jake told her sternly. 'You're probably better off in the kitchen for the moment.'

Alice was so taken aback she could hardly speak. 'I'm *terribly* sorry,' she said with freezing politeness. 'I thought this was a dinner party.'

'It is,' Jake said easily. 'The other guests aren't here yet. I just asked the guys a bit earlier to thrash out a few ideas over some drinks. There isn't any more of that mulled wine, is there?'

In the kitchen, Alice furiously put more wine on to warm. She deliberately chose a bottle her father had brought at Christmas and which had been shoved under the sink by Jake because it wasn't organic. It was, however, a first-class Bordeaux, which was a terrible waste to ruin with mulled wine herbs. But the mildly naughty thrill of watching everyone drink it would be compensation for that. And she could have an unadulterated glass or two of it while the mulled stuff warmed.

As a knock sounded on the front door, she wondered who the other guests would be. Hopefully the new blood would be better value. These hopes were dashed as soon as Alice saw it. None of the new blood looked as if it had any blood at all.

The newcomers comprised, Alice gathered, what her husband grandly called his 'panel of editorial advisers'.

'This is Dr Enoch Scarthin,' Jake beamed. 'He's our soil erosion expert.' Dr Scarthin, Alice thought, looked pretty eroded himself. He was a wizened, squinting wraith, with pitted, yellow skin. 'And this,' Jake clapped a frog-like man with bulging eyes on the back, 'is J. Larry Tabasco. He's our global warming prophet.'

As they finally sat down at table, Alice, with a sense of inevitability, found herself between Mr Tabasco and Dr Scarthin. 'Sort of a rock and a hot place,' she joked. They both looked blankly back at her.

Alice was bloodied, but unbowed. Her legal work had frequently included dining with dry sticks; besides, she had been taught as a child that there was no such thing as a bore. The fault was in yourself if you couldn't find a mutually interesting subject to discuss.

Perhaps she had even more faults in herself than she imagined. Try as she might, her every conversational seed fell on stony ground. Each gauntlet of chat remained resolutely un-picked up. Scarthin and Tabasco weren't, it seemed, interested in conversation as such. Most of what they said – mainly entirely to each other – were dense paragraphs of statistics, reeled off apparently from memory. In common with everyone else at the table, they seemed to have no boredom threshold whatsoever.

Sipping copious quantities of wine, Alice allowed her mind to wander in and out of the various discussions. No one seemed to be listening to anyone else.

'. . . yes, but we know that the high consumption Western lifestyle generates a huge amount of household waste – 28.2 million tonnes in Britain every year, 1.2 tonnes from every home . . .' shouted someone.

'. . . restrict traditional waste-disposal methods – incineration and landfill – because of their adverse effects on the environment,' yelled someone else.

'Organic household waste should be composted, instead of allowing it to rot in landfill sites where it generates potent greenhouse gases such as methane . . .' boomed another.

Alice realised, as the evening progressed, that she had been over-hasty in condemning Jessamy for asking what she did all day. It was the only question she would be asked about herself all evening.

'. . . get over the stigma we have about rubbish.' This last from Joss, eyes blazing messianically.

'Waste,' Jessamy blasted back, 'is an individual's responsibility. Follow the Three Rs – Reduce, Reuse, Recycle . . .'

It was around the seaweed pudding mark that Alice started seeing double and began to sway on her orange-box. Across the table, Jake was listening intently as Jessamy reeled off a list of annual tonnages, all the while gazing adoringly into his eyes. Beside her, the soil analyst was expounding erosion theories, while Joss, picking his teeth, looked fascinated. Alice put her hand over her mouth to press back the laughter she felt bubbling relentlessly up. Everyone looked so serious.

On her other side, the global warmer was getting heated. 'The position,' he was intoning, eyes half-closed, 'is far, far more dangerous than anyone would like to think.'

Alice hiccuped. She gave the prophet a glassy grin. 'Oh really?' she slurred. 'Actually, *actually*, I'd like to think the danger is more dangerously imminent than the most dangerous thing anyone could think of . . . *hic*.' She reached for the petrol water container and waved it unsteadily in his face. 'More reverse thrust de-ionised whatsit, Professor?' Then, spurred helplessly on by the sight of his outraged face, she dissolved into hysterical giggles.

There was a shocked silence.

'Al!' thundered Jake.

In the ensuing silence, a high, whining sound from overhead could be heard. Rosa had woken up and was demanding attention.

'Al,' Jake repeated.

She met his gaze and did not move. She felt like shouting defiantly that he should go, Rosa was his daughter too. But then her eyes dropped to the chickpea flan and she thought better of it. She got up from the table and left the room.

As she mounted the stairs, she heard the stir of conversation. 'Sorry about that,' Jake muttered. Then he dropped his voice still further '. . . can't expect much else . . . used to work for a glossy magazine company . . .' was all Alice could make out. But it was enough. In the bedroom, she held the baby to her, burning with indignation. How bloody *dare* he?

Today's separation anxiety seemed worse than usual, Hugo thought glumly as he detached a shrieking Theo from his car seat. And worse, he knew, was to come. Driving away from the nursery these days, he was increasingly beset by images, long buried, of himself as an eight-year-old at boarding school watching his father's car disappear down the drive. As he turned into the main road, the remembered sense of loss, fear and unworthiness would break over him like a wave. Could Theo really be feeling the same at not even a year old?

He carried his protesting son up the stairs and into the building. And straight into the path of the nursery head.

'A word please, Mr Fine.'

The nursery head's office stood, kennel-like, beside the main door, enabling her to leap out, Rottweiler-like, without warning. And, despite the fact she was short and blonde, resembling a guard dog in no respect other than her fierceness, the Rottweiler was how Hugo had started to think of her.

The Rottweiler, he noticed, was holding a cake. It seemed familiar to him. Then he realised why. It was his cake for the fund-raising cake stall.

'This cake, Mr Fine,' boomed the Rottweiler, holding out the confection in question.

'Yes?' Hugo said brightly. He wondered what was wrong with it; it was, after all, the biggest, brightest and costliest the supermarket could offer.

'I take it that neither you nor Mrs Fine have made it yourselves?'

Distracted briefly by the idea of Amanda in front of an oven for any purpose other than assessing its style points, Hugo paused. In order to minimise its bought appearance, he had taken the cake out of the box. But the Disney characters printed in sugar on the surface and its general air of lurid commercialism were probably a bit of a giveaway.

'Er, no,' he confessed. 'It's bought.'

'Nuts, Mr Fine.'

'It's true,' Hugo pleaded. 'From Sainsbury's. I've still got the receipt somewhere.' He began to slap his pockets for his wallet.

The Rottweiler's expression had changed from disapproving to exasperated. 'What I meant, Mr Fine, was that, as it isn't home-made, you have no idea whether your cake has nuts in it?'

'Oh. Er. No.'

'You are aware, Mr Fine, of the issues surrounding nuts and children?'

'Um, yes, absolutely.' Hugo had vaguely heard something about this.

'Then you are aware that nuts can cause *death* to infants?'

'Oh. Gosh. Right, yes. Oh dear.'

'So you will understand when I request that you take your cake away. It is not, I regret to say, suitable for inclusion on the Chicklets cake stall.'

'Oh. I see. Right, OK.' Crestfallen, Hugo took the cake, with difficulty as he was already carrying Theo. Theo, predictably, took an intense interest in the spurned patisserie and immediately tried his best to grab it. His father, now convinced that what had seemed an innocent sponge sandwich was now a hundred times more fatal than hemlock, fought desperately to keep it from the baby's thrashing grasp.

Still, at least it seemed to have distracted him from his separation anxiety.

By the time Hugo finally arrived at work, he felt as if he had been awake for several days and had overcome more challenges than the Fellowship of the Ring. He reflected wistfully on the days when his most pressing early morning appointment was a long session on the loo with yesterday's papers.

And there were, he knew, more challenges to come. Seeing Neil eyeing him beadily through the glass sides of his office, Hugo remembered what Sue had said about unsympathetic employers. The galoshes incident had been disastrous. He had a lot of ground to make up. Only a spectacular sales stunt along the lines of the station house would restore him to favour in the current climate.

Hugo rummaged through his work pile. This was a depressing business, given the number of problems Neil had landed him with recently. Lurking just below the top of the heap was the list from the demanding couple unwilling to buy a house without a green door or with a number 3 in the address. And only from a guaranteed non-divorcee.

Hugo sighed and rapped his pencil on the desk. There had to be a way round this somehow. The guaranteed non-divorcee was the trickiest bit. How could one go rummaging through the wreckage of clients' personal lives to find out that sort of thing?

He pulled out some of the other papers on the problem pile. Among them was Firth House, a property in one of

Bath's most prestigious Georgian terraces that was proving slow to sell. This was thanks to the colossal price being demanded for it by the owner, an architect called Tarquin who was the most flamboyantly gay person Hugo had ever met. The reason for the move, apparently, was that Tarquin had split with his long-term boyfriend and no longer wished to remain in, as he had sighed, a house 'just *so* full of memories. We must have had a blazing bloody row in every corner of every room.'

Hugo smiled faintly, remembering Tarquin mincing theatrically round the house during the valuation. His smile broadened. An idea was forming in his head. Could two tricky-to-solve birds be killed with one stone? He picked up the telephone.

'Tarquin?'

'*C'est moi*, sweetie. Who's this? Oh, the *divine* Hugo. How absolutely lovely. Tell me, darling, have you sold my little bolt hole yet, or not?'

'Well, I've got someone who might be interested. But I need to ask you a few things first.'

'How unutterably exciting. Fire away, scrumptious one.'

'Firth House. Has it got a number of any sort?'

'Well, it used to, darling, but I thought numbers were just *so* dull. So I named it after the heavenly Colin and his delicious bottom in *Pride and Prejudice*. Rather clever, don't you think, this being Bath and all that?'

'What was the number?' Hugo asked, crossing his fingers.

'Sweet one, I'll have to check. But actually, I think it's

seventy-eight or something utterly yawnworthy like that. Seventy something, anyway.'

Hugo punched the air. Two out of three, at a stroke. 'Tarquin?'

'Yes, oh godlike one?'

'How do you feel about painting your front door green?'

Tarquin, it transpired, felt just fine about it. Hugo replaced the receiver feeling even better. Immediately the phone rang again.

'Is that Mr Fine?' asked a fluting, birdlike voice.

'Yes.'

'It's Mrs Grimbley here.'

Grimbley, *Grimbley* . . . oh, *yes*. The picky house-hunting couple. Half of it, anyway. He sat up excitedly in his chair.

'Hello, Mrs Grimbley,' he greeted her cheerily. 'You've chosen a very good time to ring, as it happens. I think I may have found you exactly the property you want. With a green door, without a three in the number and owned *most definitely* by a guaranteed non-divorcee.'

'How very exciting, Mr Fine,' exclaimed Mrs Grimbley. 'Because we think we've narrowed it down as well.'

'How do you mean?' Hugo asked carefully.

'We had a dream last night that the house we must have was a little detached cottage with a red front door. It was number forty-two and had an apple tree in the garden. We thought you'd like to know. We thought it would make your job *so* much easier.'

250

Putting the phone down, Hugo tried valiantly to concentrate on the only cheering prospect currently visible on his horizon. Which was meeting Alice at lunchtime in the supermarket.

Chapter 16

Alice had no intention of meeting Hugo, however. Admittedly she had allowed herself to be charmed in both the bookshop and the supermarket. But as soon as she had left she had remembered he was husband to the vile Amanda Hardwick and not, therefore, someone she could feasibly be friends with.

Alice forced from her thoughts Hugo's look of tired defeat in the bookshop, his returning her purse in the supermarket and his touching desperation to have coffee. She was *not* meeting him. Even though she had promised and she always kept her promises. But in this case it was impossible.

And so, as the morning of the meeting ticked by, Alice determinedly mushed vegetables for Rosa and vowed not to stir from the Old Morgue. From time to time she looked up from this loathed task to see through the kitchen window that the early rain had stopped and the clouds were parting to reveal a sky of brilliant blue.

It *would* be a good day for an outing. And Rosa, currently mewling on the kitchen floor, clearly dissatisfied with the sand-filled Evian bottle Jake had given her, *adored* bus rides . . .

But that, Alice thought, reining herself in, was just tough. The Amanda factor wasn't the only reason that meeting Hugo was impossible. There was the Jake one too; while the precise reason for Jake's loathing of Hugo remained a mystery, Alice suspected that it was because he seemed the opposite of everything Jake stood for. It was certainly hard to imagine Hugo insisting on politically correct nursery rhymes. Or growing brassicas in human sewage. Or showing his wife up in public . . . Alice forced herself from this train of thought. The point was that meeting Hugo behind Jake's back would be a betrayal.

As she mashed, Alice's thoughts returned swiftly and resentfully to the *Get Trashed!* dinner party and what she had overhead Jake saying as she went upstairs. He had not spoken a word – of apology or otherwise – since, not even as they cleared up the following morning. But for Alice the memory festered, burning in her gut like undigested chickpea flan. While she was aware that she hadn't behaved terribly well herself, the way he had treated her was difficult to forget.

Alice looked out of the kitchen window again. It was a bright blue and gold day. An outing was almost unbearably tempting. But if Jake found out she had met Hugo he would be furious. Yet what right, given his recent behaviour, did he have to be angry about anything?

On the other hand, could she let petty point-scoring over

her own husband be reason to have coffee with Amanda Hardwick's?

Seconds later, Alice was wiping her hands and reaching for her own and Rosa's coats.

Hugo stood apprehensively at the entrance to the supermarket café. He'd been here fifteen minutes and there was no sign of Alice.

The toilets and baby changing room were just beside where he stood. Women carrying infants confidently pushed open the door. He'd even opened it for a few of them, but had seen little of what was inside. He wished the baby changing room had a clear glass window and he could watch what went on. The amount he and other clueless fathers would learn! Perhaps he could mention this on one of the Suggestions Box slips by the main entrance; on the other hand, did he want to risk a visit from the police and social services?

His initial mood of buoyant optimism was giving way to a crushing sense of disappointment. He had unthinkingly trusted that Alice would turn up, but this struck him as more and more unlikely. She was married to Jake, who vehemently disliked him, and he was married to Amanda, who Alice seemed to view in much the same light.

He was about to turn away and trudge back to the supermarket car park when he saw someone tall and fair walking rapidly towards him. It was a woman holding a baby. It was Alice.

Ten minutes later, sitting opposite her over a cup of

supermarket cappuccino, Hugo felt things weren't going quite as well as he had hoped. Conversation, to say the least, was stilted.

Alice's baby Rosa – or was it Rosie? – was staring at him in an unnerving fashion. He raised his eyebrows at her, stuck out his tongue and waggled his ears. The baby started to cry. As she jiggled her comfortingly up and down, Alice smiled at Hugo awkwardly.

Mortified, Hugo stopped the sideshow. 'So. Ahem. Rosie's four months old, did you say?'

'Rosa.' She looked at him over the rim of the huge, thick, coffee cup. 'And, actually, she's five months, now.'

'Oh God, of course, the same age as Theo.' Hugo clapped his palm to his head. The coffee from the cup in his other hand slopped over the rim and down his wrist. He felt the tepid brown stream run stickily into the bend in his elbow. Damn. Another shirt ruined and he had no idea how to get stains out.

Silence fell again. Alice started pulling her coat and bag towards her. 'Well, thanks for the coffee,' she smiled. 'I must be going.'

Under the table, Hugo twisted his hands in anguish. Here she was, sitting in front of him, the answer to all his problems. But somehow he could not frame the questions. His confidence in dealing with women, once as natural as breathing, was gone.

Yet this was his one chance. Once Alice walked out he would never see her again. He rose from the table, hands spread imploringly on the glaring blue Formica surface.

'Don't go. Please. It's just that . . . well . . . there's something I'd like to ask you.'

'What?'

Hugo shot her a wild glance. 'I was wondering,' he said hoarsely, 'whether you might know how to . . .'

'How to what?'

'How to . . . um.' He cleared his throat. 'How to put a nappy on.'

Alice, who had started to stand up, abruptly sat down. Her eyes, already wide, grew wider still and rounder as she looked at him. 'A nappy? You're asking me how to put a *nappy* on?'

'Er, well, yes. Exactly that. On a baby, obviously,' Hugo added hurriedly, before wishing he hadn't.

'You've got a five-month-old baby and you don't know how to put a nappy on?' Alice shook her head in amazement.

'I know it sounds ridiculous,' Hugo said, embarrassed. 'But the thing is, we had a maternity nurse and I suppose I never really learnt the skills. And neither did Amanda.'

'So what about the maternity nurse?' Alice asked, not particularly sympathetically.

'Er, well, she's not around any more. She left in, er, rather a hurry. The Royal Family needed her or something.'

Despite her disapproval, Alice giggled. 'The Royal Family?'

'To be honest, I think she was glad to see the back of us.' Encouraged, Hugo told Alice the story of Nurse Harris's arrival and the endless references to Lord Fairbourne. As she giggled again, Hugo felt that he would do anything to make her giggle more.

'She sounds terrifying.' Alice wondered what the strange feeling creeping through her was. It was, she realised a second or two later, the unaccustomed sensation of enjoying herself.

'She was terrifying,' Hugo agreed. 'But you're right. I was pretty pathetic not to pick anything up from her.' He sighed, remembering how he had absolutely expected Nurse Harris, and subsequently Amanda, to run Theo with little or no input from himself. It seemed incredible now.

But had it been his fault entirely? He remembered again Amanda's glowing speeches about earth having no greater joy than that of looking after a baby. Until, that was, she had actually had to look after one.

Hugo knitted his brows, realising it was impossible to explain this without sounding as if he was making excuses. But given the way Alice was looking at him – half scornfully, half amused – he had to say *something* to defend himself.

'Amanda insisted she wanted to stay at home and look after the baby,' he began. 'She said it would be a pleasure, that it was the ultimate important job and nothing she had ever done in her career had ever come close . . .' He stopped.

Alice raised an eyebrow. 'Go on,' she said.

Hugo went on. Reality, he explained, had set in. Amanda had realised that babies woke up at all times of the night, screamed for no reason, and, more worryingly, for real reasons. That they vomited, filled nappies, bit, scratched, farted and were far from being docile and adorable. Rather, they resembled wild animals. At which point she had, abruptly and utterly, lost interest.

'So she took the first job she was offered and now, to be honest, she's away rather a lot,' Hugo finished.

Alice said nothing. She had no idea why she should be surprised, yet she was. It seemed incredible that Amanda Hardwick could be as unreliable and selfish a mother as she was a journalist. Could she really have stalked out on both her son and his father with never a backward glance?

That she and Hugo, not to mention Theo, were all casualties of Amanda's spectacular self-centredness now occurred to Alice.

'So you see,' Hugo summarised, trying to sound as unself-pitying as possible, 'that's my position. My wife's away all the time and suddenly I'm in charge of a baby and frankly . . .' he paused, raking a coffee-sticky hand through messy dark hair, 'frankly, I've no idea what to do with him. He sleeps all day and he yells all night and . . .' Hugo rubbed his eyes, 'from bathing him to putting him to bed and everything in between seems to be a disaster. I mean, I don't want to make it sound as if I don't love my son, because I do, or at least I *suppose* I do . . .'

'You only *suppose*?' Alice echoed, shocked. Her hand moved to caress Rosa's head.

Hugo shrugged helplessly. 'I know that sounds awful, but Theo hasn't really taken to being with just me all that well and . . .' he blinked at Alice in despair, 'I suppose what I mean is that if I knew what to do with him, we'd have a better relationship. There's this horrible situation with the nursery, for a start.' He explained about the separation anxiety.

Alice nodded. 'But what do they say when you ring up?'

'Ring up?' Hugo's eyes were wide. 'What do you mean, ring up?'

'Well, during the day. To see how he's doing.'

He could not believe her matter of factness. Ring up the Rottweiler? Did she realise what she was saying? 'I never have,' he shuddered. 'I'm not sure I'd dare.'

'But why not? You're a parent. A paying client. You have the right to ask questions.'

'I suppose so.' This revolutionary thought had never occurred to Hugo.

'My guess,' Alice swished her coffee around the bottom of its cup, 'is that Theo is fine the minute you go out of the baby room. He's just trying to manipulate you. All babies do it.'

'Do they?'

'Well, how is he when you fetch him? Crying?'

Hugo shook his head.

'There you go then,' Alice said briskly. 'I'd put money on it that he's absolutely fine when you're not there.'

'Do you really think so?' Hugo's eyes, Alice saw with a pang, shone with emotion.

'Why don't you ask them when you go and pick him up?' she suggested. A glowing sensation was spreading through her now. It was, she realised, a long time since she had felt needed, and that her advice and opinion counted for something.

'Shit!' she suddenly exclaimed.

Hugo nodded resignedly. 'Well, I can hardly blame you for saying that. I deserve it.'

'No, I mean shit, look at the time.' Alice waved her wrist at him. 'I have to go. It takes ages to get back on the bus.'

'The bus?' Hugo looked amazed. 'Oh, of course. You only do public transport.' He tried to speak without irony. 'I remember from the antenatal classes. But surely it makes sense for you to have a car *now*? You're miles from anywhere with a baby.'

'Cars are bad for the ecosystem,' Alice muttered.

'Yes, and I've seen that bus to Bath that goes through Combe,' Hugo answered. 'That exhaust hanging off the back of it's bad for the ecosystem as well. And surely it's bad for your spinal column to carry all that shopping *and* a baby.'

Alice wished he would stop this particular line of argument. Her mother held identical views on the subject and it was hard to deny their logic. Hugo's face, however, had changed. He was looking at her aghast.

'The nappies!' he stuttered. 'You can't go yet. You said you'd show me how to put them on.'

'Nappies. Yes,' Alice bit her lip. 'Er, well, I could demonstrate on Rosa, I suppose. The only problem is that there's not really the time. Not if I'm going to make the bus.'

'Look, why don't I give you a lift? I'm going back into Bath anyway. I can take you to the bus station. Or home, if you like. Anywhere,' he pleaded, eyes wide with desperation.

'The bus station's fine,' Alice said. She smiled reassuringly at Hugo. 'Come on then.'

But Hugo's face had fallen again.

'What's the matter?' Alice asked.

'I've just remembered,' Hugo said dully. 'Last time I saw Jake he said you only ever use terry nappies. I'll never get anywhere with those. Even disposables are beyond me.'

To his surprise, a guilty blush was creeping over Alice's face. 'Erm, well,' she said. 'As a matter of fact I have started to use the occasional disposable.' She cleared her throat. 'Just in emergencies, obviously.'

'Of course,' Hugo nodded gravely. Alice flashed him a conspiratorial smile. 'So let's hit the baby changing room.'

Having dropped Alice off at the bus station, Hugo drove away on air. He was finally an initiate into the cult of correct nappy-fitting.

He needed to practise, of course, but there was no shortage of opportunity for that. And in case of real difficulty, he had managed to get Alice's telephone number.

'I'm sure I won't need to ring you,' he had persuaded. 'But it would be wonderful, just in case.'

'OK.' Alice was, in fact, more willing to give her number than she let him think. She was delighted that anyone considered her advice worth having. *Get Trashed!* all too obviously felt they could live without it.

'You see,' Hugo added as he wrote the number down, 'I know this sounds absolutely mad, and really pathetic.' He gave a short, despairing laugh. 'But when it comes to Theo, there's really no one else I can ask.'

There's really no one else I can ask. Alice felt a lump rise in her throat. He was, she recognised, lonely and helpless. Not unlike herself.

He pressed a small card into her hand. 'Here's my number. You've done so much for me. If there's anything I can do for you, ever, I don't know what, clean out your guttering or something, sort out your damp-proof courses . . . oh God, just listen to me waffling on, well, anyway, here I am. It's got my mobile on it as well.'

He drove away barely seeing the road in front. Instead, that slow smile, that fair hair, those wide, surprised blue eyes floated before him. He wondered if her bus had come yet. He wondered, with a suddenness that made him swerve, what it would be like to kiss her, to lift that fine hair and pull that angelic face to his. While it was reassuring that he could call her about Theo, he had become aware that he wanted more than that. The person he wanted her to focus on was not only his son, but himself.

At Chicklets, he had more reason than ever to thank her. The baby room staff, once he asked them, confirmed that, so far as Theo's separation sufferings went, he was dry-eyed and eating Weetabix within minutes of his father's departure. Hugo's burden of guilt and unhappiness lifted like a rocket.

Leaving the nursery with Theo, he noticed Barbara, his red-haired raincover rescuer, leaning against the wall. She was conducting what sounded like a terrifyingly high-powered conversation on her mobile. She looked terrifying too, briskly efficient in a smart dark suit with a crisp white blouse and a large shiny briefcase. Some mothers, Hugo thought enviously, his elated mood subsiding faintly, had everything so well organised.

As he passed with Theo, he caught a little of what Barbara was saying. Her tone, to his surprise, was urgent and strained.

'I'm sorry, James, but it's just not possible, we'll just have to reschedule. I absolutely can't come back to chambers today.' She paused, listening. Her face drained. Her voice, when she replied, was sharp with shock. 'What? You'll move the brief to one of the other barristers?'

Hugo heard her mobile click shut. Then silence. Then, to his astonishment, Hugo heard stifled but definite sobbing behind him. He turned to see Barbara pressed to the wall, face red and crumpled, the picture of despair. He was at her side in seconds. 'What's the matter?'

Barbara pushed a hand underneath her nose. 'Oh, nothing. No more than the usual.'

'The usual?' Hugo prompted.

Barbara gave him a watery grin. 'No sleep, no time, too much work and no sympathy from anyone *at* work when the nursery rang up to say Isabel had been sick and would I come to fetch her. I had to cancel an important meeting.' She paused and pulled a face. 'But what can you do? You're tugged this way and that between home and career . . .' She swallowed.

'I know what you mean,' Hugo said gently.

'Don't get me wrong,' Barbara said, more spiritedly. 'I like my job – well, usually. And frankly, with another on the way,' she patted her stomach, 'I can't afford to leave it.'

Theo, bored of the conversation, started to squirm and wriggle. Barbara chucked him under the chin. 'Well, thanks for the sympathy,' she said to Hugo.

'It's nothing.'

'Oh, but it is. Knowing that you're not the only struggling parent in the world is what gets you through it. Knowing other people know how you feel.' She patted his arm. 'We working parents must stick together; hold each other up.'

'Yes,' said Hugo, remembering the similar conversation he had had with Sue. He smiled at Barbara, aware of a sensation which, though rewarding, was entirely different from anything he had ever known in the property business. It came from the fellowship of adversity, rather than prosperity at the expense of some gullible idiot or other. He smiled at Barbara. They were comrades in arms. Comrades with babes in arms.

Barbara had whipped a hand-mirror out from somewhere and was examining her reflection. 'God. Look at me. Oh well, what the hell. I'd better go in and get Isabel now.'

'Hope she feels better.'

Hugo continued down the corridor. Just as he reached the front entrance, the Rottweiler shot out of her office.

'Mr Fine? Can I have a word?'

Hugo froze. After the cake ticking-off earlier, he had not been expecting another encounter so soon. 'Uh . . . yes. Of course.'

The Rottweiler, whose belligerent vermilion jacket brought

out the reds of her eyes, trotted briskly up to where Hugo stood in the corridor. She scrutinised Theo, who had now started to whimper. The corners of her small mouth pressed down in disapproval. She shook her head. 'Mr Fine. We can't have this.'

'Have what?' gasped Hugo. 'Look, he can't help it. It's separation anxiety . . . he's a bit sensitive at the moment.'

'I'm talking about *this*.' The Rottweiler pulled at Theo's trousers. 'This is how you dressed him this morning. The trousers are on back to front, for a start.'

So they were, Hugo saw. The pockets were facing the wrong way. But why did babies need pockets anyway?

He switched on his most charming smile. Time to dig out the renowned Fine magic and get the old bat on side. 'To be honest,' he said, dusting off his most melting look, 'it's a miracle those trousers are on at all. Trying to dress Theo's like, well, wrestling with an octopus, ha ha . . .'

The Rottweiler held up a hand. 'Mr Fine. If you please. I run a nursery used by over fifty parents of small children. They all manage to dress them perfectly adequately.'

Hugo was stung by the unfairness. He was a man, struggling by himself. Surely she could cut him some slack? He watched with trepidation as the Rottweiler fingered the slack on Theo's top or, to be more precise, the slack at the bottom, which hung down with two unmatched buttons on it. And which corresponded to the slack at the top with two vacant unbuttoned holes. 'We were in a bit of a hurry and—' Hugo blustered.

'Not only have you not bothered to do this up properly,'

the Rottweiler accused, 'but this item is on back to front as well. It's meant to button up the back.'

Oh, for Christ's sake. The damned shirt hadn't come with a map. Didn't the woman realise how long it had taken to do up the buttons, however badly, in the first place?

'Mr Fine.' The Rottweiler folded her arms and stared him squarely in the face. 'That children are presented neatly by their parents is one of Chicklets's most basic rules. As, having read the prospectus, you will know.'

Hugo's shoulders slumped. In point of fact, he had not read the prospectus. It was, no doubt, lurking beneath one of the piles of paper that now rose like Manhattan in every room of Fitzherbert Place.

'I'm sorry,' he muttered.

But the Rottweiler had not finished yet. 'There is a reason for this rule, Mr Fine. It encourages tidiness and cleanliness, as well as respect for others and the institution. Turning up with your child looking dishevelled not only suggests the opposite, but suggests neglect of the child itself.'

The flash of anger Hugo felt surprised him with its violence. 'Are you saying I'm neglecting my son?'

The Rottweiler pursed her lips. 'I am merely warning you that further transgressions of Chicklets's rules will be viewed in the dimmest of lights.'

Hugo's fury was replaced by a sudden wave of terror. He remembered how utterly, already, he had come to depend on the nursery routine to give structure and stimulation to Theo and allow him to work.

'And there's one other thing,' the Rottweiler said.

Hugo's heart plummeted. 'There is?'

The Rottweiler eyed him sternly. 'Is Theo up to date with his jabs?'

Hugo was relieved to be able to nod with confidence. This was one aspect of childcare he'd been particularly careful to observe, with the help of reminder notes from the health visitor.

'Absolutely. The next one's coming up soon.'

The Rottweiler looked satisfied. 'Good. There've been a couple of nasty rashes around in the nursery. But Theo should have no problems in that case.'

As they left the nursery, Theo gave vent to his frustration by means of a sustained, piercing wail. Hugo did not blame him in the least. On the contrary, he wanted to join him. The noise intensified as Hugo tried to persuade the resisting infant into the car seat.

'I sure wouldn't be making that noise if you were holding *me*,' purred someone behind them.

Laura was slinking across the car park as if coming on stage at the Moulin Rouge. Theo, rather unexpectedly, immediately stopped screaming and stared at her in amazement. Possibly, Hugo thought, because he had not seen that amount of lipstick before on anyone. Not even on his mother, who in any case must be becoming a distant memory by now.

'Amanda around?' Laura picked up uncannily on his train of thought.

'Er . . .' Hugo felt his colour rising and not only because of his car seat exertions. 'No. I'm not exactly sure when she's coming back, either.'

Laura's eyes lit up. 'So she's left you all by yourself?' She ran her tongue suggestively across her teeth.

Sod this car seat, Hugo raged silently, still struggling with the straps. So long as they remained unbuckled, he was stuck here with this terrifyingly predatory woman. He was aware that, flustered, hot and with his bottom sticking out of the car, his position was far from dignified.

'I meant to say last time we met . . .' Laura was bending into his back, suddenly close. Her breath was warm on his cheek and smelt, he thought, faintly of alcohol, 'Fergus is away a lot as well.' She was batting her eyelashes so hard Hugo could almost feel the breeze. 'So we're both in the same ship, as that woman used to say in the antenatal classes.' She laughed loudly.

Clunk! The baby was buckled in now. Hugo longed for an excuse to leave. If only Theo would have another tantrum.

But Theo, watching from his car seat, had his eyes still glued to Laura's red lips. He had lately, Hugo had noticed, developed a fascination with mouths and teeth.

'So why don't you come over for a drink sometime?'

'That's very kind.' Hugo glared meaningfully through the open back door at his son. Never would an attack of separation anxiety have been so welcome. But the baby just stared on silently at Laura.

'I think he likes me.' Laura pressed close to Hugo as she

waved to Theo. 'But then, he's a man. Most men do. Apart from bloody Fergus, that is,' she added venomously.

Theo was now smiling and gurgling at Laura. He was even waving his little fat hands. Irritation surged through Hugo. He never got that sort of treatment himself, and he fed and clothed the wretched boy, as well as got up several times a night to attend to him.

Laura turned glittering, maquillaged eyes on him. 'Come on then,' she urged. 'Let's make a date.'

Hugo shrank back, floundering for an excuse. 'Er, the thing is . . .' He paused, then bent into the back of the car. Silently apologising to Theo, he pinched the baby hard on the thigh. 'I'm sorry,' he gasped as the child gave a loud screech of protest. 'But he's terribly tired. I'd really better take him home.'

Chapter 17

As he stood outside the end-of-terrace house, Hugo remembered Neil's instructions. 'Should be pretty straightforward, Fine. Viewers – Buckley, their name is – more or less committed to buying the place once they saw it on our website. All you have to do is show them round and tie the deal up.'

Our website, Hugo had noted. Without his own insistence that Dunn and Dustard be launched into cyberspace or else lose out to the competition, Neil – who had stiffly resisted the idea at first – would no doubt still imagine the Internet to be some sort of fishing tackle. Still, there would be no prizes for pointing this out.

He looked, now, at the front of the house and for once agreed with his boss. It seemed absurdly simple to sell. End of terrace was always desirable, and this one had other plus points too. Chief of which was its quintessential Bathness:

tall, high-windowed and built in stone the colour of the middle of a Crunchie bar.

And even if the slight shabbiness of the outside – a cracked pane in the fanlight, long-defunct plants in the window box – was echoed on the inside, there were always estate agents' tricks he could resort to. Damp patches and cracks, for instance, were easily disguised with pictures or furniture, so long as the vendors hadn't decluttered the place to make it look bigger and removed every last thing.

Hugo checked his watch. He had ten minutes before the prospective buyers were due; ample time to get in and do some tweaking. Slipping the key into the lock, he entered the house.

Inside, all was hushed and gloomy. The curtains in the sitting room were drawn; bad mistake, Hugo thought impatiently. What vendors needed to push them towards the right decision was the right atmosphere. Clever lighting, abundant shiny-leaved pot plants and the delicious smell of baking bread or fresh flowers could work wonders.

Pulling back the sitting-room curtains, Hugo noticed the crack on the wall immediately. Almost simultaneously, he saw the large red-wine stain on the carpet. But before he leapt to drag the sofa over the mark, or reached for his trusty mini-hammer which, in its time, had moved endless mirrors over endless wall defects, he paused. Again, and as he had at the Osokozi bungalow, he found himself wondering whether such actions, once unquestioned, were strictly, well, *fair*.

He frowned. Odd how such thoughts crept up on him

272

these days. Odder still, how, via some hidden link, they led on to thoughts of Alice. It was almost as if she were his conscience. Certainly, after the supermarket nappy master-class, he viewed her almost as the angel to which she bore such a strong resemblance.

She had been astonishingly patient and helpful in the baby changing room. Over and over again she had shown him how the tapes attached to the sides until, eventually, he had understood. She had even shown him a few baby-dressing tricks for good measure. It had never occurred to Hugo to treat the pulling on of jumpers as a peepo game – he and Theo usually fought their way screaming through the various holes and sleeves. As for standing the child up and distracting it with a toy when attempting to put trousers on, this was genius. The Rottweiler, Hugo thought gleefully, would be in for a shock from now on.

Yet standing there, hammer in hand, he had a nagging feeling Alice might not approve of some of the grubbier aspects of his profession. He groaned. Of all the inconvenient moments to develop scruples. Especially given his current position at Dunn and Dustard. The galoshes incident was far from forgotten and for Theo's sake as well as his own he needed to get the vendors to commit this afternoon. Hugo walked towards the wall with his hammer.

Then something, suddenly, stopped him in his tracks. It was not another vision of a disapproving Alice. Rather, it was a strange, low noise like a growl. But it couldn't be. The house was empty.

It was then that Hugo saw the dog, lurking low in the gloom of the fireplace corner. Its grey-white coat blended into the pale walls, which was why he hadn't noticed it before. It was, he recognised, physically small but enormously mean-looking; one of those dogs, he thought uneasily, that occasionally hit the headlines for mauling babies or killing corgis. Staffordshire bull terrier, was it? No one had said anything about a dog on the premises, let alone a vicious-looking man-eater like this.

He smiled weakly at it. 'Good dog,' he said cajolingly. The animal looked back through nasty little eyes and growled again, deeper and louder this time. 'Lovely dog,' Hugo shakily assured it as the front door bell rang.

Hurrying down the hall he passed a hand over his fore-head. A light sweat had broken out. He opened the door and gave a sickly grin to the cheerful-looking man and woman who stood there.

'Hello, we're Sarah and Steve Buckley . . . ooh . . . are you all right?' asked the woman, peering at him with concern.

'Fine!' Hugo determinedly scraped his shattered nerves together. 'In fact, ha ha, that's my name, as it happens.'

'What is?' asked the man.

'Fine. Hugo Fine. As in parking, speeding, whatever. Ha ha. Er . . . come in.' He swung what he knew to be an over-vigorously inviting arm into the hallway. The Buckleys stepped over the threshold, exchanging glances as they did so.

'Let's go upstairs first,' Hugo suggested loudly in an

attempt to drown the growls from the sitting room.

'What was that?' asked Sarah Buckley, looking startled as Hugo bundled her up the elegant Georgian staircase.

Hugo turned a serene smile upon her. 'What was what?'

'A sort of roar,' supplied Steve Buckley, looking at Hugo quizzically.

'*Roar?*' Hugo flashed a sickly smile. The dog in the sitting room growled viciously again. 'Oh, *that* roar? One of the owner's pets, that's all. A very sweet dog. No trouble at all.'

'Sweet? *That* thing?' Steve Buckley had stopped his ascent abruptly. He was, Hugo saw with sinking heart, staring at the evil-looking beast pacing with deadly intent into the hallway. Claws grating on the floorboards, it looked up the staircase at Hugo and snarled.

'Lovely, isn't she?' Hugo gabbled. 'Elsie, her name is,' he added as the animal leapt on to the lower stairs. '*Good* Elsie,' he pleaded, as the dog's murderous eyes burnt into his own.

'Elsie?' echoed Steve Buckley, narrowing his eyes at the animal. 'It's male.'

'But very in touch with its feminine side,' Hugo assured him.

'It's a Staffordshire bull terrier, isn't it?' Sarah Buckley said nervously.

'Something like that.' Hugo did his best to sound breezy. 'They make wonderful pets. Very loyal and . . . er . . . loving.'

The dog ascended the next step. Its eyes flashed. The three people above it edged upwards.

'Loving, eh?' Steve Buckley said doubtfully. 'Well it obviously would love to eat all three of us at a sitting.'

'It's its way of showing affection,' Hugo suggested .

'I don't know about you, darling,' Steve Buckley remarked, 'but I'm not sure I can concentrate on a show-round when there's an animal like that about.'

Hugo smiled at him dazzlingly. 'I suppose I do see what you mean.'

Steve Buckley looked annoyed. 'Think you're funny or something? I was talking to Sarah, not you. Come on, darling. Let's get out of here.' With that, the Buckleys descended the stairs, neatly sidestepped the dog and, before Hugo had time to protest, were gone.

As the slam of the door echoed round the deserted hall, Hugo looked at the dog with loathing. 'You bastard,' he told it.

The dog bared its teeth, snarled, and mounted three more steps. There would, Hugo realised, be only one winner in this particular argument. Calculating that shock was his only weapon, he waited until the dog had climbed two further stairs before suddenly leaping up, emitting an earsplitting yell and dashing downwards past the surprised animal.

The next few seconds were all teetering, plunging and skidding along the hall floorboards accompanied by bloodcurdling barking. As the dog caught up, Hugo felt the agonising swipe of razor-sharp claw against his thigh. Then the sensation of teeth at his buttocks. Then he was fumbling madly at the front door; then, miraculously, slamming it behind him. As he stumbled away, head spinning, heart heaving, he heard the frustrated murderer barking in fury.

He fished for his mobile. 'Get me Neil,' he ordered Shuna, for once neither noticing or caring about her habitual surliness of tone.

A few seconds later, Neil's voice floated serenely down the line. 'In the bag then, is it?' he asked.

'Not quite, but *I* was nearly in a bloody body bag,' Hugo burst out. 'There's a maniac of a dog in there. Why the hell didn't you tell me?'

'A *dog*?' Neil sounded surprised. 'Oh yes,' he said, evidently after some thought. 'The owner did mention that her pet would be around. Said it was a sweet little thing called Chou Chou. Apparently it loves people and is no trouble at all.' Neil's tone darkened. 'You didn't upset it, did you, Fine?'

'Come on, darling,' Alice coaxed Rosa, pushing a spoonful of beetroot, okra and sweet potato mush at her daughter's mouth. Rosa's red lips, however, were obdurately closed against the pink-grey slop and would, Alice suspected, remain that way. 'Just a taste. It's not as bad as it looks. *It couldn't be*,' she added under her breath, catching the high chair as it threatened, for the thousandth time, to roll away across the floor.

Rosa's high chair was a battered supermarket trolley which Jake had 'reclaimed' from a canal. 'Imagine how useful it's going to be,' he had enthused. 'A million times better than a normal high chair.'

In practice, Alice had found it to be ugly, cumbersome and impossible to move smoothly in any particular direction. It was also much given to sudden lurches. Feeding Rosa was challenge enough without her rolling off suddenly.

She decided now to cut her losses and release Rosa from her torments. The baby immediately crawled into the dining room where Jake was working.

The *Get Trashed!* premises were temporarily unusable, owing to what the editor described as the 'large amount of potentially valuable reclaimable material' currently occupying it. Alice had welcomed her husband's being at home as an opportunity to mend the cracks in their relationship. The more she had brooded on them, the more damage Jake's cutting, disloyal words at the dinner party had inflicted. Things were not the same between them. The flattering, idealised veil through which she saw him had been rent. She hoped, given time, the hole might grow over, like the one in the ozone Jake was forever banging on about.

Her overwhelming, heart-rushing, stomach-twisting physical attraction to him was, she supposed, still there. But momentarily dormant, and in any case, certainly not in the intensity it had been. Recent attempts at sex had not been successful. Communication, meanwhile, was rare; Jake was working too hard to speak to Alice during the day and was frequently out in the evenings. Frequently with Jessamy, from what Alice could gather. Although, initially, she had striven to ignore her growing suspicions, in the end she could do so no longer.

'But what are you doing?' she asked, as he prepared once again to go off and meet his sub-editor.

'Working,' Jake said shortly.

'Working where? On what?'

On that particular occasion it turned out that he and Jessamy were picketing the local football stadium to demand that the aluminium trays from the half time pies were recycled. Alice felt her fears disperse. It sounded extremely plausible.

Besides, did Jake have any room in his life for an affair? No more, it seemed to Alice, than the cottage had room for more 'reclaimables' from refuse heaps. The Old Morgue really was beginning to look more and more like the dumps from whence most of its contents increasingly came. Inside was a sea of jars, boxes, stereos, abandoned video players and all other imaginable and unimaginable kinds of clutter. Outside, meanwhile, loos, sinks and bathtubs now covered every inch of garden. And, contrary to what she had once said to her mother, not a single one made an attractive planter.

Then there was the windchime. Made of old baked bean cans, it clanged all night and drove Alice mad. The exterior walls bristled with old shoes on strings stuffed with earth – 'fantastic hanging baskets,' Jake enthused. The only fantastic aspect to them, Alice considered, was that she herself lived within a million miles of such hideous things. Still, at least she no longer feared, as she intermittently had, that the Old

Morgue was haunted. The sheer amount of rubbish about the place meant that the only unquiet soul there was room for was herself.

And it wasn't just Alice's surroundings that had deteriorated. Her hygiene standards were under threat too. Last night, over supper, Jake had looked up and said, 'You know, Al. You don't have to flush the loo every time you use it.'

'Yes you do!' Alice's hands had flown, horrified, to her mouth. 'Jake, you can't be serious.'

But he was. And after that, the carrot soup had lost what small attraction it had. While Alice had continued, daringly, to flush when Jake was absent, fear of what she might find beneath the lid when he was present had started to give her constipation for the first time in her life. She was thankful only that her mother had no current plans to visit; following the brainwashing row, relations with her parents had been rather strained.

But while Mrs Duffield had studiously and diplomatically avoided discussing Jake in subsequent phone calls, Alice had an uncomfortable but growing feeling that her mother was right. Why had Jake's perfectly admirable enthusiasm for conservation and recycling turned into an obsession with trawling dumps for other people's rubbish?

'Hey! Al!' Jake's voice floated testily through from the dining room. 'Come and get Ro, will you? I can't do a bloody thing when she's around.'

Alice went in search of her daughter. 'It's probably time she had some sleep,' she said, jiggling the baby in her arms.

'Fine.' Jake, immersed in his page proofs, did not look up.

Alice took Rosa up into the bedroom and laid her down. While thankful the child was now too large to fit in the hammock, she was less delighted with the substitute, a cot Jake had made by taking the lid off an old ottoman he had found – where else? – on a dump. Alice had scrubbed the box out several times but it still, she thought, sniffing it critically, had an unpleasant, musty smell.

Rosa nonetheless seemed happy in it, so Alice went into the bathroom to wash vegetable purée off her clothes. She tried not to look at the ottoman lid. This, with its hideous dusty-pink padded Dralon surface, had been put into service strengthening the top of the by-now-so-clearly-collapsing-even-Jake-could-not-ignore-it changing table. Alice felt irritated every time she looked at it and considered what grubs and insects might be living beneath the lid's surface. How long it had been on the dump before Jake 'found' it did not bear thinking about.

Her eye met the bathroom cupboard. Or, rather, the former wooden wine container mounted on the wall, which did the same job. It was full of clutter, some from before she moved in. Occasionally she had thought about tidying it out, but had abandoned the idea in favour of something more pressing. Now, however, seemed the perfect time. Alice opened the door, which promptly fell off. She looked at the crammed shelves. Drawing the bathroom bin – a former paint tin – over, she began to clear them.

She was absorbed in her task when someone behind her said, 'Hey, there,' in a low, suggestive growl.

Alice stuffened as Jake snaked muscled arms around her waist and moved his hands up to caress her breasts. 'I'm sorry, Jake. I'm not really in the mood.'

'You were always in the mood *once*,' he reminded her grumpily.

'I know. I probably will be later.'

'Bloody hell!' Jake exclaimed. She realised that this was not an exclamation of anticipation. He wasn't talking about sex any more. His eye had caught the bin and what she had thrown in it. 'That's perfectly good stuff!' He was yanking out a tube of cucumber face cream.

'Jake, it's *not* good stuff. I bought it as an emergency in some village shop in Wales about five years ago. It's always been rubbish and now's the time to get rid of it.'

'But can't you use it for something else?' His eyes were wide with panic. 'It's cucumber, is it? Can't we use it for . . . I don't know . . . salad dressing?'

'Jake, it's face cream. You can't *eat* it.'

He was no longer listening. He had delved into the bin again and was looking anguished as he brought out a small, half-opened foil packet. 'You're not throwing *these* away, are you?'

Alice swallowed. 'These' had not been a particularly pleasant discovery. 'Jake, they're condoms.'

'So?'

'*Used* condoms.' He must, she assumed, have put them back as a hideous mistake.

His expression did not change. 'Yes?'

'But they've been put back in the *cupboard*.' Alice felt a thrum, like an engine, start to build in her feet. 'Jake, surely you're not telling me that you keep *used condoms*. That you *recycle* them?'

'Nothing wrong with that,' he said defensively. 'They're clean. I just rinse them out and they're as good as new.'

'Good as new for what?' Alice croaked. Then the tension in her stomach eased as she realised that – of course – he must be talking about one of his reclaimed-junk sculptures. He must at some time have used them in his art. Very Jake and Dinos Chapman.

'You're asking what they're good for?' A wide, suggestive smile split Jake's face. 'What do *you* think?'

'You're joking!' Alice felt her legs about to buckle. She fumbled behind her for the wall.

Jake's expression had become defiant. 'I'm not joking. It makes sense. The condom industry has a lot to answer for. Those poor trees suffer agonies when they're bled for the rubber.'

'Did you use a recycled condom when . . . when you met me?' Alice's heart was pounding so hard she could hardly hear her own voice.

'Um, yes, probably.' His voice was bouncy, almost self-congratulatory. As if he expected to be praised for such an admirable economy.

Alice had never understood, not really, how she had become

pregnant when Jake had been using a condom. But she did now. Condoms were not, of course, ever one hundred per cent reliable. But they were a damn sight more so when new, and not rinsed-out used ones of questionable vintage. Possibly with more holes than those bloody colanders he had nailed to all the ceilings. She felt about to burst. Her life had changed entirely because of this. She had given everything up when presented with the *fait accompli* of pregnancy. And although she had done it gladly, who was to say what her reaction would have been if she'd been given the choice? Certainly, she had been at her wits' end with Intercorp. But, as the Head of Human Resources had said at the time, a week's holiday and a change of job could easily have been the solution.

Accidents happened – Alice accepted that. One had to live with them. But what had happened to her was no accident. He had known, as she hadn't, that the protection being used during that first, passionate encounter, was almost certainly inadequate. He had sacrificed her power to determine her own future to his determination to recycle even the ludicrously, inadvisably, ridiculously unrecyclable.

She could hear her own voice in her memory, wondering over and over again why motherhood had come about so unexpectedly. And Jake's invariable reply: 'Things like this happen for a reason.'

Her fists clenched. Now, of course, she knew what that reason was. He had put the interests of a group of trees – a group of fucking *trees* – before her own.

She finally raised her eyes to meet his. 'You bastard,' she said simply. 'You stupid, irresponsible *bastard*.'

Chapter 18

Now that he'd cut four teeth Theo had the most adorable smile. Hugo stared at it, hypnotised, unable for a moment to get on with the daily business of preparing for work and nursery.

He watched his son crawling swiftly off and leapt to get to the top of the stairs first. What strength there was in those solid little legs! He would be walking soon at this rate. Hugo felt his eyes prick as he imagined his son tottering towards him in that drunken, bow-legged, saddle-sore way that babies had. And Theo talking, which must surely happen sooner or later.

He picked up his son and felt the small chubby legs grip his hip. They fitted well together these days, he and Theo. As he held the baby close, Hugo felt something else. Something squishy in the bottom region. Reluctantly, he returned to the bathroom and the baby changing unit.

Hugo hummed to himself as he wiped Theo clean. The

nursery, he knew, was at the bottom of it, so to speak. Chicklets prided itself on serving only organic food to its charges, which was, of course, admirable. The drawback was that organic food produced organic poo, which was far worse than the normal variety.

This led his thoughts neatly to Alice. Remembering the organic baby food manual she had been perusing in the bookshop, he imagined this syndrome was familiar to her too. Particularly given her fondness for vegetarian cooking. Funny, but when, on the drive to the bus station, he'd asked how the fundamentalist vegetarian party had gone, she'd been unexpectedly tight-lipped. It went, she had said briefly.

The telephone rang as he finished the nappy change. Hugo went to answer it, returning to the kitchen with the portable handset and putting it on to speakerphone as he shoved some toast under the grill.

'Are you signing with him?' demanded a testy female voice.

'*Amanda?*'

Both he and Theo stared at the handset in amazement. She had not been in touch for some weeks.

'Well, don't sound so surprised. I am his mother, you know.'

'Actually, I was beginning to forget,' Hugo muttered under his breath.

'What was that you just said?'

'Nothing. It's an awful line. Am I *singing* with him, did you say? Well, a bit, I suppose. He prefers Elvis, though.'

'*Signing*. Not singing, you idiot. Babies who sign have an

IQ twelve to fourteen points higher by the age of seven compared to children who don't and—'

'Look, Amanda, where are you? What the hell are you talking about?'

'New York. And I'm calling to ask whether my son is being given the opportunity to improve his brain by using the latest powerful but effective child development technique, namely signing.'

Hugo drew shuddering breath as he realised that the habitually absent and incommunicado Amanda was actually calling with parental advice.

It was, he knew, vital not to express the anger he felt in front of Theo. Listening to your parents rowing was powerful child development of another sort altogether. 'What is this signing?' Hugo asked through gritted teeth.

'I can't believe you've never heard of it,' Amanda snapped. 'Isn't he doing it at nursery, for Christ's sake? Everyone here is. God, the UK is just *so* backward. OK, well, the sign for milk is like milking a cow, right? You squeeze your fist and make this sign before you give Theo milk and then Theo will do it back when he wants milk—'

'Excuse me,' Hugo interrupted with freezing politeness, 'but if Theo wants milk, I know all about it, believe me. He doesn't have to make any signs. He just yells.'

'That's because he's frustrated,' Amanda cut in. 'He's disempowered because he's preverbal.'

'Come again?'

'Very young children lack the motor skills to produce speech but they do have the ability to sign.' She sounded, Hugo thought, as if she was reading it off the back of a box. 'You can't start too early . . . girls routinely outperform boys in school.'

'Amanda. Hang on. Theo is five months old.'

'Yes. Exactly. You'd better buck up and get signing if he's going to be on *University Challenge*.'

'*What?*'

'Hang on.' There was a muffled discussion on the other end of the line. 'I've got to go,' Amanda said imperiously. 'Must dash and talk about Estée Lauder. Have you got it yet, by the way?'

'Got what?' Hugo sniffed. There was a definite smell of burning in the air. He looked round with panic at the grill. Black smoke was pouring out of it.

'That stuff I sent. Look, I'll talk to you later.'

'What stuff . . . ?' The line went dead. As Hugo dragged forth the incinerated bread, there came a hammering at the door, accompanied by the revving of an engine. Knowing of old the dangers of leaving the baby in his high chair, Hugo threw both grill and toast into the sink, lifted Theo out, put him abruptly down on the floor and gave him his car keys to play with before hurrying along the hall passage.

'This number four?' bellowed the man in the brown United Parcels Service uniform. 'Got a delivery for you.'

'But I wasn't expecting anything.' Hugo glanced anxiously over his shoulder down the hallway. Was Theo where he had left him?

The deliveryman strode round to the back of the van and

flung open the doors. 'Help me down with this lot, can you?'

'I can't. I've got a baby inside.' Inside the bloody oven by now, probably. Or putting his tongue into the electric sockets.

'Won't take a minute. 'Ere you are, squire.'

'*Umph.*' Hugo reeled under the weight of the huge, heavy cardboard boxes being thrown his way. 'Look, there's been a mistake.'

The deliveryman consulted his notes. 'Nah. No mistake. Delivery to four Fitzherbert Place, this says.'

'But what is it?'

The deliveryman squinted at the clipboard. 'Trouble with these things is you can't read the writing . . . oh, 'ere we go. It's a Hideaway Hollow.'

'A what?'

'Don'arse me. A Hideaway Hollow, whatever that is.'

Hugo's distracted ears strained for Theo. He could hear nothing. No doubt he was halfway up the stairs by now. Or lying at the bottom in a stunned and crumpled heap. Desperately, he looked at the labels on the boxes. 'Tree house, it says here,' he said wildly. 'It's a tree house.'

'Well, there you are then,' said the man in brown. 'It's a tree 'ouse.'

'But I haven't ordered a tree house . . . oh, sod it. Never mind. Where do I sign?'

As the van roared off, Hugo shot back inside. To his vast relief, Theo was still sitting on the floor, chewing happily on the keys to the Toyota. Picking him up, Hugo went outside and tried with one hand to drag the heavy cardboard parcels off the pavement and up the front step. Who the hell had sent this ludicrous contraption and, more to the point, why?

Opening the first of the parcels, Hugo found a small gold envelope on which was typed, in loopy, foreign-looking typing, the word 'Theo'. Inside was a note from Amanda. It was scented and printed with pastel balloons.

My darling Theo, *Hugo read disbelievingly*. Here's a little present for you! Your Hideaway Hollow! I hope you like it. Brooklyn Beckham's got one exactly the same – they cost £8,000 and are hand-carved from real wood, not nasty plastic! From a Scandinavian redwood tree, apparently! I bet none of your friends have got one! You can only get them at Harrods. Get Daddy to put it up for you. And get him to help you send a thank-you letter to that lovely Mr Fayed. See you soon, my darling. Your loving Mommy.

A series of increasingly bizarre gifts followed where the tree house had led. A huge, barking toy dog came one week, a mini-biohazard suit from a shop near Ground Zero the next, 'because you never know' the note attached had said.

One thing he certainly didn't know, Hugo thought, was when Amanda was coming back. Or whether. Her absences stretched from one week to the next with no fixed date for her return. No doubt these stupid and extravagant presents were intended to compensate Theo for this. He, meanwhile, Hugo suspected crossly, was clearly expected just to carry on regardless.

His irritation peaked the morning he opened the door to go to nursery and found, staring him in the face, a well-built man with his fist raised. 'What the hell . . .' Hugo began.

'Sorry mate,' said the man in a broad Cockney accent. 'Was about to knock.'

Behind him, half on the pavement, was a large pink and purple van bearing the star-festooned logo 'Twinkledreams'.

'I'm 'ere to do the ceiling,' the man informed him.

Hugo stared. 'I don't understand. What ceiling?'

'You jokin' me? The one in the baby's nursery, o' course. Now look 'ere, I've come all the way from Kensin'ton. If this is some sort o' bleedin' joke—'

'Look,' Hugo cut in. 'I don't know what you're talking about. And I'm in a hurry, so . . .' He was about to disappear back into the house and shut the door behind him when his mobile shrilled.

With difficulty he fished it out, and with even more difficulty stopped Theo grabbing it. 'Amanda.'

'Just checking to see if it's there.'

Hugo exhaled hotly through his nose in annoyance. 'What the hell have you sent now?'

'A Twinkledreams ceiling.'

So that was what it was. Another insane bequest from across the Atlantic. 'We don't want a bloody Twinkledreams ceiling. Whatever that may be.'

'I can't believe you've never heard of them. Or maybe I can,' Amanda sighed martyrishly. 'Anyway, they're very trendy. The projectors built into the walls change the sky on the ceiling from dawn to dusk while Baby sleeps. Oh, and the stars twinkle.'

'But what's the point if it all happens when Theo's asleep?'

'He never sleeps,' Amanda said authoritatively.

'He does now,' Hugo returned triumphantly.

'Well, whatever,' Amanda snapped. 'Everyone who's anyone's baby's got one. They cost twenty thousand pounds. Don't you think that's lovely?'

'*Twenty thousand?*'

There was a shrill of laughter from the other end. 'You don't think *I'm* paying for it, do you? Woman in my position? Hardly, sweetie. By the way, the photographer's not there yet, is he?'

'*Photographer?* Amanda, would you mind explaining just what the hell is going on?'

Theo's bedroom, complete with new fibre-optic ceiling, was, it seemed, to be featured in a prominent US interiors magazine. The ceiling company had supplied it free in exchange for publicity. Directly she had explained this, Amanda cut off. Hugo watched helplessly as the Twinkle-dreams representative picked up his tool bag and went past into the hall.

His mobile rang again. He answered it crossly, expecting more Amanda. He did not, at first, recognise the woman's voice on the other end. It was muffled and nasal, as if the speaker had a bad cold.

'Hugo?' it sniffed.

'Alice?' Hugo immediately forgot all about Twinkledreams.

The goddess of parenting, with her serene face and dreamy blue eyes, was phoning . . . *him*?

'Can we meet?' Alice asked. 'I've had some, er, bad news.'

'Erm-God-yes-absolutely-of-course-no-problem-when?'

'Now?'

'Yeah. Great.' A date with Alice! It was unbelievable. His morning was suddenly looking up. Much as, in bemusement, Theo would shortly be doing at his ceiling.

'Couldn't be better. I've just got to drop Theo off at nursery and I'm all yours.'

'Don't you have to go to work?'

'Well, yes. But not straight away.' This was not true. Following the disastrous dog incident, he was in worse odour than ever at Dunn and Dustard. He had an opportunity to make amends today; a show-round in half an hour on the other side of Bath. But, he reasoned to himself, it was only a couple of Saab-driving yuppies looking for a second home in the country. He could easily ring them and rearrange it. 'Where do you want to meet? There's a café near the—'

'Café?' Alice said contemptuously. 'I don't want *coffee*. I know it's only half-past eight, but I want a *drink*. And a pretty fucking stiff one, if it's all the same to you.'

'You're *joking*,' Hugo gasped as, one hour and several gin and tonics later, Alice reached the climax of her tale. 'He'd been recycling the *condoms*?'

'Don't . . . don't . . .' Alice's face was creased as if suffering a migraine. Which she felt she might well be about to. Her head was thick with alcohol for the first time since Sally's wedding. She was vaguely aware that, with a baby beside her in a buggy and drinking like a fish, she was causing a mild sensation in the hotel bar. Not that she cared.

Hugo was amazed. His low opinion of Jake had turned out to be a flattering overestimation.

'I can't believe it,' he said eventually, shaking his head slowly. 'He sounds straight out of one of those weird religious sects they have in the States, where the women obey their menfolk no matter how reactionary and repressive they are.'

Alice buried her head in her hands. 'I can't believe what I've been putting up with. It's all so obvious now. My mother was absolutely right. She said he was brainwashing me.' She shook her head. 'Why did I let him? *Why?*'

Hugo shrugged. 'Love?' he suggested, colouring slightly. 'It's the oldest excuse in the book, obviously. But it's still the best. I mean, look at me. I thought I was in love with Amanda . . .' He stopped, appalled. Mentioning Amanda in front of Alice was never a good idea.

'Love.' Alice smiled ruefully. 'Yes. I *was* in love. Very much.' Her face softened as she looked at the baby asleep in her buggy. 'And I still am,' she added, extending a finger to touch Rosa's peachy cheek.

'With *Jake*?' Hugo was horrified.

'I was talking about Rosa. I don't know how I feel about Jake at the moment.'

'Well I bloody do.' Hugo said violently.

There followed one of those awkward silences he remembered from the supermarket café. He searched for a way to break it.

'We'd better have something to eat,' he suggested. 'Soak all this booze up. What do you fancy?' He peered at the bar menu.

'I don't care,' Alice said. Then a defiant light blazed in her eyes. 'Oh, actually, I do. Just for once, I'd like the most mass-produced internationally corporate hamburger imaginable, with lashings of plastic cheese and tomato ketchup, served in a white roll made of bleached flour inside an ozone-layer-destroying Styrofoam container.'

'Coming up,' grinned Hugo, waving for a waiter.

'Are you sure you've got time?' Alice met his smile with a shy one of her own. 'Thanks for listening,' she added. 'It's made me feel – well – *better*, telling you about it. You see, I'm a bit like you with Theo. There's no one else I can really talk to.'

Looking into her sad, sincere face, Hugo felt like ice cream on a hot August pavement. Rescuing his reputation at Dunn and Dustard could not have seemed less important. 'My appointment can wait,' he heard himself saying.

'What's it like being an estate agent?' Alice seized the opportunity to change the subject.

Hugo shrugged. 'OK, I suppose. You get out and about.'

She looked at him wryly. 'Jake says estate agents spend their whole time lying. Forcing people into deals that plunge them into debt, all for the sake of houses that aren't worth living in.'

'He really is a ray of sunshine, isn't he?' Hugo said crossly.

Alice picked at a bowl of vegetable chips. Up until now, Hugo had assumed they were pot pourri. 'I wonder if these are organic,' she mused.

'Shouldn't think so.'

'Great.' She took a handful and smiled at him. 'Yes, well, quite apart from what Jake says, can you honestly say that every single house you sell is as marvellous as you make it out to be?'

'A lot of the ones round here are very nice,' Hugo insisted.

'So estate agenting's not a lying profession?' Alice teased.

'Not at all – well, sometimes I suppose,' Hugo thought guiltily of the Osokozi old lady from what, now, seemed like years ago. Uncomfortably he remembered her asking him whether he would have bought the hideous bungalow himself, and how he had assured her that he would.

'Oh, look,' he said thankfully. 'Here comes the food.'

And that's not the only thing, he thought a second later, as a big-nosed woman with high heels clacked towards them across the lobby.

'Hewwwwwgooooo!' exclaimed Laura, enveloping him in an elaborate kiss. He could feel, rather than see, Alice's amazement.

'Hello, Laura,' he muttered, extracting himself from her cleavage. 'Fancy meeting you here!'

The bright, heavily mascara'd eyes flicked enquiringly from Hugo to Alice. The thickly lipsticked mouth smiled conspiratorially. Hugo remembered uncomfortably that the hotel was the same one in which Laura had met her mystery man at Christmas.

'This is Alice,' he said hurriedly, wondering why he felt so defensive. It wasn't as if he and Alice were there for the purpose Laura had been. And was again, for all he knew. 'She was at the same antenatal class as us,' he added.

'Really?' Laura, a proprietorial hand still on Hugo's shoulder, scrutinised Alice closely. 'Can't say I remember.'

Alice got to her feet. 'I'd better be going.'

'But you haven't eaten your burger,' Hugo pointed out in despair.

'Haven't time. Rosa's going to wake up in a minute.'

'Don't worry, it won't go to waste.' Laura had picked up the ketchup-slathered bun and was stuffing it into her face. 'Mm. Delicious.'

'Bye, then.' Hugo's eyes were beaming messages into Alice's, none of which she appeared to receive. She looked back blankly.

'What's that?' Laura squawked suddenly, pointing at the handles of Rosa's buggy. And, specifically, at the large white bag stretched across them. 'I know this sounds far-fetched and they're probably the most stylish buggy holdall going, but they look just like maternity knickers with the legholes sewn up.'

'That's exactly what they are,' Alice muttered, blushing. 'They're recycled.'

Laura frowned for a split second, then waved the burger in excitement. 'Oh, of course! I remember you now. You were that mad environmentalist who was going to have a home birth on a shower curtain.'

* * *

Standing, as arranged, on the side of the road, Hugo was relieved when the Saab-driving yuppies finally came into view. They'd be horrible, obviously. But at least they would stop his endless dwelling on Laura barging in on his drink with Alice.

Miserably, he remembered her hurrying off across the lobby. And then red-lipsticked, chasm-cleavaged Laura sitting heavily down in Alice's place, messily finishing the burger and telling him in loud, bitter, unsparing detail about Fergus's latest outrages. He had left as soon as he could.

And now he had these grim second-home-hunters to look forward to.

He saw, as it drew up, that their car didn't look like a Saab convertible. It looked like a battered Polo. The skinny couple emerging didn't look wealthy and arrogant, either. They were, Hugo recognised, the archetypal Young and Knackered. The man was about twenty-five, nervous and clearly worked into the ground while the woman had lank hair and smudges beneath her eyes.

'We can't really afford a house round here,' the woman confided, looking at Hugo with worried hazel eyes. 'But we thought we might be able to buy a barn and convert it.'

'Absolutely,' Hugo said briskly, watching them step carefully round the rubble. They talked in low voices, smiling anxiously at each other. Hugo watched them with a sort of pitying contempt. It was obvious that they didn't have a clue.

'We could put a kitchen here,' the girl said hopefully at one point, pointing at a patch of stony earth Hugo knew for a fact had a mineshaft beneath it. 'I don't know,' the man kept saying. 'It's probably a great bargain. I don't know anything about property.'

Eventually, the girl picked her way over the stones to Hugo.

'It's wonderful, it really is,' she smiled. 'But, this barn does seem a little . . .' her voice dropped, 'expensive.' Her eyes lingered appealingly on his. 'I just wondered . . . should we buy it? I mean, is it a bargain? If you were us . . .' her voice was a whisper now '. . . would you?'

Hugo cleared his throat. God, he hated questions like this. Obvious what he had to do, though. His professional duty. Tell them the broken pile not only had potential to be a wonderful family home, but represented a significant investment for the future. Then drive off, sale and, more importantly, commission, in the bag. He wondered why he was even hesitating. His current status at Dunn and Dustard made any other course career suicide.

He hesitated, fighting the knowledge that the only way 'Paradise Barn', as the farmer insisted it was called in the details, could be a wonderful family home was if you were a family of fieldmice.

'Would you buy it if you were us?' the woman pressed. She looked anxiously at the rubble before her.

Hugo continued to say nothing. The couple had clearly no idea what converting a barn meant in terms of expense, effort and stress. Even a barn that was actually a barn, rather than what this was – a heap of worthless stones on a slope of field that got the north wind smack in the face. It wasn't impossible that the discovery of what it did mean would drive them apart. He felt the sudden, insane urge to protect them.

'I think,' he said gently, 'that I probably wouldn't.'

She smiled at him, gloriously. 'Thanks,' she said softly. He watched them leave, long arms twined round each other. And immediately felt like kicking himself. He was losing it, he really was. If he carried on like this, he'd be out of a job.

Chapter 19

The following morning, Hugo drove Theo into Bath to the doctor's. While he was not looking forward to watching his son being stabbed with a needle, it was difficult not to feel cheerful. It *was* an absolutely beautiful day.

As he parked and carried Theo to the health centre, Hugo found himself admiring the Georgian buildings en route. He registered, with a prick of surprise, that there was a space of a good few minutes before he started to reckon what each structure was worth. And what, were he selling it, he could hope to cream off in commission. Was the habit of a lifetime weakening? Was he finally appreciating architecture for its own sake?

Recently, he had found himself admiring the contours of Fitzherbert Place. Even the house had a definite grace, despite the enormous amount of work it needed. But Hugo had now quietly abandoned Amanda's plans for refurbishment. Seeing them through involved not only time and money, but inclination. Neither he nor Theo cared if an ever-largening stain accompanied them most of the way up the staircase.

He had arrived at the health centre now. He pushed open the green-painted door into the light, airy interior. Of all he was growing to appreciate about Bath, a surgery that was clean, modern and had appointments systems was among the most revelatory of all.

The one he had used in London had been the opposite. Everyone, whatever their ailment, waited outside in a mob for it to open. Then they rioted to the reception desk where the practice manager tried in vain to establish who was first. There was always a wait of at least an hour, during which, given the exotic range of patients and ailments present, one could contract anything from TB to avian flu. Hugo had always left feeling worse than when he had arrived.

His mobile shrilled as he registered Theo at the reception desk. The possibility that it was Alice leapt wildly in his mind, to be swiftly and cruelly followed by the discovery that it was Neil. Sounding very angry. As he carried the writhing baby into the waiting area, Hugo felt his benevolent mood leak away.

'Ah. The barn conversion. Yes.'

'What happened?' Neil demanded. 'You never came back to the office. Buy it, did they?'

'Er, not exactly.'

There was an ominous silence. Then the storm broke. 'I don't *believe* it,' Neil roared. 'Those two were complete sitting ducks. Clueless. They'd have bought bloody *anything*.'

'Well, in the end it turned out to be not what they wanted.'

'Bollocks. You cocked it up, Fine. And where the fuck are you now, may I ask?'

'At the health centre. Theo's having a jab.'

'Oh, for Christ's sake. Don't bother telling us, will you? Why don't you just become a full-time nanny and have bloody done with it?'

'I did tell you about it. Or Shuna, at any rate. She put it in the diary.'

'You knew about this, did you, Shuna?' Neil yelled at his secretary. 'Fine's bloody baby getting a jab? In the diary is it . . . *no?* He *didn't* tell you? You didn't tell her, Fine,' Neil announced, returning to the receiver.

Hugo fought to keep patient. 'Well, she obviously forgot.' His ear caught Theo being announced over the doctor's intercom. 'I've got to go. I'll be in later. After I've dropped him off at nursery.'

'Nursery? *Nursery?!*' Neil was expostulating as Hugo turned the phone off.

Thanks to a skilfully wielded biscuit, Theo's jab passed without incident. Afterwards, they set off for Chicklets where, as he carried his son carefully up the stairs, Hugo spotted Barbara and Sue coming down them. Both were too absorbed in talk to see him.

'I can't go on like this,' Sue was saying despairingly. 'It's just impossible. He was up four times last night and now I've to come and take him home because he's got a few bloody spots.

You wouldn't believe the fuss the boss made about me going – and only this morning he sent one of the other girls home because she had a bloody *hangover*. A *self-inflicted* illness, for Christ's sake. How fair is that?'

'It's not,' said Barbara grimly. Judging by her clothes, she had clearly come straight from chambers again.

Hugo reached Dunn and Dustard with a cold sense of dread in his stomach. Yet, most unexpectedly, Neil actually smiled as he came in. A valuation request, it turned out, had come through half an hour ago, from someone in one of Bath's smartest areas. They had asked for Hugo personally. 'They say they've heard you're very good,' Neil added, raising an eyebrow.

'Which I am,' Hugo said immediately. 'Remember the station house?'

'I'm remembering that dog. Those bloody shoe covers. That dead-cert barn conversion.'

Shuna, listening in as usual, sniggered.

Hugo ignored them and turned his attention to the notes concerning the house valuation. He whistled. 'Wow.'

'Quite something, eh, Fine?' Neil grunted.

'You bet. Must be the most tasteless place I've ever seen. "The house is called Leather, after the nightclub the owners met in," ' Hugo quoted from the notes.

'Yeah, but the guide price is two million. Get that on our books and we stand to make some serious money. And you stand to redeem yourself, Fine. The owner's expecting you tomorrow, by the way.'

The next day, Hugo parked in the road outside Leather. As he remembered to do only rarely these days, he checked his appearance in the mirror. He was relieved he had. There was some salvage work to be done.

On his shoulder was a snail trail of snot, and the pattern on his tie included several hardened clusters of baby porridge. Below his eyes the bags hung purple, capacious and testimony to another night at the coal face of fatherhood.

He wiped himself down as best he could, raked his hair with his hands and smoothed his eyebrows with his thumbs. Then he swung his legs out of the car, squared his shoulders and set off for the house.

There was, he knew, no margin for error this time. Or for fits of misplaced conscience. The point was not what Alice would think of his conduct, but how Neil, the paymaster who controlled Theo's supply lines, saw it. No matter what the temptation to do otherwise, he would value Leather at the highest it could stand. And possibly beyond.

In contrast with – or defiance of – the gracious Georgian houses neighbouring it, Leather was of a type best described as contemporary. Its enormously high boundary wall was of brash, golden, brilliantly new stone. Its gates, unsurprisingly, were electronic, and as they swung slowly open to reveal the boxy, glassy house at the end of the curving drive, Hugo stood for a minute, stunned. It was even worse in reality than it had sounded on paper.

He crunched up the dazzlingly orange-paved brick drive to the front door. The tune that pealed out as he rang the doorbell reminded him unpleasantly of a turgid rock anthem called 'The Wind Beneath My Wings'. But surely that was a little far-fetched. Even for a house called Leather.

The shape visible through the glass doorway was singing something as it approached. 'You're the wind beneath my-hiy wings,' it declared in a husky vibrato as it opened the door.

'Laura!' Hugo clutched the folders under his arm in panic.

'Hi, sexy! Is that a tape measure in your pocket or are you just pleased to see me?'

It wasn't just the line that was bad. The clothes weren't too good either. She lounged against the door frame in a near-transparent red chiffon negligée, every available edge of which seemed to be trimmed with marabou feathers.

He struggled hard to feel relaxed rather than alarmed. Laura routinely dressed like a Bangkok ladyboy, so this was probably nothing out of the ordinary.

'I didn't realise this was your place,' he remarked with as much ease as he could muster. Although, he supposed, if there was one person in the whole of Bath he might imagine lived in Leather, it would be Laura. 'What a coincidence!' he added, knowing perfectly well it was nothing of the kind. So it was she who had requested his exclusive services. Was it merely just an excuse to see him? Or was there the remotest chance that she was serious about this sale?

'Isn't it just?' Laura beamed back.

'Especially as,' Hugo said pleasantly, 'you never mentioned you were putting it up for sale when we met at the nursery.'

'Must have slipped my mind.' She turned and beckoned him

to follow through a hallway a 747 could comfortably have parked in. Their destination was a kitchen full of spotlights, blinding whiteness and gleaming metallic surfaces. It looked, Hugo thought, more suitable for open heart surgery than anything to do with eating or entertaining.

He stared round for as long as he possibly could before reluctantly returning his gaze to Laura. In addition to the usual plastering of make-up, she wore red satin high-heeled mules to match the negligée.

'Want a drink?' Laura purred.

'Yes, please.' Hugo jumped at the chance to inject some normality into the scenario. 'Coffee would be great.'

Laura bent over to open the fridge despite the fact its handle was on a level with her elbow. That negligée left nothing to the imagination. You could see up to her tonsils. Averting his eyes, Hugo brought them back a few seconds later to see Laura holding, not the carton of milk he had expected, but a bottle of champagne. Before he could say anything she had prised off the cage and was handling the cork in a highly suggestive manner.

'Oh.' Hugo smiled uncertainly. 'That sort of drink.' His eyes slid to the kitchen clock. It was not yet ten.

Nonetheless, he accepted the bulky cut-crystal glass Laura smilingly passed him. 'Your husband around?' he asked casually, fervently hoping so. Fergus sounded horrible, but less so than being alone with his wife.

Laura's beam snapped off. '*Him*?' she spat. 'He's casting a commercial in Sweden. *If* you get my meaning.'

309

'Oh. Right.' Hugo wasn't entirely sure that he did.

'He doesn't fancy me any more.' Laura's lip suddenly trembled and her head started to wobble. She clutched his arm, nails boring in through his jacket fabric. 'Do *you* fancy me, Hugo?' she asked plaintively. 'Am I attractive?'

Hugo sighed. Another tactical cul de sac to extricate himself from. 'Fergus can't possibly mean it,' he said evasively. 'It must be his idea of a joke.'

'*Joke!*' Laura exclaimed furiously. 'Know what he said to me the other night?' Her champagne glass, he noticed, was almost empty already.

'We were lying in bed and he was doing the usual—'

'Well, there you are,' Hugo interrupted triumphantly. 'He was doing the usual. What more proof do you need that he finds you attractive?'

'When I say the usual,' Laura's eyes flashed over the rim of her glass, 'I mean that he was banging on as usual about how important he was. And so I said, "Well, of course, I only do a *little* job. Looking after Django and all that." Just to see what he'd say.'

'And what did he say?'

'He said "mm". He *agreed*!'

'Mmm,' said Hugo. He corrected himself hastily. 'I mean, er, oh dear.'

Laura walked to the kitchen window and stared angrily out. 'If I wasn't bringing up his bloody kid I'd be earning a fortune,' she snarled. 'I was before. I had a career once, you know.' She broke off and, quite suddenly, started sobbing hysterically. 'Oh God,' she howled. 'What's happened to me? What have I done with my life?'

Her moods, Hugo thought, had more swings than Theo's favourite playground. Already now the tears were drying, the angry expression smoothing. 'I want to kill him sometimes, you know,' she said quietly, addressing the marble kitchen floor.

She burst into tears again, flinging herself, sobbing, on to Hugo's chest. He felt the sooty tears soaking into his pristine white shirt and her hot, panting breath and damp skin. Her heavy perfume made his head swim. Tuberose. A scent that always made him feel slightly sick and as if he was gasping for air. He thought fleetingly of Alice, who, he imagined, never smelt of anything but soap.

'Who do you want to kill? Fergus?'

She looked at him through anguished, mascara-smudged eyes. 'No,' she gulped. 'Django.'

He started. She wanted to kill her own baby? Despite his shock, he felt a swirl of sympathy. This was obviously desperation talking. Laura was, by her own admission, neglected, bored, depressed, lonely and completely lacking in self-esteem. He gripped her shoulders firmly and held her back at arm's length. 'Er, Laura. Look, this sounds a bit serious. Isn't there someone you can talk to? A friend?'

She raised her streaked face, eyes tragic. 'I don't have any friends in Bath. Apart from Amanda, of course, and she's buggered off and left me.' She was wiping her nose on the back of her hands.

Join the club, thought Hugo.

Suddenly, the megawatt smile was back on again. She sidled up very close. 'Still,' she purred, running her hands down her hips, 'at least I haven't let myself go. Have I, Hugo?'

He swallowed. 'Er, no. No, not at all.'

'Not like that hippy from the antenatal class you were with the other day,' Laura tittered. 'What does she think she looks like? Not a scrap of slap and hair like straw. Shame, though. She'd probably scrub up well if she bothered.'

Indignation swept Hugo. How dare she talk this way about Alice?

'I saw you from the other side of the foyer.' Laura nudged him meaningfully. 'And I thought, way hey, what's naughty old Hugo up to then? But I have to say I was a little bit disappointed when I saw it was *her*. Or do I mean relieved?'

'I don't follow,' Hugo said stiffly.

'Do I have to spell it out? I thought you were up to – well, *you know* – but then I realised, when I saw *her*, that you couldn't possibly be! I mean, you're married to Amanda. Miss Well-Groomed Glossy 2005. You don't have affairs with tramps.'

Tramps! If anyone round here was a tramp . . . Hugo bit back a furious defence of Alice and fished out his notebook. The sooner he did the valuation, the sooner he could get out.

'What are you doing?' Laura breathed, tracing the line of his cheekbone with a finger.

'Taking notes for the house details. The brochure, you know.'

'Why?' She was ruffling his hair now.

'Well, there's usually a brochure when a house like this is being sold.'

'Is there?' She giggled.

'Yes.' Gently yet determinedly, he detached her hand from his head. He fought his instinct to turn on his heel and run. He needed this commission. 'So,' he said brightly, 'this is the kitchen. What about the rest of the place?'

'*Jobsworth*.' She stuck out a teasing lower lip. 'Refill?' She brandished the champagne bottle.

'I'm all right, thanks.'

'Oh, for God's sake. Live a little.' She tipped some into his own nearly full glass and slopped a lot into her empty one. She looked at him quizzically. 'OK then,' she said resignedly. 'This way.' He followed her out into the hallway.

'Oops!' she exclaimed, clacking to a halt and picking up a small black remote control that lay on a mirror-topped side-table. She pointed it at the corner of the room. 'Best de-activate the CCTV, eh?'

'CCTV throughout,' Hugo said loudly, making notes in a businesslike fashion.

Laura started her bottom-wiggling ascent of a sweeping Plexiglass staircase best described, Hugo thought, as *Gone With the Wind* meets *Star Wars*. She went up remarkably quickly, given her heels. When he got to the top, there was no sign of her.

'Laura?' he called.

'Come and find me!' sang out the teasing reply.

He followed the direction of the voice down a white-painted, cream-carpeted corridor featuring about six identical, wide white doors with Perspex globes for handles. Only one was ajar.

'Laura?' he repeated, outside it.

'In he-yah!' she trilled.

When, some time later, he could bear to think about this scene, Hugo supposed he was asking for it. He should have known, given the morning's run-up, given Laura's history in general, exactly what lay behind that bedroom door. He should have acknowledged what was glaringly obvious: that her reason for calling him to the house had nothing to do with selling it. Ultimately, he should have faked some call from the office and beaten a hasty retreat.

But he did none of these things. Instead, he pushed open the bedroom door.

It was worse than he had feared. Laura, naked apart from the red silk mules, lay in the centre of a large, rumpled, purple four-poster. Her knees were up and her legs were spread wide in an attitude reminding Hugo unpleasantly of the birthing position in Lotti's videos. The white flesh of her breasts spilt over the hands that pushed rhythmically upwards and outwards towards him. She was gyrating her pelvis and moaning.

'Come and get it, big boy,' she murmured. 'You know you want it.'

The atmosphere in the room was suffocating. The curtains were pulled, the heat was intense and the scent of tuberose overwhelming.

Desperately, he tried to get a grip on the situation. 'Er, look, Laura. I mean, it's very good of you to offer, but the thing is . . .'

Laura rolled on to her front and slithered across the bed to one of the four poster's thin brass columns. Grasping it, she pulled herself upwards and began to gyrate suggestively up and down. She was, he realised, pole-dancing, although, given the amount of alcohol she had drunk, pole-clutching was nearer the mark.

She licked a forefinger, pressed it to her clitoris and made a hissing sound. 'Sssss!' she slurred. 'I'm *hot*. Hot hot *hot*. Come on. You know you want me. You always have. I could see it in your eyes.'

As Hugo stood rooted to the spot, Laura's come-hither looks darkened to annoyance. 'Well! What are you waiting for?'

'Er, I'm, you know, well, there's Amanda . . .'

'Amanda!' She slumped down from the pole, rolled across the bed and slid off the end towards him. Her mouth was distorted in a big red sneer. 'She doesn't give a flying fuck about you. Otherwise why isn't she here?'

It was a neat summary of his situation. 'Erm, well, even so, technically at least, I'm a married man.'

'So what?' Laura shot back. 'I'm a married woman.'

'I'm a father,' Hugo argued.

'I'm a mother,' she countered.

Hugo backed away. 'Laura, I really don't think this is a good idea.'

'Why not?' she growled, approaching him like a lioness might her prey. Her unruly hair had clumped over her face and her breasts swung heavily from side to side. 'Don't I turn you on? You said I was attractive.'

'You are attractive. But . . .'

'Are you saying,' Laura snarled, 'that you don't fancy me?'

'Er . . . hang on, that's my phone.' Never had he scrambled for it so eagerly.

'Leave it!' Laura commanded.

'I can't,' Hugo had spotted Chicklets's number on the screen. 'It's Theo's nursery. It could be anything.'

'It'll be something and nothing. Always bloody is. They're always sending Django home with conjunctivitis. I just clean him up, put white foundation powder over the red bits round his eyes and send him back.'

Never, Hugo thought, pressing the little green phone icon, had he been so glad to hear from the Rottweiler.

His relief lasted approximately three seconds.

The Rottweiler, as ever, was crisp, to the point and terrifying. 'Mr Fine, I would be grateful if you could come and get Theo immediately. He has a suspect rash on his chest.'

'But he was fine when I left him.'

'That may be so. But he isn't now.'

'Well, don't you know what this rash is? He had a jab yesterday. It's probably a reaction to that.'

'Mr Fine, we are a nursery, not a hospital accident and emergency department.'

The mere mention of such places sent a chill through Hugo.

'But don't you have someone there who knows about . . . that sort of thing?' Surely, with the fees they charged? It seemed amazing that they could just ring up and suddenly all the responsibility was the parent's.

'Mr Fine, I repeat, we are a nursery. Not a sanitorium. And we would be most grateful if you came and removed your son. Now.' *Click. Burr.*

Hugo stared at the mobile, his bewilderment mixed with a growing terror.

'Hewwwwgooo!' Laura mewed at him from the bed. She was rubbing herself up against the bedpost again, one hand pushing her breasts towards him. 'I *need* you,' she lowed through pouting lips.

Distractedly, he stared at her. In the light of what he had just heard, the situation he was now in seemed more unreal and absurd than ever. 'You don't need *me*, Laura,' he said slowly. 'What you need is . . . I don't know. Therapy or something.'

'*Therapy?!*' Her eyes flashed fire. 'How fucking dare you?'

'Because it's true,' Hugo said quietly, walking out of the room.

Her outraged howl followed him down the slippery glass staircase. 'Therapy! Me? I'm not the kind of woman who needs therapy! There's nothing fucking wrong with me. You'll be sorry you said that. *Bastard.*'

Chapter 20

At Chicklets, Theo was crying. 'He's not quite himself,' the nursery assistant remarked as she pushed up Theo's Babygro to reveal a handful of faint red spots.

At the sight of them, Hugo felt relief. Only now did he realise he had been expecting something akin to bubonic plague. 'They don't look so bad,' he said.

'You never know with rashes,' the assistant replied equivocally.

'Yes, but they don't look like meningitis or anything, do they?' This, Hugo knew, was the real worry. He'd seen posters of what it looked like in the surgery only that morning. Deeply coloured spots signifying the swift, pitiless killer.

'I'd keep an eye on them, all the same,' the assistant advised. 'Get a doctor to check them out if they get worse.'

The baby's spots, so far as Hugo could see, did not get worse through the afternoon. At bedtime, as usual, he and

Theo listened to the baby's nursery rhyme tapes. This was the only part of Alice's advice that Hugo regretted taking.

It wasn't entirely her fault, he recognised. Her recommendation – that Hugo did the same things with Theo every night before putting him to bed – had been entirely open-ended. 'Babies love repetition,' was all Alice had said, and so it had proved to be, although Hugo wished nightly he had chosen something other than Theo's nursery tapes to repeat.

The tinny, inane tunes and their dreadful arrangements drove him mad and he worried about the inner lives of people forced into studios and made to sing 'The Wheels on the Bus' in unnaturally high, bright voices.

Some of the words were quite odd when you really – as he did nightly – listened to them. 'Pop Goes the Weasel', for example, was basically a paean to pub-crawling: 'Up and down the City Road/In and out the Eagle/That's the way the money goes/Pop goes the weasel.' He'd been in and out the Eagle more than a few times himself, especially during the Clerkenwell property boom. And the money had certainly gone on Eagle food. One of London's first gastropubs, he remembered.

'That's enough, Theo,' Hugo said, as a particularly hideous arrangement of 'Michael Finnegan' came at agonising last to an end. 'Bedtime.'

Theo, most unusually, did not protest either at being taken upstairs or laid down on the changing table for his pyjamas and new bedtime nappy. He did not even wail for his dummy, which Hugo was especially pleased about. While dummies had been an essential part of life when Amanda had first left, and were still vital in getting Theo off to sleep, Chicklets did not approve of them. Hugo himself had a love–hate relationship with them – while grateful for the peace they would provide, he deplored the way they made Theo look like Hannibal Lecter, wings of plastic spreading out either side of his face.

But as he undressed Theo, the possible reason for the baby's uncharacteristically placid mood became instantly, hideously obvious. The pale red spots which had sprinkled Theo's stomach and chest had changed. They had multiplied a hundredfold and glared out a dark and angry crimson, raised slightly from the skin. They looked, Hugo thought, like flock wallpaper. The meningitis poster in the doctor's surgery flashed horribly into his mind.

For a few seconds, he was too terrified to move, as if, somehow, by keeping still, he would maintain control of the situation. He dithered, baby-wipe in hand, before suddenly snapping into action and, stuffing Theo under his arm, flinging himself downstairs to the phone. With trembling hand, he called the doctor's surgery.

The recorded voice of the receptionist advised him in warm, West Country tones that the health centre was now closed. It recommended that he call NHS Direct. Flustered by this unexpected turn of events, Hugo had to call back twice to get the number accurately, then punched it on to the keypad with shaking hand. Eventually, someone came on the line and asked for his address.

'My baby's got a rash,' Hugo croaked. What the hell did his address have to do with it?

'We'll get to that. Could I just have your postcode? And your date of birth.'

'But he might have fucking meningitis,' Hugo yelled. Under his arm, Theo began to cry.

'The sooner you give me your details, sir, the sooner someone will be able to call you back.'

Hugo was aghast. 'Call me back? Can't I talk to you about it?'

'I'm one of the operators. A nurse or doctor will call you back.'

'And how long's that going to take?'

'Hopefully not longer than ten minutes. Now if you'll just give me your postcode . . .'

Hugo slammed the phone down in panic. Ten minutes! He wasn't sure how fast meningitis acted, but he knew it didn't hang about. Theo's little life could have been snuffed out by then. Hugo clasped his by now screaming son to his chest, wrapping him in the folds of the suit jacket he was still wearing from this morning. He felt like crying himself and only by a supreme effort of will managed not to.

Instead, he paced up and down, trying to calm the riot in his brain. He should, he knew, ring Amanda. She was Theo's mother. She had a right to know what was happening. She might, he hoped as he stabbed the keypad, have some idea what to do.

'Hi, Amanda Hardwick here,' said her mobile's

322

answerphone. 'Sorry I can't come to the phone right now, but if you leave a message . . .'

The panic in Hugo's head was a whirling blizzard. He wanted to run amok and scream. But he couldn't. He had to hold on, for Theo's sake. The baby's life might depend on the decisions he made now. Hugo breathed in deeply – so deeply it made his head spin. Then it came to him. Alice. Of course. He could call Alice.

Alice was upstairs when she heard the phone ring, putting Rosa to bed in the ottoman. Jake, at home on account of the rubbish still apparently filling his office, went to answer it.

'Alice?' she heard him say suspiciously. 'She's here, yes.'

Against her better judgement, Alice thought grimly. In the white heat of her first, furious anger following the condom discovery, she had been ready to leave and take Rosa with her. On the back of the humiliation of the dinner party, it was the last straw. Then her native good sense had kicked in. Emotional grand gestures, tempting though they were, often resulted in repenting at leisure. She wasn't making decisions for herself alone; Rosa's best interests were the most important thing.

A factor, minor but not insignificant, in her eventual decision to stay was that Jake seemed genuinely sorry for his actions. It was the first time Alice had heard him either apologise or admit that he was wrong.

'It was stupid of me, I know,' Jake had groaned, his

handsome face creased with regret. Of course your human rights are more important than those of the rubber trees.'

'Jake, trees don't have human rights. They're *trees*.'

Jake raked an agitated hand through his long dark hair. He turned his long, beautiful eyes on her in the most meltingly beseeching of looks. 'Oh shit, Al, I'm sorry. Please. I only did it because, I dunno . . .' He scrunched his hair again with every appearance of desperation. 'Because I'm too much of a caring person, I suppose. Come on, Al. It's not the worst crime in the world. Give me another chance. For Rosa's sake, if no one else's.'

Alice knitted her brows. The Rosa argument was a powerful one. In the dark hours of the night, when the big questions of existence closed in on her, she tried to remember that, whatever Jake's behaviour, and via however devious a route, he had brought her adored Rosa into her life. Would she really want to be without her?

On the other hand, was staying with Jake really the right thing to do? Her mother, certainly, did not think so. Alice had instantly regretted the moment of weakness in which she had told her the whole story.

Disguising her fury at the way her daughter had been treated had cost Mrs Duffield considerable effort. Resisting the urge to say 'I told you so' had cost even more. 'Of *course* you would want to have had Rosa,' she agreed. 'But ideally you'd have had the choice about whether or not to conceive her. As you know, there's not much you get to control about motherhood.'

'Tell me about it,' said Alice, ruefully.

'But most women get to make that first decision at least.'

'Oh, well,' Alice said briskly. 'Jake's been an idiot, I admit. But I'm giving it another go.'

'I see. But are you quite sure you want to stay with' – her mother's resolve broke temporarily – '*that fanatic*?'

'Mum,' Alice said firmly. 'We've got to try and make it work for Rosa's sake. Jake is her father and I want her to be secure, like I was, with two loving parents. You don't know how lucky you are, never having had a cross word with Dad.'

'But if you'd just tell me who's calling . . .' Jake's voice, irritated, floated up from downstairs. Still on the phone, Alice realised, returning from her daydream. But hadn't whoever it was rung for her? Indignantly, she went to the top of the stairs to listen. 'So you say you're a friend of hers, sure,' Jake was saying. 'But who shall I tell's calling?'

Hugo, at the other end, hadn't expected to have to get through Alice's security system first. That, after the unbelievable condom business, Jake was still around was an unpleasant surprise. 'Tell her it's a friend,' he repeated stubbornly.

'Yes, but *what* friend?' The jaunty, slightly whiny voice had a ring of insistent steel in it. Jake would, Hugo knew, put the phone down in an instant if he knew his identity. The thought of this happening with Theo possibly dying in the background brought him to the edge of murderous frenzy. With a superhuman effort, he tried to calm down.

'Just put her on, will you? It's an emergency.'

There was a distrustful silence. Hugo sensed he was about to be cut off. Then, miraculously, in the background, he heard Alice's voice. She must have just come into the room. He felt like yelling to attract her attention, but realised this would be futile.

'Someone for me, is it?' he heard her ask.

There was a thumping noise as Jake handed the receiver over.

'Hello?'

'Oh Alice,' Hugo gasped, 'thank God you're there. You've got to help me, I don't know what's wrong with him, he's—'

Alice frowned. 'Who *is* this?'

'It's Hugo.'

'*Hugo?*'

Alice felt her face glow red. Her heart raced at the memory of their last meeting. The things she had said. The amount she had drunk. What he must have thought of her.

On the other side of the room, Jake stiffened with hostility at the name. '*Him!* What does *he* want?'

'What's the matter?' Alice asked, doing her best to ignore her husband. She sensed immediately that this was not a social call.

'Theo. He's got a rash,' Hugo whimpered. 'It looks bad, Alice.'

'How bad? Have you done the glass test?'

'Glass test?'

'*What's going on?*' demanded Jake agitatedly, closing in on Alice and the phone.

'You press a clear glass over the spots,' Alice instructed while trying to bat Jake away. 'If they fade, it's not meningitis. If they don't fade, it is. Try it. I'll stay on the line while you do.'

At Hugo's end, the phone clattered to the floor. She heard him rummaging in cupboards, cursing, then the smash of several glasses falling. Throughout, in the background, was the high, keening note of a crying baby. She bit her lip.

Jake was gesturing angrily in her face again. Again she tried to make him go away. 'Hugo's in trouble,' she hissed. 'His baby's ill . . .' She stopped as, at the other end of the phone, a scraping and bumping announced that Hugo had snatched it up again. 'All our glasses are cut crystal,' he howled. 'Amanda didn't seem to buy anything else, bugger her.'

'But you must have *something*. Not even an old jam jar?' Alice's gaze trailed round her own sitting room. Jam jars were all she could see – used as candle holders, filled with earth and used as doorstops, standing on the mantelpiece collecting coins, corks and bits of scrap paper.

'He's a waste of time, Al!' Jake snarled. Suddenly, he snatched at the telephone.

Furiously, Alice slapped him away. *Didn't you hear me?* she mimed. *His baby's ill.*

Jake looked disbelieving. 'Got a cough, has it?' he jeered. 'So why don't they get one of their fleet of nannies on the case? Spoilt brat.'

'Found one,' Hugo gasped, returning to the phone. 'Used to have a really horrid scented candle in it,' he added, with the pointlessness of panic. 'Right. What did you say I should do now?'

'Press it against the spots. If they fade on contact, they're not meningitis.'

In the background, Theo's crying changed key and became harder, more desperate. Alice's fists curled with tension. When Hugo came back to the phone his voice was cracked and barely audible. It was clear he was on the verge of weeping.

'Alice, I can't bloody tell if it's fading or not. I've tried, but I just can't. I'm too fucking scared to think straight.'

'Calm down,' Alice said gently. 'It's a hard thing to do, I know, but it's important. Have you called the doctor?'

'I've rung both the doctor and NHS bloody Direct. The surgery was closed and NHS Direct was useless.'

'Useless?' Alice was surprised. 'I've always found them rather good.'

'Oh, I don't know,' Hugo said despairingly. 'I probably didn't give them enough time. It was just a voice on a phone, some receptionist, not even a nurse. I was panicking.' He took a breath, fighting vainly for control. 'Alice,' he sobbed, 'I don't know what to do. I'm *terrified*.'

Alice considered for exactly half a second. 'Right. *Here's* what you do. Call an ambulance now. Then wrap Theo up warmly. And give me your address. I'll be right over.'

She put the phone down to find Jake glaring in hot-eyed

indignation. 'His *address*? You're going over there?'

'Yes, and before you ask, I'm not hanging around for a bus either. I'm going to go to the pub. Someone there will take me. It's an emergency. He's on his own with an ill baby and he needs help.'

'Well, you've just told him to call an ambulance,' Jake snapped. 'He'll get plenty of help from them. And at the same time steal it from someone who really needs it.'

'What's that supposed to mean?' Alice was buttoning her coat with swift fingers.

'You should only call ambulances in *real* emergencies,' Jake said piously.

'And what makes you think this isn't one?' Alice asked coldly as she reached for the doorknob. 'The baby has a bad rash by the sound of it. If it's meningitis he might die if he doesn't get to hospital soon.'

Hugo, waiting for the ambulance, had the sensation of time dragging and flying at the same time. It seemed like hours before he heard the engine outside, yet, according to the kitchen's fake-rococo clock, only eight minutes had elapsed between him placing the 999 call and a green-boiler-suited man and woman arriving at his door.

'This the little fella?' asked the burly man kindly, looking at Theo. The baby's cries had subsided now to exhausted moans. Hugh nodded, his eyes pricking and a painful feeling coursing the inside of his nose. 'Right,' said the paramedic. 'Let's have a look at him.'

Hugo handed his son over and shakily locked up Fitzherbert Place. He climbed into the back of the ambulance to find the burly man examining Theo's chest. 'Real bobby dazzler this is,' he remarked cheerfully of the flock wallpaper.

'Is it dangerous?' Hugo asked jumpily.

The burly man did not look up. 'You never know with rashes,' he said evasively. 'Or babies. It's best to be safe.' He arranged Hugo and his son under the blanket on the bed and strapped them both in. He fixed a grey plastic clip to Theo's index finger. 'To keep an eye on his pulse,' he explained. The baby stared expressionlessly at the red light on the clip's end. His uncharacteristic calmness made Hugo feel more panicky than ever.

'Right. Let's get to the hospital.' The ambulanceman knocked a signal on the screen dividing the back from the driver's section. The woman was at the wheel, Hugo realised, surprised. He'd always imagined all that high-speed, wailing-siren stuff to be the work of men.

Just as the burly man pulled the doors shut, there was a mighty banging on the other side of them. He pushed them open to reveal Alice, wide-eyed, dishevelled and panting. 'Wait for me,' she gasped, climbing in. 'Is Theo all right?' she asked Hugo, placing a chill hand on his.

'Er . . .' Hugo looked fearfully at the ambulanceman. There were no clues in the broad face. 'I'm not sure.'

'We're taking him in,' the ambulanceman said. 'It's best to check.'

'And how are you?' Alice looked in concern at Hugo. He

tried to smile, despite his trembling lip, thundering heart and looming hysterical tears.

'You're the child's mother, I take it,' the ambulanceman remarked to Alice.

'No. Just an . . . er, friend.' Alice grinned awkwardly at Hugo. He squeezed her fingers gratefully, not trusting himself to speak.

He was aware as never before of the vulnerability and complexity of the tiny body laid so lightly on his own, and of his utter helplessness in the face of Theo's illness. He could not escape the black centre of his ragged, heightened impressions; the possibility that his son might die. Hugo could see it all now: the small white coffin, the empty cot, the deserted high chair, still spattered, like the rest of the kitchen, in mashed banana from teatime. Theo's clothes still dirty in the laundry basket; his last filled nappies in the dustbin, even. He closed his eyes, clutched the baby closer and felt he was going to die himself.

Alice, he sensed, had an idea of what he was going through. Her hand remained on his while she questioned the ambulanceman about his work.

'. . . What do we think is a real waste of time? Well, the biggest drain on our resources is picking up drunks,' he was saying. 'You wouldn't believe it. People come out of the pub, fall over and ring us up.'

Hugo lay there cocooned in his nightmare. His every conscious thought concentrated on the small, silent form lying on his chest, willing Theo to fight whatever it was. As the ambulance rattled on, he imagined the flock-wallpaper rash, spreading silent but deadly beneath the white Babygro, deepening in colour, pushing up ever more hideous lumps.

With an effort, he tuned in to Alice's conversation. The sound of her voice both reassured and distracted him.

'Drunks? Really? You mean drunks call ambulances? Just because they're *drunk*?'

'You bet they do. Had one the other day, young bloke who'd had a few too many. Fell over in the road outside the pub. Called an ambulance, saying he'd hurt his leg. Nothing more than a bruise, it was. That sort of thing *really* annoys us.'

'I bet,' said Alice. 'And what about this?' She gestured at Hugo and Theo.

'This?' The ambulanceman shrugged. 'That rash might be something and nothing, sure. But it might not be, either. Babies are complicated things. They can't tell you what's wrong with them. You don't want to take the risk. When we hear from the control centre that a baby's involved, it gets priority.'

'That's very interesting.' A steely expression entered Alice's eye. 'Very interesting indeed.'

'We're here!' the ambulancewoman called from the front.

Hugo felt a jolt of mixed shock, fear and relief. The doors at the back of the ambulance were opened and he and Theo were unstrapped. Within seconds they had been hurried under the red and white A&E sign into the blaze of light that was the hospital.

Chapter 21

'Oh, thank God,' Hugo croaked, the tears welling and spilling over as he looked into Dr Watson's lovely face. 'Thank *you*.'

The paediatrician handed Theo back. The baby was now happily chewing on a biscuit and looked brighter than he had all evening. 'So there's no need to worry,' the doctor said. 'We've had a good look at him. It looks quite dramatic, I know, but it's really only a viral infection. He could have picked it up anywhere. From the floor, from putting his hands in his mouth, anything.'

'I'm so sorry,' Hugo bent his head. 'I've been wasting your time. It was just that it looked so . . . *awful*.' He blinked hard.

'Don't worry, Mr Fine.' Dr Watson tossed back her shining spill of hair. 'It was a quiet evening, as it happens. And it's better to be safe than sorry, eh?' She chucked Theo under his busy, biscuit-encrusted chin. 'He'll fight it off himself, probably pretty soon, as it looks as if this is the high point.

The spots may even have gone by tomorrow, if you're lucky . . . Oh, excuse me,' she looked down at the pager at her waist, 'I'd better go. Good night.'

And off she went in her white coat, disappearing down the brilliantly lit white corridor like, Hugo thought, those visions of heaven people have from time to time.

He kissed the top of Theo's head and looked at Alice. Her eyes, he noticed before she quickly glanced away, looked wet as well. 'I don't know how to thank you,' he said quietly. 'I don't know what I would have done.'

Alice linked her arm through his. 'Oh, shush. Come on. Let's call a minicab from reception and take Theo back to bed.' She had no intention of returning immediately to the Old Morgue. There was certain to be an inquisition from Jake and what had happened was none of his business. Moreover his behaviour about the phone call had been appalling, and had seemed even more so after what the ambulanceman had said. She was, in short, disgusted with him.

'You're coming back with me?' Hugo asked in delight.

'I want to see you both settled.' As she smiled at him, Hugo felt his knees weaken for reasons that had nothing to do with Theo.

In the kitchen at Fitzherbert Place, Alice stared at the shepherdesses painted on the cupboard doors. This had to be Amanda Hardwick's work. Overlaid, it was equally obvious, with Theo's. The effect of all that pastel and carving spattered in mashed banana was quite surreal.

'Sorry about the mess,' Hugo muttered. 'I haven't had the chance to chisel it all off yet.'

Alice smiled. 'You've had other things to worry about.'

'You could say that.' Hugo hugged the now-sleeping baby carefully and close. He beckoned her into the sitting room. 'Sit down while I put Theo to bed. Help yourself to drinks – there are some around somewhere.' He wondered where, exactly. Amanda had once kept a well-stocked cocktail tray, but he had drunk it dry long since right down to the blue Curaçao. He had a feeling there were some dusty cans of Tennents around, maybe in the cupboard under the sink.

Bugger. He really wasn't very well prepared. Probably he should have got the cab driver to stop at the off-licence. But it would hardly have looked good, being picked up from hospital with a baby only to stock up on booze at the first opportunity.

Once in the nursery, Hugo settled Theo comfortably in his cot. The baby sank into sleep with a grateful sigh, a tiny sound that flooded his father with tenderness and relief. He stood there for a moment stroking the unconscious little head. The moment Theo was tucked up in bed was always his favourite of the day, and not only because things were quiet at last. It was also to do with the gratitude and pride he felt at being able to provide his baby with a safe, warm haven. Tonight, after the hideous evening they had suffered, it felt more special than ever. He tiptoed away feeling simultaneously as if he would burst with love, and tireder than ever before in his life.

By the door, Hugo stumbled over something big and soft. It was, he realised, the hideous, battery-operated barking dog that was one of Amanda's many ludicrous presents.

He made his way back down to the sitting room and Alice. She sat there, smiling and patient, on the edge of the sofa. She looked tired, but still lovely. Lovelier, he thought, because the reasons she looked tired were lovely in themselves.

'Right,' Hugo grinned, rubbing his hands together. 'Drink. Oh, and supper. You must be starving.' His own stomach was tying itself in knots of hunger.

'Can I help?' Alice bounced up.

'No, really. Leave it to me. You've done enough helping for one night.'

Hugo wasn't just being polite. He was playing for time. He did not want Alice, who he wanted so desperately to impress, to see he had no idea what he was going to cook. That he couldn't cook. That he had nothing to cook with. Who was he kidding even trying? His eye caught the well-worn menu of the Taj Mahal stuck behind the telephone. Should he ring for a takeaway? All those cartons and paper bags with the grease showing through, though. Not very sexy.

He rummaged in the cupboards. Ah, *there* were the cans of Tennents. Three left. He hoped, rather against hope, that she liked lager. There was nothing else apart from a musty brace of herbal teabags left by Amanda.

Hugo detached one of the cans, rubbed the top against his trousers to remove the dust and pulled the ring off as discreetly as he could. Carefully, he poured it into a cut-crystal gin and tonic glass and took it to Alice.

'Thanks very much.' Alice sipped it gingerly. Lager. Her least favourite drink in the world. Apart from that stuff made of grass, which Jake had brought back once and which was supposed to have amazing cleansing properties. She'd thought at the time that she could have drunk Cif and got the same result less disgustingly.

Hugo fled back into the kitchen. After a frantic search he unearthed a half-finished packet of dried penne. A start. All he needed now was sauce.

There was none, of course. A tin of sardines, a tin of chickpeas and a packet of bayleaves was all Hugo could find. In the cupboard nearest the cooker were a couple of jars of Theo's baby food. The outlook was bleak.

Doubtless there was some amazing and delicious recipe involving bayleaves, chickpeas and sardines, but he was damned if he knew what it was. Whereas – his eyes slid to the baby food jars – were there not distinct possibilities here?

No. He couldn't possibly. On the other hand . . .

Hugo examined one of the jars. Organic tomato and mozzarella flavour pasta. Well, what could be more suitable? Mix it in with the penne, and Alice would never know. He rattled around for a couple of pans, emptied the baby food into one, stuck the pasta water on to boil in the other and started to look for some plates. For the first time that evening he began to whistle.

'Supper!' he called, not long afterwards. Bringing the plates through to the sitting room, he beamed.

'That was quick,' Alice remarked, impressed, as she took the plate he handed her.

'Just a little something I rustled up,' Hugo smirked modestly.

Alice, sampling the pasta, detected a strange taste, thick, blunt, bland. She was, however, too polite to comment.

They had their feet companionably up on the sitting-room coffee table. It would, Hugo realised, be the ideal opportunity to ask Alice how things were with Jake. That he had answered the phone had not been a good sign, and the mystery of what he was still doing in her cottage – in her life at all – was a worry. Yet he shied away from the subject. He had suffered enough trauma for one evening and he feared the answer.

His eye caught a number of crumby plates stacked haphazardly beneath the coffee table. Realising how grotty they looked, he sat up and started to pull them out. 'Sorry,' he grinned awkwardly. 'It's a bit of a bachelor household here these days. Me and Theo. He doesn't mind mess. In fact, he makes most of it.'

'Is that Theo I can hear?' Her ears, ever-attuned to infant cries of distress, had picked something up on the floor above.

Hugo, midway to the kitchen with his plates, stopped and dumped them abruptly on the floor. He flew up the stairs two at a time. Alice heard him enter the nursery and murmur something reassuring to Theo, who instantly stopped crying.

She decided to make herself useful until he came down.

Picking up the heap of plates from the carpet, she carried them into the kitchen where, on the counter next to the cooker, she saw the empty jar of baby food with the red-stained pan beside it. She stared in disbelief. Could it be possible that he'd mixed it with . . .

Just then, an ear-splitting series of barks exploded somewhere above her. Theo screamed in terror. There was banging, crashing and what sounded like a struggle. It sounded as if the biggest, loudest, most savage dog in the world was loose in Theo's nursery.

The plates slid out of Alice's arms and into the sink with a smash. She shot up the stairs. On the top landing Hugo was emerging from the baby's room. He seemed remarkably free of bloodstains. Under his arm he carried what looked like a large soft toy.

'What happened?' she hissed as he closed the nursery door behind him.

Hugo shook the toy. 'This bloody dog Amanda sent. Fell over it earlier and must have switched the sodding thing back on somehow. It goes ape – or rather dog – if you come within a few inches of it.'

Alice looked at the dog. Its ears hung askew and its expression was comically doleful. It looked as if it had got the worst of the fight. Then she looked at Hugo. She thought of the tell-tale pan and empty jar in the kitchen.

Alice felt a pulling at the corners of her mouth. The pulling got harder. She began to giggle and shake. Hugo, after an initial stare of surprise, started to grin as well.

Trying not to squeal with laughter, Alice pressed her hand tightly to her mouth and went swiftly back downstairs. Hugo followed closely. Very closely. In the darkness at the bottom, he turned her towards him and gently pulled her face to his.

He kissed her for a long time. As he pulled her body closer, she yielded eagerly, sighing and twisting in pleasure as his tongue probed deeper and his exploring fingers edged up her shirt.

He pressed her backwards and downwards. On the carpet, he explored her, slowly, luxuriously, deliciously.

'Oh Alice,' Hugo groaned. He felt all the tension and misery, not only of this evening, but all the weeks and months before, flowing out of him. As his hand slipped beneath the waistband of her trousers, he felt her stiffen in resistance, then relax. Her stomach, he saw, pressing his lips to it, was smooth and taut, the warm skin stretched over her hipbones like a teenager's. Only a neat scar, faded now, hinted that a child had once grown here.

Alice, trembling with pleasure, stretched her arms above her head as he pushed downwards, to the white broderie anglaise knickers he had somehow suspected she would wear . . .

'*Woof!* Woof! Woof! *Woof!*'

His eyes snapped open.

'Bugger.' He struggled on to his elbow 'Bloody dog must have switched itself on again.' He looked at her in despair. Her eyes were creased with laughter. What a clown she must think him.

The toy was, he knew, probably broken. He had given it a good kicking earlier, after all. 'Woof! Woof!' There it went again. And, fuguing with it now, the high, plaintive sound of a woken-up Theo.

Alice scrambled to her feet and pulled her jeans up her long, pale legs. She began buttoning her shirt. She tucked a piece of hair behind an ear and gave him an awkward smile. 'I'd better be going.'

'Sure,' Hugo grimaced, cursing the dog.

'Have you got a minicab number?'

'Of course. Hang on.' Miserably, he went into the kitchen. There were, he knew, some taxi firms on the Taj Mahal menu.

'I'll call it while you sort out Theo and the, erm, dog,' Alice suggested, coming in behind him. Panicked, Hugo lunged for the counter beside the cooker to conceal the evidence of the baby food jar.

She put a hand on his arm. 'Don't worry. I've already seen it. It doesn't matter.'

Wordless, cringing, he passed her the menu and dashed upstairs to settle his son.

'Bye, then,' Alice waved from the cab as he shut her in. 'Thanks for supper.'

He looked at her in anguish. Supper! After all she'd done for him tonight, one of the lowest evenings of his life, didn't she deserve better than a can of warm lager and some ancient pasta mixed with baby food?

'Can I see you again?' he asked. 'I'd love to take you out to dinner – you know – properly. To thank you.'

'There's no need. Honestly.'

'But I want to,' Hugo insisted. 'Really, I do. What about next weekend?'

She gave him her gut-twisting, slow burn of a smile. 'That would be lovely. But you know, it really wasn't a problem, helping you. I was just glad I could. And if there's anything else, just call me.'

He waved until the tail lights of the taxi had vanished round the corner. Then he went back inside, seized the dog and marched it out to the dustbin at the back. 'That's you finished,' he snarled at it, clanging the lid down on top. The dog, however, had other ideas. Throughout the night, Hugo was woken up intermittently by the sound of wild barking with an additional metallic echo. Thank God, he thought, as he settled back to sleep each time, it was the day for the dustmen tomorrow.

Chapter 22

Hugo drove to work next day with a light heart. Theo's spots had miraculously disappeared, just as Dr Watson said they might. Almost more miraculously, Chicklets had accepted him back without a murmur.

The morning was clear and sunny, lending sparkle to the grass and highlighting the wealth of detail on the buildings. Hugo admired elegantly spare railings, gleaming brassware and shining glass in many-paned windows. The stone glittered with a thousand unnameable minerals. Unnameable by him, at least.

Hugo admired all this partly to stop himself thinking about Alice as he drove. Remembering his mouth round her nipple, he had already hit the kerb twice. And he feared the memory of her broderie anglaise knickers in heavy commuter traffic. For the sake of his car if nothing else, the dog's intervention had been a godsend.

'Don't know what you're so bloody pleased about,' snapped Neil as Hugo arrived, whistling, at Dunn and Dustard. Hugo looked in surprise at his boss's long face.

'What's up?' he asked.

'*What's up?*' Neil's piggy eyes flashed. 'What the hell happened at Leather?' he raged.

Hugo's head, which had been full of the freshness of Alice, now flooded with the depravity of Laura, stark naked and legs splayed in that suffocatingly perfumed room. He felt a sickening jolt. The entire episode had slipped his mind. An entire lifetime seemed to have passed between then and now.

'You might well look like that,' Neil barked. 'You know we've lost it, obviously.'

'Lost what?'

'Leather. The owner rang after you'd gone, saying that everything she'd heard about you was obviously wrong and that you were the most unprofessional agent she had ever met.'

Hugo felt the blood drain from his face.

'She's taking the house off our books,' Neil fumed. 'She'll be giving it straight to one of our rivals, obviously.'

Hugo remembered Laura bawling after him down the stairs: 'There's nothing fucking wrong with me. You'll be sorry you said that.' So this was how she was making him sorry. By threatening his job.

He took a deep breath. 'Look, Neil. Nothing's lost. That woman's got no intention of selling that house. She's bullshitting.'

'I just know.' Hugo was aware how weak this sounded. 'Trust me,' he added.

Neil gave Hugo a level look. Then he exploded. 'Trust *you*?' he thundered, head and neck swelling like a bullfrog's. 'You must be fucking joking, Fine. You came here full of yourself as some shit-hot London estate agent and, frankly, shit is what you've been. Everything you've touched lately has turned to it. We were going to cream off the commission from those warehouse buildings until you turned up with bags on your shoes. That barn conversion sale was a dead cert until you got involved. Then there was that dog business. And as for this bloody house – the client had even asked for you *by name*. What more of a head start could you hope for? But you arsed it up. You arsed them all up, didn't you, Fine?' Neil's breath was coming in short, hot, little bursts. 'I've had enough. Put one more foot wrong and you're out.'

Determinedly not meeting Shuna's triumphant eye, Hugo returned to his desk. Tempted though he was to tell Neil where to stick his crummy job, he resisted. Where else would he find something he was qualified to do and that allowed him to look after his son each afternoon? A large part of working parenthood, Hugo had found, was about keeping your mouth shut and your head down. And your mind on matters of expediency rather than bruised ego.

His mobile rang. Raising the instrument to his earlobe, he realised his mistake in assuming the morning could not go further downwards. It was Amanda.

'I had a missed call from you,' she accused.

'Yes. I was trying to get you last night.' He spoke in a low voice, aware of Shuna's pearl-studded ears twitching a mere couple of desks away.

'I was at a perfume launch,' Amanda said breezily. 'Nothing important, was it?'

He was about to tell her about the rash and the hospital and how terrified he had been. But Shuna's ever-present ear made him pause. And was there any need to go into detail? Everything had turned out well in the end.

'Important? Er, no. Not really.' He'd tell her if she probed. If she asked one further question that showed real concern, or that she possessed even an inkling of that maternal telepathy that alerted mothers to the fact their child was in danger.

But Amanda did not probe. She had, it turned out, other reasons for ringing. 'Now listen,' she ordered Hugo crisply. 'I need to arrange a shoot with Theo.'

'A shoot? You mean you want to take pictures of him?'

'What do you think I mean? The glorious bloody Twelfth.'

'But what are the pictures for?'

'A magazine piece,' Amanda snapped. 'Now, what's his schedule? When is he free?'

'He doesn't have a schedule. He goes to nursery, he comes back at lunchtime, I feed him, play with him, he has his tea, he plays some more and then it's bathtime—'

'Spare me the fucking details,' Amanda yelled. 'So basically he's around afternoons, yeah?'

'That's right. But what is this piece about, anyway?' Hugo

had lowered his voice again, aware that Shuna, under cover of straightening *Country Life*s on a nearby coffee table, was listening hard.

'It's about me and Theo.'

'*What* about you and Theo?'

'About my life as a working mother. How I juggle career and domestic responsibilities. Keep working while holding a home life together.'

'You're joking,' burst out Hugo.

'I most certainly am not. It's a well-known modern phenomenon. And it's *very* stressful.'

'But you *don't* juggle work and domestic responsibilities,' Hugo tried not to notice Shuna still shuffling about the coffee table.

'Yes I do. It's going to say so in the article: "Amanda Hardwick: How I Combine Career with Childcare". It's about how I've overcome the challenges of child-raising to wave a flag for the back-to-work mum.'

Skidding to the front of Hugo's mind came the challenges of child-raising he had seen at Chicklets. Sue, green with nausea but determined to make it into the office. Barbara the high-powered barrister, crying against the wall of the corridor. He himself rushing from nursery to work, increasingly fearful of putting a foot wrong in either. What did Amanda know about any of this?

And there was more. He thought of himself and Theo in the back of the ambulance, Theo with his rash, he in a state of hysterical panic. What did Amanda know about that, either? Or the more workaday scenarios – Theo yelling with bored fury in the front of a supermarket trolley, for instance. No doubt Amanda's idea of shopping with a baby was drifting round Harvey Nicks with a leopardskin papoose, personal assistant at her heels.

'I'm going to be a pin-up for working mothers,' Amanda announced smugly. 'Which is why this magazine wants to do a piece about me and Theo. About my exhausting but rewarding life as a glossy magazine editor and busy mum.'

'But you don't have a life as a busy mum. You left all that to me.'

'Don't start attacking me over my job!' Amanda shrieked. 'Have you any idea how it feels to leave your baby behind for long periods simply in order to be able to *work*?'

'What are you talking about?' Hugo clenched the phone, his knuckles white with anger. Her humbug was breathtaking. She had made it clear from the outset that she was returning to her career for her own satisfaction.

'You see! Yours is the typical male reaction!' Amanda shouted triumphantly. 'Sexist *pig*!'

By the time Hugo had recovered from this, Amanda was in full flow again.

'It's the classic dilemma of any working mother,' she was declaring. 'Frankly, you can't win. Either you're seen as a saddo stuck at home changing nappies or a ruthless careerist hellbent on satisfying your own selfish ambition.'

'I agree,' said Hugo.

'There you are!' Amanda exulted. 'You agree!'

'I agree that that's the classic dilemma of the working mother,' Hugo told her. 'But I don't agree that it's yours.'

'Typical,' Amanda snorted furiously.

'Eh?'

'This was just what I was telling this magazine editor the other day over lunch at Gary Rhodes's. Great place, by the way.'

'*Is* it?' Hugo thought crossly of his own lunches, standing up eating Weetabix or spaghetti hoops out of saucepans while listening unwillingly to *The Archers*.

'Mm. Fab champagne list and stunning views of the Gherkin. Anyway, we decided that profiling me as a working mother was more than just interesting, it was *important*. An opportunity to highlight the sacrifices that working women have to make. The compromises that have to be struck. The painful decisions that are necessary before both home and office can be juggled in harmony, blah blah blah – you get the picture. I'll be back in the next few days. I'll let you know.'

'You're coming *back*?' Hugo gasped. He hadn't realised the shoot would involve Amanda actually *with* her son.

'Well, how the hell else are they going to photograph us together?'

Hugo felt sick. He didn't want Amanda to come home. Not in the slightest. He had grown used to her absence. *Un*accustomed to her face. He and Theo were doing just fine without her. The childcare creases were being ironed out and, occasionally, he even felt he knew what he was doing. He enjoyed the sensation that he and the baby were a unit. The boys' club. Father and son.

'Gotta go,' Amanda said briskly. 'I'm due in a meeting about sea urchins' gonads.'

'What?'

'Crucial ingredient in upscale body cream. Christ, Hugo. Don't you know *anything*?'

Ending the call, Hugo found himself looking, not into Shuna's sneery features, but Neil's cross red ones. He had no idea how long his boss had been standing there.

'Now look, Fine,' he blustered. 'I'm giving you one last chance here. I need you to do a show-round this afternoon for a flat in a new development called Pride and Prejudice Palisades.'

'Right!' Shaking Amanda forcibly from his thoughts, Hugo did his best to look eager and on the ball.

Neil regarded him wearily. 'It's a pain in the arse because I was going to do it myself but something else pretty important has come up and I'm going to be out of the office a few days, probably for the rest of the week. Anyway, even you can't fuck this up. It's simple. The people interested in looking at it have practically signed already. All you have to do is turn up at half past two and open the door for them.'

Half past two. Neil had clearly forgotten that he didn't work afternoons. Dare he remind him, given the earlier scenes? Hugo thought rapidly. Far better to say yes and ring Chicklets in the hope they could hold Theo for a bit longer. Or, better still, he thought, relief swirling his body, he could ring Alice. Hadn't she said he could call her if he needed her?

* * *

Alice was sitting reading to Rosa. She was not, however, concentrating on *Peter Rabbit's Touch and Feel Book*. Her mind was on Hugo and the touching and feeling he had been doing.

She had been unable to think about anything else all morning. Hugo's face – handsome, sensitive, tired – had swum before her eyes. Her fingers, turning the pages for Rosa, tingled with the memory of tracing his lips and touching his hair.

'Look at Mrs Tittlemouse cleaning up those sticky foot-prints,' Alice murmured into the top of Rosa's honey-coloured head.

Her mind, however, was on Hugo's aftershave with its pepper-lemon tang. The delicious scent had forced comparison with what Jake smelt like these days.

The bathing issue, which her mother had found problematic all those months ago, had recently got rather more so. Jake now tended to skip, not just a day between baths like herself, but entire weeks, which meant he could be a bit high. His hair, formerly so lustrous, now looked greasy more often than not. She had also noticed, now that soap no longer controlled it, that he had a tendency to spottiness. None of this particularly assisted attempts at reconciliation, let alone sex.

Whenever, now, he attempted to hold her his incipient beard scratched her face and her nostrils filled with warm, welling unwashedness.

'Here's Tom Kitten's mother washing his face with a lovely

soft cloth . . .' If only Tom Kitten's mother could wash Rosa's father, Alice thought.

'Ooh, darling, that's the phone. I'll just get it.' Carefully, Alice placed her daughter on the floor and turned to the page where Mrs Tiggywinkle was hanging out a sheepskin rug on her line. As Rosa began to pluck curiously at the fluffy fabric, Alice crossed the room and raised the receiver. Her every vein coursed with hope that it was Hugo.

It was.

'Alice. Thank God you're there. Do you think, possibly, that you might look after Theo . . .'

'Of course,' she said smiling, when he had finished.

Alice was not smiling now. Where the hell *was* Hugo? The playground was clearing. As the sun slowly slid down the early spring sky, the last of the mothers packed their toddlers into buggies. Alice watched from the bench as they wheeled them off towards the streetlights coming on at the far side of the park.

He'd meet her and pick up Theo at three-thirty, he had said. At the very latest. And what was it now? She looked at her watch. Coming up to half past *five*.

The sky had turned from watery pale blue to a bruised deep grey. The trunks of the trees darkened and the lights in the loos went on. Two brooms were crossed in the entrance; the ancient and universally recognised symbol, Alice thought, of the toilet cleaner going about his duties.

Up until now, it had been quite a fun afternoon. Theo and

Rosa seemed to hit it off well, in that solemn, absorbed way that babies did. Theo, Alice saw, had survived his early parental challenges to become a smiley, happy, adorably cheeky child. And it was wonderful to see Rosa, who rarely encountered other children, interacting so well with a peer. As she watched them, Alice thought briefly and wistfully about Rosa having a brother. Then she put the thought away. Given her age and, particularly, circumstances, it was never going to happen.

The babies' good humour was now starting to dissipate. On Alice's knee as they sat on the bench, Rosa was wailing, waving her pink neon teddy crossly. Theo, in Rosa's pushchair, was making irritable, pre-wail noises. Alice looked at her watch again and frowned. It was very unlike Hugo to let her down like this. No doubt there was a reasonable explanation, but she was fast losing the ability to imagine what it could be.

Alice lugged them over to the swings yet again. But even Theo, whose appetite for whooshing through the air in the little cages seemed boundless, had now had enough. His bottom lip was sticking out and his formerly merry dark eyes looked hostile.

Rosa's wails rose sharply in timbre as the pink neon teddy fell from her grasp and on to the ground beneath the bench. Hurriedly, Alice bent and picked it up.

Only recently had she liberated from her knicker drawer the handful of toys, including this bear, which was all she had been able to save from the haul Rosa was sent at birth. The rest had been long ago donated to homeless shelters by Jake. Rosa, when presented with it, had fallen on the teddy with a cry of delight and pressed it to her bosom as if it were a long-lost friend. Which, Alice supposed, it was.

She was starting, now, to feel rather desperate. She had peered hard at every looming, then passing figure, but none of them had been Hugo. Soon she would have to leave. A vulnerable woman on her own with two even more vulnerable children had no business being out with them at night. And not a warm night, either.

Settling Rosa in her preferred position facing outward in her baby sling, and tucking Theo snugly into the pushchair, Alice decided to do one last lap of the park.

As she trundled the buggy along the paths she gazed miserably at the asphalt. Her annoyance at Hugo's non-appearance was spiked with disappointment. It wasn't just that she wanted to see him to relieve her of Theo, so she could take Rosa home for her tea. She wanted to see him. *Him.*

What had started as pity, then curiosity, then amusement at his ineptitude at fatherhood, had become serious attraction. Last night, after Theo's rash scare, had crystallised what she had not wanted to admit before; the pull she felt towards him whenever she saw him. Hugo was charming, and interested, and funny. His was a dashing, dark-haired handsomeness that even broken nights, food-flinging babies and an obvious inability to iron barely dented; indeed, added a stomach-flipping aspect of vulnerability. She felt a rush of pleasure at the thought of him.

And especially at the thought of him with Theo. Jake, for all his perfect-parent persona, had never been this at ease with Rosa.

Hugo may have needed help nappy-changing, but he needed no guidance where it really mattered. Theo was quite obviously the centre of his life. While the centre of Jake's life was – what? Rubbish, basically, thought Alice. He had told her he would be unavailable to help put Rosa to bed this week as he was chaining himself to wheelie bins with Joss and Jessamy in order to urge the council to recycle ninety-nine per cent of all household waste. Was it, Alice wondered, possible to recycle that much? Wasn't some waste – well – just waste?

In the centre of the park a low bridge crossed a little river. Alice paused on it, leaning over so Rosa could see the rushing water. Rosa laughed and waved her teddy happily. She was fascinated by water, particularly that she saw coming out of the bathtaps. On the rare occasions that this happened.

Theo liked water too, judging from his interested mooing noises. She stroked his head affectionately. He really was a sweet boy. Watching him chuckling as he stared at the water, so happy, so ready to be amused, she felt a stir of amazed indignation on the child's behalf. How could anyone, even Amanda Hardwick, leave this baby behind?

What sort of father too?

Her faith that Hugo would come had now almost completely faded. What on earth was he thinking of, abandoning her – and Theo – here? Had she misread him utterly? Only a moment or so ago she had thought herself practically in love with him. But was he really no better than his selfish, irresponsible wife?

Chapter 23

'Hall-oooo!' called Hugo into the darkness. His voice rolled round in a booming echo. 'Hallo! Anybody up there? Oh, sod it. *Sod it.*'

Yet again, he had thought he'd heard a movement. But yet again his ears were playing tricks on him. *Bugger.* What the hell could he do?

Precisely nothing until a resident of Pride and Prejudice Palisades came down to the underground car park in which he had so cretinously locked himself. But how was he supposed to have known that the bloody car park door, which opened simply enough with a handle from the outside, required a bloody *key* to get back out again? A key, more to the point, that he did not have.

Hugo sat on the chilly concrete steps, felt the clammy cold seeping through his pinstripe trousers and brooded on the high price he was paying for professional diligence. He'd got here before the clients to make sure the flat looked presentable. It had. And then, in a moment of over-cautious madness his old London self would have hooted with laughter at, he had decided to check the underground car park. Pick up any unsightly sweet wrappers just to be on the safe side. But then had come the clunk behind him and the realisation he was a prisoner. The realisation that his mobile didn't work underground swiftly followed. Both Alice – in the park with the children – and the office were unobtainable.

He groaned, stood up stiffly and paced the garage floor again. The unrelieved darkness was horrible. His knuckles stung and bled from banging on the stairwell door. The constant dripping from the roof was grating on his nerves. He could, Hugo thought fearfully, die down here. He could be found weeks from now, the flesh stripped from his bones by the rats he was increasingly certain he could hear.

The clients, he was glumly aware, would have been and gone hours ago. No doubt presuming the estate agent hadn't bothered to turn up to meet them. Neil, when he found out, would go spare. He would also, Hugo knew, fire him. While he had descended into the car park an employed man, he was unlikely to exit it as one.

Still. Hadn't Neil said he was away for the rest of the week? He couldn't fire him until Monday, at any rate. And there was plenty to look forward to before then. This weekend's dinner with Alice, for instance.

He thought of her anxiously. She must have been standing

by the swings for hours now. Christ only knew where she imagined he was.

Alice, in the park, was still peering into the darkening, Hugo-less distance, still wrestling with her reluctance to believe he was not coming.

She was angry. She had, she knew, better start pulling up the drawbridges. She'd given Hugo an inch – although not quite the inch he wanted, thanks to that toy dog. And, typical of his sex, he had taken a mile. Now he was taking her for granted.

In which case, he had a shock coming. She was neither enslaved nor obliged to him. That smart dinner he had promised was off, for a start. As she planned to tell him, if he ever turned up.

At the sudden sound of running footsteps, she crouched protectively over the children. She watched in alarm as the gangling figure stumbled towards her out of the dusk.

'Alice!'

'Hugo. Where the hell . . . ?' Angrily, she shook off the arms trying to embrace her. Theo, recognising his father, wailed for attention. Hugo immediately dropped to his knees by the pushchair, kissing his son and squeezing his chill little hands. He looked exhaustedly up at Alice. 'I got stuck,' he explained lamely.

'Stuck?' Alice exclaimed. 'For over three hours?'

Hugo had expected her to be cross, but this level of white-hot fury was a shock. He had genuine and dramatic reasons for his absence, albeit reasons he hesitated to tell her about, lest she thought him as much of an idiot as his eventual rescuer, an elderly gentleman who had come down in search of a battered Reliant Robin, evidently had.

His silence annoyed Alice even more. 'You're not even going to give me an explanation?' she stormed. 'Oh, what the hell does it matter? Here's your son, anyway. Now you've finally deigned to turn up, I'm taking Rosa home.'

'Alice, please,' Hugo stammered. 'I'm sorry. Really, I am. You see—'

But Alice had turned away.

'I'll ring you,' Hugo ventured.

'Don't bother.'

He was aghast. 'Not ring . . . but *Alice*! I'm sorry. Look, it's ridiculous and I didn't want to tell you but I got locked in an underground car park for half the afternoon.'

'Is that right?' Alice said disbelievingly, her stare apparently conveying the doubt that even he could be that stupid. 'Well, I'm sorry about that. But I'm going now. Goodbye.'

'But I'll see you on Saturday,' Hugo faltered. 'For dinner, remember?'

'Actually, I won't be able to make it.'

'Won't . . . ?' Hugo searched wildly for the words with which to plead that she saw reason. It wasn't as if what had happened had been his fault. Not entirely. 'But I've booked Allingham House,' he wailed.

Alice drew a sharp breath. Allingham House. She'd heard of it, of course. Everyone in Bath had. A Jacobean stately home turned wildly expensive hotel in the rolling country outside the city, it was the rural offshoot of a fashionable London club and supposedly the haunt of weekending celebrities. It had a racy, decadent reputation, a cutting-edge spa with up-to-the-minute pampering treatments and horizon pools indoors and out. Jake would never in a million years have taken her there. Alice hesitated, sorely tempted. After so long without the luxuries she had once taken for granted, the thought of a spa was almost unbearably seductive. She'd been to one once a week in New York. Nonetheless . . .

'I won't be able to make it,' she repeated.

Before Hugo could say anything more, something small and pink flew through the air and fell with a plop in the water. It was accompanied by a bloodcurdling shriek from Rosa.

'Shit,' muttered Alice.

'What's the matter?' Hugo peered into the river. 'What is it? Did she drop something?'

'Her teddy,' said Alice agitatedly. 'She absolutely loves that teddy. It's her favourite.'

Hugo stared down into the water just below the bridge. It was flowing fast and the small, bright teddy, which had initially fallen into a clump of waterlogged twigs, was already working itself free. It would be out and away in seconds. As Rosa shrieked hysterically and Alice tried in vain to comfort her, he realised he had very little choice. Any hopes he had of restoring himself in Alice's affections, not to mention quieting Rosa and the now-wiffling Theo, all rested on one thing. Rescuing that bear.

Hugo thought fast. His car was parked on the road outside the park gates; should he leap into it and race the toy downstream to the next bridge in the hope of being in time to fish it out? But, given the speed of the current, the chances of the bear getting there first were high, as, indeed, were those of it sinking to a watery grave long before. It was crucial he kept the animal in his sights.

The bear now swirled free of the twigs and, face up, began to sweep downstream at what seemed to Hugo an impossible speed. There was, he realised, only one thing for it. He dragged off his jacket and tie.

'Here,' he said, shoving the bundle of cloth at Alice. 'Hang on to this for a minute.'

He leapt over the small, white-painted paling that edged the path and plunged across the grass beside the river. It was difficult to see in the fading light but in the water just ahead of him, a small smudge of pink confirmed he was keeping pace with the teddy. As the river prepared to round a bend, Hugo's hopes began to rise that the toy might be driven into the bank by the force. Then he came violently into contact with something hard and spiky.

'Fuck!' cursed Hugo, dancing with pain as he realised he had run legs-first into a three-strand barbed-wire fence separating the park from a neighbouring field. But there was no time to feel sorry for himself, or even assess the damage. A bear's life was at stake, a child's happiness, and, almost as important, a relationship he wanted to continue. What were a few scratches compared with that?

Hugo took a few paces back, then shot forward and vaulted the barbed-wire fence. He landed in a stony clump and twisted his ankle, but the sickening pain of this was nothing beside the agony of no longer being able to see the pink blob in the river. He struggled through the thicket and out the other side to glimpse, to his joy and relief, the teddy bear some distance in front of him, swimming gamely on in what, at this point, was much deeper water.

A less joyful sight altogether was the wall and bridge now looming in front of him. He had reached the edge of the field and was now coming into the town. He could hear traffic on the other side of the wall. By the time he'd battled across what sounded like a busy road, Teddy would be long gone.

Unhesitating before the inevitable, Hugo raced to the edge of the riverbank and leapt in. He yelled aloud with the pain and cold of contact. The shock was almost heart-stopping and the water more freezing than he ever imagined. The current, too, was far more powerful than it looked.

Alice, watching anxiously from downstream, let out her own yell of horror as she saw the distant, running figure of Hugo suddenly change direction and plunge into the water. She felt suddenly sick. She had driven him to this. He had only done it to make amends. To show he was sorry for being late. And that he cared.

Oh, she hadn't meant to be horrible. Really, she hadn't meant it. She'd been tired and cross, that was all. And about what? What did an hour or so's waiting in a park matter compared to a man's life? She had not misjudged him, not remotely; that much was obvious now. Hugo's unhesitating unselfishness in racing after the bear had single-handedly restored all her faith.

As Hugo swirled out of sight under the bridge, his head a dark blob against the foaming grey water, Alice clenched her hands together in agony.

'Hugo!' she bawled. 'Just get out. The teddy doesn't matter. Get out of the river!'

But Hugo did not hear. He could hear nothing but the rush of water. He was swirling round in the centre of the stream, buffeted by the currents and bound unpleasantly about by slimy lengths of weed. The river might be narrow, but it was deeper and stronger than it looked.

Teddy was still ahead of him, though out of arm's reach. Around him, Hugo felt the powerful muscle of water increase its grip and speed. He realised, alarmed, that the anchoring jumble of rocks on the bottom was now far below the reach of his feet. Worse, he and the bear were whirling towards a boiling white mass of water. A weir, it looked like.

The chill water slapped over his ears and sloshed, dingy-tasting, into his mouth. Bowling helplessly along, Hugo looked despairingly up at the darkening sky and wondered whether his life might be worth slightly more than a small ball of neon nylon costing probably less than five pounds.

The weir approached. Panicking now, Hugo felt, beneath his legs, a tremendous energy forcing him forward upon which his frantic kicks made no impression. Twigs swirled giddily past. The teddy had vanished, and now the current had disgorged a contact lens, he could barely see anything but spray and water. Or hear anything apart from splashing and his own terrified, painful gulps.

He no longer cared about the teddy. All that mattered now was saving himself. For Theo's sake, if no one else's. He couldn't leave him alone in the world, or with Amanda, which amounted to much the same thing. The image of his son burning in his head, Hugo tried, with one last, enormous, heart-bursting effort, to thrash towards the riverbank.

He felt his foot hit, and then slip off the muddy flanks of safety. One second later he was flailing wildly in terror. The second after that, it was all over.

Something sharp was sticking in his face. Something even sharper was digging into his back and between his legs. Hugo realised, in incredulous relief, that he was impaled on a large tree branch trailing in the river. A mere few feet further on, the water tumbled over into the deadly boiling pot of the weir. The god of parenting had intervened for him.

Or perhaps the god of teddies. Because now Hugo saw that it wasn't only his life the tree had saved. Crammed soggily between some twigs nearby, was something small and bearlike. And very bright pink.

Shortly afterwards Hugo found himself seized bodily, heaved upwards and spreadeagled on the ground. He blinked up at the group of people – passers-by from the bridge, presumably – who had dragged him from the river on to the bank.

'You all right?' one of them asked him, looking quizzically at the teddy bear Hugo held fast in his hand. Hugo moved his lips to speak and found he couldn't. Instead, he registered in wonder the wide sky above, the chill earth beneath his head and the fact that he was breathing and alive.

One of his legs, he now realised, was burning with pain. He remembered, as if from years ago, the barbed wire fence.

'I've called an ambulance,' someone else said. 'It'll be here in a minute. Your leg's bleeding quite badly. Best if you go and get checked out.'

'Hugo!' Alice's face loomed, startlingly white, out of the darkening blue above him. 'I thought you'd . . .' Her breath came short and painful. Pounding across rough ground with one heavy baby in a buggy and another the same size bouncing around her neck had been a physical challenge of the most strenuous nature. Not that she had cared.

Hugo weakly raised the hand from which mud-stained, soggy Teddy dripped dejectedly on to the ground. Rosa gave a crow of delight.

The crowd started to melt away.

Alice bent low over Hugo and kissed him. 'I'm sorry,' she murmured. 'Forget everything I said. Apart from this. I love you.'

'Does that mean,' Hugo muttered, 'that dinner's still on?'

He could not make out her answer. Alice's broad smile, the whole of her face in fact, was swirling like the water in whose pitiless, deadly depths he had so recently been immersed. And then, as they say, everything went black.

Chapter 24

In the bar of Allingham House, Hugo felt swamped by weary familiarity. He felt there was something about the place that seemed to be trying too hard. From the trance music thumping in the foyer to the expectation-defying sports facilities – *red* baize snooker table, *blue* tennis courts – it reminded him of London hipness at its most self-conscious and strained. It also, he thought, eyeing the blue strobe lights sweeping the ornate plaster ceiling and the jellybean machines in a row on the wall, reminded him most uncomfortably of his wedding. There had been jellybean machines there too, at the fashionable Soho club, all of which had been emptied and the contents hurled at him and Amanda.

His eye rolled without interest over the women in caramel leather coats and with thick blonde highlights, or else strutting round in tight black trousers with their bums sticking out. Women like this would have interested him once. But not now.

He rubbed a hand over his tired face and knew it looked very different from those of the other men present. They were all of a certain age – his – and had a certain look to go with it: well-moisturised skins, done teeth and short, brushed-up hair of a determined darkness. Had he stayed in London, Hugo supposed, he'd probably be looking like that himself.

The music in the bar – a non-specific drum 'n' bass – was deafeningly loud. To reassure the clientele they weren't that old, perhaps. Or that, even if they were, they were hip.

In the intervals between tracks, Hugo could hear someone in the foyer carrying on a loud conversation in his mobile whilst simultaneously hassling the reception desk about e-mails. He cringed slightly, thinking he'd probably been guilty of such behaviour himself once. Now it struck him only as ridiculously self-important and rude.

Alice was not yet here. At his suggestion, she had arrived earlier in the afternoon and gone straight to the hotel spa.

'But isn't that a bit extravagant?' she had worried. 'Won't you have to book a room so I can do that?'

'Yes. But it doesn't matter.' Hugo had waved a breezy hand. 'You deserve it.'

'Deserve it? I almost got you killed rescuing a bloody teddy bear.'

'Least I could do. You came with me to the hospital when Theo was ill. You showed me how to put on nappies . . .'

'Oh, please. That was nothing.' Alice waggled her hands, embarrassed. 'But – this room thing. It'll cost a fortune.'

'I don't care.' Hugo genuinely didn't. The fact he couldn't afford it couldn't have bothered him less. Since his near-miss brush with death, he had resolved to live more in the moment. What was a few hundred quid if it brought joy to the woman he loved? Besides, having a room might come in handy for all sorts of things. You never know.

He wondered what excuse Alice had given Jake for her absence. The nature of their cohabitation remained vague. From the little he could gather from Alice, they seemed to have settled into an uneasy mutual living and shared childcare arrangement. During dinner, Hugo hoped, there would be an opportunity to raise the thorny question of their spouses and how to handle them.

For him, it had been relatively easy to oganise the evening. Certain of the Chicklets staff offered a babysitting service and it had been a simple matter to sign one of them up for tonight. Rather more effort had gone into cleaning up Fitzherbert Place to a level passing muster in the eyes of a health-conscious nursery nurse. He needn't have worried, however. From the moment he had showed her Theo's room, the nurse's eyes had shot to the dawn-to-dusk Twinkledreams ceiling and remained there. She had been, quite simply, amazed by it and Hugo doubted she would notice anything else all evening. Except, hopefully, Theo.

Hugo raised his hand for more whisky.

As the waiter brought over his drink, Hugo noticed, slumped in the distressed leather armchair opposite, a decrepit heap of flesh that reminded him of portraits of Henry VIII. Except that the slumped and sleeping man, his advanced age notwithstanding, wore a back-to-front baseball cap, a pair of bright orange combat trousers and a camouflage-print nylon T-shirt stretched tightly over his man breasts. His white, veiny feet, in open sandals bristling with Velcro, tapped with aficionado zeal to the omnipresent music. Hope I die, Hugo thought, before I get old. Especially if I get old like *that*.

He sat up hurriedly in his chair. Alice was coming into the bar. Or so he had thought from a distance, but was it her, really? The figure walking towards him had Alice's willowy build and swinging gait but, as it approached, the familiarity receded. Her hair did not hang, poker-straight, to her shoulders in Alice fashion. This woman's hair, shining thick and brilliant, was caught up in a fashionably tumbling manner that framed the long, thoughtful face.

And the face looked different; shaped and dramatised with skilful make-up. The eyes were smoky, the lips painted to a rosy fullness and the high cheekbones glowed. The clothes she wore were infinitely more sophisticated than Alice's usual off-the-skip wardrobe; a clinging skirt in elegant pale blue with a matching tight cashmere top. The high breasts, slim waist and long legs thus revealed were having their effect on the other men in the bar. Even Henry VIII had woken up and was staring appreciatively. The caramel-coated women, meanwhile, were giving Alice an entirely different sort of appraisal through slitted, jealous eyes.

'Hi! Like my new look?' Alice bent over and kissed Hugo on the cheek. A wave of delicious spa smells broke warmly over him from her cleavage.

'Fantastic,' he said sincerely. 'The spa was good, then?'

'I got a bit carried away.' Alice delightedly spread her fingers to display a new manicure. 'All those treatments. I haven't had anything like them since I was in New York. I just couldn't resist. I even went to the hotel boutique and bought these afterwards.' She gestured down at her clothes.

A lump swelled in Hugo's throat. He had always thought Alice was beautiful, albeit in a gentle, understated way. He could see now that he was wrong. Given the right clothes and make-up she was beautiful in the most dramatically obvious way imaginable.

'What's your room like?' he asked.

A faint pastel pink spread over Alice's cheek. She looked at him shyly through her hair.

Hugo was intrigued. 'What's the matter with it?'

Alice tucked one of her shining locks behind her ear. She ran a quick, nervous tongue over her lips. 'Nothing. Nothing really. It's lovely. Actually, it's quite amazing.'

'In what way?' Hugo probed.

'There's just, I don't know, something about it,' Alice confessed. 'There's a huge mosaic bath just opposite the bed. It's got candles all round it. Then there's a massive shower room with a decking floor and a shelf full of enormous bottles of body lotion. Huge sofas all over the place. The bed is colossal, and surrounded by all these aphrodisiac oils . . .' She began to giggle. 'I suppose what I'm saying is that it's not terribly, well, *subtle*.'

'You mean you've never seen so many places to shag in your life?'

Alice squealed with laughter and nodded.

Hugo raised an eyebrow. He'd sold a thousand penthouses just like it and knew exactly the sort of thing. Pretending he didn't, however, could potentially reap dividends. 'You know,' he said soberly, 'I can't visualise it at all. You'll have to show me.'

Her face flinched with alarm. 'Oh, no. I, er, couldn't.'

'I see,' Hugo said tightly.

Alice stopped laughing. Her eyes grew round with concern. 'You're not offended? I mean, it's wonderful being here. You're so sweet to treat me.'

'Well it's *slightly* disappointing you're not entirely happy with the room . . .'

'Oh, I am,' Alice said desperately. 'Really, Hugo . . .'

He raised a hand to silence her. 'But I'll forgive you completely if you take me there and show me what you mean.'

'I suppose,' he said, ten minutes later, 'that it's all meant to be a bit ironic.'

There was, Hugo was aware, nothing remotely ironic about the need swelling urgently in his trousers. Nobody, even the most committed post-modernist, had ironic erections. He tried to keep his eyes from Alice's breasts, tried too to stop his mouth watering and his hands shaking. He had so nearly had her before. He felt he would burst if he didn't have her now.

'. . . shower head's the size of a dustbin lid,' Alice was saying.

He paced towards her over the warmed stone floor. Alice was standing by the bed with her back to him, reaching up for the bottles on a rack just above it. 'Just look at some of these names,' she was giggling. 'Love Potion Number Nine, Eau Erotique . . .'

He felt her stop and stiffen as he wound his arms about her waist. 'Oh, Alice.' He buried his nose in her wonderful-smelling hair.

Her nipples brushed his hands as she turned round in his embrace. 'Hugo.' She took his face in her hands and pulled his mouth into hers.

Hugo's hand, under her skirt now, had made a discovery. 'You're not . . .'

She looked boldly into his eyes. 'Wearing any knickers. I know. I'd have told you at some stage. Had to get you in here somehow.'

He frowned. 'You *wanted* me to come in here?'

'Why else do you think I told you about the, erm, facilities?'

'But you didn't want me to see.'

Alice raised her eyes, mock-exasperated. 'For such a Mr Sophisticated,' she teased, 'you know very little about women.'

'Hey, hang on a minute . . .'

'Let's not waste time talking,' she murmured, leading him towards the bed.

'Steady,' she whispered as he tore at her skirt. 'We've got all the time in the world. Well, until dinner, anyway.'

Sometime later, Alice looked down at Hugo. Radiant with satisfied desire just a moment or two before, her expression was now still and sober.

'What's up?' He placed his hands on the slim hips that still straddled him, feeling his loins stir again.

'You *know* what's up, Hugo. Us. You and me. We're both married. With children.'

'Er, yes. I was going to talk to you about that.'

'What the hell are we going to do?'

Dinner was served in a long restaurant with a long blue banquette down one side. Opposite this, spaced at regular close intervals, were small square tables equipped with candles, mini bottles of brown sauce and another chair on the far side. Most couples seemed to comprise one person talking into a mobile while the other smoked lavishly all over them. The few conversations between couples both present all seemed to be about screenplays and treatments.

'But I don't think any of them actually *work* in the film business,' Alice hissed. 'The woman who did my massage said that most guests were journalists doing spa features. I was the first paying customer she'd had all weekend.'

Hugo smiled. The dinner was going well. Apart from the food, which seemed to be straining as hard for effect as most of their fellow diners. He and Alice had already sniggered over the reindeer shepherd's pie. Why mess with a classic? As for the lamprey and chorizo brochettes . . .

'Oh well,' Alice had said. 'It makes a change from mung beans, let me tell you.' Yet, despite the laughter, a shadow lay over their table: the fact that, at the end of the evening, they would have to part and return to their responsibilities. Separate families and separate lives. Separate spouses, with only their lunacy in common.

'Oh, Hugo.' Alice, face fragile in the candlelight, was clawing at her bread roll with newly manicured fingers. 'It's all such a mess.'

Hugo's mind slid back to the bedroom. The sex had been fantastic, but best of all had been lying with her afterwards. It had seemed the most natural, wonderful thing in the world. He wanted to wake with her like that every morning. Or as many mornings as he might have left. Life, as he had recently learnt, was shockingly unpredictable and could be very short. One had to snatch at happiness where one could.

He reached across the brown sauce bottle and wound her fingers through his. 'Well,' he said in a low voice, aware of the couples sitting close on either side, 'we have two choices. We either carry on like this, seeing each other secretly . . .' He stopped and took a swig of wine. While this was an entirely feasible and indeed time-honoured way forward, it wasn't ideal. Neither he nor Alice were cloak-and-dagger people.

Alice's unhappy face mirrored his doubts. 'I suppose so,' she said reluctantly, crumbling more bread.

'Or,' said Hugo, 'we break with the mad spouses. We

bring it all out in the open, get divorces and start a new life together.'

Alice's eyes widened. '*Divorces?*' Her throat contracted in a nervous swallow.

Hugo forked up some more of the reindeer shepherd's pie and smiled at her worried expression. 'Well, why not? I'm married to someone who's never here and clearly never wants to be, while you're married to a fanatic who'd rather be out chaining himself to dustbins or finding new ways to reuse shoelaces. Meanwhile, life is slipping away right in front of us. We've got to grab it a bit more, Alice. Seize the day. Make things happen.'

Her face darkened. 'That's what Jake said when we first met. He was always going on about having the courage of one's convictions.'

'Yes, well.' Hugo did not feel this was a particularly helpful example. '*That* was different. You had no idea what convictions he was talking about and if you had you'd never have married him.'

'No,' Alice said slowly. It was so difficult, now that the spell was broken, to recall the extent of the fascination Jake had once had for her.

Hugo leant towards her. 'You love me, don't you?'

'Yes. I do. But . . .' She bit her lip.

'But what?'

'But what about the *children?*' Alice burst out unhappily.

He stared at her, amazed. 'Well, they'd live with us, of course. Bloody hell, you didn't think I meant we'd be without them?' He felt his eyes sting at the thought. 'We'd all live together. You'd be a fantastic stepmother to Theo.'

Alice smiled wistfully. 'I was only thinking in the park how lovely it would be for Rosa to have a brother.'

'There you are then,' Hugo said triumphantly.

'But it won't be easy,' Alice warned.

'You never know, Alice. I mean, obviously, when most couples split up, that's true. There are all sorts of battles . . .'

When most couples split up. The statistics and likelihood of it happening were, Alice knew, horrifically high. Yet somehow she had never imagined it happening to her. For her, she had thought, marriage would last for ever. Just as it had for her parents. But it hadn't. She looked down and twisted her hands.

'. . . Amanda, I'm sure, won't put up any sort of fight,' Hugo continued optimistically. 'She'll be glad to see the back of Theo. It's long enough since she's seen the front of him. She'll be relieved not to have the responsibility.' He paused, thinking of the conversation about the photoshoot. That Amanda now seriously considered herself the ultimate working mother did not seem possible, even given her capacity for self-delusion. It was a fad, a front, a publicity stunt. Perhaps Amanda herself had realised how ridiculous it was; there had, to Hugo's great relief, been no further mention of the interview.

'So what about Jake?' he asked.

Alice laid down her forkful of lamprey. 'What about him? I hardly see him. If he's working at home, he shuts himself away and doesn't want Rosa or me anywhere near him. And at night he's never in.'

'So where is he?'

She shrugged. 'Out protesting with the *Get Trashed!* lot.'

'*Every* night? You're sure?'

'Pretty sure.'

'There aren't any women on the staff?'

Her brow wrinkled. 'Well, there's Jessamy. And yes, before you ask, she probably does fancy him. But I'm fairly certain his only interest in her is how effectively she can chain herself to a wheelie bin.'

'Really?' Hugo was unconvinced. 'What does she look like?'

'She's about six feet tall with bright purple hair and she's a part-time goat psychologist.'

Hugo smirked. 'She sounds right up his street. But if you say he doesn't fancy her . . .'

'I do.' Alice poked him chidingly. 'He's not interested in other women, I'm sure of that. He hasn't got time. At the moment, he's too busy going to burger chains and telling them they should be recycling plastic cutlery instead of throwing it away.'

'Christ.' Hugo rubbed his eyes. If further proof were needed of Jake's insanity, here it was. Who but a lunatic went out rescuing chip forks when they could be in with the divine Alice?

'You know,' Alice mused, toying with her chorizo, 'the more I think about it, the more I just can't understand why he wanted to marry me in the first place. It just seems one of the weirdest things ever. It was easy for me – I was swept off my feet and I wanted a baby. And I thought he did too – he said he did, and that he'd devote the rest of his life to us. But it turned out that he had other priorities.' She shook her head and stared at the candlewick glowing in its lick of flame.

'Just like Amanda,' Hugo pointed out. 'They've both got other irons in the fire that are much more important to them. There's no reason why they'd want to hang on to either us or the children.' His voice was hopeful. 'So you see, it's just a case of persuading them round to our point of view.'

'You forget one thing,' Alice said quietly. 'Amanda hates me and Jake hates you. Even if they agreed to split with us they'd never allow us to be with each other.'

It was a good point and Hugo untastingly finished his pie as he considered it. 'I suppose the best thing,' he said eventually, 'is to do it in two stages. The first is to leave Amanda and Jake and set up house on our own. Separately. And then once they've got used to that and the system is proved to be working, we start to float the idea of you and me being together.'

Alice thought about this. In truth, living alone with Rosa would make very little difference to the baby. Deciding to stay with Jake had not been a success. Not from the point of view of their own relationship and not from that of Jake and their daughter. Thanks to the amount of time he spent shut up working in the sitting room, or out being an eco-vigilante, Rosa had started to look at him with an obvious lack of recognition.

Hugo bent earnestly over the table. 'I know how we should do this. Believe me, I'm a salesman.'

'Isn't that a contradiction in terms?' she teased.

Hugo rolled his eyes. 'I mean it's my job to sell people things.'

'But you sell houses. Houses are different. We're talking about people and their lives.'

Hugo shook his head. 'Darling, houses are all about people and their lives. You're not selling them bricks and mortar. You're selling an idea about bricks and mortar. A dream of how they could live there. And what we need to sell Jake and Amanda is a dream about how their lives would be easier and better on their own.'

'I suppose so,' said Alice. It would certainly be no hardship to leave Jake on his own. Despite the incursions of *Get Trashed!* into her savings – incursions which, now she had put a stop to them, had not helped the domestic atmosphere either – she could probably buy somewhere just big enough for a single woman and a baby. Somewhere miles from any reclaimed vitreous enamel or vegetation-sprouting second-hand footwear.

'So that's the plan,' Hugo said decisively. 'If we handle Jake and Amanda carefully, it'll be fine. The important thing is that there should be no sudden shocks. They mustn't find out what we're up to until we want them to know.'

'You make it sound so easy.' As Alice stretched over to kiss him, Hugo felt a stirring in his groin.

'Well, well, well.' The voice coming from behind them had

a nasty, victorious note. 'The devoted husband and father, if I'm not very much mistaken.'

Hugo looked up in horror to see Laura smiling down at him. It was not a nice smile. With her oily trowels of make-up and the light from the candles licking her features, she looked, he thought, like a particularly evil gargoyle.

'And the eco-princess!' Laura exclaimed, scrutinising Alice. Her eyes slid back to Hugo. 'Fancy seeing you two here!'

Her voice was full of bitter triumph. She had obviously seen them kissing. It felt, Hugo thought, like being a mouse in the paws of a particularly sadistic cat.

Laura cocked her head at Alice. 'I was right. She *has* scrubbed up well, after all.'

'Laura,' Hugo said at last.

Her teeth shone sticky in the candlelight. 'Fergus is back for the weekend so he brought me here for dinner for a treat. And *what* a treat it's turning out to be!'

Lurking in the gloom behind her was the Henry VIII in the baseball cap he had spotted slumped in the bar. The anti-dog poo guru and consummate wife-neglecter at last, thought Hugo. Any other time, he might have been interested.

Now, however, he felt only a low, thrumming dread. Why had he stayed at Leather, and not run away as soon as he saw her? Only an idiot could not have seen what was obviously about to happen. And why, furthermore, had he ever mentioned therapy? He had not realised that, while hell had no fury like a woman scorned, it had nothing on a woman scorned then told she needed a psychiatrist.

'No need to ask if Amanda's still away then?' He could see, in Laura's eyes, the light of revenge. The dread escalated alarmingly.

Chapter 25

Amanda closed her eyes and stretched her arms out against the warm marble. She wriggled her toes in the boiling waters of the Jacuzzi. Some of the jets were directed, apparently deliberately, to give really quite delicious sensations. Her jetlag was fading by the minute.

Not that her jetlag was too serious. It was, in fact, hardly noticeable. Admittedly she'd come in on the overnight flight, but in the all-singing, all-dancing, all-champagne-serving flatbed first-class cabin. Her glimpse into the hellish abyss of Economy was, thankfully, long behind her.

She looked critically around the room. Those alcoves containing Roman-style oil-burners were a bit ten minutes ago, really. The whole place felt below the standard of spas she knew in the States, notably the one in Utah last week with the electric yoghurt body wraps.

Merely having one's meridians rebalanced, the main

treatment on offer here, seemed dull in comparison. On the other hand, why struggle on with meridians all over the place? Life for working mothers like her was hard enough as it was. As she planned to tell the newspaper this very afternoon.

'Amazing coincidence,' she observed to Laura. 'I can't believe you rang and said you needed to talk to me the very second I was getting into my cab at Heathrow.'

'Incredible,' Laura replied, resplendent in a swimming costume of a pink so hot it made Amanda's eyes ache. 'And so great you could come straight to the spa to meet me, rather than going home first.'

Amanda wiggled a slender brown foot. Laura's call, as it happened, had fitted in quite well. A quick spa session, she had decided, would be just the thing to add extra glow for the camera.

'Especially as you must be desperate to see Theo,' Laura added.

'*Theo?* Who . . . ? Oh, of *course*, absolutely . . .' Shit, she'd almost forgotten her own baby's name. Amanda looked warily at the other woman and saw with relief that, somewhat incredibly, she did not appear to have noticed.

Amanda was far from being a perceptive soul, but even she now sensed something not quite right with Laura. Her entire manner was odd. As was her appearance – bloated, bloodshot, spotty and caked in make-up even in the water.

Amanda was smugly aware of looking infinitely better herself. So there was, after all, *something* to be said for flogging herself to death to keep career and family life on track. Perhaps all that effort made the blood flow faster or something. Cleared out the system. Clever her. She could suggest that to the interviewer as well.

'I'll see Theo this afternoon, anyway,' Amanda said airily. 'Hopefully his looks will have improved since I last saw him . . . not that that was very long ago, of course.'

'He must be so excited that you're coming,' Laura added, choosing her words carefully, 'that Hugo must be in quite a state as well.'

Amanda breezily examined her nails. 'Oh, they've got no idea I'm here yet. I thought it would be fun if it was a surprise for them.'

She wondered impatiently what Laura wanted so desperately to talk about. She'd better come to the point of whatever it was quickly. Didn't she realise some people had work to do, national newspaper magazines to see?

Laura, as a stay-at-home mother, obviously had all the time in the world. She didn't realise how lucky she was, frankly. 'Better get dressed, I suppose,' Amanda sighed. 'No rest for the wicked. I've got a tough afternoon ahead.'

'Doing what?' Laura asked, having failed to recognise the nudge.

Amanda's well-moisturised and lightly tanned jaw worked crossly over a piece of sushi. 'Photoshoot with Theo,' she groaned. 'It'll be exhausting.'

'Photoshoot? Sounds like fun,' Laura said enviously.

'No, it sounds like work,' Amanda corrected her. 'They want to talk to me about how I combine my busy working life with being a successful mother. While at the same time keeping a happy, flourishing marriage on track.'

Laura gave her what, had Amanda been capable of noticing, was a curious look. 'Is that right?'

'Uh-huh.' Amanda yawned ostentatiously. 'So come on, then. What's the problem? You said you wanted to talk to me about a problem you had.'

A look of despair crossed Laura's face. 'Yes, it sort of touches on what you've just been saying. Being a successful mum. The happy bit especially,' she added dolefully.

Amanda smiled with satisfaction. 'Oh, I see. You want to know how I manage?' She gave a mock-rueful laugh. 'Frankly, darling, I wish I knew how I did it myself. But by all means ask. I'll tell you what I know.'

'Erm, well . . .' Laura hesitated. Then it all spilt out, uncontainable as vomit. How unstimulating Laura was finding motherhood. How abandoned she felt by Fergus. How unfulfilled – to say the least – she felt by Django. How guilty she felt about everything.

Amanda stared at her, appalled. Was *this* all Laura wanted to tell her? Moan on about *herself*, in other words?

'But of *course* Fergus is useless,' she said irritably. 'Wake up and smell the coffee, Laura. Men *are* completely useless. Look at Hugo. *Hopeless*. If I want anything doing properly, I have to do it myself. *Every* time.'

Laura seemed hardly to be listening. 'I'm beginning to wonder,' she said slowly, 'whether or not I should be having therapy. What do you think, Amanda? I mean, you're my friend.'

Friend? What was Laura going on about? Amanda rarely gave friends a thought. They seemed, on the whole, an irrelevance and inconvenience, always wanting help of some sort or other. She had never had time for them; Laura was an acquaintance at the most. She was of no professional or personal use whatsoever.

'Because frankly,' Laura spoke with a sob in her voice, 'a friend's what I need at the moment. There's no one else I can talk to. Or who wants to listen.'

Amanda cast her a thoughtful look. On the other hand, she could probably do with some friends. They were fashionable at the moment. She'd seen lots of articles about them being the new family and how female networking was the new black. 'I've discovered so much more about my *friends*,' she pictured herself telling the magazine journalist. 'Motherhood has definitely extended my ability to empathise.'

'Yes,' she said slowly, savouring the curious sensation of uttering the sentence for the very first time. 'I am your friend.'

'So you'll tell me the truth?' Laura demanded, her eyes searching Amanda's. 'Just as I wouldn't hold back if there was something I felt you should know about?'

'Ye-es,' said Amanda.

'Do you think,' Laura asked, 'that I should have therapy?'

'Therapy?' Amanda repeated, the 'r' revealing a shining row of bleached white teeth. 'But what for? There's nothing wrong with you. You're a bit fed up, sure. But hey, aren't we all? Some of us – *some of us*,' she repeated with emphasis, 'are fed up and have to hold down a career as well.'

Laura looked down into the bubbling water and frowned. 'I don't think it's ordinary fed up. I've been thinking about killing myself, actually.'

Amanda gasped. What Laura was saying was too awful to be true. How could *anyone* be quite so self-indulgent?

'Killing yourself!' she exclaimed. 'But how *can* you be unhappy when you don't even have to work? You should try changing places with me if you want to know what *real* pressure is.'

She reached behind with manicured hand for the glass of chilled champagne. Not vintage, admittedly, but it would do. She closed her eyes again, enjoying the sensation of cold alcohol swirling around inside her system and hot, bubbling water swirling around outside it. 'Look,' she said, sitting up in the water. 'I'm sorry, but I've got to be frank with you. Reveal unpalatable truths. That's what friendship's all about, isn't it? You just said so.'

Laura nodded dumbly.

'Well, what I think is that you should be counting your blessings.'

'I know. Healthy son, nice house, all that.'

'Not *just* that,' Amanda said briskly. 'Think how much luckier you are than me, for example. I mean, I envy you, I really do.'

'You do?' Laura looked stunned.

'Absolutely I do. I envy you for the fact you don't seem to *need* to have your brain stimulated with a career.'

Laura opened her mouth to object. 'But . . .'

'You don't need to be fulfilled at work,' Amanda steamrollered on. 'You can't imagine the strain,' she sighed, 'of trying to keep all these balls in the air and not dropping any of them. Being mother to Theo, trying to hold a demanding job down *and* keep a successful marriage going!'

Laura tried once more to interrupt. But Amanda took no notice.

'Life's just *so* demanding,' she continued, 'I can't *tell* you how wonderful it is to be here. To have a break, to enjoy a spot of pampering at last. It's dreadful, never having a second to spare for this kind of thing.' Amanda raised a smooth, tanned leg, exfoliated the previous week in Utah, out of the water. 'But everyone else has to come first – Theo most of all, obviously. And then, at the back of the queue, little old me.' She examined her smooth, waxed armpits. 'People are always telling me they don't know how I do it.' She smiled wearily. 'And, do you know something, Laura?'

'Well, yes, actually, I do,' Laura said quickly. 'Something that you should know as w—'

'*I'm* not sure how I do it either. So goodness knows what I'm going to tell the journalist!' Amanda tittered delightedly.

'I can think of one thing you're not going to tell them,' Laura said grimly, climbing out of the water.

Amanda observed with satisfaction the patches of cellulite on Laura's thighs. *Serious* orange peel, that. It was shocking how some people let themselves go when they had babies.

'What do you mean, you can think of one thing I'm not going to tell them?' she said absently, her eyes still on Laura's upper legs.

Laura, midway into her bathrobe, turned. 'Well, I'm only telling you this because you're my friend, obviously. Unpalatable truths and all that.'

'Of course.' Amanda jerked her damp head emphatically up and down. 'So what is it? Shoot.'

'Your husband's been shagging that eco-hippy from the antenatal class.'

It was, Hugo thought, like death. He did not know when the blow would come, only that it would.

That it could come at any moment made him jittery. It could come now, for example, as he sought to clean up Theo after the latter had detonated the most substantial nappyload of his short life. Theo was suffering from a nursery tummy bug that he had, with his usual generosity, not hesitated to share with his father. Hugo's current inner turmoil therefore had more than one aspect.

His sole consolation was that Amanda might strike from overseas. She had, he knew, been in New York again. And while obviously Laura could and would reach her there to tell her she had caught him with Alice, the prospect of being shouted at over the phone from three thousand miles away seemed less appalling than facing Amanda's rage in person.

In his brighter moments he imagined she wouldn't care; what was a fling, after all? But then he would remember that it was a fling with Alice, the woman Amanda held single-handedly responsible for the end of her Intercorp career.

In his lower moments he worried about Alice. He had not

spoken to her since the Allingham House dinner.

Alice had thrown down her big white napkin like a flag of surrender and dashed out of the restaurant, shoulders rigid with pent-up sobs. He had followed. The ever-pounding drum and bass in the foyer had provided a soundtrack to their misery until the taxi came to take her away.

Only then had she looked at him, her eyes wide with fear. 'What the hell's going to happen now? What are we going to do?'

'Run away together?'

'And what about the children?' She clutched him with white-knuckled hands. 'What about them?'

Hugo swallowed. 'Don't worry,' he assured her as he shut the gleaming car door. 'It'll be fine. If it all comes out in the open, so what? It might be for the best. Speed things up a bit.'

He knew, from Alice's face, white and unhappy against the dark plush car seats, that she did not share his optimism. He wasn't sure that he shared it himself.

Hugo had just hosed Theo down in the bathtub and was attempting to dry his squirming, resisting body when he heard someone slam into the house. 'You there?' a familiar voice bellowed. Hugo froze. *Amanda*. Unexpected, unannounced and obviously back from New York directly on hearing the news from Laura.

His wife did not mince her words. 'You bastard,' she shrieked, stomping up the stairs and into the bathroom.

'Laura told you then,' Hugo said resignedly, holding both hands over Theo's ears.

Amanda, he saw, looked extraordinary. Her career as a magazine editor seemed not only to have gone to her head, but everywhere else as well. Her hair was platinum blonde and hung to her shoulders. She wore an arresting outfit involving a black and white patterned miniskirt, matching crop top revealing several feet of belly and, over these a long dressing-gown-like garment of the same material as the rest. Silver high-heeled boots and wraparound shades completed the ensemble. Hugo realised, looking at her, that he had become more provincial than he had suspected. He had completely forgotten that people dressed like this. Theo, meanwhile, was staring at her in amazement.

'Of course Laura fucking told me,' Amanda raged. 'She's my *friend*. She's loyal to me, not that that's a concept *you'd* understand.'

'Loyal!' Hugo snorted. 'I don't think you'd have thought so if you'd seen her coming on to me the other day. Rubbing herself up against the bedpost, completely nude and pissed as a fart. The woman's insane.'

Amanda's eyes blazed. 'You sad fantasist sicko. Coming on to *you*? Oh *sure*. Well you would say that, wouldn't you. Anything to get yourself off the hook.'

'Eh?—'

'How bloody dare you?' Amanda yelled. 'Shagging that mealy-mouthed, career-destroying . . .'

'I don't see that your career's been destroyed,' Hugo broke in. 'I'd say the opposite, if anything.'

Amanda narrowed her eyes and placed both red-taloned

hands on her hips. 'I wouldn't say anything if I were you,' she snarled. 'Save it for your solicitor. And the divorce court.'

Hugo clutched Theo so hard that the baby yelped. 'What exactly do you mean by that?'

'What the hell do you think I mean?' Amanda's voice was raucously triumphant. 'What do women – or should I say *mothers* – in my position normally mean?'

He stared at her for several agonised seconds. '*Theo?*'

'Yes, Theo. Quite frankly, now he's so presentable, it's about time he stopped rotting in the sticks and lived somewhere decent. He can,' Amanda said decisively, 'come to London with me.' She swept a withering glance over Hugo's foam-spattered, damp-wrinkled suit. 'It's about time I took him in hand. Took him . . . well, everywhere. To premieres. Mother and baby spas. On educational holidays. The Galápagos Islands, that sort of thing. He's got a lot of ground to cover before Cambridge. You can't start too soon.'

'The Galápagos Islands . . . ?'

'He needs a proper christening as well.'

'But we haven't been near a church the whole time we've lived here.'

'Not *here*,' Amanda said witheringly. 'He'll be christened in London. Obviously. St George's Hanover Square with a couple of celebrity godfathers, that sort of thing.'

'Celebrity g—' Hugo could hardly frame the words.

'As far as his school goes,' Amanda added decisively, 'I'll call in a few favours and get him in at that prep school where

Jeremy Paxman's kids go, as well as Sebastian Faulks's and Jade Jagger's.'

'But Theo's happy here,' Hugo objected. 'He likes Chicklets. And they think there'll be a full-time place for him soon.'

Amanda was not listening. 'Great school. Richard Curtis was a human fruit machine at the summer fête last year. We sent a photographer to cover it.'

'But you can't . . . just *uproot* him like that,' Hugo burst out. 'He lives here, not London. *This* is his home.'

'Well, it won't be soon,' Amanda said lightly. 'So you'd better start getting used to the idea.'

Hugo's voice was barely above a whisper now. 'You mean you're going for custody of him? But you can't. You don't know anything about Theo.'

'I know *best*.'

He frowned. 'What do you mean, you know best?'

'Because I am, may I remind you, his mother. Mothers know best.'

'And I'm his father. I've been looking after him on my own for months.'

Amanda yawned. 'Oh, change the bloody record, can't you?'

'But childcare's hard work. Twenty-four seven . . . you can't imagine,' Hugo heard his voice switch from steely fury to desperate pleading. 'Amanda, come on. You wouldn't want to do it.'

'Well the funny thing is,' Amanda drawled, 'I really rather fancy having a go at it again.' She chucked her son under his soft chin with her long, hard nails. 'Theo's turned into quite a little doll now he's finally got some hair – thank God it didn't stay ginger. He can come with me to the fashion shows and be *Class*'s little mascot.'

Hugo was feeling sick for reasons unconnected with Theo's stomach bug. 'But you can't—' he began, then stopped.

She could, he suspected. And if things got really nasty . . .

He remembered pictures of fathers in the papers, chaining themselves to cranes, stopping the traffic and throwing purple powder at the Prime Minister. And all because they'd been denied access to their children after divorce. Was that what lay in store for him? Could it really happen? After all he and Theo had been through together?

'Just watch me,' Amanda said with bitter triumph. 'I'll . . .' But before the unnamed threat could be issued, a noise outside distracted her. She went over and opened the window to see. 'Fuck! It's the bloody journalists.'

'Journalists?'

Amanda flashed him a glance of furious impatience. 'I rang you about it, dumbo. That interview. They want to talk to me about how I combine a brilliant career with a happy marriage and successful motherhood. *Dahhhhhhling!*' she exclaimed, teetering towards Theo on perilous heels. 'Are you ready for your close-up?'

Like an eagle with its prey she swooped him up and crushed him closely to her before peeling him off and thrusting him hurriedly at Hugo. 'Oh, *disgusting*, he's just wiped his filthy snotty nose all over my sleeve. Here, take him. *Quick.*'

She rushed to the wash basin and dabbed frantically at the damage with a baby sponge. 'Doesn't he realise it's crêpe de Chine?' she snarled.

As the doorbell rang, she teetered back from the basin and snatched Theo again. Ripped from his father, the baby started up a thin, tired wail.

'Oh, shut up,' Amanda snapped, grabbing a dummy from the bathside and ramming it in his mouth.

Hugo watched Amanda glance in the mirror, check her hair and plaster on a huge showbiz smile before lurching to the stairs under the clearly awkward and unfamiliar weight of a baby. 'Careful,' he warned.

She paused and looked viciously over her shoulder. 'No. You be careful. You'd better bloody play ball with this interview. Otherwise you'll be *really* sorry.'

Hugo immediately saw this as a straw to clutch at. Was Amanda saying, albeit unpleasantly, that if he remained discreet, smiling and supportive during the interview she would simmer down and see reason? That there was room for debate, negotiation and, hopefully, the changing of minds?

'Hey-there-how-are-ya-come-*in*,' he heard her cry to the group of people at the front door. From the top of the stairs he watched them enter: the handsome photographer with the emphatically tousled hair, his tiny blonde female assistant, the interviewer with her cropped hair, techo-glasses, knee boots and tight-fitting houndstooth-check coat. They all stared unapologetically round.

'This is my husband,' Amanda said as Hugo came down the stairs.

The journalist smiled at him glassily. 'And aren't you the lucky man? Married to this superwoman!' She gestured at Amanda. 'Imagine it makes you feel a bit indequate at times.'

'Er, yes,' admitted Hugo. Rarely, certainly, had he felt less adequate than he did at the moment.

The journalist made a note. Amanda's expression, Hugo saw, encouraged, was approving.

For the next two hours he fetched and carried cups of tea for the crew while Amanda sat on the sofa with Theo and held forth about her mothering, editing and home-making abilities.

'You must be *so* proud of her,' the journalist gushed as, yet again, Hugo appeared with his tray.

He forced his chin up and down. 'Oh, I am.' Catching Amanda's expectant expression he realised that rather more was required. 'Amanda is . . . *amazing*.'

'The way she juggles everything!' the journalist added admiringly.

'It's just . . . unbelievable,' Hugo agreed.

'And how hands-on are you?' the journalist enquired. 'With the baby, I mean?'

Hugo glanced at Theo, who was playing happily with the photographer's light meter. He sensed Amanda's drill-like stare. 'Oh,' he said, in an attempt at breeziness. '*Quite* hands on. I try, you know.' He gave a self-deprecating laugh.

'But she's a hard act to follow, huh?' prompted the journalist.

Hugo said nothing, not trusting himself to.

'He's so *good*!' the journalist remarked of Theo. 'You really *have* got it down to a fine art.'

'Thanks!' said Hugo, a split second before Amanda could claim credit. He shot her an apologetic glance, realising his mistake. Yet it was, for him, a matter of huge pride and yet bitter regret that Theo did not burst into tears or have a tantrum. At one time he would have obliged royally, and put Amanda at an obvious disadvantage. But Theo, as a rule, did not indulge in such behaviour any more. As Hugo had relaxed and blossomed into his role as a father, Theo had relaxed and blossomed into his as a baby.

'You're too kind!' prinked Amanda. She held out her teacup to Hugo. 'More tea please . . . *darling*.'

'We're out of milk,' Hugo said. 'Darling,' he added hurriedly.

Amanda rolled her eyes at the journalist. 'Men! Typical! You ask them to remember *one thing*! Oh well,' she added with theatrical brightness. 'You know what they say. If you want something doing, don't just ask a busy person. Ask a stressed-out, juggling, multi-tasking working mother!'

As the journalist tittered and made yet more notes, Hugo silently ground his teeth.

'So,' he said to Amanda, when, much, much later, the door finally closed behind the magazine crew, 'I did everything you wanted. I played ball.'

'You certainly did,' she agreed.

'So can we talk about *us* now? About Theo?'

'If you like,' Amanda said. 'But I can't see why.'

'Because you were talking about divorce,' Hugo reminded her in the most non-confrontational tone he could manage. 'And taking Theo away.' He pressed his nose into the warm head of the baby who, as Amanda had busied herself with farewells, he was holding again.

'So what's changed?' Amanda asked lightly.

Hugo wanted to shout with the shock of it. So she had tricked him. She had no intention of negotiating and never had. She had only hinted as much to buy his silence and complicity during a prize piece of personal publicity. He stared at Amanda with loathing. So this was it. This was war.

'You wait,' he said in a low, furious voice. 'I'll fight you for Theo every inch of the way.'

'Well, the best of British in that case.' Amanda shrugged on her coat. 'You're going to need it. You've just committed yourself to print in a national newspaper saying that I'm a fantastic wife and mother. If you weren't going to lose before, you're definitely going to lose now.'

Chapter 26

Alice had been watching and waiting for the right moment to discuss the future with Jake. It had not yet come, due mostly to his almost continuous absence from the cottage. His increasing *Get Trashed!* commitments, followed by more and more evenings spent eco-agitating, meant opportunities to talk were confined to first thing in the morning or last thing at night. Neither of which were an ideal time to broach the possible break-up of their family.

She thought constantly of Hugo. Lying alone in bed as, night after night, Jake stayed out late, she relived the memory of his lips on her eyes, mouth, neck and breasts. She ached too to know how he was, and how matters stood with Amanda. But only a fool, in the circumstances, would try something as rash as getting in touch. Matters with Jake needed to be resolved first. She had thought long and hard about their conversation in the restaurant and now felt more optimistic. Given her legal background, her gift for argument, perhaps she could persuade Jake that Hugo's solution really was best for them all.

She had almost fallen asleep the night she heard the front door of the cottage slam hard. And, immediately afterwards, heavy, angry footsteps on the stairs.

In the ottoman, Rosa stirred and whimpered. Alice, beneath the duvet, froze even more than she was doing already, given the always inadequate heating.

The bedroom door opened to reveal a crack of light. 'Al!' hissed Jake. 'I want to talk to you downstairs. Now.'

She crept guiltily out from beneath the duvet. He had, she miserably guessed, found out about Hugo. But how?

'Woad!' exploded Jake by way of explanation when she arrived barefoot and shivering in the sitting room to find her suspicions were correct.

'Woad?' Alice clutched her washed-out, over-sized second-hand T-shirt about her.

'Woad!' Jake repeated.

'You mean that stuff the Ancient Britons used to wear to scare off the Romans?' How had that helped in his deductions?

'And which is emerging as a viable alternative to the potentially cancerous artificial indigo dyes currently being used for jeans.'

Alice frowned. 'What? I don't understand.'

Jake rummaged in his pocket. 'And I didn't, either, when I first found this,' he snarled, waving a crumpled piece of white cotton at her.

Alice stared at it, at first bemused and then with heart-speeding recognition. It was the handkerchief Hugo had lent to her when they had met in the bookshop. Jake must have found it in the washing pile. And, of course, it had Hugo's initials on it.

Oh, how *Othello* of her. How *bloody* stupid of her. Alice's fists clenched. She should have hidden the handkerchief immediately. But then, at the time there had been no need. Far from being desperate to see Hugo, as now, she had been anxious to get away from him.

'I couldn't work out who H D E F was,' Jake growled, his eyes long and glittering in the light filtering through the ceiling colander. 'And then, at the fashion show, it suddenly all made sense.'

'Fashion show?' It was all making less and less sense to Alice. What was Jake, of all people, doing at a fashion show?

'London Fashion Week,' Jake snapped. 'Me and Jess have been there tonight campaigning for wider use of planet-friendly dyes.'

'I see,' said Alice faintly. 'That's where the woad comes in.'

'Yes, and that's where I saw that stuck-up trout from the antenatal class. That editor woman.' Jake paused. Alice felt a stab of panic.

'Amanda?'

'Who tells me,' Jake went on acidly, 'that you're fucking her husband.' He waved the handkerchief. 'Hugo Dennis Eric Fine?'

Now, in the midst of catastrophe, Alice found herself dwelling on Hugo's middle names. He hadn't struck her as either a Dennis or an Eric.

'You know what I could do?' Jake thundered. 'Leave . . .'

Hope soared within her. 'Well, if you're sure . . .' Him disappearing would solve everything. She had not expected such a simple, quick resolution.

'. . . and take Ro with me.'

'Take Rosa?' Alice said sharply.

'Don't think I'd leave her with you, do you? What sort of bloody mother are you anyway?' His face twisted with disgust. 'That oily bastard of an estate agent. Al, how bloody could you? How grubby could you get?'

Alice resisted saying that, so far as grubbiness went, both Allingham House and Hugo were cleaner than Jake and the Old Morgue. There were more important points to make. 'You *can't* take Rosa,' she exploded. 'You've got no legal rights to. The courts—'

'Legal rights? Courts?' Jake smiled coldly. 'Who needs legal rights? With my network of underground eco-contacts, I could disappear just like that.' He snapped his fingers. The sharp sound echoed in Alice's ears. 'There's the German beetle camp, for a start.'

'Beetle . . . ?'

'A group in Germany who've built a whole city of tunnels under a rare beetle breeding ground they're saving from developers.'

Alice immediately imagined Rosa in an underground

passage, beetles teeming above and German hippies teeming below. She clamped a horrified hand to her mouth.

'Matter of fact,' Jake remarked, inspecting a clod of crud on his grubby red check shirt, 'I've been thinking of going abroad for some time, *Get Trashed!* being about to bite the dust and all that.'

'Is it?' Alice was aware things had not been going well. But this badly? Had the end of her cash handouts spelt the end for the magazine?

'Yes.' He gave her a hard stare. 'So pissing off with Rosa rather fits in with my plans.'

One of the hopes Hugo was clinging to was that Barbara, the barrister mother at Chicklets, would represent him in the battle with Amanda. At the first opportunity he cornered her at the nursery and petitioned her to come for a quick coffee. Barbara, however, refused.

'I'm sorry,' she said. Her eyes were bloodshot with exhaustion. Rarely had Hugo seen a woman quite so tired. 'Isabel was up all night with her teething. I'm knackered and I'm putting my client's case this morning.'

'I'll be quick,' Hugo said. 'I'll tell you now.' There, in Chicklets's foyer, keeping his voice as low as possible, he sketched out the situation as best he could.

To his intense disappointment, Barbara was shaking her head before he finished. 'Not for me,' she said.

'You don't want to represent me?' Was it disapproval that was stopping her?

'I'd love to if I could. But it's not the way the system works. You can't appoint barristers directly. You need a solicitor to do that.'

'Oh,' said Hugo, crestfallen. 'I see.'

'And anyway, this would be a family case and my speciality is fraud.'

Hugo gave a mirthless laugh. 'Believe me, this is much more about fraud than family.'

Barbara chortled. 'Oh dear. But in any case you need a solicitor first and foremost. I can give you the name of a good one. And do, above all, go for counselling.'

'Counselling?' Hugo was unpleasantly reminded of Laura. 'Bit late for that, isn't it?'

Barbara shook her head. 'A willingness to try counselling rather than just giving up on the marriage impresses courts in divorce cases.'

'But the marriage is . . .' began Hugo.

'Over? Well of course it is. But what we're talking about here is who gets custody of Theo. The odds'll be stacked against you, you know that?'

Hugo nodded miserably. Barbara rubbed his arm comfortingly. 'Don't worry. You've got a good chance. You're obviously devoted to Theo and you're in reliable employment.'

'That's important?' Hugo thought anxiously of the underground car park fiasco.

Barbara looked at him in surprise. 'Of course it is. A jobless father is unlikely to be granted custody at the expense of an employed mother.'

'Oh. Right.' Hugo bit his lip.

'So a job plus the therapy will stand you in good stead.'

But Hugo's stead, as it happened, stood good only as long as it took to get from the nursery to Dunn and Dustard.

Learning – in glorious technicolour from Shuna followed by reluctant precis from Hugo – of the occurrences in the underground car park, Neil summarily fired him. 'I'm sorry, Fine. But you're a liability, let's face it.' Hugo tried desperately to reason with him. 'But, Neil. Come *on*, mate. You don't know what this means. Amanda's divorcing me—'

'And so am I,' expostulated Neil, who was, as usual, in no mood to be gracious. Again as usual, he reeled off the list of Hugo's crimes against estate agenting. 'And you still haven't managed to find a place for the Grimbleys,' he finished, 'let alone sell that raving poofter's place in Charlotte Crescent.'

'Neil, for God's sake,' pleaded Hugo. 'You've got to give me another chance.'

'Sorry, Fine. You've had your chances.'

As Hugo miserably absorbed this, Barbara's voice echoed in his ears. 'A jobless father is unlikely to be granted custody at the expense of an employed mother.' Especially a self-declared high-achieving, juggling, multi-tasking mother like Amanda. He didn't have to close his eyes to imagine her in some sharp suit in the courtroom, briefed to the nines, working that dynamically capable chic for all it was worth. And what it was worth, ultimately, was Theo.

The thought of his son being taken from him made Hugo feel desperate. It seemed impossibly unfair that it could happen, and yet, especially now, he did not doubt that it would.

There was, as Hugo saw it, but one option left to him. He pushed past Neil, disappeared into the loos and burst into tears.

Looking back, some time later, on the days that subsequently passed, it seemed miraculous to Hugo that he survived them. In some ways, of course, he had no choice; Theo, at least temporarily, was still in his charge and as exacting a taskmaster as ever. But at night, when the baby was finally silent in his cot, Hugo, in bed, would stare hopelessly into the darkness and try not to think about the even blacker hole that was his future. Whether Alice was still part of that future, he was miserably unaware. All attempts to get in touch with her had met with a wall of silence and on one occasion the closed and unyielding door of the Old Morgue. That had been the lowest point of all.

Hugo had, however, summoned up the resolve to take Barbara's advice and contacted both solicitor and counsellor. But after the initial outlay of effort and expense, both initiatives seemed increasingly hopeless. He had lost his job and he had played into Amanda's hands over the magazine article. Through fair means or foul, and her own indomitable will, Amanda would get what she wanted. She always did. Today, for example, in the waiting room of the Northanger Advice and Support Centre, he felt he was merely going through the motions.

He heard one of the counsellors' doors open, but did not look up. If Dr Hasselblad was ready, he'd say so. Footsteps came out. Hugo heard the footsteps pause, then change direction towards him.

He gritted his teeth and clenched his knuckles. Please God it wasn't Amanda. Certainly, it shouldn't be. They had different, separate counselling times, after she had reluctantly accepted her own solicitor's advice that if Hugo was going, she should as well.

The shoes were, he noticed, getting nearer. A pair of flat brown brogue toes stopped just under his nose.

'Hugo?' It was Laura's voice. 'Is that you?'

He jerked his head up, shocked. *Her!* Sounding as untroubled as if she had spotted him from across the road. Had she no shame?

He looked at her resentfully from under his brows, noting the absence of the usual hot-pink and heaving bosom. Instead she wore a grey polo neck jumper and jeans almost as sober as the shoes.

'What the hell do you want?' he hissed.

She looked, he saw, nervous. 'Er . . . how are you?' she asked. 'You look, er . . .'

'Awful?' Hugo prompted sarcastically, aware of his hot, tired eyes and creased clothes. He scraped a hand through his hair; the tangles were worse than he had realised. How many days had gone by since last he had brushed it were anyone's guess. He needed to raise his standards. The hedge backwards look was as likely to impress a divorce court as having no job.

'Yes,' said Laura quietly. 'Awful.'

He glared at her. 'Can't think why. Because I *feel* great, obviously. Never better. My marriage has broken up and I'm about to lose my son. Both thanks in no small part to you. So do me a favour, will you, and piss off.'

He had expected – hoped – that Laura would leave after this. He had dropped his head again, but the flat brown toes in front of him did not walk away. Instead, they turned at an angle and Hugo felt the bench beside him give as she sat down.

'Hugo,' Laura said, in a low voice. 'Listen to me.'

He immediately doubled his guard. Into his tired, anxious mind crept the idea that whatever this woman was up to was part of his wife's evil plan. She was Amanda's friend, after all. Her self-styled 'loyal' friend, incredibly. 'Listen to you? Are you joking? Leave me alone. Haven't you done enough damage?'

'I understand why you're saying that . . .' Laura began.

'I should think you bloody do,' cut in Hugo, shaking off the hand she now placed on his arm.

'. . . but I wanted to thank you,' Laura finished.

'Thank me?' He snapped his head to the side to look at her, so hard he felt his neck crunch. '*Thank me?* You're in the wrong movie, Laura. I'm in the one where the husband who's looked after the child almost all its life loses it on a whim of his feckless egomaniac absentee wife's after her friend tells her he's been having an affair. I'm not sure which one you're in.'

Laura met his gaze steadily. 'I'm in the one where the hopeless mother who wanted to kill herself and her child goes to therapy on the advice of her friend's husband and finds she's a classic postnatal depressive. She realises she isn't a lunatic after all. And after a few sessions she starts to see where she's been going wrong. With her marriage, with her son and . . .' Laura paused and looked down, 'she realises as well that certain unpleasant and vengeful acts, such as telling her friend about her husband's infidelity instead of talking first to the husband himself and allowing him to make amends, came about out of spite and a wish to destroy. To make everyone else feel as unhappy as she did.'

There was a silence. Hugo said nothing. He had some time ago passed the stage of being unable to believe his ears.

Laura's make-up-less eyes flicked earnestly up at him. 'So that's why I wanted to thank you. You were the only person who suggested therapy might be the answer. I was furious at first but then I thought about it and I realised you were right. You probably saved my life.'

Hugo did not react. What did she expect him to do? Cheer?

'I haven't been going to counselling for long,' Laura added earnestly. 'But I'm already discovering so much.' She placed her hand shyly back on Hugo's arm. 'The importance of being honest, for one thing. I know I'm not the perfect mother. I just do my best, like any mother does. I'm also trying to accept Fergus's limitations as a husband, and not expect from him what he can't give. And, along the way, I'm hopefully getting to know myself a bit more. Find out who's there beneath all that slap and cleavage. And alcohol.' She gave him a rueful smile.

Hugo did not return it. 'Sounds like you're pretty busy,' he sourly observed.

'I've got a long way to go, obviously,' Laura eagerly admitted. But I'm going to get there. I'm beginning to think, too, that counselling might be where it's at for me. As a career, I mean.'

Hugo shrugged. 'A moving story,' he remarked bitterly. 'I'm thrilled for you, Laura, really, I am. I'm so glad you're finding yourself. It makes me feel so much better now that I'm losing just about everything.'

'You *were* having an affair,' Laura pointed out.

Hugo flared like a match at this piece of staggering impertinence. He rounded on her furiously. 'What about you in that hotel foyer with God knows who at Christmas? What about the moves you made on *me*?'

She dropped her eyes.

'It wasn't just an affair, anyway,' he muttered, wanting to make the point, even to Laura, that his and Alice's relationship could not be bracketed with her own grubby liaisons. 'We were going to tell them – eventually.'

'Were you?' Laura had raised a disbelieving eyebrow.

He addressed the floor again. 'It was a question of timing. We were going to tell them, but not straight away. We needed time, we thought, and they needed time, to help them see what was so obvious. That we were all with the wrong people, basically. Jake doesn't want to be with Alice and Amanda doesn't want to be with me. And neither of them wants to be with their children.'

'But Amanda's Theo's mother,' Laura pointed out. 'How do you know she doesn't want to be with him?'

Hugo flung up his head. 'Because she disappeared a few weeks after he was born. Because she thought ludicrous Hollywood presents – all, incidentally, blagged for free – were the same as being at home looking after him. Because I couldn't get her on her mobile the night I took him to hospital thinking he was about to die. Because she's prepared to wreck a happy, stable home, albeit an unconventional one, so she can tart him around fashion shows and send him to school with celebrity children.'

He buried his head in his hands, grinding his eyes as if to grind out the pain. 'Yes,' he added in a choked voice. 'Amanda is his mother. And an example to us all, the way she manages to combine a brilliant career with raising a child and keeping a marriage going.'

He looked fiercely at Laura, who was staring back at him in shock. 'I never realised . . .' she stammered. 'I mean, it was obvious there were a few self-confusion issues going on there, but . . .'

'*Self-confusion?*' Hugo spat. 'Is that what the counsellors call it?'

'I'm sorry,' Laura said, in a voice barely above a whisper. Her eyes, which looked wet, were fixed to the floor.

Hugo glanced impatiently at the therapist's still-closed door. He was anxious for the session to start. Not because the counsellor had, so far, said anything particularly useful, but so he could bring to an end this surreal and ridiculous exchange with Laura. Dr Hasselblad was over-running by almost half an hour. Who did he have in there? Some suicide case?

'I'm so sorry,' Laura repeated. 'If I could turn the clock back and not have told Amanda, I would do. It was none of my business. If I could do anything to help, to make things better, to make amends, I would.'

Hugo flicked her a look. 'There isn't anything you can do,' he said quietly.

'But I'm *so sorry*.' Rummaging for a tissue, Laura scraped at her nose with it.

He shrugged. 'I don't know what you expect me to say.'

'Anything you like,' Laura suggested. 'Scream at me. Hit me if you want.' She sounded almost eager.

A faltering ray of illumination filtered into Hugo's brain.

'So that's what this is all about,' he said with grim satisfaction. 'Amanda wants me to hit you to finally prove I'm unstable, violent and unfit to be a father.'

Laura looked at him in horror. 'Of *course* not!'

Hugo shook his head disbelievingly. 'Well you can tell her there's no need for tricks like that. I won't win the court case. On top of everything else, I've lost my job now as well.' He looked at her bitterly. 'You had a hand in that too. Game, set and match. Congratulations.'

'Oh, Hugo, I'm so—'

'Look, I don't care how sorry you are. It's too late. The damage is done.'

She was twisting her hands in anguish. 'But there might be something I could . . .'

'There's nothing you can do,' he snapped. 'Except leave me alone. Just *go away*.'

He could hear chairs scraping behind Dr Hasselblad's door. The protracted session was finally coming to an end. Without another word, Laura got up and left.

Seconds later, Dr Hasselblad's door opened. Hugo, standing up, glanced casually but curiously at who might be coming out.

It was Alice.

Chapter 27

It was vital, Alice had recognised, for her to end the relationship with Hugo. Whatever her own passionate personal feelings, they had to be put aside for the greater good. Jake was a bottle of marital nitro-glycerine, ready to explode with devastating consequences at the slightest unscheduled wobble. Alice was desperate to keep everything as calm as possible. Which meant, so far as was possible, preserving the status quo.

In exchange for promising to give *Get Trashed!* an emergency cash transfusion, she secured from Jake the assurance that he would support her efforts to get their marriage back on track. A solicitor she contacted advised that counselling sessions for them both could be helpful and although, historically, Alice had regarded all therapists as quacks, historically she had not been in the situation she found herself in now. Tired, despondent and above all, desperate. No source of help could be ruled out.

A professional person's view of the matters troubling them might even be useful. If things ever got to court, the fact that the counselling had been her initiative would show a willingness, if not an ability, to make amends.

While she had not seen Hugo since the fateful night at the hotel, she had rehearsed what she would do if, as was not completely unexpected, she met him in the street. Night after night before sleep finally, belatedly, claimed her, she rehearsed her cool but friendly response.

What she had never rehearsed for, never expected, was to emerge from a counselling session to see, standing before her, the very reason she was there in the first place.

Not only was Alice unprepared for the sight of Hugo, she was unprepared for what he would look like. Bleary-eyed, wild-haired and as sunken-cheeked as a Schiele drawing. Sleepless black shadows dragged beneath each reddened eye.

A great wave of tender concern smashed over her head. Hugo looked, she thought, as if he had been under torture. Even his voice sounded broken. 'Alice,' he said, in a parched sort of way that made her want to gather him to her breast and hug everything better.

'What are you doing here?' she hissed.

His smile was sickly. 'Relationship therapy. You?'

She looked away. 'Same.'

'Jake knows then?' She looked, he thought, so beautiful with a soft pink scarf – surely not from the dump – bringing out the flush in her cheeks and warming her pale sheet of hair.

'Yes. And I gather from him Amanda knows as well.'

Hugo nodded. 'So basically we're both here to keep our marriages going.' He snorted.

Alice, looking at the floor, felt him catch at her hand. A thrill of fear juddered through her as she snatched it away.

'Oh God, Alice, don't do that.' He sounded appalled. 'It's as if you hate me or something.'

'Of course I don't hate you.' Her eyes snagged fleetingly on his. 'It's just that I don't dare . . . Look, I can't see you again. Ever.'

Hugo drove a frustrated fist into his palm. 'It's so bloody *unfair*. People have flings for years before anyone finds out. If they ever do. Some people have entire secret families. And look at us. One night and our whole world's fallen apart.'

'We've committed adultery,' Alice said quietly. 'It's a big thing, Hugo. It doesn't matter how many times it happened. Once or a million times, it's all the same. We broke a promise.'

'And what about *them*?' Hugo's voice was a shout of anguish. 'What about the promises *they* broke? Amanda was going to give up her career and be the world's best mother. Jake dragged you back from New York on the understanding that life with him would be just bloody fantastic. And look what happened. Amanda pissed off within days of Theo being born and Jake turned you into an eco-prisoner.'

'I know,' Alice whispered. 'But none of that matters now. All that matters is that I get to stay with Rosa.'

'But you could divorce him for unreasonable behaviour. Believe me, I've been looking into it. I know. Five minutes in your house and any court would come down on your side. I drove past it only this morning. The place is a bloody bomb site.'

'You drove past this morning?' Her breath caught in her throat.

'I drive past most days,' he confessed. 'Just in case I might see you. I never do, though.'

There was silence. Then he added, 'You could leave him, you know. Get custody of Rosa.'

She shuddered a no. 'He's threatened to take her away. I think he means it.'

'*What?* He's threatened *what*? Hell, Alice. That's probably grounds for divorce in itself.'

She banged clenched fists to each of her sides. 'Stop talking about divorce. I don't *want* a divorce.'

Hugo felt as if an iron hand had closed round his throat. 'You don't want . . . ?'

'I don't want to rock the boat. And I suppose now I feel that I deserve what's happened. I don't want any more upheaval. I want us all to stay together as a family.'

Hugo stared, disbelieving. 'Oh, for Christ's sake, Alice. What sort of self-punishing crap is that? You *don't* deserve what's happened. What you deserve is a break.'

She twisted her hands. 'Well, none of that matters now. What's more important than anything is giving Rosa a happy, secure childhood. With both her parents, like I had.'

'Even if one of her parents is a bloody lunatic? You said yourself you had no idea why he married you.'

'He seems to be taking to counselling, though,' Alice told him defensively. 'Maybe this was what he needed. It might make a difference. He might change. He has a bit, already. I think the counsellor's noticed the hygiene problem. He's washing again . . .' Her voice was almost pleading.

'You think so?' Hugo said ominously. 'Alice, you may be convincing yourself, but you don't convince me. A leopard doesn't change his spots. Even if he washes them.'

His scepticism, she knew, was understandable. But, much to Alice's own amazement, Jake really had taken to therapy with enormous enthusiasm. Slightly but definitely, his temper and general attitude had improved since the sessions had started. As had his personal hygiene. Beside washing, he had started shaving again and that lank, greasy look she so hated had finally gone from his hair.

'He's got some moisturiser in the bathroom cupboard, the first I've ever seen him use,' she added. 'He's even started wearing aftershave, which he never has before.'

'*Aftershave!*' Hugo exclaimed, wondering what that had to do with anything. Hastily, he collected himself. 'Look, we're wasting valuable time. When do you usually have your counselling? And what time is his?'

'Every Wednesday at nine,' she muttered. 'And Jake's is at twelve. Why?'

'Mine's usually on Wednesdays at eleven. Today it got moved, that's why I'm here now. But Alice, listen, I could move it to the same time as you. Get a different counsellor, or whatever. You could keep Dr Hasselblad – he's been no bloody good to me anyway.' He clutched her. 'We could see each other then. Before or after. Accidentally, or so it would seem.' He swallowed. 'What do you think?'

For a second, Alice wavered. Then she shook his hand off. 'No,' she said firmly. 'What would be the point?'

He felt the hope seep out of him, like air from a sagging balloon. 'The point?' he repeated. 'That we'd see each other at least. Go for a coffee or—'

'We can't.'

'Oh, Alice. Please. I can't bear it . . .'

'Well you'll have to,' she said sharply. 'We'll both have to.'

Hugo tried to squash the rising lump in his throat. 'You're right,' he said defeatedly. 'Seeing the people we love in the context of trying to find a way to stay with the people we don't is just . . .'

'. . . not the way to keep our children.' Alice moved towards the door.

Hugo gave a hollow chortle. 'Oh, I've already lost Theo.'

This had an electric effect. She whipped round, appalled. 'What – has there been a hearing already?'

'No, but it'll be soon. And I'm not expecting to come out of it all that well. You'll be co-respondent, obviously.' He smiled at her ruefully.

Alice flinched. Co-respondent in a divorce. The other woman. The evil temptress. Not a role she had ever imagined for herself.

'But they can't give Amanda Theo,' she protested. 'The

Children's Act favours the primary carer, and that's you.'

'I know. But apparently courts always imagine it's the mother. And you know what Amanda's like. She'll put on an Oscar winner of a performance in order to get her own way.'

Alice tried to banish the vision of the evil Amanda, Cruella de Vil-like, sinking her red shining talons into the puppylike Theo. 'She *can't*. I mean . . . they *won't*. You must have a good chance? With your track record of looking after him. And your job, of course.'

'I got sacked. Alice, I don't have a job.' He turned up his palms helplessly.

Alice looked back at him in despair.

'So you're probably right,' Hugo said with forced flippancy. 'There is no point in any of it. This is it then. This is goodbye.'

She sat at the back of the bus all the way home, sobbing quietly into her scarf and feeling as if a razor was twisting in her heart.

She was terrified for Hugo. His fear of losing Theo was probably justified. As she herself well knew, court cases involving Amanda Hardwick meant disaster. And he had lost his job into the bargain. Alice groaned. She felt sick and choked, as much by circumstance as by the black fumes pouring out of the vehicle's exhaust.

Home, she pushed open the battered door of the Old Morgue. Jake, just behind it, shoved at her the whimpering Rosa. 'I've got to go out,' he announced, clearly in a tremendous rush.

'Oh, right. Where?'

'Counselling,' Jake called cheerily over his shoulder, dodging through the vitreous enamel cluttering the path.

Alice fed Rosa and switched on the garish primary-coloured cassette player she had recently bought for her song tapes. The player was plastic, apparently indestructible and probably had a life expectancy to rival Stonehenge, yet, incredibly, had attracted no adverse comment from Jake. Another example, Alice supposed, of the mellowing effect counselling was having.

Rosa, who loved music, was bouncing triumphantly up and down to 'Miss Polly had a Dolly' when the telephone rang. It was Alice's mother.

'How are things, darling?' she asked, more gaily than she felt. As Alice's chief confidante, she was aware of the threatened kidnap. So far, she had managed to keep her own volcanic feelings on the subject heroically under wraps.

'Oh, you know,' Alice said absently, smiling at Rosa, who was pushing up the volume dial with her fat little hands. 'Bobby Shaftoe' blared out deafeningly.

'No, darling, I don't know. Tell me.'

Alice paused, then it all came out in a rush. 'I saw Hugo this morning. At the therapist's.' She closed her eyes briefly. 'It was . . . horrible. He was so upset.'

'And what about you?' her mother probed.

'I was pretty upset too, obviously. But, Mum, I feel so dreadful about the affair. It was wrong. *Really* wrong. I've caused such a lot of trouble. Made such a mess of everything.'

'Darling, these things happen,' Mrs Duffield said soothingly.

But not to you and Dad. Alice thought hotly. 'Well, they're not happening any more,' she said firmly. 'I told him there was no future for us and we were better off trying to rebuild the marriages we had.'

There was a pause at her mother's end. 'Why did you say that, darling?' Mrs Duffield asked carefully.

Alice felt a prick of annoyance. Was her mother, secure on her lofty pinnacle of unbroken wedded fidelity, patronising her?

'Look, Mum,' she said, exasperated, 'we've been through all this before. You know it's because I want Rosa to have both her parents.'

'You don't think it's a high price to pay? Spending the rest of your life with Jake? After all he's put you through?'

'Honestly, Mum, he's improved. I think the therapy's helping a bit. He's very keen on it . . .'

'*Improved?*' Her mother's self-discipline finally gave way. 'Believe me, darling, people like him don't improve. You're far better off being a single mum, for Rosa's sake as well as yours. Just divorce him.'

'Mu-um!' exclaimed Alice. 'What are you saying?'

'Only what I've been wanting to say for ages.' Mrs Duffield was now in full, furious flow. 'You'd have a case for unreasonable behaviour. Jake dragged you back from New York on the understanding that life with him would be just fantastic. And look what happened. He turned you into an eco-prisoner. In ghastly surroundings. Five minutes in your house and any court would come down on your side. The place is a—'

'Bloody bomb site. I know,' Alice admitted. 'That's just what Hugo said. He said everything you've just said.'

'You know, darling, the more I hear about this Hugo the more I like him. Him rescuing Rosa's teddy was just adorable. Heroic.'

A pang went through Alice at the memory. 'That's beside the point.'

'Is it? Why?'

'Because the whole Hugo thing's impossible. I'm staying with Jake and that's that. I've got a responsibility to Rosa and—'

'But the man's a lunatic,' her mother broke in. 'You said yourself you had no idea why he married you. Don't tell me all that's changed, all of a sudden.'

Was Hugo, Alice wondered, actually in touch with her mother? Or were they just employing the same scriptwriter?

'Look,' she conceded. 'It won't be ideal. Not at first, anyway. And possibly not ever. But I'm not sure I deserve to be enjoying myself, anyway. Not after what I've done.'

'But you can't stay with a madman who doesn't love you just to punish yourself. Darling, where's the logic in that? And what good does it do Rosa?'

Alice took a deep breath. She felt tired, defensive and, increasingly, angry. 'I know Jake and I will never live up to the standards of you and Dad. But I wanted her to have something like the same security and happiness that I did.'

Her mother sighed. 'So you keep saying. But I think I should tell you something.'

'*What's that?*' Alice shouted. Rosa had pushed the volume of her nursery tape up again.

Humpty Dumpty sat on a wall . . .

'The standards of your father and me aren't quite so high as you think.' Her mother's voice was tight. 'As a matter of fact, we very nearly split up when you were very young.'

'What?'

'I never told you this because I never thought I would have to. But I had an affair as well. You were about three at the time.'

Humpty Dumpty had a great fall . . .

'But . . .' Alice grasped the receiver as if it were the only stable thing in a teetering world. *Mum and Dad . . .* an *affair* . . . it was impossible. She shook her head hard, as if to expel her mother's words from her ears.

'Your father was very hurt when he found out. It was dreadful. Getting back together was a very delicate and difficult business. Making it work even more so.'

Alice's swift legal brain had by now come to her rescue. 'There you are,' she exclaimed, triumphant. 'You got back together with Dad. So you should know exactly what I'm going through with Jake. You should be cheering me on, not telling me to get divorced and how wonderful Hugo is.'

'That's where you're wrong,' Mrs Duffield said gently. 'It's because your father and I got back together that I'm advising you to stay apart.'

Alice frowned. 'I don't follow.'

Her mother hesitated. 'It took a great deal of heart-searching, generosity on your father's part particularly and facing up to uncomfortable truths for us both to make it work again. It wasn't easy. In fact, it was very hard. Rebuilding shattered trust is almost impossible. But we did it.'

'And so will we,' Alice cut in. 'And Rosa won't know anything was ever wrong. Just as I didn't.'

'Your father,' her mother replied gently, 'is a very special man. But Jake is not, in my view, a special man, at least not in that sense. Darling, what I'm saying is that I really doubt that you, even with all your good intentions, could make that marriage work after everything that's happened. You're much better off getting out of it.'

. . . All the king's horses and all the king's men. Couldn't put Humpty together again.

'Thanks, Mum,' Alice said. 'I appreciate your support, I really do. Thanks a *lot*.' She slammed the receiver down angrily.

Chapter 28

Hugo was mooching miserably around Theo's empty nursery. He often found himself here these days; it was, he supposed, a way of preparing himself for the approaching time when the nursery was vacant permanently.

On his way out, he stumbled into Theo's activity centre-cum-baby walker and accidentally set it going. 'Hey there! Let's play!' As the toy's tinny American accents echoed eerily through the room, Hugo jumped. He looked nervously at the pile of toys, a garish jumble of staring cartoon eyes, plastic smiles and rigid limbs protruding at dramatic angles. They struck him as rather sinister. With no Theo to make sense of them, they looked like something out of a horror film.

He looked at his watch, noting with relief that it would soon be time to fetch his son from Chicklets. The morning, like every morning since he had lost his job, had dragged. After dropping Theo at nursery he had called the solicitor, certain, as always, that the morning post would have brought Amanda's divorce papers and with them the date for the hearing. But as it happened, the post hadn't.

The delay was, Hugo felt sure, another of Amanda's torture tactics. While the date he awaited would obviously mark the end of everything he lived for, he was almost beginning to look forward to it. The limbo he was in was debilitating, a halfway house, a living death.

He should, he supposed, probably be keeping Theo at home with him. He had, after all, nothing else to do and he should make the most of their last few weeks, days, hours, or whatever it was, together. Now he was no longer earning, Chicklets's fees were eating into his dwindling savings as well.

But the thought of his lively, merry baby, used now to the company of other infants, cooped up with no one but his miserable self and even more miserable attempts at catering was unendurable. Theo deserved better. To withdraw him from Chicklets would, anyway, be to cut the last tie to their old, happy life together. It was not something he felt able to do.

Hugo tramped downstairs, noting vaguely that the stain on the staircase wall was bigger than ever. He'd never got round to doing anything about it. Still, it would be someone else's problem soon.

The divorce would obviously mean number four Fitzherbert Place would be sold. No doubt an eager young couple, bright-eyed and enthusiastic about their escape to the picturesque provinces, would buy it and set about it with heritage paints and architectural salvage catalogues. In no time at all they would transform it into a tasteful family home. He hoped they would be happy, whoever they were.

He locked the front door and got into the car for Chicklets, wondering how many of these once-routine, taken-for-granted trips he had left.

Arriving at the nursery, Hugo was almost glad to see the Rottweiler shoot out of her office in trademark style. It brought an element of normality at least.

'Mr Fine. A word, if you please. In my office.'

He followed the nursery head into her lair and looked round at the surprising number of flickering computer screens. It reminded him of an air traffic control centre. He had no idea that running a kindergarten was so technical.

'I want to talk to you about Theo,' the Rottweiler said, settling herself at the other side of her vast desk.

'Fire away,' Hugo said comfortably. For once, he was in no hurry to leave. 'It's not the nappies again, is it?'

He had been pulled up short a few days ago about Theo's habit, apparently recently acquired, of filling his nappy en route to the nursery. 'Nursery regulations,' the Rottweiler had sternly pointed out, 'demand that babies are presented at Chicklets with clean bottoms.'

Nursery regulations had thereafter seen Hugo stop every two minutes on the way to Chicklets, get out of the car, go round to the back seat, remove Theo from his restraints and lift him up and sniff his rear to make sure all was well. The amused gazes of passing drivers had to be borne, as well as the outraged howls of a Theo recognising he had been rumbled.

'No,' the Rottweiler said. 'It's not nappies. It's about Theo's biting, Mr Fine.'

'*Biting?*'

'Your son, Mr Fine, has been biting other children.'

'Oh, no.' Hugo stared in wide-eyed despair at the surface of the desk. A warm wave of shame flooded him. He remembered how furious and indignant he had been on the few occasions Theo had been on the receiving end of such attacks from his peers. No doubt other mothers and fathers would now be baying for Theo's blood. Thank goodness nursery policy forbade the naming of miscreants.

'I don't understand,' he said. 'He never bites at home.'

The Rottweiler waggled her pen. 'Immaterial, Mr Fine. We need to find out why he is doing it here. And put a stop to it.'

'I don't know,' Hugo said miserably. 'It can't be because he's hungry. He loves his food and he gets lots of it here and at home.'

The Rottweiler looked faintly exasperated. 'Hunger, Mr Fine, is rarely the cause. Young children do not tend to have cannibalistic tendencies. Nor is biting unusual amongst pre-talkers. Sometimes it's just one of the many ways, albeit not a particularly nice one, that they use to express themselves. It can be stopped with firm discouragement.'

Hugo grasped at this straw. 'Oh, right. So we'll just all try and firmly discourage him, then?'

The nursery head waggled her pen again, warningly. 'But sometimes, Mr Fine, very occasionally, biting can be caused by something else. Something more specific. An expression of anger or frustration about something.' She leant forward, her bulging blue eyes enquiring. 'Is there anything that Theo is perhaps reacting to at the moment? Any problems at home, for instance?'

Hugo felt himself shrivel in the intensity of her stare. That the Rottweiler had guessed all was not well was obvious. And unsurprising; he was, after all, the physical embodiment of domestic breakdown. Unwashed, unbrushed, unironed, unpolished. Unhappy.

Even so, for all his personal degradation, he had imagined his efforts to protect his son from the worst of the pre-divorce fallout to have been successful.

So brilliantly successful, he thought bitterly now, that Theo was biting other children to express his unhappiness, even at this early stage. No one had as yet been near a courtroom.

'Oh God,' he said, into the hand that had flown to his mouth and was pressing hard against it to stop the howls that wanted to come. He flicked a terrified glance at the Rottweiler, imagining her in the dock supporting Amanda. 'I regret to say that Mr Fine's abilities as a parent were inadequate, if well-meaning . . .' The prospect of social workers and separation orders crowded horribly into his mind. Perhaps he wouldn't have to wait for the divorce to lose Theo.

'Oh God,' he repeated to the Rottweiler. 'You want to throw him out, don't you? Well, of course you do. Nobody wants a baby that *bites* . . .' His voice broke on the last word.

'On the contrary, Mr Fine,' the Rottweiler said briskly, 'we should be very sorry to see Theo go. He is a happy, loving little boy. What we want is to find a solution. Help him through this.'

Hugo wondered whether, in his misery, he was hearing all right. He had never suspected the Rottweiler to have an understanding streak. He had always assumed her function was to make parents' lives as difficult as possible.

Across the desk, the Rottweiler's stern features relaxed. 'Mr Fine,' she said, in a gentle voice he had not heard before, 'while I am unaware of the precise nature of your personal difficulties, I would like to just say this. If there is anything I, or Chicklets, can do to help – an extra hour of care here and there, say – do please let me know. We are here to support you and, of course, Theo in any way we can.'

Hugo felt his body slump sideways in amazement. He managed, just in time, to stop himself falling off his chair; managed, even, to stammer out his incredulous thanks.

'You are very welcome, Mr Fine.' The Rottweiler tactfully glanced away from his glistening eyes. 'We are, of course, aware of the many difficulties facing the working mother – sorry, *parent* – at Chicklets. And of your case in particular, may I say.'

'How do you mean?' croaked Hugo.

'*Ahem.* It was fairly evident at first that you were having – how shall I put it? – something of a challenging time with Theo. But we all admired the way you overcame those challenges in order to build a really extraordinarily close and loving bond with your son.'

Hugo was too surprised to speak.

'In addition, you have always been quick to co-operate with nursery rules and support us whenever you can. You are a model parent, Mr Fine. Believe me, I wish there were more like you around.'

'A model parent,' Hugo gasped. '*Me?*'

'Now,' the Rottweiler reached for a kettle on a table behind and switched it on. 'May I suggest a cup of tea. With sugar,' she added, flicking Hugo an amused glance. 'I believe that it's good for shock.'

Theo had recently become extremely attached to a game in which a pile of coloured wooden rings was pushed on to a stake. Accordingly, for most of the afternoon following their return from Chicklets, Hugo sat patiently beside the baby in his nursery, cheering and clapping whenever his son managed to re-impale a ring. Theo soon made the connection between effort and reward and was eventually cheering himself wildly, bouncing up and down in excitement. Hugo laughed back, trying not to wonder how many such opportunities he had left. Model parent or no model parent. The Rottweiler's opinion, he had glumly concluded, would count for little in the battle with Amanda. Given the dastardly tricks she no doubt had up her designer sleeve.

Clunk. As Theo, having successfully negotiated a particularly big, thick ring, erupted once again in self-applause, Hugo forced away his worries in a frenzy of clapping and cheering.

'A touching sight,' someone observed caustically from the nursery doorway.

'*Amanda*. How the hell—'

'Did I get in?' She reached into the pocket of her shiny black leather coat and shook a handful of jangling metal. 'I've still got my keys.'

As she stalked, spike-heeled, into the room, Theo stopped pushing his rings on his stick and stared up at her from the floor, his small face solemn, his big eyes grave. Hugo glanced at him in concern. The baby was soaking up the tension like a sponge. Some poor infant at Chicklets would suffer the consequences of this tomorrow.

Amanda stared at Hugo. 'You look like shit,' she said frankly.

Hugo was getting used to such remarks. 'Suppose I haven't been having the best time recently,' he remarked sarcastically. He wondered what she wanted. No doubt to trap him into saying something else she could use in court.

Amanda strode round the nursery, hands thrust in the pockets of her coat. He did not invite her to take it off.

He noticed her precise make-up and the way her hair shone with the obviously recent attentions of someone expensive. Besides her, both he and Theo, whose face retained ample evidence of the beans he had had for lunch, looked more than a little crumpled.

Hugo edged protectively closer to Theo, whose attention had returned to his rings and stick. He watched his wife warily. Another possibility for her visit struck him. But if Amanda thought she was coming for the baby now, she was mistaken. The courts, as yet, had ruled nothing. They had not even sat. For the moment, Theo's home was with him at Fitzherbert Place.

'Why are you here?' he asked.

'To talk.'

'What is there to talk about?' His first suspicions had been correct, then. 'I thought we were talking through our solicitors, anyway.'

Amanda's back was now towards him, so he could not read the expression on her face. It would, he was sure, be triumphant, and more than a little contemptuous. Fitzherbert Place, she would be thinking, was a dump. The sooner she pulled her equity out of it, not to mention her son, the better.

'I've come to tell you,' Amanda said, after what seemed the longest pause in history, 'that I was wrong.'

Hugo's fingers edged tighter round Theo's warm little side. 'Wrong?' he croaked. 'About what?'

'About everything.' She was still addressing the far wall. Or, perhaps, the chest of drawers against it.

'You mean . . . ?' Hope roared up within him like an erupting volcano. 'You mean that you don't want a divorce?'

Brilliant possibilities reeled dizzily through his head. The threat of separation from the baby finally lifted. Theo, him and Amanda, all together again as a family. And while this last was hard to imagine, he would make it work for Theo's sake. He *would*, however badly Amanda behaved. He had a new perspective on that now. The worst, most arrogant and

Wendy Holden

eye-wideningly selfish excesses of his wife were sheer delight compared to the terror he had lived with these past few weeks.

Amanda turned. Hugo's face was blazing so brilliantly with hope she felt she could warm her hands on it. She shook her head. 'No,' she said shortly. 'I don't mean that. I still want a divorce.'

'You do?' The volcano became a chilly chasm.

'You and I were never going to work out. Besides,' Amanda added casually, flexing a finger with a big ring on it, 'I've met someone else.'

Hugo closed his eyes. Just when he felt he could bear the emotional roller coaster no longer, here came another sickening twist. Theo was to have a stepfather. His primary male role model was to be not him, but . . .

'Who?' Hugo demanded. 'Who have you met?'

The head of the magazine company, it turned out. 'Fantastic guy called Rick,' Amanda enthused. 'Bald, admittedly, but quite sexy. Shit-hot businessman, though. And as rich as fuck, obviously.'

Hugo reflected dejectedly that maybe a shit-hot business-man who was as rich as fuck was rather a good model for Theo. Better than he was at any rate. 'And you're going to marry him?'

'Maybe.' Amanda gave a coquettish little smile. There was a pause.

'So,' Hugo eventually said, dully. 'What *were* you wrong about then?'

438

'Sorry?' Amanda said blankly. Her thoughts were obviously still with Rick. Or, more likely, his money.

'You said you'd come to tell me you were wrong about something.'

'Oh, yeah.' Amanda ran her hands absently through her expensive hair. 'I was wrong,' she said, checking her lipstick on one of Theo's cot mirrors, 'about *me*.'

'*You?*'

Amanda started to walk around the nursery again, trying not to skewer the scattered toys with her heels. 'I've been thinking about myself,' she announced.

'Ye-es?' So what was new? The chances of Amanda ever thinking about anyone else were non-existent.

'I've realised a few things,' Amanda continued. 'Things I never realised before. For instance, while some women are born to be mothers, for others, career is what matters.'

Hugo narrowed his eyes. Only to Amanda was that a revelation. He could not imagine what all this was leading up to and the suspense made his muscles ache.

'It's been so tough,' Amanda declared, turning tragic eyes on him. 'You know, keeping the whole thing going. The job, Theo, you and me. The juggling. That whole hideous working-mother thing.'

Hugo felt the familiar fury rise. Not this self-deluding rubbish again. Remembering Barbara, almost collapsing with exhaustion in Chicklets's foyer while she tried to concentrate on helping him, he wanted to shout at Amanda to get real. Or get lost. Why should he waste one of the last afternoons he and Theo had together listening to this?

'You know,' Amanda sighed, 'one of the worst things of all is that I haven't been able to talk to anyone about the terrible strain I've been under.'

Not much, thought Hugo. Only the entire readership of whatever magazine had interviewed her.

'Because, of course, I've never had the time,' Amanda continued martyrishly. 'Until now. Last night I had a very long talk on the phone with Laura. She rang me. Really *forced* me to open up about everything.'

'Did she now?' Hugo said sardonically. It must, he thought, have been like forcing open a box of teabags.

Amanda nodded eagerly. 'It was such a relief. We talked endlessly about *me*, for once. About the pressures *I* was under. The uncertainty *I* felt. And my frustration, as a perfectionist, at not being able to do everything – work, wife, motherhood – absolutely brilliantly.'

Hugo's glance slid to Theo's activity centre. Could he, he wondered, batter Amanda to death with it?

'And Laura – you know . . .' Amanda shook her head disbelievingly. 'Well, she was *amazing*. I'd completely underestimated her. I had no idea how *wise* she was.'

Hugo could think of many words to describe Laura. Wise was not one of them.

'She helped me realise what I'd just refused to let myself accept.' Amanda's eyes were wide with wonder. 'That some women just weren't born to be mothers. But that the journey

– having the baby and all that – was a necessary part of the pathway to greater self-realisation.'

'I see.' Hugo's tone was determinedly neutral despite the outraged boiling of his insides. 'So Theo and I were a sort of experiment?'

'Exactly that,' Amanda nodded delightedly. 'Becoming a mother myself was the crucial step to realising that, actually, it wasn't my bag at all. And Laura's showed me that if that's the sort of woman you are then it's best to admit it and accept your other strengths. That it's a strength to admit your weaknesses.' She looked distantly at Theo. 'And, you know, I've got so many strengths. I'm a great writer, for a start. Great words person. Great editor. *Class* is doing fantastically.'

Hugo thought gloomily of the no doubt also fantastic salary that had mysteriously never made it to Fitzherbert Place.

Amanda bent over the cot mirror again and inspected her mascara. 'Rick's desperate for me to do more. Be editor-in-chief of a range of titles.'

'Congratulations.' Hugo miserably imagined the long days at the aspirational nursery that this would mean for Theo.

'Thank you.' Amanda nodded graciously. 'But here's the dub, as they say.'

'Rub.'

'What?'

'Here's the rub. That's the phrase.' So much for the great words person.

'Oh, right. Well, anyway, what I wanted to tell you is that Laura helped me *see*.'

'See what?'

'That I deserved a break, after everything I'd been through. And that us splitting up was a natural pause, a chance to reassess the way I wanted to live the rest of my life. A chance to get off this awful pressurised, over-achieving mummy-go-round. A chance to start my new life with Rick free of ties and responsibilities. *Hugo*,' Amanda said, looking wildly into his eyes. 'she helped me to be *honest* with myself.'

Hugo was unsure whether to laugh or cry. Or simply scream and jump out of the window. 'Amanda, forgive me for being stupid,' he said.

'Oh, I forgave you for that ages ago.'

'But just what is all this leading up to?'

Amanda raked her hands through her hair excitedly. 'Laura convinced me that taking Theo with me to London would be the worst possible thing for my career. Not to mention complicating the start of my new life with Rick.'

Hugo felt as shocked as if a shire horse had kicked him in the balls. 'What? She convinced you of *what*?'

'That Theo would be better off here with you. You know, among all the people and places he's used to. The nursery and all that.'

Were it not for the fact he was already sitting down, Hugo would, he felt, have sunk to his knees. God bless Laura. She had wanted to help him and she had. Bringing her new counselling skills to bear on Amanda's vanity, selfishness and self-delusion, she had twisted them to an outcome suiting everyone.

'So you'll get custody in the divorce,' Amanda said breezily. 'We can sort out access, alimony and all that crap later on.'

All that crap. The kind of crap that routinely ruined lives. Including his own, or so he had expected.

'Alimony?' he queried, the word putting a brake on his rising joy. 'You know I'm skint. I lost my job.'

'So I heard.' Amanda looked at him almost affectionately. 'Loser. I'll be paying *you*, obviously. Upkeep for Theo.' She looked at her watch. 'Shit, is that the time? Must dash, got a lipstick launch at the Grosvenor House later. Bye, darling,' she flung absently in Theo's direction, before darting out of the door in her heels.

'Ayiyiyiyi,' said the baby triumphantly, sliding the last of his wooden rings on to his stake.

Chapter 29

Hugo could hardly believe his luck. The clouds had parted. He and Theo were to remain together. Amanda, meanwhile, was to start a new life with her shit-hot businessman who was as rich as fuck. Following the divorce, which had miraculously swung from bitterly acrimonious to almost impossibly amicable, he, Hugo, would be free to marry whoever he wanted.

All that remained to make his happiness complete was to persuade Alice that staying with her husband was a mistake. But this, obviously, was not going to be easy. He had to find a way to help her extricate herself. A way that would appease her obviously rampant guilt while ensuring she did not lose Rosa.

No ordinary display of logic would work, he knew. No normal line of argument would have any effect whatsoever. Not least because she would not allow him to talk to her.

His telephone calls went unanswered. And when, again, he gathered the courage to knock on the Old Morgue's door, it remained, as before, resolutely shut. He had tried shouting through the letter box, but to no avail. The only life in the place, it seemed, was in the clanging of the garden's bean-can windchimes and the plant-stuffed footwear festooning the walls.

Only one other possibility of meeting Alice remained. He knew where and when she attended her counselling sessions. He could lie in wait.

When, with an electric jerk of the heart, he saw Alice finally come out of the clinic, he noticed she looked as doleful as the rainy day. Her sessions were obviously just as uplifting as his had been. Among the many joys of his current situation was no longer having to bother with Dr Hasselblad.

From the warmth of his car he watched her walk down the wet street to the bus stop. Once she was standing there, he started the engine and drove past, slowing down as if spotting her by chance.

'Alice! Want a lift?'

Excitement spasmed across her face at the sound and sight of him. Then, clearly with an effort, she arranged her features into a blank. 'I can't talk to you,' she hissed, blinking the raindrops off her eyelashes.

'Come on, Alice,' he urged. 'Get in the car. I've got some news for you. Great news.'

'I *can't*.' Her eyes flicked about her in terror. 'Jake might see me. *His* therapy session is any minute now.'

'Alice. Come on. It's pissing down.'

'*Please*,' she begged. 'Just go away. Leave me alone.'

Hugo hesitated. He could not drive off without telling her what had happened. It wasn't the best method of communication, granted, still less the most private. But what else could he do?

'Amanda's getting married again!' he roared from the driver's window. 'To a shit-hot businessman who's as rich as fuck!'

The rest of the bus queue cheered. 'Good for her!' boomed a solid old lady, waving a walking stick in the air.

'She's agreed I get custody of Theo!' Hugo yelled.

More cheers. An emotional fight to the death, meanwhile, was playing out over Alice's face. Her expression was half exultation, half wanting to sink into the pavement.

'So don't you see, Alice?' Hugo bellowed. 'Once the divorce goes through I can marry again. I'll have Theo. So all you have to do is divorce Jake for unreasonable behaviour and you, me, Rosa and Theo can all live together. Happily ever after.'

The crowd at the bus stop went wild. 'Go on, dear,' the old lady urged Alice. 'He looks like such a nice young man. *I* would.'

'Well, don't let me stop you,' snapped Alice. She turned furiously on her heel and stormed down the street, heedless of the puddles. Heedless himself of the hoots of the cars behind him, Hugo crawled alongside her, shouting and pleading, to little effect. After a few minutes of angry marching, Alice turned abruptly into an alleyway and was thereafter lost from sight.

Hugo continued to cruise round the neighbouring streets, but without success. Eventually, accepting defeat, he parked and stared morosely at the steering wheel. So near and yet so far. While a miracle had occurred with Amanda, nothing short of outing Jake as number two to Osama bin Laden would convince Alice there was no future in her marriage.

In fact, did Hugo but know it, nothing could be further from the truth. Alice's hopes for a stable marital future had just sustained something of a body blow.

Admittedly, there had been clues. The moisturiser in the bathroom cupboard had recently been joined by toner and facial scrub. Jake's aftershave collection, moreover, had doubled in size to two bottles. He now bathed every day, flushed the lavatory with wild abandon and a number of T-shirts that were definitely new had leavened his otherwise second-hand wardrobe. But it wasn't this that ultimately blew his cover.

Alone one night in the cottage with Rosa – Jake being out demonstrating with Joss and Jessamy – Alice had answered the phone. On the other end was a Joss not only not demonstrating, but clearly unaware he was supposed to be. 'Oh right,' he said, sounding surprised. 'So he's out somewhere with Jess, is he?'

'It would seem so,' Alice replied tightly, deafened by the crash of a million pennies dropping simultaneously.

How could she have been so stupid? So blind? Why had she discounted Jessamy as a threat?

Empty days had passed, and weeks begun and ended while Alice fought with herself over what to do. On the one hand, she felt she deserved this betrayal, having been unfaithful herself. On the other, they had agreed to stay together for Rosa's sake. Her unhappiness grew. Jake's wardrobe and aftershave, meanwhile, grew ever more assertive. The course of action Alice eventually settled on was continuing to attend her counselling sessions. Perhaps Dr Hasselblad had the answers. Meeting Hugo at the clinic that morning, however, had only increased the questions.

Hugo, unaware of any of this, got out of the car and walked towards the town centre. Determindly, he told himself there was no point moping about Alice. There was too much to do. A job to find, for instance.

He had tried most of the big Bath estate agencies by now. But it was possible an untapped couple of independents lurked in some side street. A smaller agency might be more suitable anyway, being possibly more disposed to accept the part-time arrangement he wanted.

Although Chicklets had offered a full-time place, his afternoons with Theo were, Hugo had decided, too precious to give up. But the fact he wasn't a woman, yet wanted to work mornings only, seemed to confound most of the agencies he approached. 'It's an unusual request – for a man,' he heard time and time again. Explaining that it was for childcare reasons seemed only to worsen the situation.

Get real, Hugo wanted to shout as he walked out under supercilious stares. Men are parents too. And guess what, it's the way things are going.

When he wasn't fantasising about family life with Alice, Hugo imagined himself head of a flourishing estate agency staffed entirely by part-timers. Men especially, with childcare responsibilities. He had, he recognised, come a long way from the days when parting yuppies from their bonuses was his only business ambition.

Realising he was about to pass his old employers, Dunn and Dustard, Hugo slowed down. He was unable to resist looking in the window to see if any of the old faithfuls were still there. Tarquin's immovable town house, for example.

A number of other people were loitering outside the agency's windows. This was not unusual; the pavement outside frequently hosted knots of day-trippers squinting at prices and fantasising about life amid Regency splendour.

Tarquin's house was indeed still there. As were the familiar paragraphs accompanying its photograph. 'An unparalleled opportunity to purchase this peerless property . . .' Alliteration, Hugo thought, was a wonderful thing. But it still hadn't shifted the house.

'Quite honestly, darling, I'm in despair,' sighed a camp, nasal voice beside him. 'I mean, the Ancient Mariner got off lightly. If he really wanted to know what a serious albatross was, he should have tried selling Firth House. And if only somebody would, frankly.'

Hugo was surprised to recognise Tarquin himself. He wore a shaggy grey fur coat, red velvet trousers and an air of comic dismay. Having initially imagined the complaint was addressed to him, Hugo now saw that he was wrong. Tarquin was talking to the tall, broad-shouldered, long-haired man through whose arm his own was tightly threaded. And who bore, Hugo noticed, a powerful resemblance to Jake.

Possibly, he realised, a split second later, because he *was* Jake.

The two of them pulled away from the window and walked slowly together down the street. Hugo stared after them. Hadn't Alice just said Jake was at counselling?

That night, Alice had put Rosa to bed and was gloomily descending the staircase when, to her surprise, she heard a rattling at the door. Terror churned in her stomach. Jake was, as usual, allegedly at some demonstration, and no one was expected, also as usual. Was this the moment she had subconsciously feared ever since moving to the English countryside? The moment a madman with a knife burst in and stabbed her to death?

It was not a madman with a knife, however. It was her husband.

'You're back early,' Alice remarked.

'Yes.'

'Was the demonstration cancelled?'

Jake shook his head. His silky hair slid from side to side, shining in the light from the colanders on the ceiling. 'There wasn't a demonstration.'

'Ah.' Much as she had suspected. But why was he admitting it? Alice sensed something momentous. Was he about to announce he was leaving her for Jessamy?

'I know I said that's where I was going.' Jake's voice was gentle, as if addressing an invalid. 'But I wasn't. I was . . .' He looked uncharacteristically uncomfortable. 'I was . . . I am . . . seeing someone else.'

'I know,' Alice said calmly.

He started. 'You *know*?'

'Of course. You're having an affair with Jessamy, aren't you?'

'*Jessamy?*'

'Oh, come off it, Jake,' Alice snapped. 'You've been spending every evening with her for months. You said you were out with her and Joss, but I happen to know that you weren't because Joss called you one night when—'

'Jessamy's got nothing to do with it,' Jake interrupted loudly. 'She's just a friend. A work colleague.'

'Is that right?' She threw him a scorching glance of disbelief.

'Yes.' He looked boldly back. 'I haven't been seeing her. I've been seeing, erm, Tarquin.'

'You mean,' Alice said slowly, 'that you're having an affair with . . . *a man?*'

'Yes.'

'Called . . . *Tarquin?*'

'Yes.'

'You mean . . . you're gay?'

He did not meet her eye. 'It's always been there, Al,' he groaned. 'And I've always been scared of it. I've tried to suppress it. Get it to go away. But it wouldn't.'

Alice's throat was dry. She was so surprised she could barely speak. 'But . . . the sex. With me. You seemed to enjoy it.'

'I did.'

'But if you're gay . . . ?'

'Al, loads of gay men are in straight relationships or even married before they finally face up to their true inclinations. Some of them never do, of course . . .'

'Thank goodness you had the courage, eh?' Alice said bitterly.

'Al, I'm sorry. I really wanted to make it work. I hoped that being married . . . having a wife . . .'

She frowned, working out what he was saying. 'That's . . . why you married me? To force yourself . . . to be straight?' She burst out laughing. It was all so unbelievable.

He dropped his head. 'Something like that.'

Alice was not laughing now. She shook her head as the memories flowed back. 'It must have been so easy for you at Sally's wedding. I was single and desperate, or so you no doubt thought. Easy pickings. Go on, admit it,' she snarled, voice rising unsteadily. 'Wasn't it like that?'

He sighed. 'You were very . . . receptive. And very beautiful,' he added quickly.

She ignored the compliment. 'And you were pretty full-on.

Flying out to New York. Bursting into my office with a million red roses. And then all that perfect father stuff. The antenatal classes . . .' Her throat blocked with fury and she stopped.

He raked an agitated hand through his hair. 'I know. I know. I was acting, I admit it.'

'*Acting!* Too fucking right. You should be in LA polishing your Oscars.'

'I thought that, even if marriage didn't work, being a father would . . . I dunno . . . sort me out for good.'

His eyes were burning as he looked at her, but burning differently than before. Where they had once been messianic, bullying, they seemed now to be pleading for understanding. 'It *had* to work. But it didn't. I knew it as soon as Rosa was born. I realised how wrong I had been and I was terrified. I started making excuses not to be with you straight away.'

'Taking my flowers to the addiction centre, for instance.'

'Al, believe me, if it could have been any other way . . .'

'But it could have been,' she blasted. 'You could have been *nicer* to us. Allowed Rosa to go to nursery and me to start some sort of new career. But no. You became a funda-mentalist enviro-maniac. Made me –' what had Hugo and her mother said? – 'a virtual bloody *eco-prisoner*. But why? What was all that about? What did that have to do with being gay?'

'Everything. When I met Tarquin for the first time, I realised what might happen. So I went into overdrive with work. Wouldn't allow myself to think about anything else. Got completely and utterly obsessed with the whole recycling business . . .'

'But who *is* Tarquin?' Alice demanded. 'Where did you meet him?'

'Tarquin's an architect. He came to a *Get Trashed!* seminar about sustainable housing.' Jake allowed a smile to flicker across his features. 'He was extremely interested in the possibilities of grass-roofed underground developments. Or so I thought. In fact, he'd just got out of a long-term bad relationship and was interested in . . . well . . .'

'You?'

He shot her a haunted look. 'God, Al—'

'Stop calling me Al.'

'You've no idea how I tried to resist him, Alice. But he was very persistent.'

Witheringly: 'It must have been hell.'

'So the more persistent he got, the more extreme the environmental stuff got. I tried to bury myself in it.'

'Bury all of us in it, you mean. You could hardly see the cottage for those heaps you started bringing home from the dump. Those loos. And baths. And basins.' She stopped as a horrible thought struck her. '*The condoms!*' she shrieked 'You hadn't, I mean . . . used them . . . on *men*?'

His hair flew about his head in a desperate negative. 'No. I promise you. I never had . . . I never thought I would. I was determined not to fall in love with Tarquin.'

'My mother knew there was something weird about it all.

Why didn't I listen to her?' Alice wailed. 'She was right all along.'

'I'm sorry, Al,' Jake said in a crushed whisper. '*Alice*, I mean. All I can say is that I was confused. Confused, angry and scared. And, yes, I took it all out on you . . . and Rosa.'

'You *bastard*. And you made me suffer so much over the Hugo thing. You were going to run away with Rosa.'

'I wouldn't have, Al. It was just an empty threat. I was panicking. I would only have been running away from myself.'

'Is that Dr Hasselblad speaking?' Alice asked sourly.

'Ah.' Jake raised his eyebrows in a *mea culpa* expression. 'The counselling sessions.'

In a flash, she understood. 'You mean you didn't go to them? You were seeing . . . *Tarquin* instead?' She pushed a hank of hair out of her eyes. 'Jesus.'

His voice was pathetically eager. 'But Alice, Tarquin's been better than any counselling. He's really helped me get to know myself. Face up to things I never dared to before.'

'Like what?' she asked wearily.

'That I'm a bloody idiot, for a start. Tarquin and I were out for dinner one night—'

'Dinner!' Alice's eyes flew open. She and Jake had never been out for dinner in the entire time she had lived at the Old Morgue.

'Yes.' He slid her a guilty look. 'I'm afraid that we've been having quite a lot of dinners. Possibly when you thought I was out chaining myself to wheelie bins. You see, Tarquin's very fond of good food . . .'

'He's not the only one,' Alice said resentfully.

'Anyway,' Jake continued, 'there I was, telling him about the moral and ethical ramifications of everything he was about to eat. He helped me see I wasn't making the world a better place. I was just annoying people when they were trying to eat.'

Alice's stare was steely. 'You know,' she said with sudden vehemence, 'I don't care about any of this. I don't want to know. It's your business. Frankly, you make me sick.'

'Alice—'

'You're a bully, a hypocrite and a shameless manipulator. You've messed up my life and not only mine . . .'

'Alice. Please. What I want you to understand is that Tarquin's helped me to think straight. Best of all,' Jake added, eyes and voice glowing with sincerity, 'he's helped me be *honest* with myself.'

Alice was now too angry to speak. How dare he stand there singing the praises of his boyfriend? She felt about for something to throw at him.

Jake sailed on serenely. 'He's helped me realise that becoming a husband and father was what I needed to do in order to realise what a completely *useless* husband and father I am. And that the best thing to do now is to just stop pretending. Accept that I'm not Superdad, or ever likely to be.'

'I see,' Alice's hand had by now closed over a jam jar on a table behind. Filled with earth from the garden, it was doing duty as a paperweight. She lifted it slowly as she spoke, her voice shaking with anger. 'So Rosa and I were a sort of experiment?'

'Exactly that.'

Behind her back, Alice raised the jar, preparing to hurl it into his face. '*Experiment!*' she snarled.

'Hey. Don't be cross. It's a good thing. Tarquin's helped me see that if that's the sort of guy you are then it's best to admit it and accept your other strengths.'

Her fingers tensed for the throw. 'Alice,' Jake urged softly, 'what I'm leading up to is that I don't think there's any point in trying to keep the marriage going. You and Rosa are better off without me.'

The jam jar crashed to the floor and shattered. Earth spilled everywhere. 'You mean . . . ?'

He started in shock at the noise and looked in surprise at the filthy floor. 'Er . . . yes. You can divorce me for adultery. Or unreasonable behaviour. Or both. Or whatever you like. I won't contest it. And you can marry whoever once it's over. Even that oily bastard Hugo.' He grinned. But Alice was not yet ready to make jokes.

'Rosa?' Her throat was so full she could barely get the syllables out.

'You'll have custody, obviously. But we need to work out access. I think, at last, I really am ready to be a good father. Properly this time, I mean. And a support to you, as well. *Get Trashed!*'s going much more commercial. Tarquin's got some great ideas. It'll be a proper business. Diversifying in lots of ways. You'll start seeing a return on your investment soon. Oh, Alice, it's been such a bloody mess. But hopefully now . . .'

Alice did not hear the last few sentences. Jake's gabbling had died in her ears. She collapsed on an orange-box chair in a dead faint.

Chapter 30

Hugo peeled his face from the white-coated chest of an exceptionally pretty woman. His rush through the hospital was such that he had failed to consider the possibility that the corner he was heading for might have someone coming round it.

'Sorry,' he gasped, mortified.

Dr Watson, Consultant Paediatrician, recovered her breath. She looked sharply at Hugo. 'Don't I know you?'

'We've met before,' Hugo admitted, his stomach flipping as he remembered the last time. 'My baby son had a rash.'

The doctor nodded. 'Of course. Nasty-looking one, wasn't it? And how is he now? Walking?'

Hugo nodded, grinning at the thought. Theo thundering about on his fat little legs was a sight of which he never tired.

'So what brings you back here?' the doctor asked.

'A class.' Hugo's grin widened. 'An antenatal class.'

'You're having another baby? Congratulations.'

'Thanks.'

'Well, I'll leave you to it. You know your way, obviously. Good luck. I might see you on the great day if I'm doing the rounds.' Hugo watched the doctor walk off, swinging her great mass of shining black hair.

Actually, he realised, he didn't know his way. He had forgotten. It was almost a year and a half since he had last attempted to find the antenatal classes and the grey-linoed bowels of the hospital were as much of a mystery now as they had been then.

He pelted onwards down the corridor, then past a couple of bends. It took a further five minutes of rising panic before finally, thankfully, he found the right door.

He knocked and opened it to see Alice smiling back at him from the middle of a horseshoe of people. He stumbled thankfully towards the empty orange plastic chair next to her. 'Sorry I'm late,' he announced to the class at large.

In the centre of the horseshoe stood a thin-faced woman with wire-framed glasses and a bright, toothy smile. 'Welcome,' she said to Hugo. 'Now you are here we can start. My name is Lotti . . .'

It had been Alice's idea to come to the classes on the grounds that she could remember next to nothing of the first ones, thanks to Amanda's distracting, hate-filled stares. He had agreed on the very similar grounds that Jake's nauseous personification of perfect fatherhood had had much the same effect on him.

As Lotti got out the poster of the upside-down baby, Hugo's

thoughts wound irresistibly backwards. It was now almost nine months since Alice had made that breathless, shouting, crying phone call in which she had confirmed in hysterical bursts Hugo's half-formed suspicions regarding Jake and Tarquin. And, more significantly, the implications of all that for their own future together. The fact that they had one, in other words.

The marriages to Jake and Amanda were dissolved, in the end, with little more than a sigh. Shortly after, Alice moved into Fitzherbert Place and a little after that, it was discovered that Theo and Rosa, between who the early promise of friendship had blossomed into near inseparability, were to be joined in the nursery by someone else. When Alice, beaming, had waved the pregnancy tester at him, Hugo felt that his cup of joy hadn't just run over. He felt it was flooding down the street like a fire hydrant.

He had immediately suggested a wedding. Yet Alice resisted. 'I made all those vows once,' she said. 'And I broke them. It's meaningless to make them again.' He could not argue with this logic. In his heart, anyway, Hugo felt more than married to Alice. He felt welded to her, with a love forged through the fire of the most abject adversity he had ever known.

Alice, for her part, felt like a horse let out of the starting gate once the marriage to Jake was finally over. She had found work in a local chambers as a media legal expert and was now much in demand with the battalions of publications and TV companies flocking to Bath from London in search of cheaper rents, less stressed staff and a better quality of life.

No matter what the volume of work, however, Alice stuck to her resolve of part-time employment. Never again, she had decided, would her work–life balance get as seriously skewed as it had during her years in New York. She had no intention, moreover, of letting Hugo hog all the children all the time.

Hugo, when he wasn't with Theo and Rosa, was delighted with the success of his estate agency. To begin with, the banks had balked at lending the money to begin a business in which every employee worked part-time and was a parent. Phrases like 'serious motivational question marks' were bandied about until Hugo forced home the obvious point that no worker was quite so committed as a well-rewarded part-timer with childcare responsibilities and an understanding boss. And, once it was set up and underway, a free nursery into the bargain.

The banks eventually accepted that no one but an idiot would let such a Holy Grail slip through their fingers. And Hugo did not employ idiots. On the contrary, those he did employ, mostly London refugees as he himself had been, were so razor-keen, experienced and capable that Fine Properties soon eclipsed most of the other agencies in Bath in terms of sales success. They could, Hugo was sure, have even sold Firth House. Except that Tarquin no longer wanted to sell it.

Tarquin's lovely town house in its gracious crescent was these days no longer an albatross. Rather, it was the goose that laid the golden eggs, or at least contained them. It was more than earning its keep as a multi-tasker: while the top three floors were the luxurious home of himself and Jake, the bottom two and the cellar housed the burgeoning and hugely lucrative business that *Get Trashed!* was fast becoming.

The more populist approach that Tarquin had first suggested, and which Jake had sketched out to Alice, had been a massive success. Few famous people had passed on the opportunity to contribute to or be interviewed for the launch issue of what was effectively the world's first environmental glossy. Flying off to LA to catch Brad Pitt, or New York to see David Bowie, had effectively quashed what weak ideological resistance Jessamy especially had initially put up. Seeing the magazine on all, rather than none, of the newsstands, thanks to a distribution deal put together by Amanda, had also helped win them over.

Amanda, from the throne of editor-in-chief of a vast range of consumer titles, had been quick to see the possibilities of the new *Get Trashed!*. 'Sort of *Heat* meets Friends of the Earth newsletter,' she explained to her media mogul new husband. 'We've got to buy it, darling. Celebrities with a conscience are the new black.'

On the back of the higher profile, increased investment and changed emphasis of *Get Trashed!* had come a wave of media ventures. Prime among these was *Get Trashed!* TV, a production company that had not only spotted the publication's potential as a programme format, but also Jake's to front it.

'Dustbin Hotman: the bloke who makes litter luscious' had been the coverline of the issue of *TV Times* with Jake on the front. Designer-dishevelled and heart-stoppingly handsome, his dazzling smile had been flanked by an empty bean can in one hand and a jam jar in the other. A second series was already in production while the first one was airing, much to the delight of Rosa, who bounced on her bottom throughout each episode pointing at the screen and saying 'Dada'. Jake's relationship with his daughter and ex-wife was positively flourishing now he was no longer living a lie. And almost as importantly, a steely effort had been made on Alice's part in particular to let bygones be bygones.

Amanda's relationship with Theo and Hugo was equally cordial, although Hugo kept having to remind her that, while her offers of work experience for Theo were very welcome, he was as yet on the young side. 'Can't start too early if he's going to be the new William Randolph Hearst,' Amanda boomed back.

Laura, meanwhile, was becoming a celebrity. Her therapy-with-a-twist slot in *Get Trashed!* in which readers aired their difficulties in getting partners to recycle and speculated, often luridly, on the reasons for their refusal, was one of the magazine's most-read pages and had translated especially felicitously to television. As a result of which Laura now also had a counselling spot on breakfast TV and had become a household name.

Hugo, whose idea the page had been in the first place – although Amanda, to whom he had suggested it, subsequently took all the credit – was especially pleased that Fergus had to play second fiddle to his famous wife. Not that he seemed to mind. On the frequent paparazzi shots of them together, often with Django, attending film premieres and television awards, he looked like a battered version of Michael Douglas proudly squiring a gap-toothed Catherine Zeta-Jones-look-a-like.

'Yugo!' someone foreign-accented was saying. 'Yugo!'

Hugo blinked, remembering where he was. Back in the antenatal class with Lotti beaming at him.

'Sorry,' Hugo said, startled. 'I was miles away. What did you say?'

'I am asking everyone how they feel about having a baby,' Lotti explained, blinking earnestly at him through her glasses. 'Give the people a chance to air their anxieties, you know? It's goot to do it in this situation, where we are all in the same ship together.'

'Boat,' smiled Hugo.

'Oh yes,' said Lotti. 'You are right. Boat. So, Yugo. How do you feel about becoming a daddy?'

Déjà vu swept Hugo. His heart thundered. His gut surged with nausea and his hands twisted together. He opened his mouth and closed it again. He looked at Alice, who was watching him with concern.

'Becoming a father?' he forced out eventually from a constricted throat.

'That's right, Yugo. I want you to tell the class how you feel. Any worries you might have, you can share them with us.'

Hugo took a deep breath. He reached for Alice's hand and squeezed it. 'I feel,' he said slowly, 'that it's going to be the absolute best thing. The best thing ever in the best possible world.'

Pastures Nouveaux

Wendy Holden

From SW7 to rural heaven . . .

Cash-strapped Rosie and her boyfriend Mark are city folk longing for a tiny country cottage. Rampantly nouveaux-riches Samantha and Guy are also searching for rustic bliss – a mansion complete with mile-long drive and hot and cold running gardeners.

The village of Eight Mile Bottom seems quiet enough, despite a nosy postman, a reclusive rock star, a glamorous Bond Girl and a ghost with a knife in its back. But there are unexpected thrills in the hills. The local siren seduces Guy while a farmer fatale rocks Rosie's relationship. Then a mysterious millionaire makes an offer she can't refuse. But should she?

Praise for *Pastures Nouveaux*

'Delicious mayhem. With this updated version of *Cold Comfort Farm*, Holden has pulled it off yet again. Simply divine' *The Times*

'Pacy pastiche of city dwellers gone country . . . an entertaining novel which will no doubt delight' *Daily Mail*

'Clever, naughty, affectionate and good-natured . . . a comic romp engineered with aplomb and dash' *The Sunday Times*

'People will adore this book' *Independent*

'Hilarious look at townies who move to the country' *Mirror*

'Holden at her funniest and most perceptive . . . spot on' *Mail on Sunday*

0 7472 6616 6

headline

Bad Heir Day

Wendy Holden

She thought she'd met Lord Right. But then it all went wrong.

Anna's boyfriend Seb is impossibly handsome, impossibly rich and generally just impossible. When eventually he dumps her, she vows to give up men and throw herself into her career. Which is how she ends up personal assistant to bestselling author Cassandra. The social climber from hell, Cassandra has a huge house in Kensington, a philandering rock star husband and the spawn of Satan for a son. So when desperate-to-escape Anna meets dashing Jamie, charming heir to a castle in Scotland, she can't believe her luck. And she probably shouldn't . . .

'The perfect antidote to the blues' *The Times*

'Devilishly witty' *Elle*

'Savagely amusing; the satire is deadly, the plot addictive and the pace exhilarating' *Metro*

'So delicious, funny and heart-warming that I turned straight back to page one after I'd finished it in order to guzzle it all over again' *Fiona Walker*

'Restores the pun to literary respectability, an amazing feat' *Esquire*

'Fulfils the old definition of comedy' *The Sunday Times*

'A witty trip through the lives of Kensington wives; in this satirical romp, Holden has created a wonderfully machiavellian nanny mafia' *Literary Review*

'Romps through high society, crackling with barbed one-liners. An *Upstairs Downstairs* for the millennium' *Woman & Home*

'Fiendishly witty' *Marie Claire*

0 7472 6130 X

headline

Azur Like It

Wendy Holden

Love in a hot climate.

A comic romance in the South of France.

Kate, a journalist in a small northern town, is fed up with covering black-pudding championships for the *Slackmucklethwaite Mercury* and living with Mum, Dad and Gran in a semi called Wits End. When evil tycoon Peter Hardstone takes over the paper, slashes budgets and sacks staff, Kate's career hits an all-time low.

Gloom turns to glamour once Hardstone's sexy son arrives to work on the *Mercury*. And when Kate's sent with him to cover the glittering Cannes Film Festival, she can't believe her luck. But it's not all fun and games in the playground of the rich. Behind the glitz and sunshine lies a dark mystery that becomes Kate's most challenging newspaper assignment yet.

Praise for AZUR LIKE IT

'Deliciously, wickedly and infectiously naughty. I defy anyone to read it without a smile on their lips' *Daily Mail*

'Laugh aloud blockbuster' *In Style*

'Deliciously witty satire ... Another sure-fire bestseller' *Heat*

'Ms Holden always heads straight to the No. 1 spot with tongue firmly in cheek' *Glamour*

0 7553 0066 1

headline

Fame Fatale

Wendy Holden

Unbridled lust. Unlimited excess. Unbelievable egos . . .

Ruthless hack Belinda wants a rich and famous man. Her problem is her job: interviewing Z-list celebs for a tabloid's Tea Break slot means zero opportunity for megastar-bagging.

Unassuming Grace just wants a quiet life. Her problems include an egomaniac boyfriend, a matchmaking mother and a publishing job with the authors from hell.

Scheming Belinda finally finds fame, while Grace has it thrust upon her in the shape of a handsome film star. But life among the A-list is anything but easy. Amid unbridled lust, unlimited excess and unbelievable egos, the girls' lives spectacularly collide. And then the real problems begin.

Praise for *Fame Fatale*:

'A hilarious, touching romp through stardom, sex and addiction to celebrity' *Cosmopolitan*

'A frothy, naughty, Evelyn-Waugh-on-speed take on literary and media life, pulled off with great aplomb by a writer firing on all cylinders. A real hoot' *Daily Mail*

'Wicked wit . . . totally fun' *Mirror*

'High-speed satire . . . perfect' *Glamour*

'Holden is on delicious form . . . needle-sharp and witty' *The Sunday Times*

0 7472 6615 8

headline